BEN-HUR

BEN-HUR

by

LEW WALLACE

Abridged Edition

PRINTED IN   GREAT BRITAIN
DEAN &   SON Ltd.
41/43 Ludgate Hill   LONDON E.C.4

MADE AND PRINTED IN GREAT BRITAIN BY PURNELL AND SONS LTD.
PAULTON (SOMERSET) AND LONDON

603 03036 x

CONTENTS

BOOK FIRST

BOOK SECOND

BOOK THIRD

BOOK FOURTH

6

BOOK FIFTH

BOOK SIXTH

BOOK SEVENTH

BOOK EIGHTH

BOOK FIRST

CHAPTER I

IN THE DESERT

THE Jebel es Zubleh is a mountain fifty miles and more in length, and so narrow that its tracery on the map gives it a likeness to a caterpillar crawling from the south to the north. Standing on its red-and-white cliffs, and looking off under the path of the rising sun, one sees only the Desert of Arabia, where the east winds, so hateful to the vine-growers of Jericho, have kept their playgrounds since the beginning. Its feet are well covered by sands tossed from the Euphrates, there to lie; for the mountain is a wall to the pasture-land of Moab and Ammon on the west —lands which else had been of the desert a part.

The Arab has impressed his language upon everything south and east of Judea; so, in his tongue, the old Jebel is the parent of numberless wadies which, intersecting the Roman road—now a dim suggestion of what once it was, a dusty path for Syrian pilgrims to and from Mecca— run their furrows, deepening as they go, to pass the torrents of the rainy season into the Jordan, or their last receptacle, the Dead Sea. Out of one of these wadies—or, more particularly, out of that one which rises at the extreme end of the Jebel, and, extending east of north, becomes at length the bed of the Jabbok River—a traveller passed, going to the table-lands of the desert. To this person the attention of the reader is first besought.

Judged by his appearance, he was quite forty-five years old. His beard, once of the deepest black, flowing broadly over his breast, was streaked with white. His face was brown as a parched coffee-berry, and so hidden by a red *kufiyeh* (as the kerchief of the head is at this day called by the children of the desert) as to be but in part visible. Now and then he raised his eyes, and they were large and dark. He was clad in the flowing garments so universal in the East; but their style may not be described more particularly, for he sat under a miniature tent, and rode a great white dromedary.

Exactly at noon the dromedary, of its own will, stopped, and uttered the cry or moan, peculiarly piteous, by which its kind always protest against an overload, and sometimes crave attention and rest. The master thereupon bestirred himself, waking, as it were, from sleep. He threw the curtains of the *houdah* up, looked at the sun, surveyed the country on every side long and carefully, as if to identify an appointed place. Satisfied with the inspection, he drew a deep breath and nodded, much as to say, "At last, at last!" A moment after, he crossed his hands upon his breast, bowed his head, and prayed silently. The pious duty done, he prepared to dismount. From his throat proceeded the sound heard doubtless by the favourite camels of Job—*Ikh! ikh!*— the signal to kneel. Slowly the animal obeyed, grunting the while. The rider then put his foot upon the slender neck, and stepped upon the sand.

The man as now revealed was of admirable proportions, not so tall as powerful. Loosening the silken rope which held the *kufiyeh* on his head, he brushed the fringed folds back until his face was bare—a strong face, almost negro in colour; yet the low, broad forehead, aquiline nose, the outer corners of the eyes turned slightly upward, the hair profuse, straight, harsh, of metallic lustre, and falling to the shoulder in many plaits, were signs of origin impossible to disguise. So looked the Pharaohs and the later Ptolemies; so looked Mizraim, father of the Egyptian race. He went first to the litter, and, from the cot or box opposite the one he had occupied in coming, produced a sponge and a small gurglet of water, with which he washed the eyes, face, and nostrils of the camel; that done, from the same depository he drew a circular cloth, red-and-white striped, a bundle of rods, and a stout cane. The latter, after some manipulation, proved to be a cunning device of lesser joints, one within another, which, when united together, formed a centre pole higher than his head. When the pole was planted, and the rods set around it, he spread the cloth over them, and was literally at home—a home much smaller than the habitations of emir and sheik, yet their counterpart in all other respects. From the litter again he brought a carpet or square rug, and covered the floor of the tent on the side from the sun.

All was now ready. He stepped out: lo! in the east a dark speck on the face of the desert. He stood as if rooted to the ground; his eyes dilated; his flesh crept chilly, as if touched by something supernatural. The speck grew; became large as a hand; at length assumed defined proportions. A little later, full into view swung a duplication of his own dromedary, tall and white, and bearing a *houdah*, the travelling litter of Hindostan. Then the Egyptian crossed his hands upon his breast, and looked to heaven.

"God only is great!" he exclaimed, his eyes full of tears, his soul in awe.

The stranger drew nigh—at last stopped. Then he, too, seemed just waking. He beheld the kneeling camel, the tent, and the man standing prayerfully at the door. He crossed his hands, bent his head, and prayed silently; after which, in a little while, he stepped from his camel's neck to the sand, and advanced towards the Egyptian, as did the Egyptian towards him. A moment they looked at each other; then they embraced—that is, each threw his right arm over the other's shoulder, and the left round the side, placing his chin first upon the left, then upon the right breast.

"Peace be with thee, O servant of the true God!" the stranger said.

"And to thee, O brother of the true faith!—to thee peace and welcome," the Egyptian replied, with fervour.

The new-comer was tall and gaunt, with lean face, sunken eyes, white hair and beard, and a complexion between the hue of cinnamon and bronze. He, too, was unarmed. His costume was Hindostani; over the skull-cap a shawl was wound in great folds, forming a turban; his body garments were in the style of the Egyptian's, except that the *aba* was shorter, exposing wide flowing breeches gathered at the ankles. In place of sandals, his feet were clad in half-slippers of red leather, pointed at the toes. Save the slippers, the costume from head to foot was of white linen. The air of the man was high, stately, severe. Visvamitra, the greatest of the ascetic heroes of the Iliad of the East, had in him a perfect representative. He might have been called a Life drenched with the wisdom of Brahma—Devotion Incarnate. Only in his eyes was there proof of humanity; when he lifted his face from the Egyptian's breast, they were glistening with tears.

They looked to the north, where, already plain to view, a third camel, of the whiteness of the others, came careening like a ship. They waited, standing together—waited until the new-comer arrived, dismounted, and advanced towards them.

"Peace to you, O my brother!" he said, while embracing the Hindoo.

And the Hindoo answered, "God's will be done!"

The last comer was all unlike his friends; his frame was slighter; his complexion white; a mass of waving light hair was a perfect crown for his small but beautiful head; the warmth of his dark-blue eyes certified a delicate mind, and a cordial, brave nature. He was bare-headed and unarmed. Under the folds of the Tyrian blanket which he wore with unconscious grace appeared a tunic, short-sleeved and low-necked, gathered to the waist by a band, and reaching nearly to the knee; leaving the neck, arms, and legs bare. Sandals guarded his feet. Fifty years, probably more, had spent themselves upon him, with no other effect, apparently, than to tinge his demeanour with gravity and temper his words with forethought. The physical organization and the brightness of soul were untouched. No need to tell the student from what kindred he was sprung; if he came not himself from the groves of Athené, his ancestry did.

CHAPTER 2

THE THREE STRANGERS

To speak in the style of the period, the meeting just described took place in the year of Rome 747. The month was December, and winter reigned over all the regions east of the Mediterranean. Such as ride upon the desert in this season go not far until smitten with a keen appetite. The company under the little tent were not exceptions to the rule. They were hungry, and ate heartily; and, after the wine, they talked.

"To a wayfarer in a strange land nothing is so sweet as to hear his name on the tongue of a friend," said the Egyptian, who assumed to be president of the repast. "Before us lie many days of companionship. It is time we knew each other. So, if it be agreeable, he who came last shall be first to speak."

"Hear me, brethren," said the Greek. "The door of my heritage looks over an arm of the sea, over the Thermaic Gulf. One day I saw a man flung overboard from a ship sailing by. He swam ashore. I received and took care of him. He was a Jew, learned in the history and laws of his people; and from him I came to know that the God of my prayers did indeed exist, and had been for ages their lawmaker, ruler, and king. What was that but the Revelation I dreamed of! My faith had not been fruitless; God answered me!"

"As He does all who cry to Him with such faith," said the Hindoo.

"When the Jew was gone, and I was alone again, I chastened my soul with a new prayer—that I might be permitted to see the King when He was come, and worship Him. One night I sat by the door of my cave trying to get nearer the mysteries of my existence, knowing which is to know God; suddenly, on the sea below me, or rather in the darkness that covered its face, I saw a star begin to burn; slowly it arose and drew nigh, and stood over the hill and above my door, so that its light shone full upon me. I fell down and slept, and in my dream I heard a voice say:

" 'O Gaspar! Thy faith hath conquered! Blessed art thou! with two others, come from the uttermost parts of the earth, thou shalt see Him that is promised, and be a witness for Him, and the occasion of testimony in His behalf. In the morning arise, and go meet them, and keep trust in the Spirit that shall guide thee.'

"And in the morning I awoke with the Spirit as a light within me surpassing that of the sun. I put off my hermit's garb, and dressed myself as of old. From a hiding-place I took the treasure which I had brought from the city. A ship went sailing past. I hailed it, was taken aboard, and landed at Antioch. There I bought the camel and his furniture. Through the gardens and orchards that enamel the banks of the Orontes, I journeyed to Emesa, Damascus, Bostra, and Philadelphia; thence hither. And so, O brethren, you have my story. Let me now listen to you."

The Egyptian and the Hindoo looked at each other; the former waved his hand; the latter bowed, and began:

"Our brother has spoken well. May my words be as wise."

He broke off, reflected a moment, then resumed:

"You may know me, brethren, by the name of Melchior. I speak to you in a language which, if not the oldest in the world, was at least the soonest to be reduced to letters—I mean the Sanscrit of India. I am a Hindoo by birth. My people were the first to walk in the fields of knowledge, first to divide them, first to make them beautiful.

"One night I walked by the shores of the lake, and spoke to the listening silence, 'When will God come and claim His own? Is there to be no redemption?' Suddenly a light began to glow tremulously out on the water; soon a star arose, and moved towards me, and stood overhead. The brightness stunned me. While I lay upon the ground, I heard a voice of infinite sweetness say, 'Thy love hath conquered. Blessed art thou, O son of India! The redemption is at hand. With two others, from far quarters of the earth, thou shalt see the Redeemer, and be a witness that He hath come. In the morning arise, and go meet them; and put all thy trust in the Spirit which shall guide thee.'

"And from that time the light has stayed with me; so I knew it was the visible presence of the Spirit. In the morning I started to the world by the way I had come. In a cleft of the mountain I found a stone of vast worth, which I sold in Hurdwar. By Lahore and Cabool, and Yezd, I came to Ispahan. There I bought the camel, and thence was led to Bagdad, not waiting for caravans. Alone I travelled, fearless, for the Spirit was with me, and is with me yet. What glory is ours, O brethren! We are to see the Redeemer—to speak to Him—to worship Him! I am done."

The vivacious Greek broke forth in expressions of joy and congratulations; after which the Egyptian said, with characteristic gravity:

"I salute you, my brother. You have suffered much, and I rejoice in your triumph. If you are both pleased to hear me, I will now tell you who I am, and how I came to be called. Wait for me a moment."

He went out, and tended the camels; coming back, he resumed his seat.

"Your words, brethren, were of the Spirit," he said, in commencement; "and the Spirit gives me to understand them. I am Balthasar the Egyptian. I believed in prayer; and to make my appeals pure and strong, like you, my brethren, I went out of the beaten ways, I went where man had not been, where only God was. Above the fifth cataract, above the meeting of rivers in Sennar, up the Bahr el Abiad, into the far unknown of Africa, I went. There, in the morning, a mountain blue as the sky flings a cooling shadow wide over the western desert, and, with its cascades of melted snow, feeds a broad lake nestling at its base on the east. The lake is the mother of the great river. For a year and more the mountain gave me a home. The fruit of the palm fed my body, prayer my spirit. One night I walked in the orchard close by the little sea. 'The world is dying. When wilt Thou come? Why may I not see the redemption, O God?' So I prayed. The glassy water was sparkling with stars. One of them seemed to leave its place, and rise to the surface, where it became a brilliancy burning to the eyes. Then it moved towards me, and stood over my head, apparently in hand's reach. I fell down and hid my face. A voice, not of the earth, said, 'Thy good works have conquered. Blessed art thou, O son of Mizraim! The redemption cometh. With two others, from the remotenesses of the world, thou shalt see the Saviour, and testify for Him. In the morning arise, and go meet them. And when ye have all come to the holy city of Jerusalem, ask of the people, Where is He that is born King of the Jews? for we have seen His star in the East, and are sent to worship Him. Put all thy trust in the Spirit which will guide thee.'

"And the light became an inward illumination not to be doubted, and has stayed with me, a governor and a guide. It led me down the river to Memphis, where I made ready for the desert. I bought my camel, and came hither without rest, by way of Suez and Kufileh, and up through the lands of Moab and Ammon. God is with us, O my brethren!"

He paused, and thereupon, with a prompting not their own, they all arose and looked at each other.

"He we go to find was called 'King of the Jews'; by that name we are bidden to ask for Him. But, now that we have met, and heard from each other, we may know Him to be the Redeemer, not of the Jews alone, but of all the nations of the earth. The patriarch who survived the Flood had with him three sons, and their families, by whom the world was repeopled. From the old Aryana-Vaêjo, the well-remembered Region of Delight in the heart of Asia, they parted. India and the far

East received the children of the first; the descendants of the youngest, through the North, streamed into Europe; those of the second overflowed the deserts about the Red Sea, passing into Africa; and though most of the latter are yet dwellers in shifting tents, some of them became builders along the Nile."

By a simultaneous impulse the three joined hands.

"Could anything be more divinely ordered?" Balthasar continued. "When we have found the Lord, the brothers, and all the generations that have succeeded them, will kneel to Him in homage with us. And when we part to go our separate ways, the world will have learned a new lesson—that Heaven may be won, not by the sword, not by human wisdom, but by Faith, Love, and Good Works."

There was silence, broken by sighs and sanctified with tears; for the joy that filled them might not be stayed. It was the unspeakable joy of souls on the shores of the River of Life, resting with the Redeemed in God's presence.

Presently their hands fell apart, and together they went out of the tent. The desert was still as the sky. The sun was sinking fast. The camels slept.

A little while after, the tent was struck, and, with the remains of the repast, restored to the cot; then the friends mounted, and set out single file, led by the Egyptian. Their course was due west, into the chilly night. The camels swung forward in steady trot, keeping the line and the intervals so exactly that those following seemed to tread in the tracks of the leader. The riders spoke not once.

By and by the moon came up. And as the three tall, white figures sped, with soundless tread, through the opalescent light, they appeared like spectres flying from hateful shadows. Suddenly, in the air before them, not farther up than a low hilltop, flared a lambent flame; as they looked at it, the apparition contracted into a focus of dazzling lustre. Their hearts beat fast; their souls thrilled; and they shouted as with one voice, "The Star! the Star! God is with us!"

CHAPTER 3

JOSEPH AND MARY

In an aperture of the western wall of Jerusalem hang the "oaken valves" called the Bethlehem or Joppa Gate. The area outside of them is one of the notable places of the city. Long before David coveted

Zion, there was a citadel there. When at last the son of Jesse ousted the Jebusite, and began to build, the site of the citadel became the north-west corner of his new wall, defended by a tower much more imposing than the old one. The location of the gate, however, was not disturbed, for the reasons, most likely, that the roads which met and merged in front of it could not well be transferred to any other point, while the area outside had become a recognised market-place. In Solomon's day there was great traffic at the locality, shared in by traders from Egypt, and the rich dealers from Tyre and Sidon. Nearly three thousand years have passed, and yet a kind of commerce clings to the spot. A pilgrim wanting a pin or a pistol, a cucumber or a camel, a house or a horse, a loan or a lentil, a date or a dragoman, a melon or a man, a dove or a donkey, has only to inquire for the article at the Joppa Gate. Some-times the scene is quite animated, and then it suggests, What a place the old market must have been in the days of Herod the Builder! And to that period and that market the reader is now to be transferred.

Following the Hebrew system, the meeting of the wise men described in the preceding chapters took place in the afternoon of the twenty-fifth day of the third month of the year; that is to say, on the twenty-fifth day of December. The year was the second of the 193rd Olympiad, or the 747th of Rome; the sixty-seventh of Herod the Great, and the thirty-fifth of his reign; the fourth before the beginning of the Christian era. The hours of the day, by Judean custom, begin with the sun, the first hour being the first after sunrise.

It was the third hour of the day, and many of the people had gone away; yet the press continued without apparent abatement. Of the new-comers, there was a group over by the south wall, consisting of a man, a woman, and a donkey, which requires extended notice.

The man stood by the animal's head, holding a leading-strap, and leaning upon a stick which seemed to have been chosen for the double purpose of goad and staff. His dress was like that of the ordinary Jews around him, except that it had an appearance of newness. The mantle dropping from his head, and the robe or frock which clothed his person from neck to heel, were probably the garments he was accustomed to wear to the synagogue on Sabbath days. His features were exposed, and they told of fifty years of life, a surmise confirmed by the grey that streaked his otherwise black beard. He looked around him with the half-curious, half-vacant stare of a stranger and provincial.

The donkey ate leisurely from an armful of green grass, of which there was an abundance in the market. In its sleepy content, the brute did not admit of disturbance from the bustle and clamour about; no more was it mindful of the woman sitting upon its back in a cushioned pillion. An outer robe of dull woollen stuff completely covered her person, while a white wimple veiled her head and neck. Once in a while, impelled by curiosity to see or hear something passing, she drew the wimple aside, but so slightly that the face remained invisible.

At length the man was accosted.

"Are you not Joseph of Nazareth?"

The speaker was standing close by.

"I am so called," answered Joseph, turning gravely around. "And you—ah, peace be unto you! my friend, Rabbi Samuel!"

"The same give I back to you." The Rabbi paused, looking at the woman, then added, "To you, and unto your house and all your helpers, be peace."

With the last word, he placed one hand upon his breast, and inclined his head to the woman, who, to see him, had by this time withdrawn the wimple enough to show the face of one but a short time out of girl-hood. Thereupon the acquaintances grasped right hands, as if to carry them to their lips; at the last moment, however, the clasp was let go, and each kissed his own hand, then put its palm upon his forehead.

"There is so little dust upon your garments," the Rabbi said, familiarly, "that I infer you passed the night in this city of our fathers."

"No," Joseph replied, "as we could only make Bethany before the night came, we stayed in the khan there, and took the road again at daybreak."

"The journey before you is long, then—not to Joppa, I hope."

"Only to Bethlehem."

The countenance of the Rabbi, theretofore open and friendly, became lowering and sinister, and he cleared his throat with a growl instead of a cough.

"Yes, yes—I see," he said. "You were born in Bethlehem, and wend thither now, with your daughter, to be counted for taxation, as ordered by Cæsar. The children of Jacob are as the tribes in Egypt were—only they have neither a Moses nor a Joshua. How are the mighty fallen!"

Joseph answered, without change of posture or countenance,—

"The woman is not my daughter."

But the Rabbi clung to the political idea; and he went on, without noticing the explanation, "What are the Zealots doing down in Galilee?"

"I am a carpenter, and Nazareth is a village," said Joseph cautiously. "The street on which my bench stands is not a road leading to any city. Hewing wood and sawing plank leave me no time to take part in the disputes of parties."

"But you are a Jew," said the Rabbi earnestly. "You are a Jew, and of the line of David. It is not possible you can find pleasure in the payment of any tax except the shekel given by ancient custom to Jehovah."

Joseph held his peace.

"I do not complain," his friend continued, "of the amount of the tax—a denarius is a trifle. Oh no! The imposition of the tax is the offence. And, besides, what is paying it but submission to tyranny? Tell me, is it true that Judas claims to be the Messiah? You live in the midst of his followers."

"I have heard his followers say he was the Messiah," Joseph replied.

At this point the wimple was drawn aside, and for an instant the whole face of the woman was exposed. The eyes of the Rabbi wandered that way, and he had time to see a countenance of rare beauty, kindled by a look of intense interest; then a blush overspread her cheeks and brow, and the veil was returned to its place.

The politician forgot his subject.

"Your daughter is comely," he said, speaking lower.

"She is not my daughter," Joseph repeated.

The curiosity of the Rabbi was aroused; seeing which, the Nazarene hastened to say further, "She is the child of Joachim and Anna of Bethlehem, of whom you have at least heard; for they were of great repute——"

"Yes," remarked the Rabbi deferentially, "I know them. They were lineally descended from David. I knew them well."

"Well, they are dead now," the Nazarene proceeded. "They died in Nazareth. Joachim was not rich, yet he left a house and garden to be divided between his daughters Marian and Mary. This is one of them; and to save her portion of the property, the law required her to marry her next of kin. She is now my wife."

"And you were——"

"Her uncle."

"Yes, yes! And as you were both born in Bethlehem, the Roman compels you to take her there with you to be also counted."

The Rabbi clasped his hands, and looked indignantly to heaven, exclaiming, "The God of Israel still lives! The vengeance is His!"

With that he turned and abruptly departed. A stranger near by, observing Joseph's amazement, said quietly, "Rabbi Samuel is a Zealot. Judas himself is not more fierce."

Joseph, not wishing to talk with the man, appeared not to hear, and busied himself gathering in a little heap the grass which the donkey had tossed abroad; after which he leaned upon his staff again, and waited.

In another hour the party passed out the gate, and, turning to the left, took the road to Bethlehem. The descent into the valley of Hinnom was quite broken, garnished here and there with straggling wild olive-trees. Carefully, tenderly, the Nazarene walked by the woman's side, leading-strap in hand. On their left, reaching to the south and east round Mount Zion, rose the city wall, and on their right the steep prominences which form the western boundary of the valley.

Slowly they passed the Lower Pool of Gihon, out of which the sun was fast driving the lessening shadow of the royal hill; slowly they proceeded, keeping parallel with the aqueduct from the Pools of Solomon, until near the site of the country-house on what is now called the Hill of Evil Counsel; there they began to ascend to the plain of Rephaim. The sun streamed garishly over the stony face of the famous locality, and under its influence Mary, the daughter of Joachim, dropped the wimple entirely, and bared her head. Joseph told the story of the Philistines surprised in their camp there by David. He was tedious in the narrative, speaking with the solemn countenance and lifeless manner of a dull man. She did not always hear him.

Wherever on the land men go, and on the sea ships, the face and figure of the Jew are familiar. The physical type of the race has always been the same; yet there have been some individual variations. "Now he was ruddy, and withal of a beautiful countenance, and goodly to look to." Such was the son of Jesse when brought before Samuel. The fancies of men have been ever since ruled by the description. Poetic licence has extended the peculiarities of the ancestor to his notable descendants. So all our ideal Solomons have fair faces, and hair and beard chestnut in the shade, and of the tint of gold in the sun. Such, we are also made believe, were the locks of Absalom the beloved. And, in the absence of authentic history, tradition has dealt no less lovingly by her whom we are now following down to the native city of the ruddy king.

She was not more than fifteen. Her form, voice, and manner belonged to the period of transition from girlhood. Her face was perfectly oval, her complexion more pale than fair. The nose was faultless; the lips, slightly parted, were full and ripe, giving to the lines of the mouth warmth, tenderness, and trust; the eyes were blue and large, and shaded by drooping lids and long lashes; and, in harmony with all, a flood of golden hair, in the style permitted to Jewish brides, fell unconfined down her back to the pillion on which she sat. The throat and neck had the downy softness sometimes seen which leaves the artist in doubt whether it is an effect of contour or colour. To these charms of feature and person were added others more indefinable—an air of purity which only the soul can impart, and of abstraction natural to such as think much of things impalpable. Often, with trembling lips, she raised her eyes to heaven, itself not more deeply blue; often she crossed her hands upon her breast, as in adoration and prayer; often she raised her head like one listening eagerly for a calling voice. Now and then, midst his slow utterances, Joseph turned to look at her, and, catching the expression kindling her face as with light, forgot his theme, and with bowed head, wondering, plodded on.

So they skirted the great plain, and at length reached the elevation Mar Elias; from which, across a valley, they beheld Bethlehem, the old, old House of Bread, its white walls crowning a ridge, and shining above the brown scumbling of leafless orchards. They paused there, and rested, while Joseph pointed out the places of sacred renown; then they went down into the valley to the well which was the scene of one of the marvellous exploits of David's strong men. The narrow space was crowded with people and animals. A fear came upon Joseph—a fear lest, if the town were so thronged, there might not be house-room for the gentle Mary. Without delay, he hurried on, past the pillar of stone marking the tomb of Rachel, up the gardened slope, saluting none of the many persons he met on the way, until he stopped before the portal of the khan that then stood outside the village gates, near a junction of roads.

CHAPTER 4

AT BETHLEHEM

To understand thoroughly what happened to the Nazarene at the khan, the reader must be reminded that Eastern inns were different from the inns of the Western world. They were called khans, from the Persian, and, in simplest form, were fenced enclosures, without house or shed, often without a gate or entrance. Their sites were chosen with reference to shade, defence, or water. Such were the inns that sheltered Jacob when he went to seek a wife in Padan-Aram. Their like may be seen at this day in the stopping-places of the desert. On the other hand, some of them, especially those on the roads between great cities, like Jerusalem and Alexandria, were princely establishments, monuments to the piety of the kings who built them. In ordinary, however, they were no more than the house or possession of a sheik, in which, as in headquarters, he swayed his tribe. Lodging the traveller was the least of their uses; they were markets, factories, forts; places of assemblage and residence for merchants and artisans quite as much as places of shelter for belated and wandering wayfarers. Within their walls, all the year round, occurred the multiplied daily transactions of a town.

The singular management of these hostelries was the feature likely to strike a Western mind with most force. There was no host or hostess; no clerk, cook, or kitchen; a steward at the gate was all the assertion of government or proprietorship anywhere visible. Strangers arriving stayed at will without rendering account. A consequence of the system was, that whoever came had to bring his food and culinary outfit with him, or buy them of dealers in the khan. The same rule held good as to his bed and bedding, and forage for his beasts. Water, rest, shelter, and protection were all he looked for from the proprietor, and they were gratuitous. The peace of synagogues was sometimes broken by brawling disputants, but that of the khans never. The houses and all their appurtenances were sacred! a well was not more so.

The khan at Bethlehem, before which Joseph and his wife stopped, was a good specimen of its class, being neither very primitive nor very princely. The building was purely Oriental; that is to say, a quad-rangular block of rough stones, one storey high, flat-roofed, externally unbroken by a window, and with but one principal entrance—a door-way, which was also a gateway, on the eastern side, or front. The road ran by the door so near that the chalk dust half covered the lintel. A fence of flat rocks, beginning at the north-eastern corner of the pile, extended many yards down the slope to a point from whence it swept westwardly to a limestone bluff; making what was in the highest degree essential to a respectable khan—a safe enclosure for animals.

In a village like Bethlehem, as there was but one sheik, there could not well be more than one khan; and, though born in the place, the Nazarene, from long residence elsewhere, had no claim to hospitality in the town. Moreover, the enumeration for which he was coming might be the work of weeks or months; Roman deputies in the provinces were proverbially slow; and to impose himself and wife for a period so un-certain upon acquaintances or relations was out of the question. So, before he drew nigh the great house, while he was yet climbing the slope, in the steep places toiling to hasten the donkey, the fear that he might not find accommodations in the khans became a painful anxiety; for he found the road thronged with men and boys who, with great ado, were taking their cattle, horses, and camels to and from the valley, some to water, some to the neighbouring caves. And when he was come close by, his alarm was not allayed by the discovery of a crowd investing the door of the establishment, while the enclosure adjoining, broad as it was, seemed already full.

"We cannot reach the door," Joseph said, in his slow way. "Let us stop here, and learn, if we can, what has happened."

The wife, without answering, quietly drew the wimple aside. The look of fatigue at first upon her face changed to one of interest. She found herself at the edge of an assemblage that could not be other than a matter of curiosity to her, although it was common enough at the khans on any of the highways which the great caravans were accustomed to traverse. There were men on foot, running hither and thither, talking shrilly and in all the tongues of Syria; men on horseback screaming to men on camels; men struggling doubtfully with fractious cows and frightened sheep; men peddling bread and wine; and among the mass a herd of boys apparently in chase of a herd of dogs. Everybody and everything seemed to be in motion at the same time. Possibly the fair spectator was too weary to be long attracted by the scene; in a little while she sighed, and settled down on the pillion, and, as if in search of peace and rest, or in expectation of some one, looked off to the south, and up to the tall cliffs of the Mount of Paradise, then faintly reddening under the setting sun.

While she was thus looking, a man pushed his way out of the press, and, stopping close by the donkey, faced about with an angry brow. The Nazarene spoke to him.

"As I am what I take you to be, good friend—a son of Judah—may I ask the cause of this multitude?"

The stranger turned fiercely; but, seeing the solemn countenance of Joseph, so in keeping with his deep, slow voice and speech, he raised his hand in half-salutation, and replied,—

"Peace be to you, Rabbi! I am a son of Judah, and will answer you. I dwell in Beth-Dagon, which, you know, is in what used to be the land of the tribe of Dan."

"On the road to Joppa from Modin," said Joseph.

"Ah, you have been in Beth-Dagon," the man said, his face softening yet more. "What wanderers we of Judah are! I have been away from the ridge—old Ephrath, as our father Jacob called it—for many years. When the proclamation went abroad requiring all Hebrews to be numbered at the cities of their birth—That is my business here, Rabbi."

Joseph's face remained stolid as a mask, while he remarked, "I have come for that also—I and my wife."

The stranger glanced at Mary and kept silence. She was looking up at the bald top of Gedor. The sun touched her upturned face, and filled the violet depths of her eyes; and upon her parted lips trembled an aspiration which could not have been to a mortal.

"Of what was I speaking? Ah! I remember. I was about to say that when I heard of the order to come here I was angry. Then I thought of the old hill and the town, and the valley falling away into the depths of Cedron; of the vines and orchards, and fields of grain, unfailing since the days of Boaz and Ruth; of the familiar mountains—Gedor here, Gibeah yonder, Mar Elias there—which, when I was a boy, were the walls of the world to me; and I forgave the tyrants, and came—I, and Rachel my wife, and Deborah and Michal, our roses of Sharon."

The man paused again, looking abruptly at Mary, who was now looking at him and listening. Then he said, "Rabbi, will not your wife go to mine? You may see her yonder with the children, under the leaning olive-tree at the bend of the road. I tell you"—he turned to Joseph, and spoke positively—"I tell you the khan is full. It is useless to ask at the gate."

Joseph's will was slow, like his mind; he hesitated, but at length replied, "The offer is kind. Whether there be room for us or not in the house, we will go see your people. Let me speak to the gate-keeper myself. I will return quickly."

And, putting the leading-strap in the stranger's hand, he pushed into the stirring crowd.

The keeper sat on a great cedar block outside the gate. Against the wall behind him leaned a javelin. A dog squatted on the block by his side.

"The peace of Jehovah be with you," said Joseph, at last confronting the keeper.

"What you give, may you find again; and, when found, be it many times multiplied to you and yours," returned the watchman gravely, though without moving.

"I am a Bethlehemite," said Joseph, in his most deliberate way. "Is there not room for——"

"There is not."

"You may have heard of me—Joseph of Nazareth. This is the house of my fathers. I am of the line of David."

The appeal was not without effect. The keeper of the gate slid down from the cedar block, and, laying his hand upon his beard, said respectfully, "Rabbi, I cannot tell you when this door first opened in welcome to the traveller, but it was more than a thousand years ago; and in all that time there is no known instance of a good man turned away, save when there was no room to rest him in. If it has been so with the stranger, just cause must the steward have who says no to one of the line of David." Then the keeper's eyes sought the ground in thought. Suddenly he raised his head.

"If I cannot make room for you," he said, "I cannot turn you away. Rabbi, I will do the best I can for you. How many are of your party?"

Joseph reflected, then replied, "My wife and a friend with his family, from Beth-Dagon, a little town over by Joppa; in all, six of us."

"Very well. You shall not lie out on the ridge. Bring your people, and hasten; for, when the sun goes down behind the mountain, you know the night comes quickly, and it is nearly there now."

"I give you the blessing of the houseless traveller; that of the sojourner will follow."

So saying, the Nazarene went back joyfully to Mary and the Beth-Dagonite. In a little while the latter brought up his family, the women mounted on donkeys. The wife was matronly, the daughters were images of what she must have been in youth; and as they drew nigh the door, the keeper knew them to be of the humble class.

"This is she of whom I spoke," said the Nazarene; "and these are our friends."

The party were conducted into a wide passage paved with stone, from which they entered the court of the khan. To a stranger the scene would have been curious; but they noticed the lewens that yawned darkly upon them from all sides, and the court itself, only to remark how crowded they were. By a lane reserved in the stowage of the cargoes, and thence by a passage similar to the one at the entrance, they emerged into the enclosure adjoining the house, and came upon camels, horses, and donkeys, tethered and dozing in close groups; among them were the keepers, men of many lands; and they, too, slept, or kept silent watch. They went down the slope of the crowded yard slowly, for the dull carriers of the women had wills of their own. At length they turned into a path running towards the grey limestone bluff overlooking the khan on the west.

"We are going to the cave," said Joseph laconically.

The guide lingered till Mary came to his side.

"The cave to which we are going," he said to her, "must have been a resort of your ancestor David. From the field below us and from the well down in the valley he used to drive his flocks to it for safety; and afterwards, when he was king, he came back to the old house here for rest and health, bringing great trains of animals. The mangers yet remain as they were in his day. Better a bed upon the floor where he has slept than one in the court-yard or out by the roadside. Ah, here is the house before the cave!"

The building was low and narrow, projecting but a little from the rock to which it was joined at the rear, and wholly without a window. In its blank front there was a door, swung on enormous hinges, and thickly daubed with ochreous clay. While the wooden bolt of the lock was being pushed back, the women were assisted from their pillions. Upon the opening of the door the keeper called out,—

"Come in!"

The guests entered, and stared about them. It became apparent immediately that the house was but a mask or covering for the mouth of a natural cave or grotto, probably forty feet long, nine or ten high, and twelve or fifteen in width. The light streamed through the doorway, over an uneven floor, falling upon piles of grain and fodder, and earthenware and household property, occupying the centre of the chamber. Along the sides were mangers, low enough for sheep, and built of stones laid in cement. There were no stalls or partitions of any kind. Dust and chaff yellowed the floor, filled all the crevices and hollows, and thickened the spider-webs, which dropped from the ceiling like bits of dirty linen; otherwise the place was cleanly, and, to appearance, as comfortable as any of the arched lewens of the khan proper. In fact, a cave was the model and first suggestion of the lewen.

"Come in!" said the guide. "These piles upon the floor are for travellers like yourselves. Take what of them you need."

Then he spoke to Mary.

"Can you rest here?"

"The place is sanctified," she answered.

"I leave you then. Peace be with you all!"

When he was gone, they busied themselves making the cave habitable.

CHAPTER 5

THE RAY FROM HEAVEN

At a certain hour in the evening the shouting and stir of the people in and about the khan ceased: at the same time, every Israelite, if not already upon his feet, arose, solemnized his face, looked towards Jerusalem, crossed his hands upon his breast, and prayed; for it was the sacred ninth hour, when sacrifices were offered in the temple on Moriah, and God was supposed to be there. When the hands of the worshippers fell down, the commotion broke forth again; everybody hastened to bread, or to make his pallet. A little later, the lights were put out, and there was silence, and then sleep.

   .   .   .   .

About midnight someone on the roof cried out, "What light is that in the sky? Awake, brethren, awake and see!"

The people, half asleep, sat up and looked; then they became wide-awake, though wonder-struck. And the stir spread to the court below, and into the lewens; soon the entire tenantry of the house and court and enclosure were out gazing at the sky.

And this was what they saw. A ray of light, beginning at a height immeasurably beyond the nearest stars, and dropping obliquely to the earth; at its top, a diminishing point; at its base, many furlongs in width; its sides blending softly with the darkness of the night; its core a roseate electrical splendour. The apparition seemed to rest on the nearest mountain south-east of the town, making a pale corona along the line of the summit. The khan was touched luminously, so that those upon the roof saw each other's faces, all filled with wonder.

Steadily, through minutes, the ray lingered, and then the wonder changed to awe and fear; the timid trembled; the boldest spoke in whispers.

"Saw you ever the like?" asked one.

"It seems just over the mountain there. I cannot tell what it is, nor did I ever see anything like it," was the answer.

"Can it be that a star has burst and fallen?" asked another, his tongue faltering.

"When a star falls, its light goes out."

"I have it!" cried one confidently. "The shepherds have seen a lion, and made fires to keep him from the flocks."

The men next the speaker drew a breath of relief, and said, "Yes, that is it! The flocks were grazing in the valley over there to-day."

A bystander dispelled the comfort.

"No, no! Though all the wood in all the valleys of Judah was brought together in one pile and fired, the blaze would not throw a light so strong and high."

After that there was silence on the house-top, broken but once again while the mystery continued.

"Brethren!" exclaimed a Jew of venerable mien, "what we see is the ladder our father Jacob saw in his dream. Blessed be the Lord God of our fathers!"

CHAPTER 6

THE BIRTH OF CHRIST

A MILE and a half, it may be two miles, south-east of Bethlehem, there is a plain separated from the town by an intervening swell of the mountain. At the side farthest from the town, close under a bluff, there was an extensive *mârâh*, or sheepcot, ages old. In some long-forgotten foray, the building had been unroofed and almost demolished. The enclosure attached to it remained intact, however, and that was of more importance to the shepherds who drove their charges thither than the house itself.

The day of the occurrences which occupy the preceding chapters, a number of shepherds, seeking fresh walks for their flocks, led them up to this plain; and from early morning the groves had been made ring with calls, and the blows of axes, the bleating of sheep and goats, the tinkling of bells, the lowing of cattle, and the barking of dogs. When the sun went down, they led the way to the *mârâh*, and by nightfall had everything safe in the field; then they kindled a fire down by the gate, partook of their humble supper, and sat down to rest and talk, leaving one on watch.

There were six of these men, omitting the watchman; and after-while they assembled in a group near the fire, some sitting, some lying prone.

Such were the shepherds of Judea! In appearance, rough and savage as the gaunt dogs sitting with them around the blaze; in fact, simple-minded, tender-hearted; effects due, in part, to the primitive life they led, but chiefly to their constant care of things lovable and helpless.

While they talked, and before the first watch was over, one by one the shepherds went to sleep, each lying where he had sat.

By the gate, hugging his mantle close, the watchman walked; at times he stopped attracted by a stir among the sleeping herds, or by a jackal's cry off on the mountain-side. The midnight was slow coming to him; but at last it came. His task was done; now for the dreamless sleep with which labour blesses its wearied children! He moved towards the fire, but paused; a light was breaking around him, soft and white, like the moon's. He waited breathlessly. The light deepened; things before invisible came to view; he saw the whole field, and all it sheltered. A chill sharper than that of the frosty air—a chill of fear —smote him. He looked up; the stars were gone; the light was dropping as from a window in the sky; as he looked, it became a splendour; then, in terror, he cried,—

"Awake, awake!"

Up sprang the dogs, and, howling, ran away.

The herds rushed together bewildered.

The men clambered to their feet, weapons in hand.

"What is it?" they asked in one voice.

"See!" cried the watchman, "the sky is on fire!"

Suddenly the light became intolerably bright, and they covered their eyes, and dropped upon their knees; then, as their souls shrank with fear, they fell upon their faces blind and fainting, and would have died had not a voice said to them,—

"Fear not!"

And they listened.

"Fear not: for, behold, I bring you good tidings of great joy, which shall be to all people."

The voice, in sweetness and soothing more than human, and low and clear, penetrated all their being, and filled them with assurance. They rose upon their knees, and, looking worshipfully, beheld in the centre of a great glory the appearance of a man, clad in a robe intensely white; above its shoulders towered the tops of wings shining and folded; a star over its forehead glowed with steady lustre, brilliant as Hesperus; its hands were stretched towards them in blessing; its face was serene and divinely beautiful.

They had often heard, and, in their simple way, talked, of angels; and they doubted not now, but said in their hearts, The glory of God is about us, and this is he who of old came to the prophet by the river of Ulai.

Directly the angel continued,—

"For unto you is born this day, in the city of David, a Saviour, which is Christ the Lord!"

Again there was a rest, while the words sank into their minds.

"And this shall be a sign unto you," the annunciator said next. "Ye shall find a babe, wrapped in swaddling-clothes, lying in a manger."

The herald spoke not again; his good tidings were told; yet he stayed awhile. Suddenly the light, of which he seemed the centre, turned roseate and began to tremble; then up, far as the men could see, there was flashing of white wings, and coming and going of radiant forms, and voices as of a multitude chanting in unison,—

"Glory to God in the highest, and on earth peace, goodwill towards men!"

Not once the praise, but many times.

Then the herald raised his eyes as seeking approval of one far off; his wings stirred, and spread slowly and majestically, on their upper side white as snow, in the shadow vari-tinted, like mother-of-pearl; when they were expanded many cubits beyond his stature, he arose lightly, and, without effort, floated out of view, taking the light up with him. Long after he was gone, down from the sky fell the refrain in measure mellowed by distance, "Glory to God in the highest, and on earth peace, goodwill towards men."

When the shepherds came fully to their senses, they stared at each other stupidly, until one of them said, "It was Gabriel, the Lord's messenger unto men."

None answered.

"Christ the Lord is born; said he not so?"

Then another recovered his voice, and replied, "That is what he said."

"And did he not also say, in the city of David, which is our Bethlehem yonder. And that we should find Him a babe in swaddling-clothes?"

"And lying in a manger."

The first speaker gazed into the fire thoughtfully, but at length said, like one possessed of a sudden resolve, "There is but one place in Bethlehem where there are mangers; but one, and that is in the cave near the old khan. Brethren, let us go see this thing which has come to pass. The priests and doctors have been a long time looking for the Christ. Now He is born, and the Lord has given us a sign by which to know Him. Let us go up and worship Him."

"But the flocks!"

"The Lord will take care of them. Let us make haste."

Then they all arose and left the *mârâh*.

.   .   .   .   .

Around the mountain and through the town they passed, and came to the gate of the khan, where there was a man on watch.

"What would you have?" he asked.

"We have seen and heard great things to-night," they replied.

"Well, we, too, have seen great things, but heard nothing. What did you hear?"

"Let us go down to the cave in the enclosure, that we may be sure; then we will tell you all. Come with us, and see for yourself."

"It is a fool's errand."

"No, the Christ is born."

"The Christ! How do you know?"

"Let us go and see first."

The man laughed scornfully.

"The Christ indeed. How are you to know Him?"

"He was born this night, and is now lying in a manger, so we were told; and there is but one place in Bethlehem with mangers."

"The cave?"

"Yes. Come with us."

They went through the court-yard without notice, although there were some up even then talking about the wonderful light. The door of the cavern was open. A lantern was burning within, and they entered unceremoniously.

B

"I give you peace," the watchman said to Joseph and the Beth-Dagonite. "Here are people looking for a Child born this night, whom they are to know by finding Him in swaddling-clothes and lying in a manger."

For a moment the face of the stolid Nazarene was moved; turning away, he said, "The Child is here."

They were led to one of the mangers, and there the Child was. The lantern was brought, and the shepherds stood by mute. The little one made no sign; it was as others just born.

"Where is the mother?" asked the watchman.

One of the women took the baby, and went to Mary, lying near, and put it in her arms. Then the bystanders collected about the two.

"It is the Christ!" said a shepherd at last.

"The Christ!" they all repeated, failing upon their knees in worship. One of them repeated several times over,—

"It is the Lord, and His glory is above the earth and heaven."

And the simple men, never doubting, kissed the hem of the mother's robe, and with joyful faces departed. In the khan, to all the people aroused and pressing about them, they told their story; and through the town, and all the way back to the *mârâh*, they chanted the refrain of the angels, "Glory to God in the highest, and on earth peace, good-will towards men!"

The story went abroad, confirmed by the light so generally seen; and the next day, and for days thereafter, the cave was visited by curious crowds, of whom some believed, though the greater part laughed and mocked.

CHAPTER 7

HEROD AND THE MAGI

THE eleventh day after the birth of the Child in the cave, about mid-afternoon, the three wise men approached Jerusalem by the road from Shechem. After crossing brook Cedron, they met many people, of whom none failed to stop and look after them curiously.

They came, at length, to a tower of great height and strength, over-looking the gate which, at that time, answered to the present Damascus Gate, and marked the meeting-place of the three roads from Shechem, Jericho, and Gibeon. A Roman guard kept the passage-way. By this time the people following the camels formed a train sufficient to draw the idlers hanging about the portal; so that when Balthasar stopped to speak to the sentinel, the three became instantly the centre of a close circle eager to hear all that passed.

"I give you peace," the Egyptian said, in a clear voice.

The sentinel made no reply.

"We have come great distances in search of One who is born King of the Jews. Can you tell us where He is?"

The soldier raised the visor of his helmet, and called loudly. From an apartment at the right of the passage an officer appeared.

"Give way," he cried to the crowd which now pressed closer in; and as they seemed slow to obey, he advanced twirling his javelin vigorously, now right, now left; and so he gained room.

"What would you?" he asked of Balthasar, speaking in the idiom of the city.

And Balthasar answered in the same,—

"Where is He that is born King of the Jews?"

"Herod?" asked the officer, confounded.

"Herod's kingship is from Cæsar; not Herod."

"There is no other King of the Jews."

"But we have seen the star of Him we seek, and come to worship Him."

The Roman was perplexed.

"Go farther," he said at last. "Go farther. I am not a Jew. Carry the question to the doctors in the temple, or to Hannas the priest, or, better still, to Herod himself. If there be another King of the Jews, he will find him."

Thereupon he made way for the strangers, and they passed the gate. But, before entering the narrow street, Balthasar lingered to say to his friends, "We are sufficiently proclaimed. By midnight the whole city will have heard of us and of our mission. Let us to the khan now."

Yet later in the evening the wise men were lying in a lewen of the khan awake. The stones which served them as pillows raised their heads so they could look out of the open arch into the depths of the sky; and as they watched the twinkling of the stars, they thought of the next manifestation. How would it come? What would it be? They were in Jerusalem at last; they had asked at the gate for Him they sought; they had borne witness of His birth; it remained only to find Him; and as to that, they placed all trust in the Spirit. Men listening for the voice of God, or waiting a sign from Heaven, cannot sleep.

While they were in this condition, a man stepped in under the arch, darkening the lewen.

"Awake!" he said to them; "I bring you a message which will not be put off."

They all sat up.

"From whom?" asked the Egyptian.

"Herod the king."

Each one felt his spirit thrill.

"Are you not the steward of the khan?" Balthasar asked next.

"I am."

"What would the king with us?"

"His messenger is without; let him answer."

"Tell him, then, to abide our coming."

"You were right, O my brother!" said the Greek, when the steward was gone. "The question put to the people on the road, and to the guard at the gate, has given us quick notoriety. I am impatient; let us up quickly."

They arose, put on their sandals, girt their mantles about them, and went out.

"I salute you; and give you peace, and pray your pardon; but my master, the king, has sent me to invite you to the palace, where he would have speech with you privately."

Thus the messenger discharged his duty.

A lamp hung in the entrance, and by its light they looked at each other, and knew the Spirit was upon them. Then the Egyptian stepped to the steward, and said, so as not to be heard by the others, "You know where our goods are stored in the court, and where our camels are resting. While we are gone, make all things ready for our departure, if it should be needful."

"Go your way assured; trust me," the steward replied.

"The king's will is our will," said Balthasar to the messenger. "We will follow you."

The streets of the Holy City were narrow then as now, but not so rough and foul; for the great builder, not content with beauty, enforced cleanliness and convenience also. Following their guide, the brethren proceeded without a word. Through the dim starlight, made dimmer by the walls on both sides, sometimes almost lost under bridges connecting the house-tops, out of a low ground they ascended a hill. At last they came to a portal reared across the way. In the light of fires blazing before it in two great braziers, they caught a glimpse of the structure, and also of some guards leaning motionlessly upon their arms. They passed into a building unchallenged. Then by passages and arched halls; through courts, and under colonnades not always lighted; up long flights of stairs, past innumerable cloisters and chambers, they were conducted into a tower of great height. Suddenly the guide halted, and, pointing through an open door, said to them,—

"Enter. The king is there."

The air of the chamber was heavy with the perfume of sandalwood, and all the appointments within were effeminately rich. Upon the floor, covering the central space, a tufted rug was spread, and upon that a throne was set. The visitors had but time, however, to catch a confused idea of the place—of carved and gilt ottomans and couches; of fans and jars and musical instruments; of golden candlesticks glittering in their own lights; of walls painted in the style of the voluptuous Grecian school, one look at which had made a Pharisee hide his head with holy horror. Herod, sitting upon the throne to receive them, clad as when at the conference with the doctors and lawyers, claimed all their minds.

At the edge of the rug, to which they advanced uninvited, they prostrated themselves. The king touched a bell. An attendant came in, and placed three stools before the throne.

"Seat yourselves," said the monarch graciously.

"From the North Gate," he continued, when they were at rest, "I had this afternoon report of the arrival of three strangers curiously mounted, and appearing as if from far countries. Are you the men?"

The Egyptian took the sign from the Greek and the Hindoo, and answered, with the profoundest salaam, "Were we other than we are, the mighty Herod, whose fame is as incense to the whole world, would not have sent for us. We may not doubt that we are the strangers."

Herod acknowledged the speech with a wave of the hand.

"Who are you? Whence do you come?" he asked, adding significantly, "Let each speak for himself."

In turn they gave him account, referring simply to the cities and lands of their birth, and the routes by which they came to Jerusalem. Somewhat disappointed, Herod plied them more directly.

"What was the question you put to the officer at the gate?"

"We asked him, where is He that is born King of the Jews."

"I see now why the people were so curious. You excite me no less. Is there another King of the Jews?"

The Egyptian did not blanch.

"There is one newly born."

An expression of pain knit the dark face of the monarch, as if his mind were swept by a harrowing recollection.

"Not to me, not to me!" he exclaimed.

Possibly the accusing images of his murdered children flitted before him; recovering from the emotion, whatever it was, he asked steadily, "Where is the new king?"

"That, O king, is what we would ask."

"You bring me a wonder—a riddle surpassing any of Solomon's," the inquisitor said next. "As you see I am in the time of life when curiosity is as ungovernable as it was in childhood, when to trifle with it is cruelty. Tell me further, and I will honour you as kings honour each other. Give me all you know about the newly born, and I will join you in the search for Him; and when we have found Him, I will do what you wish; I will bring Him to Jerusalem, and train Him in king-craft; I will use my grace with Cæsar for His promotion and glory. Jealousy shall not come between us, so I swear. But tell me first how so widely separated by seas and deserts, you all came to hear of Him."

"I will tell you truly, O king."

"Speak on," said Herod.

Balthasar raised himself erect, and said solemnly,—

"There is an almighty God."

Herod was visibly startled.

"He bade us come hither, promising that we should find the Redeemer of the World; that we should see and worship Him, and bear witness that He was come; and, as a sign, we were each given to see a star. His Spirit stayed with us. O king, His Spirit is with us now!"

An overpowering feeling seized the three. The Greek with difficulty restrained an outcry. Herod's gaze darted quickly from one to the other; he was more suspicious and dissatisfied than before.

"You are mocking me," he said. "If not, tell me more. What is to follow the coming of the new king?"

"The salvation of men."

"From what?"

"Their wickedness."

"How?"

"By the divine agencies—Faith, Love, and Good Works."

"Then"—Herod paused, and from his look no man could have said with what feeling he continued—"you are the heralds of the Christ. Is that all?"

Balthasar bowed low.

"We are your servants, O king."

The monarch touched a bell, and the attendant appeared.

"Bring the gifts," the master said.

The attendant went out, but in a little while returned, and, kneeling before the guests, gave to each one an outer robe or mantle of scarlet and blue, and a girdle of gold. They acknowledged the honours with Eastern prostrations.

"A word further," said Herod, when the ceremony was ended.

"To the officer of the gate, and but now to me, you spoke of seeing a star in the east."

"Yes," said Balthasar. "His star, the star of the newly born."

"What time did it appear?"

"When we were bidden come hither."

Herod arose, signifying the audience was over. Stepping from the throne towards them, he said, with all graciousness,—

"If, as I believe, O illustrious men, you are indeed the heralds of the Christ just born, know that I have this night consulted those wisest in things Jewish, and they say with one voice He should be born in Bethlehem of Judea. I say to you, go thither; go and search diligently for the young Child; and when you have found Him, bring me word again, that I may come and worship Him. To your going there shall be no let or hindrance. Peace be with you!"

And, folding his robe about him, he left the chamber.

Directly the guide came, and led them back to the street, and thence to the khan, at the portal of which the Greek said, impulsively, "Let us to Bethlehem, O brethren, as the king has advised."

"Yes," cried the Hindoo. "The Spirit burns within me."

"Be it so," said Balthasar, with equal warmth. "The camels are ready."

They gave gifts to the steward, mounted into their saddles, received directions to the Joppa Gate, and departed. At their approach the great valves were unbarred, and they passed out into the open country, taking the road so lately travelled by Joseph and Mary. As they came up out of Hinnom, on the plain of Rephaim, a light appeared, at first widespread and faint. Their pulses fluttered fast. The light intensified rapidly; they closed their eyes against its burning brilliance: when they dared look again, lo! the star, perfect as any in the heavens, but low down and moving slowly before them. And they folded their hands, and shouted, and rejoiced with exceeding great joy.

"God is with us! God is with us!" they repeated, in frequent cheer, all the way, until the star, rising out of the valley beyond Mar Elias, stood still over a house up on the slope of the hill near the town.

CHAPTER 8

THE CHILD CHRIST

IT was now the beginning of the third watch, and at Bethlehem the morning was breaking over the mountains in the east, but so feebly that it was yet night in the valley. The watchman on the roof of the

old khan, shivering in the chilly air, was listening for the first distinguishable sounds with which life, awakening, greets the dawn, when
a light came moving up the hill towards the house. He thought it a
torch in some one's hand; next moment he thought it a meteor; the
brilliance grew, however, until it became a star. Sore afraid, he cried
out, and brought everybody within the walls to the roof. The phenomenon, in eccentric motion, continued to approach; the rocks, trees, and
roadway under it shone as in a glare of lightning; directly its brightness
became blinding. The more timid of the beholders fell upon their knees,
and prayed, with their faces hidden; the boldest covering their eyes,
crouched, and now and then snatched glances fearfully. Afterwhile the
khan and everything thereabout lay under the intolerable radiance.
Such as dared look beheld the star standing still directly over the house
in front of the cave where the Child had been born.

In the height of this scene, the wise men came up, and at the gate
dismounted from their camels, and shouted for admission. When the
steward so far mastered his terror as to give them heed, he drew the bars
and opened to them. The camels looked spectral in the unnatural light,
and, besides their outlandishness, there were in the faces and manner
of the three visitors an eagerness and exaltation which still further
excited the keeper's fears and fancy; he fell back, and for a time could
not answer the question they put to him.

"Is not this Bethlehem of Judea?"

But others came, and by their presence gave him assurance.

"No, this is but the khan; the town lies farther on."

"Is there not here a Child newly born?"

The bystanders turned to each other marvelling, though some of them
answered, "Yes, yes."

"Show us to Him!" said the Greek impatiently.

"Show us to Him!" cried Balthasar, breaking through his gravity;
"for we have seen His star, even that which ye behold over the house,
and are come to worship Him."

The Hindoo clasped his hands, exclaiming, "God indeed lives! Make
haste, make haste! The Saviour is found. Blessed, blessed are we above
men!"

The people from the roof came down and followed the strangers as
they were taken through the court and out into the enclosure; at sight
of the star yet above the cave, though less candescent than before, some
turned back afraid; the greater part went on. As the strangers neared
the house, the orb arose; when they were at the door, it was high up
overhead vanishing; when they entered, it went out lost to sight. And
to the witnesses of what then took place came a conviction that there

was a divine relation between the star and the strangers, which extended also to at least some of the occupants of the cave. When the door was opened, they crowded in.

The apartment was lighted by a lantern enough to enable the strangers to find the mother, and the Child awake in her lap.

"Is the Child thine?" asked Balthasar of Mary.

And she who had kept all the things in the least affecting the little one, and pondered them in her heart, held it up in the light, saying,—

"He is my son!"

And they fell down and worshipped Him.

They saw the Child was as other children: about its head was neither nimbus nor material crown; its lips opened not in speech; if it heard their expressions of joy, their invocations, their prayers, it made no sign whatever, but, baby-like, looked longer at the flame in the lantern than at them.

In a little while they arose, and, returning to the camels, brought gifts of gold, frankincense, and myrrh, and laid them before the Child, abating nothing of their worshipful speeches; of which no part is given, for the thoughtful know that the pure worship of the pure heart was then what it is now, and has always been—an inspired song.

And this was the Saviour they had come so far to find!

Yet they worshipped without a doubt.

Why?

Their faith rested upon the signs sent them by Him whom we have since come to know as the Father; and they were of the kind to whom His promises were so all-sufficient that they asked nothing about His ways. Few there were who had seen the signs and heard the promises— the Mother and Joseph, the shepherds, and the three—yet they all believed alike; that is to say, in this period of the plan of salvation, God was all, and the Child nothing. But look forward, O reader! A time will come when the signs will all proceed from the Son. Happy they who then believe in Him!

Let us wait that period.

BOOK SECOND

> "There is a fire
> And motion of the soul which will not dwell
> In its own narrow being, but aspire
> Beyond the fitting medium of desire:
> And, but once kindled, quenchless evermore,
> Preys upon high adventure, nor can tire
> Of aught but rest."
>
> *Childe Harold*

CHAPTER I

ROME AND JUDEA

IT is necessary now to carry the reader forward twenty-one years, to the beginning of the administration of Valerius Gratus, the fourth imperial governor of Judea—a period which will be remembered as rent by political agitations in Jerusalem, if, indeed, it be not the precise time of the opening of the final quarrel between the Jew and the Roman.

In the interval Judea had been subjected to changes affecting her in many ways, but in nothing so much as her political status. Herod the Great died within one year after the birth of the child—died so miserably that the Christian world had reason to believe him overtaken by the divine wrath.

Judea had been a Roman province eighty years and more—ample time for the Cæsars to study the idiosyncrasies of the people—time enough, at least, to learn that the Jew, with all his pride, could be quietly governed if his religion were respected. Proceeding upon that policy, the predecessors of Gratus had carefully abstained from interfering with any of the sacred observances of their subjects. But he chose a different course: almost his first official act was to expel Hannas from the high-priesthood, and give the place to Ishmael, son of Fabus.

A month after Ishmael took the office, the Roman found it necessary to visit him in Jerusalem. When from the walls, hooting and hissing him, the Jews beheld his guard enter the north gate of the city, and march to the Tower of Antonia, they understood to real purpose of the visit—a full cohort of legionaries was added to the former garrison, and the keys of their yoke could now be tightened with impunity. If the procurator deemed it important to make an example, alas for the first offender!

With the foregoing explanations in mind, the reader is invited to look into one of the gardens of the palace on Mount Zion. The time was noonday in the middle of July, when the heat of summer was at its highest.

The garden was bounded on every side by buildings, which in places arose two stories, with verandas shading the doors and windows of the lower story, while retreating galleries, guarded by strong balustrades, adorned and protected the upper. In all directions the grade sloped gently from the centre, where there was a reservoir, or deep marble basin, broken at intervals by little gates which, when raised, emptied the water into sluices bordering the walks—a cunning device for the rescue of the place from the aridity too prevalent elsewhere in the region.

Not far from the fountain there was a small pool of clear water nourishing a clump of cane and oleander, such as grow on the Jordan and down by the Dead Sea. Between the clump and the pool, unmindful of the sun shining full upon them in the breathless air, two boys, one about nineteen, the other seventeen, sat engaged in earnest conversation.

They were both handsome, and, at first glance, would have been pronounced brothers. Both had hair and eyes black; their faces were deeply browned; and, sitting, they seemed of a size proper for the difference in their ages.

The elder was bareheaded. A loose tunic, dropping to the knees, was his attire complete, except sandals and a light-blue mantle spread under him on the seat. The costume left his arms and legs exposed, and they were brown as the face; nevertheless, a certain grace of manner, refinement of features, and cultured voice decided his rank. The tunic, of softest woollen, grey-tinted, at the neck, sleeves, and edge of the skirt bordered with red, and bound to the waist by a tasselled silken cord, certified him the Roman he was. And if in speech he now and then gazed haughtily at his companion, and addressed him as an inferior, he might almost be excused, for he was of a family noble even in Rome—a circumstance which in that age justified any assumption. In the terrible wars between the first Cæsar and his great enemies, a Messala had been the friend of Brutus. After Philippi, without sacrifice of his honour, he and the conqueror became reconciled. Yet later, when Octavius disputed for the empire, Messala supported him. Octavius, as the Emperor Augustus, remembered the service, and showered the family with honours. Among other things, Judea being reduced to a province, he sent the son of his old client or retainer to Jerusalem, charged with the receipt and management of the taxes levied in that region; and in that service the son had since remained, sharing the palace with the high priest. The youth just described was his son, whose habit it was to carry about with him all too faithfully a remembrance of the relation between his grandfather and the great Romans of his day.

The associate of Messala was slighter in form, and his garments were of fine white linen and of the prevalent style in Jerusalem; a cloth covered his head, held by a yellow cord, and arranged so as to fall away from the forehead down low over the back of the neck. An observer skilled in the distinctions of race, and studying his features more than his costume, would have soon discovered him to be of Jewish descent. The forehead of the Roman was high and narrow, his nose sharp and aquiline, while his lips were thin and straight, and his eyes cold and close under the brows. The front of the Israelite, on the other hand, was low and broad; his nose long, with expanded nostrils; his upper lip, slightly shading the lower one, short and curving to the dimpled corners, like a cupid's bow; points which, in connection with the round chin, full eyes, and oval cheeks, reddened with a wine-like glow, gave his face the softness, strength, and beauty peculiar to his race. The comeliness of the Roman was severe and chaste, that of the Jew rich and voluptuous.

"Did you say the new procurator is to arrive to-morrow?"

The question proceeded from the younger of the friends, and was couched in Greek, at the time, singularly enough, the language everywhere prevalent in the politer circles of Judea.

"Yes, to-morrow," Messala answered.

"Who told you?"

"I heard Ishmael, the new governor in the palace—you call him high priest—tell my father so last night. The news had been more credible, I grant you, coming from an Egyptian, who is of a race that has forgotten what truth is, or even from an Idumæan, whose people never knew what truth was; but, to make quite certain, I saw a centurion from the Tower this morning, and he told me preparations were going on for the reception.

A perfect idea of the manner in which the answer was given cannot be conveyed, as its fine points continually escape the power behind the pen. The reader's fancy must come to his aid; and for that he must be reminded that reverence as a quality of the Roman mind was fast breaking down, or rather, it was becoming unfashionable. The colour in the Jewish lad's cheeks deepened, and he may not have heard the rest of the speech, for he remained silent, looking absently into the depths of the pool.

"Our farewell took place in this garden. 'The peace of the Lord go with you!'—your last words. 'The gods keep you!' I said. Do you remember? How many years have passed since then?"

"Five," answered the Jew, gazing into the water.

"Well, you have reason to be thankful to—whom shall I say? The gods? No matter. You have grown handsome; the Greeks would call you beautiful—happy achievement of the years! If Jupiter would stay content with one Ganymede, what a cup-bearer you would make for the emperor! Tell me, my Judah, how the coming of the procurator is of such interest to you."

Judah bent his large eyes upon the questioner; the gaze was grave and thoughtful, and caught the Roman's, and held it while he replied, "Yes, five years. I remember the parting; you went to Rome; I saw you start, and cried, for I loved you. The years are gone, and you have come back to me accomplished and princely—I do not jest; and yet—yet—I wish you were the Messala you went away."

The fine nostril of the satirist stirred, and he put on a longer drawl as he said, "No, no; not a Ganymede—an oracle, my Judah. A few lessons from my teacher of rhetoric hard by the Forum—I will give you a letter to him when you become wise enough to accept a suggestion which I am reminded to make you—a little practice of the art of mystery, and Delphi will receive you as Apollo himself. At the sound of your solemn voice, the Pythia will come down to you with her crown. Seriously, O my friend, in what am I not the Messala I went away? I once heard the greatest logician in the world. His subject was Disputation. One saying I remember—'Understand your antagonist before you answer him.' Let me understand you."

The lad reddened under the cynical look to which he was subjected; yet he replied firmly, "You have availed yourself, I see, of your opportunities; from your teachers you have brought away much knowledge and many graces. You talk with the ease of a master; yet your speech carries a sting. My Messala, when he went away, had no poison in his nature; not for the world would he have hurt the feelings of a friend."

The Roman smiled as if complimented, and raised his patrician head a toss higher.

"O my solemn Judah, we are not at Dodona or Pytho. Drop the oracular, and be plain. Wherein have I hurt you?"

The other drew a long breath, and said, pulling at the cord about his waist, "In the five years, I, too, have learned somewhat. Hillel may not be the equal of the logician you heard, and Simeon and Shammai are no doubt inferior to your master hard by the Forum. Their learning goes not out into forbidden paths; those who sit at their feet arise enriched simply with knowledge of God, the law, and Israel; and the effect is love and reverence for everything that pertains to them. Attendance at the Great College, and study of what I heard there, have taught me that Judea is not as she used to be. I know the space that lies between an independent kingdom and the petty province Judea is. I were meaner, viler, than a Samaritan not to resent the degradation of my country. Ishmael is not lawfully high priest, and he cannot be while the noble Hannas lives; yet he is a Levite; one of the devoted who for thousands of years have acceptably served the Lord God of our faith and worship. His——"

Messala broke in upon him with a biting laugh.

"Oh, I understand you now. Ishmael, you say, is a usurper, yet to believe an Idumæan sooner than Ishmael is to sting like an adder. By the drunken son of Semele, what it is to be a Jew! All men and things, even heaven and earth, change; but a Jew never."

The Jew arose, his face much flushed.

"Do not leave me," said Messala.

The other stopped irresolute.

"Gods, Juda, how hot the sun shines!" cried the patrician, observing his perplexity. "Let us seek a shade."

Judah answered coldly,—

"We had better part. I wish I had not come. I sought a friend and find a——"

"Roman," said Messala quickly.

The hands of the Jew clenched, but controlling himself again, he started off. Messala arose, and, taking the mantle from the bench, flung it over his shoulder, and followed after; when he gained his side, he put his hand upon his shoulder and walked with him.

"This is the way—my hand thus—we used to walk when we were children. Let us keep it as far as the gate."

Apparently Messala was trying to be serious and kind, though he could not rid his countenance of the habitual satirical expression. Judah permitted the familiarity.

"You are a boy; I am a man; let me talk like one."

The complacency of the Roman was superb. Mentor lecturing the young Telemachus could not have been more at ease.

They were now at the gate. Judah stopped, and took the hand gently from his shoulder, and confronted Messala, tears trembling in his eyes.

"I understand you, because you are a Roman; you cannot understand me—I am an Israelite. You have given me suffering to-day by convincing me that we can never be the friends we have been—never! Here we part. The peace of the God of my fathers abide with you!"

Messala offered him his hand; the Jew walked on through the gateway. When he was gone, the Roman was silent awhile; then he, too, passed through, saying to himself, with a toss of the head,—

"Be it so. Eros is dead, Mars reigns!"

CHAPTER 2

JUDAH'S HOME

FROM the entrance to the Holy City, equivalent to what is now called St. Stephen's gate, a street extended westwardly, on a line parallel with the northern front of the Tower of Antonia, though a square from that famous castle. Keeping the course as far as the Tyropœon Valley, which it followed a little way south, it turned and again ran west until a short distance beyond what tradition tells us was the Judgment Gate, from whence it broke abruptly south. The traveller or the student familiar with the sacred locality will recognise the thoroughfare described as part of the Via Dolorosa—with Christians of more interest, though of a melancholy kind, than any street in the world. As the purpose in view does not at present require dealing with the whole street, it will be sufficient to point out a house standing in the angle last mentioned as marking the change of direction south, and which, as an important centre of interest, needs somewhat particular description.

The building fronted north and west, probably four hundred feet each way, and, like most pretentious Eastern structures, was two stories in height, and perfectly quadrangular. The western windows were four in number, the northern only two, all set on the line of the second story in such manner as to overhang the thoroughfares below.

Not long after the young Jew parted from the Roman at the palace up on the Market-place, he stopped before the western gate of the house described, and knocked. The wicket (a door hung in one of the valves of the gate) was opened to admit him. He stepped in hastily, and failed to acknowledge the low salaam of the porter.

To get an idea of the interior arrangement of the structure, as well as to see what more befell the youth, we will follow him.

The passage into which he was admitted appeared not unlike a narrow tunnel with panelled walls and pitted ceiling. There were benches of stone on both sides, stained and polished by long use. Twelve or fifteen steps carried him into a court-yard, oblong north and south, and in every quarter, except the east, bounded by what seemed the fronts of two-storey houses; of which the lower floor was divided into lewens, while the upper was terraced and defended by strong balustrading.

Clearing the second passage, the young man entered a second court, spacious, square, and set with shrubbery and vines, kept fresh and beautiful by water from a basin erected near a porch on the north side. The lewens here were high, airy, and shaded by curtains striped alternate white and red. The arches of the lewens rested on clustered columns. A flight of steps on the south ascended to the terraces of the upper storey, over which great awnings were stretched as a defence against the sun. Another stairway reached from the terraces to the roof, the edge of which, all around the square, was defined by a sculptured cornice, and a parapet of burned-clay tiling, sexangular and bright red. In this quarter, moreover, there was everywhere observable a scrupulous neatness, which, allowing no dust in the angles, not even a yellow leaf upon a shrub, contributed quite as much as anything else to the delightful general effect; insomuch that a visitor, breathing the sweet air, knew, in advance of introduction, the refinement of the family he was about calling upon.

A few steps within the second court, the lad turned to the right, and, choosing a walk through the shrubbery, part of which was in flower, passed to the stairway, and ascended to the terrace—a broad pavement of white-and-brown flags closely laid, and much worn. Making way under the awning to a doorway on the north side, he entered an apartment which the dropping of the screen behind him returned to darkness. Nevertheless he proceeded, moving over a tiled floor to a divan, upon which he flung himself, face downwards, and lay at rest, his forehead upon his crossed arms.

About nightfall a woman came to the door and called; he answered, and she went in.

"Supper is over, and it is night," she said.

He stirred himself, and sat up.

"Very well. Bring me something to eat."

"What do you want?"

"What you please, Amrah."

She laid her hand upon his forehead; then, as satisfied, went out, saying, "I will see."

After a while she returned, bearing on a wooden platter a bowl of milk, some thin cakes of white bread broken, a delicate paste of brayed wheat, a bird broiled, and honey and salt. On one end of the platter there was a silver goblet full of wine, on the other a brazen hand-lamp lighted.

The room was then revealed: its walls smoothly plastered; the ceiling broken by great oaken rafters, brown with rain stains and time; the floor of small diamond-shaped white-and-blue tiles, very firm and enduring; a few stools with legs carved in imitation of the legs of lions; a divan raised a little above the floor, trimmed with blue cloth, and partially covered by an immense striped woollen blanket or shawl—in brief, a Hebrew bedroom.

The same light also gave the woman to view. Drawing a stool to the divan, she placed the platter upon it, then knelt close by ready to serve him. Her face was that of a woman of fifty, dark-skinned, dark-eyed, and at the moment softened by a look of tenderness almost maternal. A white turban covered her head, leaving the lobes of the ear exposed, and in them the sign that settled her condition—an orifice bored by a thick awl. She was a slave, of Egyptian origin, to whom not even the sacred fiftieth year could have brought freedom; nor would she have accepted it, for the boy she was attending was her life. She had nursed him through babyhood, tended him as a child, and could not break the service. To her love he could never be a man.

He spoke but once during the meal.

"You remember, O my Amrah," he said, "the Messala who used to visit me here days at a time."

"I remember him."

"He went to Rome some years ago, and is now back. I called upon him to-day."

A shudder of disgust seized the lad.

"I knew something had happened," she said, deeply interested. "I never liked the Messala. Tell me all."

But he fell into musing, and to her repeated inquiries only said, "He is much changed, and I shall have nothing more to do with him."

When Amrah took the platter away, he also went out, and up from the terrace to the roof.

The reader is presumed to know somewhat of the uses of the housetop in the East. In the matter of customs, climate is a lawgiver everywhere. The Syrian summer day drives the seeker of comfort into the darkened lewen; night, however, calls him forth early, and the shadows deepening over the mountain-sides seem veils dimly covering Circean singers; but they are afar off, while the roof is close by, and raised above the level of the shimmering plain enough for the visitation of cool airs, and sufficiently above the trees to allure the stars down closer, down at least into brighter shining. So the roof became a resort— became playground, sleeping-chamber, boudoir, rendezvous for the family, place of music, dance, conversation, reverie, and prayer.

The lad whom we are following walked slowly across the house-top to a tower built over the north-west corner of the palace. Had he been a stranger, he might have bestowed a glance upon the structure as he drew nigh it, and seen all the dimness permitted—a darkened mass, low, latticed, pillared, and domed. He entered, passing under a half-raised curtain. The interior was all darkness, except that on four sides there were arched openings like doorways, through which the sky, lighted with stars, was visible. In one of the openings, reclining against a cushion from a divan, he saw the figure of a woman, indistinct even in white floating drapery. At the sound of his steps upon the floor, the fan in her hand stopped, glistening where the starlight struck the jewels with which it was sprinkled, and she sat up, and called his name.

"Judah, my son!"

"It is I, mother," he answered, quickening his approach.

Going to her, he knelt, and she put her arms around him, and with kisses pressed him to her bosom.

CHAPTER 3

JUDAH'S MOTHER

THE mother resumed her easy position against the cushion, while the son took place on the divan, his head in her lap. Both of them, looking out of the opening, could see a stretch of lower house-tops in the vicinity, a bank of blue-blackness over in the west which they knew to be mountains, and the sky, its shadowy depths brilliant with stars. The city was still. Only the winds stirred.

"Amrah tells me something has happened to you," she said, caressing his cheek. "When my Judah was a child, I allowed small things to trouble him, but he is now a man. He must not forget"—her voice became very soft—"that one day he is to be my hero."

She spoke in the language almost lost in the land, but which a few— and they were always as rich in blood as in possessions—cherished in its purity, that they might be more certainly distinguished from Gentile peoples—the language in which the loved Rebekah and Rachel sang to Benjamin.

The words appeared to set him thinking anew; after a while, however, he caught the hand with which she fanned him, and said, "To-day, O my mother, I have been made to think of many things that never had place in my mind before."

The young Israelite proceeded then, and rehearsed his conversation with Messala, dwelling with particularity upon the latter's speeches in contempt of the Jews, their customs, and much pent round of life.

Afraid to speak the while, the mother listened, discerning the matter plainly. Judah had gone to the palace on the Market-place, allured by love of a playmate whom he thought to find exactly as he had been at the parting years before; a man met him, and, in place of laughter and references to the sports of the past, the man had been full of the future, and talked of the glory to be won, and of riches and power. Unconscious of the effect, the visitor had come away hurt in pride, yet touched with a natural ambition; but she, the jealous mother, saw it, and, not knowing the turn the aspiration might take, became at once Jewish in her fear. What if it lured him away from the patriarchal faith? In her view, that consequence was more dreadful than any or all others. She could discover but one way to avert it, and she set about the task, her native power reinforced by love to such degree that her speech took a masculine strength and at times a poet's fervour.

"There never has been a people," she began, "who did not think themselves at least equal to any other; never a great nation, my son, that did not believe itself the very superior. When the Roman looks down upon Israel and laughs, he merely repeats the folly of the Egyptian, the Assyrian, and the Macedonian; and as the laugh is against God, the result will be the same."

Her voice became firmer.

"As for what you shall do, my boy—serve the Lord, the Lord God of Israel, not Rome. For a child of Abraham there is no glory except in the Lord's way, and in them there is much glory."

"I may be a soldier then?" Judah asked.

"Why not? Did not Moses call God a man of war?"

There was then a long silence in the summer chamber.

"You have my permission," she said finally; "if only you serve the Lord instead of Cæsar."

He was content with the condition, and by and by fell asleep. She arose then, and put the cushion under his head, and, throwing a shawl over him and kissing him tenderly, went away.

CHAPTER 4

THE ACCIDENT

WHEN Judah awoke, the sun was up over the mountains; the pigeons were abroad in flocks, filling the air with the gleams of their white wings; and off south-east he beheld the Temple, an apparition of gold in the blue of the sky. These, however, were familiar objects, and they received but a glance; upon the edge of the divan, close by him, a girl scarcely fifteen sat singing to the accompaniment of a *nebel*, which she rested upon her knee, and touched gracefully.

She put the instrument down, and, resting her hands in her lap, waited for him to speak. And as it has become necessary to tell somewhat of her, we will avail ourselves of the chance, and add such particulars of the family into whose privacy we are brought as the reader may wish to know.

The favours of Herod had left surviving him many persons of vast estate. Where this fortune was joined to undoubted lineal descent from some famous son of one of the tribes, especially Judah, the happy individual was accounted a Prince of Jerusalem—a distinction which sufficed to bring him the homage of his less favoured countrymen, and the respect, if nothing more, of the Gentiles with whom business and social circumstance brought him into dealing. Of this class none had won in private or public life a higher regard than the father of the lad whom we have been following. With a remembrance of his nationality which never failed him, he had yet been true to the king, and served him faithfully at home and abroad. In faith he was a Hebrew, observant of the law and every essential rite; his place in the synagogue and Temple knew him well; he was thoroughly learned in the Scriptures; he delighted in the society of the college-masters, and carried his reverence for Hillel almost to the point of worship. Yet he was in no sense a Separatist; his hospitality took in strangers from every land; the carping Pharisees even accused him of having more than once entertained Samaritans at his table. Had he been a Gentile, and lived, the world might have heard of him as the rival of Herodes Atticus: as it was, he perished at sea some ten years before this second period of our story, in the prime of life, and lamented everywhere in Judea. We are already acquainted with two members of his family—his widow and son; the only other was a daughter—she whom we have seen singing to her brother.

Tirzah was her name, and as the two looked at each other, their resemblance was plain. Her features had the regularity of his, and were of the same Jewish type; they had also the charm of childish innocency of expression. Home-life and its trustful love permitted the negligent attire in which she appeared. A chemise buttoned upon the right shoulder, and passing loosely over the breast and back and under the left arm, but half concealed her person above the waist, while it left the arms entirely nude. A girdle caught the folds of the garment, marking the commencement of the skirt. The coiffure was very simple and becoming—a silken cap, Tyrian-dyed; and over that a striped scarf of the same material, beautifully embroidered, and wound about in thin folds so as to show the shape of the head without enlarging it; the whole finished by a tassel dropping from the crown point of the cap. She had rings, ear and finger; anklets and bracelets, all of gold; and around her neck there was a collar of gold, curiously garnished with a network of delicate chains, to which were pendants of pearl. The edges of her eyelids were painted, and the tips of her fingers stained. Her hair fell in two long plaits down her back. A curled lock rested upon each cheek in front of the ear. Altogether it would have been impossible to deny her grace, refinement, and beauty.

"Very pretty, my Tirzah, very pretty!" he said, with animation.

"The song?" she asked.

"Yes—and the singer too."

Amrah entered the summer chamber, bearing a platter, with wash-bowl, water, and napkins.

Not being a Pharisee, the ablution was short and simple with Judah. The servant then went out, leaving Tirzah to dress his hair. When a lock was disposed to her satisfaction, she would unloose the small metallic mirror which, as was the fashion among her fair country-women, she wore at her girdle, and gave it to him, that he might see the triumph, and how handsome it made him. Meanwhile they kept up their conversation.

"What do you think, Tirzah?—I am going away."

She dropped her hands with amazement.

"Going away! When? Where? For what?"

"A soldier," he replied, with a certain pride of voice.

Tears came into her eyes.

"You will be killed."

"If God's will, be it so. But, Tirzah, the soldiers are not all killed."

She threw her arms around his neck, as if to hold him back.

"War is a trade," he continued, more soberly. "To learn it thoroughly, one must go to school, and there is no school like a Roman camp."

"You would not fight for Rome?" she asked, holding her breath.

"And you—even you hate her. The whole world hates her. In that, O Tirzah, find the reason of the answer I give you—Yes, I will fight for her, if, in return, she will teach me how one day to fight against her."

"When will you go?"

Amrah's steps were then heard returning.

"Hist!" he said. "Do not let her know of what I am thinking."

The faithful slave came in with breakfast, and placed the waiter holding it upon a stool before them; then, with their white napkins upon her arm, she remained to serve them. They dipped their fingers in a bowl of water, and were rinsing them, when a noise arrested their attention. They listened, and distinguished martial music in the street on the north side of the house.

"Soldiers from the Prætorium! I must see them," he cried, springing from the divan, and running out.

In a moment more he was leaning over the parapet of tiles which guarded the roof at the extreme north-east corner, so absorbed that he did not notice Tirzah by his side, resting one hand upon his shoulder.

Their position—the roof being the highest one in the locality—commanded the house-tops eastward as far as the huge irregular Tower of Antonia, the garrison and military head-quarters for the governor. The street, not more than ten feet wide, was spanned here and there by bridges, open and covered, which, like the roofs along the way, were beginning to be occupied by men, women, and children, called out by the *music*. The word is used, though it is hardly fitting; what the people heard when they came forth was rather an uproar of trumpets and the shriller *litui* so delightful to the soldiers.

The array after a while came into view of the two upon their house, the house of the Hurs. First, a vanguard of the light-armed—mostly slingers and bowmen—marching with wide intervals between their ranks and files; next a body of heavy-armed infantry, bearing large shields, and *hastæ longæ*, or spears identical with those used in the duels before Ilium; then the musicians; and then an officer riding alone, but followed closely by a guard of cavalry; after them again, a column of infantry also heavy-armed, which, moving in close order, crowded the street from wall to wall, and appeared to be without end.

The brawny limbs of the men; the cadenced motion from right to left of the shields; the sparkle of scales, buckles, and breastplates and helms, all perfectly burnished; the plumes nodding above the tall crests; the sway of ensigns and iron-shod spears; the bold, confident step, exactly timed and measured; the demeanour, so grave, yet so watchful; the machine-like unity of the whole moving mass—made an impression upon Judah, but as something felt rather than seen. Two objects fixed his attention—the eagle of the legion first—a gilded effigy perched on a tall shaft, with wings outspread until they met above its head. He knew that, when brought from its chamber in the Tower, it had been received with divine honours.

The officer riding alone in the midst of the column was the other attraction. His head was bare; otherwise he was in full armour. At his left hip he wore a short sword; in his hand, however, he carried a truncheon, which looked like a roll of white paper. He sat upon a purple cloth instead of a saddle, and that, and a bridle with a forestall of gold and reins of yellow silk broadly fringed at the lower edge, completed the housings of the horse.

While the man was yet in the distance, Judah observed that his presence was sufficient to throw the people looking at him into angry excitement. They would lean over the parapets or stand boldly out, and shake their fists at him; they followed him with loud cries, and spit at him as he passed under the bridges; the women even flung their sandals, sometimes with such good effect as to hit him. When he was nearer, the yells became distinguishable—"Robber, tyrant, dog of a Roman! Away with Ishmael! Give us back our Hannas!"

When quite near, Judah could see that, as was but natural, the man did not share the indifference so superbly shown by the soldiers; his face was dark and sullen, and the glances he occasionally cast at his persecutors were full of menace; the very timid shrank from them.

Now the lad had heard of the custom, borrowed from a habit of the first Cæsar, by which chief commanders, to indicate their rank, appeared in public with only a laurel vine upon their heads. By that sign he knew this officer—VALERIUS GRATUS, THE NEW PROCURATOR OF JUDEA!

To say truth now, the Roman under the unprovoked storm had the young Jew's sympathy; so that when he reached the corner of the house, the latter leaned yet farther over the parapet to see him go by, and in the act rested a hand upon a tile which had been a long time cracked and allowed to go unnoticed. The pressure was strong enough to displace the outer piece, which started to fall. A thrill of horror shot through the youth. He reached out to catch the missile. In appearance the motion was exactly that of one pitching something from him. The effort failed—nay, it served to push the descending fragment farther out over the way. He shouted with all his might. The soldiers of the guard looked up; so did the great man, and that moment the missile struck him, and he fell from the seat as dead.

The cohort halted; the guards leaped from their horses, and hastened to cover the chief with their shields. On the other hand, the people who witnessed the affair, never doubting that the blow had been purposely dealt, cheered the lad as he yet stooped in full view over the parapet, transfixed by what he beheld, and by anticipation of the consequences flashed all too plainly upon him.

A mischievous spirit flew with incredible speed from roof to roof along the line of march, seizing the people, and urging them all alike. They laid hands upon the parapets and tore up the tiling and the sun-burnt mud of which the house-tops were for the most part made, and with blind fury began to fling them upon the legionaries halted below. A battle then ensued. Discipline, of course, prevailed. The struggle, the slaughter, the skill of one side, the desperation of the other, are alike unnecessary to our story. Let us look rather to the wretched author of it all.

He arose from the parapet, his face very pale.

"O Tirzah, Tirzah! What will become of us?"

She had not seen the occurrence below, but was listening to the shouting and watching the mad activity of the people in view on the houses. Something terrible was going on, she knew; but what it was, or the cause, or that she or any of those dear to her were in danger, she did not know.

"What has happened? What does it all mean?" she asked, in sudden alarm.

"I have killed the Roman governor. The tile fell upon him."

An unseen hand appeared to sprinkle her face with the dust of ashes —it grew white so instantly. She put her arm around him, and looked wistfully, but without a word, into his eyes. His fears had passed to her, and the sight of them gave him strength.

"I did not do it purposely, Tirzah—it was an accident," he said, more calmly.

"What will they do?" she asked.

He looked off over the tumult momentarily deepening in the street and on the roofs, and thought of the sullen countenance of Gratus. If he were not dead, where would his vengeance stop? And if he were dead, to what height of fury would not the violence of the people lash the legionaries? To evade an answer, he peered over the parapet again, just as the guard were assisting the Roman to remount his horse.

"He lives, he lives, Tirzah! Blessed be the Lord God of our fathers!"

With that outcry, and a brightened countenance, he drew back and replied to her question.

"Be not afraid, Tirzah. I will explain how it happened, and they will remember our father and his services, and not hurt us."

He was leading her to the summer-house, when the roof jarred under their feet, and a crash of strong timbers being burst away, followed by a cry of surprise and agony, arose apparently from the court-yard below. He stopped and listened. The cry was repeated; then came a rush of many feet, and voices lifted in rage blent with voices in prayer; and then the screams of women in mortal terror. The soldiers had beaten in the north gate, and were in possession of the house. The terrible sense of being hunted smote him. His first impulse was to fly; but where? Nothing but wings would serve him. Tirzah, her eyes wild with fear, caught his arm.

"O Judah, what does it mean?"

The servants were being butchered—and his mother! Was not one of the voices he heard hers? With all the will left him, he said, "Stay here, and wait for me, Tirzah. I will go down and see what is the matter, and come back to you."

His voice was not steady as he wished. She clung closer to him.

Clearer, shriller, no longer a fancy, his mother's cry arose. He hesitated no longer.

"Come, then, let us go."

The terrace or gallery at the foot of the steps was crowded with soldiers. Other soldiers with drawn swords ran in and out of the chambers. At one place a number of women on their knees clung to each other or prayed for mercy. Apart from them, one with torn garments, and long hair streaming over her face, struggled to tear loose from a man all whose strength was tasked to keep his hold. Her cries were shrillest of all; cutting through the clamour, they had risen distinguishably to the roof. To her Judah sprang—his steps were long and swift, almost a winged flight—"Mother, mother!" he shouted. She stretched her hands towards him; but when almost touching them he was seized and forced aside. Then he heard some one say, speaking loudly,—

"That is he!"

Judah looked, and saw—Messala.

"What, the assassin—that?" said a tall man, in legionary armour of beautiful finish. "Why, he is but a boy."

"Gods!" replied Messala, not forgetting his drawl. "A new philosophy! What would Seneca say to the proposition that a man must be old before he can hate enough to kill? You have him; and that is his mother; yonder his sister. You have the whole family."

With the last words he disappeared. Judah understood him, and, in the bitterness of his soul, prayed to heaven.

"In the hour of Thy vengeance, O Lord," he said, "be mine the hand to put it upon him!"

By great exertion, he drew nearer the officer.

"Oh, sir, the woman you hear is my mother. Spare her, spare my sister yonder. God is just, He will give you mercy for mercy."

The man appeared to be moved.

"To the Tower with the women!" he shouted, "but do them no harm. I will demand them of you." Then to those holding Judah, he said, "Get cords, and bind his hands, and take him to the street. His punishment is reserved."

The mother was carried away. The little Tirzah, in her home attire, stupefied with fear, went passively with her keepers. Judah gave each of them a last look, and covered his face with his hands, as if to possess himself of the scene fadelessly. He may have shed tears, though no one saw them.

The mother, daughter, and entire household were led out of the north gate, the ruins of which choked the passage-way. The cries of the domestics, some of whom had been born in the house, were most pitiable. When, finally, the horses and all the dumb tenantry of the place were driven past him, Judah began to comprehend the scope of the procurator's vengeance. The very structure was devoted. Far as the order was possible of execution, nothing living was to be left within its walls. If in Judea there were others desperate enough to think of assassinating a Roman governor, the story of what befell the princely family of Hur would be a warning to them, while the ruin of the habitation would keep the story alive.

The officer waited outside while a detail of men temporarily restored the gate.

In the street the fighting had almost ceased. Upon the houses here and there clouds of dust told where the struggle was yet prolonged. The cohort was, for the most part, standing at rest, its splendour, like its ranks, in no wise diminished. Borne past the point of care for himself, Judah had heart for nothing in view but the prisoners, among whom he looked in vain for his mother and Tirzah.

Suddenly, from the earth where she had been lying, a woman arose, and started swiftly back to the gate. Some of the guards reached out to seize her, and a great shout followed their failure. She ran to Judah, and, dropping down, clasped his knees, the coarse black hair powdered with dust veiling her eyes.

"O Amrah, good Amrah," he said to her, "God help you; I cannot."

She could not speak.

He bent down and whispered, "Live, Amrah, for Tirzah and my mother. They will come back, and——"

A soldier drew her away; whereupon she sprang up and rushed through the gateway and passage into the vacant court-yard.

"Let her go," the officer shouted. "We will seal the house, and she will starve."

The men resumed their work, and, when it was finished there, passed round to the west side. That gate was also secured, after which the palace of the Hurs was lost to use.

The cohort at length marched back to the Tower, where the procurator stayed to recover from his hurts and dispose of his prisoners. On the tenth day following, he visited the Market-place.

Next day a detachment of legionaries went to the desolated palace, and, closing the gates permanently, plastered the corners with wax, and at the sides nailed a notice in Latin:

"THIS IS THE PROPERTY OF
THE EMPEROR."

In the haughty Roman idea, the sententious announcement was thought sufficient for the purpose—and it was.

BOOK THIRD

"Cleopatra. . . . . Our size of sorrow,
Proportion'd to our cause, must be as great
As that which makes it.—
                    Enter, below, DIOMEDES.
                                    How now? is he dead?
    Diomedes. His death's upon him, but not dead."
                        Antony and Cleopatra (Act iv. Sc. xiii.)

CHAPTER I

QUINTUS ARRIUS

THE city of Misenum gave name to the promontory which it crowned,
a few miles south-west of Naples. An account of ruins is all that remains
of it now; yet in the year of our Lord 24—to which it is desirable to
advance the reader—the place was one of the most important on the
western coast of Italy.

In the old time, moreover, there was a gateway in the wall at a certain
point fronting the sea—an empty gateway forming the outlet of a street
which, after the exit, stretched itself, in the form of a broad mole, out
many stadia into the waves.

The watchman on the wall above the gateway was disturbed, one
cool September morning, by a party coming down the street in noisy
conversation. He gave one look, then settled into his drowse again.

There were twenty or thirty persons in the party, of whom the greater
number were slaves with torches which flamed little and smoked much,
leaving on the air the perfume of the Indian nard. The masters walked
in advance arm-in-arm. One of them, apparently fifty years old, slightly
bald, and wearing over his scant locks a crown of laurel, seemed,
from the attentions paid him, the central object of some affectionate
ceremony.

"No, my Quintus," said one, speaking to him with the crown, "it is
ill of Fortune to take thee from us so soon. Only yesterday thou didst
return from the seas beyond the Pillars. Why, thou hast not even got
back thy land legs."

With these words, the party passed the gateway, and came upon the
mole, with the bay before them beautiful in the morning light. To the

veteran sailor the plash of the waves was like a greeting. He drew a long breath, as if the perfume of the water were sweeter than that of the nard, and held his hand aloft.

"My gifts were at Præneste, not Antium—and see! Wind from the west. Thanks, O Fortune, my mother!" he said earnestly.

The friends all repeated the exclamation, and the slaves waved their torches.

"She comes—yonder!" he continued, pointing to a galley outside the mole. "What need has a sailor for other mistress? Is your Lucrece more graceful, my Caius?"

He gazed at the coming ship, and justified his pride. A white sail was bent to the low mast, and the oars dipped, arose, poised a moment, then dipped again, with wing-like action, and in perfect time. From the folds of his toga he drew a roll of paper, and passed it to them, saying, "Received while at table last night from—Sejanus."

The name was already a great one in the Roman world; great, and not so infamous as it afterwards became.

"Sejanus!" they exclaimed with one voice, closing in to read what the minister had written.

> "*Sejanus to C. Cæcilius Rufus, Duumvir.*
>
> "Rome, *XIX. Kal. Sept.*
>
> "Cæsar hath good report of Quintus Arrius, the tribune. In particular he hath heard of his valour, manifested in the western seas; insomuch that it is his will that the said Quintus be transferred instantly to the East.
>
> "It is our Cæsar's will, further, that you cause a hundred triremes, of the first class, and full appointment, to be despatched without delay against the pirates who have appeared in the Ægean, and that Quintus be sent to command the fleet so despatched.
>
> "Details are thine, my Cæcilius.
>
> "The necessity is urgent, as thou wilt be advised by the reports enclosed by thy perusal and the information of the said Quintus.
>
> "Sejanus."

Arrius gave little heed to the reading. As the ship drew more plainly out of the perspective, she became more and more an attraction to him. The look with which he watched her was that of an enthusiast. At length he tossed the loosened folds of his toga in the air; in reply to the signal, over the *aplustre*, or fan-like fixture at the stern of the vessel, a scarlet flag was displayed; while several sailors appeared upon the bulwarks, and swung themselves hand over hand up the ropes to the *antenna*, or yard, and furled the sail. The bow was put round, and the time of the oars increased one-half; so that at racing speed she bore down directly towards him and his friends. He observed the manœuvring with a perceptible brightening of the eyes. Her instant answer to the rudder, and the steadiness with which she kept her course, were especially noticeable as virtues to be relied upon in action.

The vessel was of the class called *naves liburnicæ*—long, narrow, low in the water, and modelled for speed and quick manœuvre. The bow was beautiful.

The simplicity of the upper works declared the oars the chief dependence of the crew. A mast, set a little forward of midship, was held by fore and back stays and shrouds fixed to rings on the inner side of the bulwarks. The tackle was that required for the management of one great square sail and the yard to which it was hung. Above the bulwark the deck was visible.

Save the sailors who had reefed the sail, and yet lingered on the yard, but one man was to be seen by the party on the mole, and he stood by the prow helmeted and with a shield.

The hundred and twenty oaken blades, kept white and shining by pumice and the constant wash of the waves, rose and fell as if operated by the same hand, and drove the galley forward with a speed rivalling that of a modern steamer.

In the midst of the rounding-to, a trumpet was blown brief and shrill, and from the hatchways out poured the marines, all in superb equipment, brazen helms, burnished shields, and javelins. While the fighting-men thus went to quarters as for action, the sailors proper climbed the shrouds and perched themselves along the yard. The officers and musicians took their posts. There was no shouting or needless noise. When the oars touched the mole, a bridge was sent out from the helmsman's deck. Then the tribune turned to his party and said, with a gravity he had not before shown,—

"Duty now, O my friends."

He took the chaplet from his head, and gave it to the dice-player.

"Take thou the myrtle, O favourite of the tesseræ!" he said. "If I return, I will seek my sesterce again; if I am not victor, I will not return. Hang the crown in thy atrium."

To the company he opened his arms, and they came one by one and received his parting embrace.

"The gods go with thee, O Quintus!" they said.

"Farewell," he replied.

To the slaves waving their torches he waved his hand; then he turned to the waiting ship, beautiful with ordered ranks and crested helms, and shields and javelins. As he stepped upon the bridge, the trumpets sounded, and over the *aplustre* rose the *vexillum purpureum*, or pennant of a commander of a fleet.

CHAPTER 2

THE ROMAN GALLEY

A PRUDENT man was Arrius—prudent, and of the class which, while enriching the altars at Præneste and Antium, was of opinion, neverthe-less, that the favour of the blind goddess depended more upon the votary's care and judgment than upon his gifts and vows. All night as master of the feast he had sat at table drinking and playing; yet the odour of the sea returned him to the mood of the sailor, and he would not rest until he knew his ship. Knowledge leaves no room for chances. Having begun with the chief of the rowers, the sailing-master, and the pilot, in company with the other officers—the commander of the marines, the keeper of the stores, the master of the machines, the over-seer of the kitchen fires—he passed through the several quarters. Nothing escaped his inspection. When he was through, of the community crowded within the narrow walls he alone knew perfectly all there was of material preparation for the voyage and its possible incidents; and, finding the preparation complete, there was left him but one thing further—thorough knowledge of the *personnel* of his command. As this was the most delicate and difficult part of his task, requiring much time, he set about it his own way.

At noon that day the galley was skimming the sea off Pæstum. The wind was yet from the west, filling the sail to the master's content. The watches had been established. On the foredeck the altar had been set and sprinkled with salt and barley, and before it the tribune had offered solemn prayers to Jove and to Neptune and all the Oceanidæ, and, with vows, poured the wine and burned the incense. And now, the better to study his men, he was seated in the great cabin, a very martial figure.

The cabin, it should be stated, was the central compartment of the galley, in extent quite sixty-five by thirty feet, and lighted by three broad hatchways. A row of stanchions ran from end to end, support-ing the roof, and near the centre the mast was visible, all bristling with axes and spears and javelins. To each hatchway there were double stairs descending right and left, with a pivotal arrangement at the top to allow the lower ends to be hitched to the ceiling; and, as these were now raised, the compartment had the appearance of a skylighted hall.

The reader will understand readily that this was the heart of the ship, the home of all aboard—eating-room, sleeping-chamber, field of exercise, lounging-place off duty—uses made possible by the laws which reduced life there to minute details and a routine relentless as death.

At the after-end of the cabin there was a platform, reached by several steps. Upon it the chief of the rowers sat; in front of him a sounding-table, upon which, with a gavel, he beat time for the oarsmen; at his right a clepsydra, or water-clock, to measure the reliefs and watches. Above him, on a higher platform, well guarded by gilded railing, the tribune had his quarters, overlooking everything, and furnished with a couch, a table, and a *cathedra*, or chair, cushioned, and with arms and high back—articles which the imperial dispensation permitted of the utmost elegance.

Thus at ease, lounging in the great chair, swaying with the motion of the vessel, the military cloak half draping his tunic, sword in belt, Arrius kept watchful eye over his command, and was as closely watched by them. He saw critically everything in view, but dwelt longest upon the rowers. The reader would doubtless have done the same; only he would have looked with much sympathy, while, as is the habit with masters, the tribune's mind ran forward of what he saw, inquiring for results.

The spectacle was simple enough of itself. Along the sides of the cabin, fixed to the ship's timbers, were what at first appeared to be three rows of benches; a closer view, however, showed them a succession of rising banks, in each of which the second bench was behind and above the first one, and the third above and behind the second. To accommodate the sixty rowers on a side, the space devoted to them permitted nineteen banks separated by intervals of one yard, with a twentieth bank divided so that what would have been its upper seat or bench was directly above the lower seat of the first bank. The arrangement gave each rower when at work ample room, if he timed his movements with those of his associates, the principle being that of soldiers marching with cadenced step in close order. The arrangement also allowed a multiplication of banks, limited only by the length of the galley.

As to the rowers, those upon the first and second benches sat, while those upon the third, having longer oars to work, were suffered to stand. The oars were loaded with lead in the handles, and near the point of balance hung to pliable thongs, making possible the delicate touch called feathering, but, at the same time, increasing the need of skill, since an eccentric wave might at any moment catch a heedless fellow and hurl him from his seat. Each oar-hole was a vent through which the labourer opposite it had his plenty of sweet air. Light streamed down upon him from the grating which formed the floor of the passage between the deck and the bulwark over his head. In some respects, therefore, the condition of the men might have been much worse. Still, it must not be imagined that there was any pleasantness in their lives. Communication between them was not allowed. Day after day they filled their places without speech; in hours of labour they could not see each other's faces; their short respites were given to sleep and the snatching of food. They never laughed; no one ever heard one of them sing. What is the use of tongues when a sigh or a groan will tell all men feel, while, perforce, they think in silence? Existence with the poor wretches was like a stream under ground sweeping slowly, laboriously on to its outlet, wherever that might chance to be.

In the labour of the rowers there was not enough art to give occupation to their minds, rude and simple as they were. The reach forward, the pull, the feathering the blade, the dip, were all there was of it; motions most perfect when most automatic. Even the care forced upon them by the sea outside grew in time to be a thing instinctive rather than of thought. So, as the result of long service, the poor wretches became imbruted—patient, spiritless, obedient—creatures of vast muscle and exhausted intellects, who lived upon recollections generally few but dear, and at last lowered into the semi-conscious alchemic state wherein misery turns to habit, and the soul takes on incredible endurance.

From right to left, hour after hour, the tribune, swaying in his easy-chair, turned with thought of everything rather than the wretchedness of the slaves upon the benches. Their motions, precise, and exactly the same on both sides of the vessel, after a while became monotonous; and then he amused himself singling out individuals. With his stylus he made note of objections, thinking, if all went well, he would find among the pirates of whom he was in search better men for the places.

There was no need of keeping the proper names of the slaves brought to the galleys as to their graves; so, for convenience, they were usually identified by the numerals painted upon the benches to which they were assigned. As the sharp eyes of the great man moved from seat to seat on either hand, they came at last to number sixty, which, as has been said, belonged properly to the last bank on the left-hand side, but, wanting room aft, had been fixed above the first bench of the first bank. There they rested.

The bench of number sixty was slightly above the level of the platform, and but a few feet away. The light glinting through the grating over his head gave the rower fairly to the tribune's view—erect, and, like all his fellows, naked, except a cincture about the loins. There were, however, some points in his favour. He was very young, not more than twenty. Furthermore, Arrius was not merely given to dice; he was a connoisseur of men physically, and when ashore indulged a habit of visiting the gymnasia to see and admire the most famous athletæ. From some professor, doubtless, he had caught the idea that strength was as much of the quality as the quantity of the muscle, while superiority in performance required a certain mind as well as strength. Having adopted the doctrine, like most men with a hobby, he was always looking for illustrations to support it.

The reader may well believe that while the tribune, in the search for the perfect, was often called upon to stop and study, he was seldom perfectly satisfied—in fact, very seldom held as long as on this occasion.

In the beginning of each movement of the oar, the rower's body and face were brought into profile view from the platform; the movement ended with the body reversed, and in a pushing posture. The grace and ease of the action at first suggested a doubt of the honesty of the effort put forth; but it was speedily dismissed; the firmness with which the oar was held while in the reach forward, its bending under the push, were proofs of the force applied; not that only, they as certainly proved the rower's art, and put the critic in the great armchair in search of the combination of strength and cleverness which was the central idea of his theory.

In course of the study, Arrius observed the subject's youth; wholly unconscious of tenderness on that account, he also observed that he seemed of good height, and that his limbs, upper and nether, were singularly perfect. The arms, perhaps, were too long, but the objection was well hidden under a mass of muscle which, in some movements, swelled and knotted like kinking cords. Every rib in the round body was discernible; yet the leanness was the healthful reduction so strained after in the palæstræ. And altogether there was in the rower's action, a certain harmony which besides addressing itself to the tribune's theory, stimulated both his curiosity and general interest.

Very soon he found himself waiting to catch a view of the man's face in full. The head was shapely, and balanced upon a neck broad at the base, but of exceeding pliancy and grace. The features in profile were of Oriental outline, and of that delicacy of expression which has always been thought a sign of blood and sensitive spirit. With these observations, the tribune's interest in the subject deepened.

"By the gods," he said to himself, "the fellow impresses me! He promises well. I will know more of him."

Directly the tribune caught the view he wished—the rower turned and looked at him.

"A Jew! and a boy!"

Under the gaze then fixed steadily upon him, the large eyes of the slave grew larger—the blood surged to his very brows—the blade lingered in his hands. But instantly, with an angry crash, down fell the gavel of the hortator. The rower started, withdrew his face from the inquisitor, and, as if personally chidden, dropped the oar half feathered. When he glanced again at the tribune, he was vastly more astonished—he was met with a kindly smile.

Meantime the galley entered the straits of Messina, and, skimming past the city of that name, was after a while turned eastward, leaving the cloud over Ætna in the sky astern.

Often as Arrius returned to his platform in the cabin he returned to study the rower, and he kept saying to himself, "The fellow hath a spirit. A Jew is not a barbarian. I will know more of him."

CHAPTER 3

THE GALLEY SLAVE

THE fourth day out, and the *Astræa*—so the galley was named—speeding through the Ionian Sea. The sky was clear, and the wind blew as if bearing the good-will of all the gods.

As it was possible to overtake the fleet before reaching the bay east of the island of Cythera, designated for assemblage, Arrius, somewhat impatient, spent much time on deck. He took note diligently of matters pertaining to his ship, and, as a rule, was well pleased. In the cabin, swinging in the great chair, his thought continually reverted to the rower on number sixty.

"Knowest thou the man just come from yon bench?" he at length asked of the hortator.

A relief was going on at the moment.

"From number sixty?" returned the chief.

"Yes."

The chief looked sharply at the rower then going forward.

"As thou knowest," he replied, "the ship is but a month from the maker's hand, and the men are as new to me as the ship."

"He is a Jew," Arrius remarked thoughtfully.

"The noble Quintus is shrewd."

"He is very young," Arrius continued.

"But our best rower," said the other. "I have seen his oar bent almost to breaking."

"Of what disposition is he?"

"He is obedient; further I know not. Once he made request of me."

"For what?"

"He wished me to change him alternately from the right to the left."

"Did he give a reason?"

"He had observed that the men who are confined to one side become misshapen. He also said that some day of storm or battle there might be sudden need to change him, and he might then be unserviceable."

"*Perpol!* The idea is new. What else hast thou observed of him?"

"He is cleanly above his companions."

"In that he is Roman," said Arrius approvingly. "Have you nothing of his history?"

"Not a word."

The tribune reflected awhile, and turned to go to his own seat.

"If I should be on deck when his time is up," he paused to say, "send him to me. Let him come alone."

About two hours later Arrius stood under the aplustre of the galley; in the mood of one who, seeing himself carried swiftly towards an event of mighty import, has nothing to do but wait—the mood in which philosophy vests an even-minded man with the utmost calm, and is ever so serviceable. The pilot sat with a hand upon the rope by which the rudder paddles, one on each side of the vessel, were managed. In the shade of the sail some sailors lay asleep, and up on the yard there was a look-out. Lifting his eyes from the solarium set under the aplustre for reference in keeping the course, Arrius beheld the rower approaching.

"The chief called thee the noble Arrius, and said it was thy will that I should seek thee here. I am come."

Arrius surveyed the figure, tall, sinewy, glistening in the sun, and tinted by the rich red blood within—surveyed it admiringly, and with a thought of the arena; yet the manner was not without effect upon him: there was in the voice a suggestion of life at least partly spent under refining influences; the eyes were clear and open, and more curious than defiant. To the shrewd, demanding, masterful glance bent upon it, the face gave back nothing to mar its youthful comeliness—nothing of accusation or sullenness or menace, only the signs which a great sorrow long borne imprints, as time mellows the surface of pictures. In tacit acknowledgment of the effect, the Roman spoke as an older man to a younger, not as a master to a slave.

"The hortator tells me thou art his best rower."

"The hortator is very kind," the rower answered.

"Hast thou seen much service?"

"About three years."

"At the oar?"

"I cannot recall a day of rest from them."

"The labour is hard; few men bear it a year without breaking, and thou—thou art but a boy."

"The noble Arrius forgets that the spirit hath much to do with endurance. By its help the weak sometimes thrive, when the strong perish."

"From thy speech, thou art a Jew."

"My ancestors further back than the first Roman were Hebrews."

"The stubborn pride of thy race is not lost in thee," said Arrius, observing a flush upon the rower's face.

"Pride is never so loud as when in chains."

"What cause hast thou for pride?"

"That I am a Jew."

Arrius smiled.

"I have not been to Jerusalem," he said; "but I have heard of its princes. I knew one of them. He was a merchant, and sailed the seas. He was fit to have been a king. Of what degree art thou?"

"I must answer thee from the bench of a galley. I am of the degree of slaves. My father was a prince of Jerusalem, and, as a merchant, he sailed the seas. He was known and honoured in the guest-chamber of the great Augustus."

"His name?"

"Ithamar, of the house of Hur."

The tribune raised his hand in astonishment.

"A son of Hur—thou?"

After a silence, he asked,—

"What brought thee here?"

Judah lowered his head, and his breast laboured hard. When his feelings were sufficiently mastered, he looked the tribune in the face, and answered,—

"I was accused of attempting to assassinate Valerius Gratus, the procurator."

"Thou!" cried Arrius, yet more amazed, and retreating a step. "Thou that assassin! All Rome rang with the story. It came to my ship in the river by Lodinum.

The two regarded each other silently.

"Dost thou admit thy guilt?" asked Arrius sternly.

The change that came upon Ben-Hur was wonderful to see, it was so instant and extreme. The voice sharpened; the hands arose tight-clenched; every fibre thrilled; his eyes flamed.

"Thou hast heard of the God of my fathers," he said; "of the infinite Jehovah. By His truth and almightiness, and by the love with which He hath followed Israel from the beginning, I swear I am innocent!

"I was a boy, too young to be a conspirator. Gratus was a stranger to me. If I had meant to kill him, that was not the time or the place. He was riding in the midst of a legion, and it was broad day. I could not have escaped. I was of a class most friendly to Rome. My father had been distinguished for his services to the emperor. We had a great estate to lose. Ruin was certain to myself, my mother, my sister. I had no cause for malice, while every consideration—property, family, life, conscience, the Law—to a son of Israel as the breath of his nostrils —would have stayed my hand, though the foul intent had been ever so strong. I was not mad. Death was preferable to shame; and believe me, I pray, it is so yet."

"Who was with thee when the blow was struck?"

"I was on the house-top—my father's house. Tirzah was with me —at my side—the soul of gentleness. Together we leaned over the parapet to see the legion pass. A tile gave way under my hand, and fell upon Gratus. I thought I had killed him. Ah, what horror I felt!"

"Where was thy mother?"

"In her chamber below."

"What became of her?"

Ben-Hur clenched his hands, and drew a breath like a gasp.

"I do not know. I saw them drag her away—that is all I know. Out of the house they drove every living thing, even the dumb cattle, and they sealed the gates. The purpose was that she should not return. I, too, ask for her. Oh, for one word! She, at least, was innocent."

For once the tribune was at loss, and hesitated. His power was ample. He was monarch of the ship. His prepossessions all moved him to mercy. His faith was won. Yet, he said to himself, there was no haste —or, rather, there was haste to Cythera; the best rower could not then be spared; he would wait; he would learn more; he would at least be sure this was the prince Ben-Hur, and that he was of a right disposition. Ordinarily, slaves were liars.

"It is enough," he said aloud. "Go back to thy place."

Ben-Hur bowed; looked once more into the master's face, but saw nothing for hope. He turned away slowly, looked back, and stopped, and the tribune went to him.

"If thou wert free, what wouldst thou do!"

"The noble Arrius mocks me!" Judah said, with trembling lips.

"No; by the gods, no!"

"Then I will answer gladly. I would give myself to duty the first of life. I would know no other. I would know no rest until my mother and Tirzah were restored to home. I would give every day and hour to their happiness. I would wait upon them; never a slave more faithful. They have lost much, but, by the God of my fathers, I would find them more!"

The answer was unexpected by the Roman. For a moment he lost his purpose.

"I spoke to thy ambition," he said, recovering. "If thy mother and sister were dead, or not to be found, what wouldst thou do?"

A distinct pallor overspread Ben-Hur's face, and he looked over the sea. There was a struggle with some strong feeling; when it was conquered, he turned to the tribune.

"What pursuit would I follow?" he asked.

"Yes."

"Tribune, I will tell thee truly. Only the night before the dreadful day of which I have spoken, I obtained permission to be a soldier. I am of the same mind yet; and, as in all the earth there is but one school of war, thither I would go."

"The palæstra!" exclaimed Arrius.

"No; a Roman camp."

"But thou must first acquaint thyself with the use of arms."

Now a master may never safely advise a slave. Arrius saw his indiscretion, and, in a breath, chilled his voice and manner.

"Go now," he said, "and do not build upon what has passed between us. Perhaps I do but play with thee. Or,"—he looked away musingly —"or, if thou dost think of it with any hope, choose between the renown of a gladiator and the service of a soldier. The former may come of the favour of the emperor; there is no reward for thee in the latter. Thou art not a Roman. Go!"

A short while after Ben-Hur was upon his bench again.

CHAPTER 4

A GLEAM OF HOPE

In the Bay of Antemona, east of Cythera the island, the hundred galleys assembled. There the tribune gave one day to inspection. He sailed then to Naxos, the largest of the Cyclades, midway the coasts of Greece and Asia, like a great stone planted in the centre of a highway, from which he could challenge everything that passed; at the same time, he would be in position to go after the pirates instantly, whether they were in the Ægean or out on the Mediterranean.

As the fleet, in order, rowed in towards the mountain shores of the island, a galley was descried coming from the north. Arrius went to meet it. She proved to be a transport just from Byzantium, and from her commander he learned the particulars of which he stood in most need.

The pirates were from all the farther shores of the Euxine. Even Tanais, at the mouth of the river which was supposed to feed Palus Mæotis, was represented among them. Their preparations had been with the greatest secrecy. The first known of them was their appearance off the entrance to the Thracian Bosphorus, followed by the destruction of the fleet in station there. Thence to the outlet of the Hellespont everything afloat had fallen their prey. There were quite sixty galleys in the squadron, all well manned and supplied. A few were biremes, the rest stout triremes. A Greek was in command, and the pilots, said to be familiar with all the eastern seas, were Greek. The plunder had been incalculable. The panic, consequently, was not on the sea alone; cities, with closed gates, sent their people nightly to the walls. Traffic had almost ceased.

Where were the pirates now?

To this question, of most interest to Arrius, he received answer.

After sacking Hephæstia, on the island of Lemnos, the enemy had coursed across to the Thessalian group, and, by last account, disappeared in the gulfs between Eubœa and Hellas.

Such were the tidings.

Then the people of the island, drawn to the hill-tops by the rare spectacle of a hundred ships careering in united squadron, beheld the advance division suddenly turn to the north, and the others follow, wheeling upon the same point like cavalry in a column. News of the piratical descent had reached them, and now, watching the white sails until they faded from sight up between Rhene and Syros, the thoughtful among them took comfort, and were grateful. What Rome seized with strong hand she always defended: in return for their taxes, she gave them safety.

Arrius judged that the robbers might be found somewhere below Thermopylæ. Welcoming the chance, he resolved to enclose them north and south, to do which not an hour could be lost; even the fruits and wines and women of Naxos must be left behind. So he sailed away without stop or tack until, a little before nightfall, Mount Ocha was seen upreared against the sky, and the pilot reported the Eubœan coast.

At a signal the fleet rested upon its oars. When the movement was resumed, Arrius led a division of fifty of the galleys, intending to take them up the channel, while another division, equally strong, turned their prows to the outer or seaward side of the island, with orders to make all haste to the upper inlet, and descend sweeping the waters.

To be sure, neither division was equal in number to the pirates; but each had advantages in compensation, among them, by no means least, a discipline impossible to a lawless horde, however brave. Besides, it was a shrewd count on the tribune's side, if, peradventure, one should be defeated, the other would find the enemy shattered by his victory, and in condition to be easily overwhelmed.

Meantime Ben-Hur kept his bench, relieved every six hours. The rest in the Bay of Antemona had freshened him, so that the oar was not troublesome, and the chief on the platform found no fault.

People generally are not aware of the ease of mind there is in knowing where they are, and where they are going. The sensation of being lost is a keen distress; still worse is the feeling one has in driving blindly into unknown places. Custom had dulled the feeling with Ben-Hur, but only measurably.

In his long service, by watching the shifting of the meagre sunbeams upon the cabin floor when the ship was under way, he had come to know, generally, the quarter into which she was sailing. This, of course, was only of clear days like those good fortune was sending the tribune. The experience had not failed him in the period succeeding the departure from Cythera. Thinking they were tending towards the old Judean country, he was sensitive to every variation from the course. With a pang he had observed the sudden change northward which, as has been noticed, took place near Naxos; the cause, however, he could not even conjecture; for it must be remembered that, in common with his fellow-slaves, he knew nothing of the situation, and had no interest in the voyage.

Now he had been in many battles without having seen one. From his bench he had heard them above and about him, until he was familiar with all their notes, almost as a singer with a song. So, too, he had become acquainted with many of the preliminaries of an engagement, of which, with a Roman as well as a Greek, the most invariable was the sacrifice to the gods. The rites were the same as those performed at the beginning of a voyage, and to him, when noticed, they were always an admonition.

A battle, it should be observed, possessed for him and his fellow-slaves of the oar an interest unlike that of the sailor and marine; it came, not of the danger encountered, but of the fact that defeat, if survived, might bring an alteration of condition—possibly freedom—at least a change of masters, which might be for the better.

In good time the lanterns were lighted and hung by the stairs, and the tribune came down from the deck. At his word the marines put on their armour. At his word again the machines were looked to, and spears, javelins, and arrows, in great sheaves, brought and laid upon the floor, together with jars of inflammable oil, and baskets of cotton balls wound loose like the wicking of candles. And when, finally, Ben-Hur saw the tribune mount his platform and don his armour, and get his helmet and shield out, the meaning of the preparations might not be any longer doubted, and he made ready for the last ignominy of his service.

To every bench, as a fixture, there was a chain with heavy anklets. These the hortator proceeded to lock upon the oarsmen, going from number to number, leaving no choice but to obey, and, in event of disaster, no possibility of escape.

In the cabin, then, a silence fell, broken at first only by the sough of the oars turning in the leathern cases. Every man upon the benches felt the shame, Ben-Hur more keenly than his companions. He would have put it away at any price. Soon the clanking of the fetters notified him of the progress the chief was making in his round. He would come to him in turn; but would not the tribune interpose for him?

The thought may be set down to vanity or selfishness, as the reader pleases; it certainly, at that moment, took possession of Ben-Hur. He believed the Roman would interpose; anyhow, the circumstances would test the man's feelings. If, intent upon the battle, he would but think of him, it would be proof of his opinion formed—proof that he had been tacitly promoted above his associates in misery—such proof as would justify hope.

Ben-Hur waited anxiously. The interval seemed like an age. At every turn of the oar he looked towards the tribune, who, his simple preparations made, lay down upon the couch and composed himself to rest; whereupon number sixty chid himself, and laughed grimly, and resolved not to look that way again.

The hortator approached. Now he was at number one—the rattle of the iron links sounded horribly. At last number sixty! Calm from despair, Ben-Hur held his oar at poise, and gave his foot to the officer. Then the tribune stirred—sat up—beckoned to the chief.

A strong revulsion seized the Jew. From the hortator, the great man glanced at him; and when he dropped his oar all the section of the ship on his side seemed aglow. He heard nothing of what was said; enough that the chain hung idly from its staple in the bench, and that the chief, going to his seat, began to beat the sounding-board. The notes of the gavel were never so like music. With his breast against the leaded handle, he pushed with all his might—pushed until the shaft bent as if about to break.

The chief went to the tribune, and, smiling, pointed to number sixty. "What strength!" he said.

"And what spirit!" the tribune answered. "*Perpol!* He is better without the irons. Put them on him no more."

So saying, he stretched himself upon the couch again.

The ship sailed on hour after hour under the oars in water scarcely rippled by the wind. And the people not on duty slept, Arrius in his place, the marines on the floor.

Once—twice—Ben-Hur was relieved; but he could not sleep. Three years of night, and through the darkness a sunbeam at last! At sea adrift and lost, and now land! Dead so long, and, lo! the thrill and stir of resurrection. Sleep was not for such an hour.

The deeper darkness before the dawn was upon the waters, and all things going well with the *Astræa*, when a man, descending from the deck, walked swiftly to the platform where the tribune slept, and awoke him. Arrius arose, put on his helmet, sword, and shield, and went to the commander of the marines.

"The pirates are close by. Up and ready!" he said, and passed to the stairs, calm, confident, insomuch that one might have thought, "Happy fellow! Apicius has set a feast for him."

CHAPTER 5

THE SEA FIGHT

Every soul aboard, even the ship, awoke. Officers went to their quarters. The marines took arms, and were led out, looking in all respects like legionaries. Sheaves of arrows and armfuls of javelins were carried on deck. By the central stairs the oil-tanks and fire-balls were set ready for use. Additional lanterns were lighted. Buckets were filled with water. The rowers in relief assembled under guard in front of the chief. As Providence would have it, Ben-Hur was one of the latter. Overhead he heard the muffled noises of the final preparations—of the sailors furling sail, spreading the nettings, unslinging the machines, and hanging the armour of bull-hide over the sides. Presently quiet settled about the galley again; quiet full of vague dread and expectation, which, interpreted, means *ready*.

At a signal passed down from the deck, and communicated to the hortator by a petty officer stationed on the stairs, all at once the oars stopped.

What did it mean?

A sound like the rowing of galleys astern attracted Ben-Hur, and the *Astræa* rocked as if in the midst of countering waves. The idea of a fleet at hand broke upon him—a fleet in manœuvre—forming probably for attack. His blood started with the fancy.

Another signal came down from the deck. The oars dipped, and the galley started imperceptibly. No sound from without, none from within, yet each man in the cabin instinctively poised himself for a shock; the very ship seemed to catch the sense, and hold its breath, and go crouched tiger-like.

In such a situation time is inappreciable; so that Ben-Hur could form no judgment of distance gone. At last there was a sound of trumpets on deck, full, clear, long blown. The chief beat the sounding-board until it rang; the rowers reached forward full length, and, deepening the dip of their oars, pulled suddenly with all their united force. The galley, quivering in every timber, answered with a leap. Other trumpets joined in the clamour—all from the rear, none forward—from the latter quarter only a rising sound of voices in tumult heard briefly. There was a mighty blow; the rowers in front of the chief's platform reeled, some of them fell; the ship bounded back, recovered, and rushed on more irresistibly than before. Shrill and high arose the shrieks of men in terror; over the blare of trumpets, and the grind and crash of the collision, they arose; then under his feet, under the keel, pounding, rumbling, breaking to pieces, drowning, Ben-Hur felt something overridden. The men about him looked at each other afraid. A shout of triumph from the deck—the beak of the Roman had won! But who were they whom the sea had drunk? Of what tongue, from what land were they?

No pause, no stay! Forward rushed the *Astræa*; and, as it went, some sailors ran down, and plunging the cotton balls into the oil-tanks, tossed them dripping to comrades at the head of the stairs: fire was to be added to other horrors of the combat.

Directly the galley heeled over so far that the oarsmen on the uppermost side with difficulty kept their benches. Again the hearty Roman cheer, and with it despairing shrieks. An opposing vessel, caught by the grappling-hooks of the great crane swinging from the prow, was being lifted into the air that it might be dropped and sunk.

The shouting increased on the right hand and on the left; before, behind, swelled an indescribable clamour. Occasionally there was a crash, followed by sudden peals of fright, telling of other ships ridden down, and their crews drowned in the vortices.

Nor was the fight all on one side. Now and then a Roman in armour was borne down the hatchway, and laid bleeding, sometimes dying, on the floor.

Sometimes, also, puffs of smoke, blended with steam, and foul with the scent of roasting human flesh, poured into the cabin, turning the dimming light into yellow murk. Gasping for breath the while, Ben-Hur knew they were passing through the cloud of a ship on fire, and burning up with the rowers chained to the benches.

The *Astræa* all this time was in motion. Suddenly she stopped. The oars forward were dashed from the hands of the rowers, and the rowers from their benches. On deck, then, a furious trampling, and on the sides a grinding of ships afoul of each other. For the first time the beating of the gavel was lost in the uproar. Men sank on the floor in fear, or looked about seeking a hiding-place. In the midst of the panic a body plunged or was pitched headlong down the hatchway, falling near Ben-Hur. He beheld the half-naked carcase, a mass of hair blackening the face, and under it a shield of bull-hide and wicker-work—a barbarian from the white-skinned nations of the North whom death had robbed of plunder and revenge. How came he there? An iron hand had snatched him from the opposing deck—no, the *Astræa* had been boarded! The Romans were fighting on their own deck? A chill smote the young Jew: Arrius was hard pressed—he might be defending his own life. If he should be slain! God of Abraham fore-fend! The hopes and dreams so lately come, were they only hopes and dreams?

A very short space lay between him and the stairs of the hatchway aft. He took it with a leap, and was half-way up the steps—up far enough to catch a glimpse of the sky blood-red with fire, of the ships alongside, of the sea covered with ships and wrecks, of the fight closed in about the pilot's quarter, the assailants many, the defenders few—when suddenly his foothold was knocked away, and he pitched back-ward. The floor, when he reached it, seemed to be lifting itself and breaking to pieces; then, in a twinkling, the whole after-part of the hull broke asunder, and, as if it had all the time been lying in wait, the sea, hissing and foaming, leaped in, and all became darkness and surging water to Ben-Hur.

It cannot be said that the young Jew helped himself in this stress. Besides his usual strength, he had the indefinite extra force which nature keeps in reserve for just such perils to life; yet the darkness, and the whirl and roar of water, stupefied him. Even the holding his breath was involuntary.

The influx of the flood tossed him like a log forward into the cabin, where he would have drowned but for the refluence of the sinking motion. As it was, fathoms under the surface the hollow mass vomited him forth, and he arose along with the loosed debris. In the act of rising, he clutched something, and held to it. The time he was under seemed an age longer than it really was; at last he gained the top; with a great gasp he filled his lungs afresh, and, tossing the water from his hair and eyes, climbed higher upon the plank he held, and looked about him.

Death had pursued him closely under the waves; he found it waiting for him when he was risen—waiting multiform.

Smoke lay upon the sea like a semi-transparent fog, through which here and there shone cores of intense brilliance. A quick intelligence told him that they were ships on fire. The battle was yet on; nor could he say who was victor. Within the radius of his vision now and then ships passed, shooting shadows athwart lights. Out of the dun clouds farther on he caught the crash of other ships colliding. The danger, however, was closer at hand. When the *Astræa* went down, her deck, it will be recollected, held her own crew, and the crews of the two galleys which had attacked her at the same time, all of whom were ingulfed. Many of them came to the surface together, and on the same plank or support of whatever kind continued the combat, begun possibly in the vortex fathoms down. Writhing and twisting in deadly embrace, sometimes striking with sword or javelin, they kept the sea around them in agitation, at one place inky-black, at another aflame with fiery reflections. With their struggles he had nothing to do; they were all his enemies: not one of them but would kill him for the plank upon which he floated. He made haste to get away.

About that time he heard oars in quickest movement, and beheld a galley coming down upon him. The tall prow seemed doubly tall, and the red light playing upon its gilt and carving gave it an appearance of snaky life. Under its foot the water churned to flying foam.

He struck out, pushing the plank, which was very broad and unmanageable. Seconds were precious—half a second might save or lose him. In the crisis of the effort, up from the sea, within arm's reach, a helmet shot like a gleam of gold. Next came two hands with fingers extended—large hands were they, and strong—their hold once fixed, might not be loosed. Ben-Hur swerved from them appalled. Up rose the helmet and the head it encased—then two arms, which began to beat the water wildly—the head turned back, and gave the face to the light. The mouth gaping wide; the eyes open, but sightless, and the bloodless pallor of a drowning man—never anything more ghastly! Yet he gave a cry of joy at the sight, and as the face was going under again, he caught the sufferer by the chain which passed from the helmet beneath the chin, and drew him to the plank.

The man was Arrius, the tribune.

For a while the water foamed and eddied violently about Ben-Hur, taxing all his strength to hold to the support and at the same time keep the Roman's head above the surface. The galley had passed, leaving the two barely outside the stroke of its oars. Right through the floating men, over heads helmeted as well as heads bare, she drove, in her wake nothing but the sea sparkling with fire. A muffled crash, succeeded by a great outcry, made the rescuer look again from his charge. A certain savage pleasure touched his heart—the *Astræa* was avenged.

After that the battle moved on. Resistance turned to flight. But who were the victors? Ben-Hur was sensible how much his freedom and the life of the tribune depended upon that event. He pushed the plank under the latter until it floated him, after which all his care was to keep him there. The dawn came slowly. He watched its growing hopefully, yet sometimes afraid. Would it bring the Romans or the pirates? If the pirates, his charge was lost.

At last morning broke in full, the air without a breath. Off to the left he saw the land, too far to think of attempting to make it. Here and there men were adrift like himself. In spots the sea was blackened by charred and sometimes smoking fragments. A galley up a long way was lying to with a torn sail hanging from the tilted yard, and the oars all idle. Still farther away he could discern moving specks, which he thought might be ships in fight or pursuit, or they might be white birds a-wing.

An hour passed thus. His anxiety increased. If relief came not speedily, Arrius would die. Sometimes he seemed already dead, he lay so still. He took the helmet off, and then, with greater difficulty, the cuirass; the heart he found fluttering. He took hope at the sign, and held on. There was nothing to do but wait, and, after the manner of his people, pray.

CHAPTER 6

FREE AND ADOPTED

THE throes of recovery from drowning are more painful than the drowning. These Arrius passed through, and at length, to Ben-Hur's delight, reached the point of speech.

Gradually, from incoherent questions as to where he was, and by whom and how he had been saved, he reverted to the battle. The doubt of the victory stimulated his faculties to full return, a result aided not a little by a long rest—such as could be had on their frail support. After a while he became talkative.

"Our rescue, I see, depends upon the result of the fight. I see also what thou hast done for me. To speak fairly, thou hast saved my life at the risk of thy own. I make the acknowledgment broadly; and whatever cometh, thou hast my thanks. More than that, if fortune doth but serve me kindly, and we get well out of this peril, I will do thee such favour as becometh a Roman who hath power and opportunity to prove his gratitude. Yet, yet it is to be seen if, with thy good intent, thou hast really done me a kindness; or, rather, speaking to thy good-will" —he hesitated—"I would exact of thee a promise to do me, in a certain event, the greatest favour one man can do another—and of that let me have thy pledge now."

"If the thing be not forbidden, I will do it," Ben-Hur replied.

"Then pledge me. By the Gods——"

"Nay, good tribune, I am a Jew."

"By thy God, then, or in the form most sacred to those of thy faith —pledge me to do what I tell thee now, and as I tell thee; I am waiting, let me have thy promise."

"Noble Arrius, I am warned by thy manner to expect something of gravest concern. Tell me thy wish first."

"Wilt thou promise then?"

"That were to give the pledge, and—Blessed be the God of my fathers! yonder cometh a ship!"

"Look for the flag now."

"She hath none."

"Nor any other sign?"

"She hath a sail set, and is of three banks, and cometh swiftly—that is all I can say of her."

"A Roman in triumph would have out many flags. She must be an enemy. Hear, now," said Arrius, becoming grave again, "hear, while yet I may speak. If the galley be a pirate, thy life is safe; they may not give thee freedom; they may put thee to the oar again; but they will not kill thee. On the other hand, I——"

The tribune faltered.

"*Perpol!*" he continued resolutely. "I am too old to submit to dishonour. In Rome, let them tell how Quintus Arrius, as became a Roman tribune, went down with his ship in the midst of the foe. This is what I would have thee do. If the galley prove a pirate, push me from the plank and drown me. Dost thou hear? Swear, thou wilt do it."

"I will not swear," said Ben-Hur firmly; "neither will I do the deed."

Both became silent, waiting.

Ben-Hur looked often at the coming ship. Arrius rested with closed eyes, indifferent.

"Art thou sure she is an enemy?" Ben-Hur asked.

"I think so," was the reply.

"She stops, and puts a boat over the side."

"Dost thou see her flag?"

"Is there no other sign by which she may be known if Roman?"

"If Roman, she hath a helmet over the mast's top."

"Then be of cheer. I see the helmet."

Still Arrius was not assured.

"The men in the small boat are taking in the people afloat. Pirates are not humane."

"They may need rowers," Arrius replied, recurring possibly to times when he had made rescues for the purpose.

Ben-Hur was very watchful of the actions of the strangers.

"The ship moves off," he said.

"Whither?"

"Over on our right there is a galley which I take to be deserted. The new-comer heads towards it. Now she is alongside. Now she is sending men aboard."

Then Arrius opened his eyes and threw off his calm.

"Thank thou thy God," he said to Ben-Hur, after a look at the galleys, "thank thou thy God, as I do my many gods. A pirate would sink, not save, yon ship. By the act and the helmet on the mast I know a Roman. The victory is mine. Fortune hath not deserted me. We are saved. Wave thy hand—call to them—bring them quickly. I shall be duumvir, and thou! I knew thy Father, and loved him. He was a prince indeed. He taught me a Jew was not a barbarian. I will take thee with me. I will make thee my son. Give thy God thanks, and call the sailors. Haste! The pursuit must be kept. Not a robber shall escape. Hasten them!"

Judah raised himself upon the plank, and waved his hand, and called with all his might; at last he drew the attention of the sailors in the small boat, and they were speedily taken up.

Arrius was received on the galley with all the honours due a hero so the favourite of Fortune. Upon a couch on the deck he heard the particulars of the conclusion of the fight. When the survivors afloat upon the water were all saved and the prize secured, he spread his flag of commandant anew, and hurried northward to rejoin the fleet and perfect the victory. In due time the fifty vessels coming down the channel closed in upon the fugitive pirates, and crushed them utterly; not one escaped. To swell the tribune's glory, twenty galleys of the enemy were captured.

Upon his return from the cruise, Arrius had warm welcome on the mole at Misenum. The young man attending him very early attracted the attention of his friends there; and to their questions as to who he was the tribune proceeded in the most affectionate manner to tell the story of his rescue and introduce the stranger, omitting carefully all that pertained to the latter's previous history. At the end of the narrative he called Ben-Hur to him, and said, with a hand resting affectionately upon his shoulder,—

"Good friends, this is my son and heir, who, as he is to take my property—if it be the will of the gods that I leave any—shall be known to you by my name. I pray you all to love him as you love me."

Speedily as opportunity permitted, the adoption was formally perfected. And in such manner the brave Roman kept his faith with Ben-Hur, giving him happy introduction into the imperial world. The month succeeding Arrius's return, the *armilustrium* was celebrated with the utmost magnificence in the theatre of Scaurus. One side of the structure was taken up with military trophies; among which by far the most conspicuous and most admired were twenty prows, complemented by their corresponding aplustra, cut bodily from as many galleys; and over them, so as to be legible to the eighty thousand spectators in the seats, was this inscription:

TAKEN FROM THE PIRATES IN THE GULF OF EURIPUS,

BY

QUINTUS ARRIUS,

DUUMVIR.

BOOK FOURTH

CHAPTER I

AT ANTIOCH

THE month to which we now come is July, the year that of our Lord 29, and the place Antioch, then Queen of the East, and next to Rome the strongest, if not the most populous, city in the world.

A transport galley entered the mouth of the river Orontes from the blue waters of the sea. It was in the forenoon. The heat was great, yet all on board who could avail themselves of the privilege were on deck— Ben-Hur among others.

The five years had brought the young Jew to perfect manhood. Though the robe of white linen in which he was attired somewhat masked his form, his appearance was unusually attractive. For an hour and more he had occupied a seat in the shade of the sail, and in that time several fellow passengers of his own nationality had tried to engage him in conversation, but without avail. His replies to their questions had been brief, though gravely courteous, and in the Latin tongue. The purity of his speech, his cultivated manners, his reticence, served to stimulate their curiosity the more.

The galley, in coming, had stopped at one of the ports of Cyprus, and picked up a Hebrew of most respectable appearance, quiet, reserved, paternal. Ben-Hur ventured to ask him some questions; the replies won his confidence, and resulted finally in an extended conversation.

It chanced also that as the galley from Cyprus entered the receiving bay of the Orontes, two other vessels which had been sighted out in the sea met it and passed into the river at the same time; and as they did so, both the strangers threw out small flags of brightest yellow. There was much conjecture as to the meaning of the signals. At length a passenger addressed himself to the respectable Hebrew for information upon the subject.

"Yes, I know the meaning of the flags," he replied; "they do not signify nationality—they are merely marks of ownership."

"Has the owner many ships?"

"He has."

"You know him?"

"I have dealt with him."

The passengers looked at the speaker as if requesting him to go on. Ben-Hur listened with interest.

"He lives in Antioch," the Hebrew continued, in his quiet way. "That he is vastly rich has brought him into notice, and the talk about him is not always kind. There used to be in Jerusalem a prince of very ancient family named Hur."

Judah strove to be composed, yet his heart beat quicker.

"The prince was a merchant, with a genius for business. He set on foot many enterprises, some reaching far East, others West. In the great cities he had branch houses. The one in Antioch was in charge of a man said by some to have been a family servant called Simonides, Greek in name, yet an Israelite. The master was drowned at sea. His business, however, went on, and was scarcely less prosperous. After a while misfortune overtook the family. The prince's only son, nearly grown, tried to kill the procurator Gratus in one of the streets of Jerusalem. He failed by a narrow chance, and has not since been heard of. In fact, the Roman's rage took in the whole house—not one of the name was left alive. Their palace was sealed up, and is now a rookery for pigeons; the estate was confiscated; everything that could be traced to the ownership of the Hurs was confiscated. The procurator cured his hurt with a golden salve."

The passengers laughed.

"You mean he kept the property," said one of them.

"They say so," the Hebrew replied; "I am only telling a story as I received it. And, to go on, Simonides, who had been the prince's agent here in Antioch, opened trade in a short time on his own account, and in a space incredibly brief became the master merchant of the city. In imitation of his master, he sent caravans to India; and on the sea at present he has galleys enough to make a royal fleet. They say nothing goes amiss with him. His camels do not die, except of old age; his ships never founder; if he throw a chip into the river, it will come back to him gold."

"How long has he been going on thus?"

"Not ten years."

"He must have had a good start."

"Yes, they say the procurator took only the prince's property ready at hand—his horses, cattle, houses, land, vessels, goods. The money could not be found, though there must have been vast sums of it. What became of it has been an unsolved mystery."

"Not to me," said a passenger, with a sneer.

"I understand you," the Hebrew answered. "Others have had your idea. That it furnished old Simonides his start is a common belief. The procurator is of that opinion—or he has been—for twice in five years he has caught the merchant, and put him to torture."

Judah gripped the rope he was holding with crushing force.

"It is said," the narrator continued, "that there is not a sound bone in the man's body. The last time I saw him he sat in a chair, a shapeless cripple, propped against cushions."

"So tortured!" exclaimed several listeners in a breath.

"Disease could not have produced such a deformity. Still the suffering made no impression upon him. All he had was his lawfully, and he was making lawful use of it—that was the most they wrung from him. Now, however, he is past persecution. He has a licence to trade signed by Tiberius himself."

"He paid roundly for it, I warrant."

"These ships are his," the Hebrew continued, passing the remark. "It is a custom among his sailors to salute each other upon meeting by throwing out yellow flags, sight of which is as much as to say, 'We have had a fortunate voyage.'"

The story ended there.

CHAPTER 2

DISAPPOINTED

WHEN the city came into view, the passengers were on deck, eager that nothing of the scene might escape them. The respectable Jew already introduced to the reader was the principal spokesman.

The ship turned and made slowly for her wharf under the wall, bringing even more fairly into view the life with which the river at that point was possessed. Finally, the lines were thrown, the oars shipped, and the voyage was done. Then Ben-Hur sought the respectable Hebrew.

"Let me trouble you a moment before saying farewell."

The man bowed assent.

"Your story of the merchant has made me curious to see him. You called him Simonides?"

"Yes. He is a Jew with a Greek name."

"Where is he to be found?"

The acquaintance gave a sharp look before he answered.

"I may save you mortification. He is not a money-lender."

"Nor am I a money-borrower," said Ben-Hur, smiling at the other's shrewdness.

The man raised his head and considered an instant.

"One would think," he then replied, "that the richest merchant in Antioch would have a house for business corresponding to his wealth; but if you would find him in the day, follow the river to yon bridge, under which he quarters in a building that looks like a buttress of the wall. Before the door there is an immense landing, always covered with cargoes come and to go. The fleet that lies moored there is his. You cannot fail to find him."

"I give you thanks."

"The peace of our fathers go with you."

"And with you."

With that they separated.

Next day early, to the neglect of the city, Ben-Hur sought the house of Simonides. Through an embattled gateway he passed to a continuity of wharves; thence up the river midst a busy press, to the Seleucian Bridge, under which he paused to take in the scene.

There, directly under the bridge, was the merchant's house, a mass of grey stone, unhewn, referrable to no style, looking, as the voyager had described it, like a buttress of the wall against which it leaned. Two immense doors in front communicated with the wharf. Some holes near the top, heavily barred, served as windows. Weeds waved from the crevices, and in places black moss splotched the otherwise bald stones.

The doors were open. Through one of them business went in; through the other it came out; and there was hurry, hurry in all its movements.

On the wharf there were piles of goods in every kind of package, and groups of slaves, stripped to the waist, going about in the *abandon* of labour.

Below the bridge lay a fleet of galleys, some loading, others unloading. A yellow flag blew out from each mast-head. From fleet and wharf, and from ship to ship, the bondmen of traffic passed in clamorous counter-currents.

Above the bridge, across the river, a wall rose from the water's edge, over which towered the fanciful cornices and turrets of an imperial palace. But, with all its suggestions, Ben-Hur scarcely noticed it. Now, at last, he thought to hear of his people—this, certainly, if Simonides had indeed been his father's slave. But would the man acknowledge the relation? That would be to give up his riches and the sovereignty of trade so royally witnessed on the wharf and river. And what was of still greater consequence to the merchant, it would be to forgo his career in the midst of amazing success, and yield himself voluntarily once more a slave. Simple thought of the demand seemed a monstrous audacity. Stripped of diplomatic address, it was to say, You are my slave; give me all you have, and—yourself.

At length a man approached and spoke to him.

"What would you have?"

"I would see Simonides, the merchant."

"Will you come this way?"

By a number of paths left in the stowage, they finally came to a flight of steps; ascending which he found himself on the roof of the depot, and in front of a structure which cannot be better described than as a lesser stone house built upon another, invisible from the landing below, and out west of the bridge under the open sky. The roof, hemmed in by a low wall, seemed like a terrace, which, to his astonishment, was brilliant with flowers; in the rich surrounding, the house sat squat, a plain square block, unbroken except by a doorway in front. A dustless path led to the door, through a bordering of shrubs of Persian rose in perfect bloom. Breathing a sweet attar-perfume, he followed the guide.

At the end of a darkened passage within they stopped before a curtain half parted. The man called out,—

"A stranger to see the master."

A clear voice replied, "In God's name, let him enter."

A Roman might have called the apartment into which the visitor was ushered his atrium. The walls were panelled; each panel was comparted like a modern office desk, and each compartment crowded with labelled folios all filemot with age and use. Between the panels, and above and below them, were borders of wood once white, now tinted like cream, and carved with marvellous intricacy of design. Above a cornice of gilded balls, the ceiling rose in pavilion style until it broke into a shallow dome set with hundreds of panes of violet mica, permitting a flood of light deliciously reposeful. The floor was carpeted with grey rugs so thick that an invading foot fell half buried and soundless.

In the midlight of the room were two persons—a man resting in a chair high-backed, broad-armed, and lined with pliant cushions; and at his left, leaning against the back of the chair, a girl well forward into womanhood. At sight of them Ben-Hur felt the blood redden his fore-head; bowing, as much to recover himself as in respect, he lost the lifting of the hands, and the shiver and shrink with which the sitter caught sight of him—an emotion as swift to go as it had been to come. When he raised his eyes the two were in the same position, except that the girl's hand had fallen and was resting lightly upon the elder's shoulder; both of them were regarding him fixedly.

"If you are Simonides, the merchant, and a Jew"—Ben-Hur stopped an instant—"then the peace of the God of our father Abraham upon you and—yours."

The last word was addressed to the girl.

"I am the Simonides of whom you speak, by birthright a Jew," the man made answer, in a voice singularly clear. "I am Simonides, and a Jew; and I return you your salutation, with prayer to know who calls upon me."

Ben-Hur looked as he listened, and where the figure of the man should have been in healthful roundness, there was only a formless heap sunk in the depths of the cushions, and covered by a quilted robe of sombre silk. Over the heap shone a head royally proportioned—the ideal head of a statesman and conqueror—a head broad of base and dome-like in front, such as Angelo would have modelled for Cæsar. White hair dropped in thin locks over the white brows, deepening the blackness of the eyes shining through them like sullen lights. The face was bloodless, and much puffed with folds, especially under the chin. In other words, the head and face were those of a man who might move the world more readily than the world could move him—a man to be twice twelve times tortured into the shapeless cripple he was without a groan, much less a confession; a man to yield his life, but never a pur-pose or a point; a man born in armour, and assailable only through his loves. To him Ben-Hur stretched his hands, open and palm up, as he would offer peace at the same time he asked it.

"I am Judah, son of Ithamar, late head of the House of Hur, and a prince of Jerusalem."

The merchant's right hand lay outside the robe—a long, thin hand, articulate to deformity with suffering. It closed tightly; otherwise there was not the slightest expression of feeling of any kind on his part; nothing to warrant an inference of surprise or interest; nothing but this calm answer.

"The princes of Jerusalem, of the pure blood, are always welcome in my house; you are welcome. Give the young man a seat, Esther."

The girl took an ottoman near by, and carried it to Ben-Hur. As she arose from placing the seat, their eyes met.

Ben-Hur did not take the offered seat, but said, deferentially, "I pray the good master Simonides that he will not hold me an intruder. Coming up the river yesterday, I heard he knew my father."

"I knew the Prince Hur. We were associated in some enterprises lawful to merchants who find profit in lands beyond the sea and the desert. But sit, I pray you—and, Esther, some wine for the young man. Nehemiah speaks of a son of Hur who once ruled the half part of Jerusalem; an old house; very old, by the faith! In the days of Moses and Joshua even some of them found favour in the sight of the Lord, and divided honours with those princes among men. It can hardly be that their descendant, lineally come to us, will refuse a cup of wine-fat of the genuine vine of Sorek, grown on the south hill-sides of Hebron."

By the time of the conclusion of this speech, Esther was before Ben-Hur with a silver cup filled from a vase upon a table a little removed from the chair. She offered the drink with downcast face. He touched her hand gently to put it away. Again their eyes met; whereat he noticed that she was small, not nearly to his shoulder in height; but very graceful, and fair and sweet of face, with eyes black and inexpressibly soft. She is kind and pretty, he thought, and looks as Tirzah would were she living. Poor Tirzah! Then he said aloud,—

"No, thy father—if he is thy father?"—he paused.

"I am Esther, the daughter of Simonides," she said, with dignity.

"Then, fair Esther, thy father, when he has heard my further speech, will not think worse of me if yet I am slow to take his wine of famous extract; nor less I hope not to lose grace in thy sight. Stand thou here with me a moment!"

Both of them, as in common cause, turned to the merchant. "Simonides!" he said firmly, "my father, at his death, had a trusted servant of thy name, and it has been told me that thou art the man!"

There was a sudden start of the wrenched limbs under the robe, and the thin hand clenched.

"Esther, Esther!" the man called sternly; "here, not there, as thou art thy mother's child and mine—here, not there, I say!"

The girl looked once from father to visitor; then she replaced the cup upon the table, and went dutifully to the chair. Her countenance sufficiently expressed her wonder and alarm.

Simonides returned to his calm, and answered coldly, "Hear me to the end. Because I am that I am, before I make return to thy demand touching my relations to the Prince Hur, and as something which of right should come first, do thou show me proofs of who thou art. Is thy witness in writing? Or cometh it in person?"

The demand was plain, and the right of it indisputable. Ben-Hur blushed, clasped his hands, stammered, and turned away at loss.

"Master Simonides," he said at length, "I can only tell my story; and I will not that unless you stay judgment so long, and with good-will deign to hear me."

"Speak," said Simonides, now indeed master of the situation—"speak, and I will listen the more willingly that I have not denied you to be the very person you claim yourself."

Ben-Hur proceeded then, and told his life hurriedly, yet with the feeling which is the source of all eloquence.

The tears ran down Esther's cheeks; but the man was wilful: in a clear voice, he replied,—

"I have said I knew the Prince Ben-Hur. I remember hearing of the misfortune which overtook his family. I remember the bitterness with which I heard it. He who wrought such misery to the widow of my friend is the same who, in the same spirit, hath since wrought upon me. I will go further, and say to you, I have made diligent quest concerning the family, but—I have nothing to tell you of them. They are lost."

Ben-Hur uttered a great groan.

"Then—then it is another hope broken!" he said, struggling with his feelings. "I am used to disappointments. I pray you pardon my intrusion; and if I have occasioned you annoyance, forgive it because of my sorrow. I have nothing now to live for but vengeance. Farewell."

At the curtain he turned, and said simply, "I thank you both."

"Peace go with you," the merchant said.

Esther could not speak for sobbing.

And so he departed.

CHAPTER 3

THE STORY OF SIMONIDES

SCARCELY was Ben-Hur gone, when Simonides seemed to wake as from sleep: his countenance flushed; the sullen light of his eyes changed to brightness; and he said cheerily,—

"Esther, ring—quick!"

She went to the table, and rang a service-bell.

One of the panels in the wall swung back, exposing a doorway which gave admittance to a man who passed round to the merchant's front, and saluted him with a half-salaam.

"Malluch, here—nearer—to the chair," the master said imperiously. "I have a mission, which shall not fail though the sun should. Hearken! A young man is now descending to the store-room—tall, comely, and in the garb of Israel; follow him, his shadow not more faithful; and every night send me report of where he is, what he does, and the company he keeps; and if, without discovery, you overhear his conversations, report them word for word, together with whatsoever will serve to expose him, his habits, motives, life. Understand you? Go quickly! Stay, Malluch: if he leave the city, go after him—and, mark you, Malluch, be as a friend. If he bespeak you, tell him what you will to the occasion most suited, except that you are in my service; of that, not a word. Haste—make haste!"

The man saluted as before, and was gone.

Then Simonides rubbed his wan hands together, and laughed.

Esther sat on the arm of the chair nursing his hand and waiting his speech, which came at length in the calm way, the mighty will having carried him back to himself.

"Well, thou art a good child, Esther, of genuine Jewish shrewdness, and of years and strength to hear a sorrowful tale. Wherefore give me heed, and I will tell you of myself, and of thy mother, and of many things pertaining to the past not in thy knowledge or thy dreams— things withheld from the persecuting Roman for a hope's sake, and from thee that thy nature should grow towards the Lord straight as the reed to the sun. . . . I was born in a tomb in the valley of Hinnom, on the south side of Zion. My father and mother were Hebrew bond-servants, tenders of the fig and olive trees growing, with many vines, in the King's Garden hard by Siloam; and in my boyhood I helped them. They were of the class bound to serve for ever. They sold me to the Prince Hur, then, next to Herod the King, the richest man in Jerusalem. From the garden he transferred me to his storehouse in Alexandria of Egypt, where I came of age. I served him six years, and in the seventh, by the law of Moses, I went free."

Esther clapped her hands lightly.

"Oh, then, thou art not his father's servant!"

"Nay, daughter, hear. Now, in those days there were lawyers in the cloisters of the Temple who disputed vehemently, saying the children of servants bound for ever took the condition of their parents; but the Prince Hur was a man righteous in all things, and an interpreter of the law after the straitest sect, though not of them. He said I was a Hebrew servant bought, in the true meaning of the great lawgiver, and, by sealed writings, which I yet have, he set me free.

"And my mother?" Esther asked.

"Thou shalt hear all, Esther; be patient. Before I am through thou shalt see it were easier for me to forget myself than thy mother. . . . At the end of my service, I came up to Jerusalem to the Passover. My master entertained me. I was in love with him already, and I prayed to be continued in his service. He consented, and I served him yet another seven years, but as a hired son of Israel. In his behalf I had charge of ventures on the sea by ships, and of ventures on land by caravans eastward to Susa and Persepolis, and the lands of silk beyond them. Perilous passages were they, my daughter; but the Lord blessed all I undertook. I brought home vast gains for the prince, and richer knowledge for myself, without which I could not have mastered the charges since fallen to me. . . . One day I was a guest in his house in Jerusalem. A servant entered with some sliced bread on a platter. She came to me first. It was then I saw thy mother, and loved her, and took her away in my secret heart. After a while a time came when I sought the prince to make her my wife. He told me she was a bond-servant for ever; but if she wished, he would set her free that I might be gratified. She gave me love for love, but was happy where she was, and refused her freedom. I prayed and besought, going again and again after long intervals. She would be my wife, she all the time said, if I would become her fellow in servitude. Our father Jacob served yet other seven years for his Rachel. Could I not as much for mine? But thy mother said I must become as she, to serve for ever. I came away, but went back. Look, Esther, look here."

He pulled out the lobe of his left ear.

"See you not the scar of the awl?"

"I see," she said; "and, oh, I see how thou didst love my mother!"

"Love her, Esther! She was to me more than the Shulamite to the singing king, fairer, more spotless; a fountain of gardens, a well of living waters, and streams from Lebanon. The master, even as I required him, took me to the judges, and back to his door, and thrust the awl through my ear into the door, and I was his servant for ever. So I won my Rachel. And was ever love like mine?"

Esther stooped and kissed him, and they were silent, thinking of the dead.

"My master was drowned at sea, the first sorrow that ever fell upon me," the merchant continued. "There was mourning in his house, and in mine here in Antioch, my abiding-place at the time. Now, Esther, mark you! When the good prince was lost, I had risen to be his chief steward, with everything of property belonging to him in my management and control. Judge you how much he loved and trusted me! I hastened to Jerusalem to render account to the widow. She continued

me in the stewardship. I applied myself with greater diligence. The
business prospered, and grew year by year. Ten years passed; then
came the blow which you heard the young man tell about—the accident,
as he called it, to the Procurator Gratus. The Roman gave it out an
attempt to assassinate him. Under that pretext, by leave from Rome,
he confiscated to his own use the immense fortune of the widow and
children. Nor stopped he there. That there might be no reversal of the
judgment, he removed all the parties interested. From that dreadful
day to this the family of Hur have been lost. The son, whom I had
seen as a child, was sentenced to the galleys. The widow and daughter
are supposed to have been buried in some of the many dungeons of
Judea, which, once closed upon the doomed, are like sepulchres sealed
and locked. They passed from the knowledge of men as utterly as if the
sea had swallowed them unseen. We could not hear how they died—
nay, not even that they were dead."

Esther's eyes were dewy with tears.

"Thy heart is good, Esther, good as thy mother's was; and I pray
it have not the fate of most good hearts—to be trampled upon by the
unmerciful and blind. But hearken further. I went up to Jerusalem
to give help to my benefactress, and was seized at the gate of the city
and carried to the sunken cells of the Tower of Antonia; why, I knew
not, until Gratus himself came and demanded of me the moneys of the
House of Hur, which he knew, after our Jewish custom of exchange,
were subject to my draft in the different marts of the world. He required me to sign to his order. I refused. He had the houses, lands,
goods, ships, and movable property of those I served; he had not their
moneys. I saw, if I kept favour in the sight of the Lord, I could rebuild
their broken fortunes. I refused the tyrant's demands. He put me to
torture; my will held good, and he set me free, nothing gained. I came
home and began again, in the name of Simonides of Antioch, instead of
the Prince Hur of Jerusalem. Thou knowest, Esther, how I have
prospered; that the increase of the millions of the prince in my hands
was miraculous; thou knowest how, at the end of three years, while
going up to Cæsarea, I was taken, and a second time tortured by Gratus
to compel a confession that my goods and moneys were subject to his
order of confiscation; thou knowest he failed as before. Broken in body,
I came home and found my Rachel dead of fear and grief for me. The
Lord our God reigned, and I lived. From the emperor himself I bought
immunity and licence to trade throughout the world. To-day—praised
be He who maketh the clouds His chariot and walketh upon the winds!
—to-day, Esther, that which was in my hands for stewardship is multiplied into talents sufficient to enrich a Cæsar."

He lifted his head proudly; their eyes met; each read the other's thought. "What shall I with the treasure, Esther?" he asked, without lowering his gaze.

"My father," she answered, in a low voice, "did not the rightful owner call for it but now?"

Still his look did not fail.

"And thou, my child; shall I leave thee a beggar?"

"Nay, father, am not I, because I am thy child, his bond-servant? And of whom was it written, 'Strength and honour are her clothing, and she shall rejoice in time to come'?"

A gleam of ineffable love lighted his face as he said, "The Lord hath been good to me in many ways; but thou, Esther, art the sovereign excellence of His favour."

He drew her to his breast and kissed her many times.

"Hear now," he said, with clearer voice—"hear now why I laughed this morning. The young man faced me, the apparition of his father in comely youth. My spirit arose to salute him. I felt my trial-days were over, and my labours ended. Hardly could I keep from crying out. I longed to take him by the hand and show the balance I had earned, and say, 'Lo, 'tis all thine! and I am thy servant, ready now to be called away.' And so I would have done, Esther, so I would have done, but that moment three thoughts rushed to restrain me. I will be sure he is my master's son—such was the first thought; if he is my master's son, I will learn somewhat of his nature. Of those born to riches, bethink you, Esther, how many there are in whose hands riches are but breeding curses"—he paused, while his hands clutched, and his voice shrilled with passion—"Esther, consider the pains I endured at the Roman's hands; nay, not Gratus's alone: the merciless wretches who did his bidding the first time and the last were Romans, and they all alike laughed to hear me scream. Consider my broken body, and the years I have gone shorn of my stature; consider thy mother yonder in her lonely tomb, crushed of soul as I of body; consider the sorrows of my master's family if they are living, and the cruelty of their taking-off if they are dead; consider all, and, with Heaven's love about thee, tell me, daughter, shall not a hair fall or a red drop run in expiation? Tell me not, as the preachers sometimes do—tell me not that vengeance is the Lord's. Does He not work His will harmfully as well as in love by agencies? Has He not His men of war more numerous than His prophets? Is not His the law, Eye for eye, hand for hand, foot for foot? Oh, in all these years I have dreamed of vengeance, and prayed and provided for it, and gathered patience from the growing of my store, thinking and promising, as the Lord liveth, it will one day buy me punishment of the wrong-doers! And when, speaking of his practice with arms, the young man said it was for a nameless purpose, I named the purpose even as he spoke—vengeance! and that, Esther, that it was—the third thought which held me still and hard while his pleading lasted, and made me laugh when he was gone."

Esther caressed the faded hands, and said, as if her spirit with his were running forward to results, "He is gone. Will he come again?"

"Ay, Malluch the faithful goes with him, and will bring him back when I am ready."

"And when will that be, father?"

"Not long, not long. He thinks all his witnesses dead. There is one living who will not fail to know him, if he be indeed my master's son."

"His mother?"

"Nay, daughter, I will set the witness before him; till then let us rest the business with the Lord. I am tired. Call Abimelech."

Esther called the servant, and they returned into the house.

CHAPTER 4

EXPLORING

WHEN Ben-Hur sallied from the great warehouse, it was with the thought that another failure was to be added to the many he had already met in the quest for his people; and the idea was depressing exactly in proportion as the objects of his quest were dear to him; it curtained him round about with a sense of utter loneliness on earth, which, more than anything else, serves to eke from a soul cast down its remaining interest in life.

It was about the fourth hour of the day when he passed out the gate, and found himself one of a procession apparently interminable, moving to the famous Grove of Daphne. The road was divided into separate ways for footmen, for men on horses, and men in chariots; and those again into separate ways for outgoers and incomers. The lines of division were guarded by low balustrading, broken by massive pedestals, many of which were surmounted with statuary. Right and left of the road extended margins of sward perfectly kept, relieved at intervals by groups of oak and sycamore trees, and vine-clad summer-houses for the accommodation of the weary, of whom, on the return side, there were always multitudes. The ways of the footmen were paved with red stone, and those of the riders strewn with white sand compactly rolled, but not so solid as to give back an echo to hoof or wheel. The number and variety of fountains at play were amazing, all gifts of visiting kings, and called after them. Out south-west to the gates of the Grove, the magnificent thoroughfare stretched a little over four miles from the city.

At last there was a clapping of hands, and a burst of joyous cries; following the pointing of many fingers, he looked and saw upon the brow of a hill the templed gate of the consecrated Grove. The hymns swelled to louder strains; the music quicked time; and, borne along by the impulsive current, and sharing the common eagerness, he passed in, and, Romanized in taste as he was, fell to worshipping the place.

Rearward of the structure which graced the entrance-way—a purely Grecian pile—he stood upon a broad esplanade paved with polished stone; around him a restless exclamatory multitude, in gayest colours, relieved against the iridescent spray flying crystal-white from fountains; before him, off to the south-west, dustless paths radiated out into a garden, and beyond that into a forest, over which rested a veil of pale-blue vapour. Ben-Hur gazed wistfully, uncertain where to go.

He came to a flock of sheep. The shepherd was a girl, and she beckoned him, "Come!"

Farther on, the path was divided by an altar—a pedestal of black gneiss, capped with a slab of white marble deftly foliated, and on that a brazier of bronze holding a fire. Close by it, a woman, seeing him, waved a wand of willow, and as he passed called him, "Stay!" And the temptation in her smile was that of passionate youth.

On yet further, he met one of the processions; at its head a troop of little girls, nude except as they were covered with garlands, piped their shrill voices into a song; then a troop of boys, also nude, their bodies deeply sun-browned, came dancing to the song of the girls; behind them the procession, all women, bearing baskets of spices and sweets to the altars—women clad in simple robes careless of exposure. As he went by they held their hands to him, and said, "Stay, and go with us."

But he pursued his way indifferent, and came next to a grove luxuriant, in the heart of the vale at the point where it would be most attractive to the observing eye. As it came close to the path he was travelling, there was a seduction in its shade, and through the foliage he caught the shining of what appeared a pretentious statue; so he turned aside, and entered the cool retreat.

The grass was fresh and clean. The trees did not crowd each other; and they were of every kind native to the East, blended well with strangers adopted from far quarters; here grouped in exclusive companionship palm trees plumed like queens; there sycamores, over-topping laurels of darker foliage; and evergreen oaks rising verdantly, with cedars vast enough to be kings on Lebanon; and mulberries; and terebinths so beautiful it is not hyperbole to speak of them as blown from the orchards of Paradise.

The statue proved to be a Daphne of wondrous beauty. Hardly, however, had he time to more than glance at her face: at the base of the pedestal a girl and a youth were lying upon a tiger's skin asleep in each other's arms; close by them the implements of their service—his axe and sickle, her basket—flung carelessly upon a heap of fading roses.

The exposure startled him. Back in the hush of the perfumed thicket he discovered, as he thought, that the charm of the great Grove was peace without fear, and almost yielded to it; now, in this sleep in the day's broad glare—this sleep at the feet of Daphne—he read a further chapter to which only the vaguest allusion is sufferable. The law of the place was Love, but Love without Law.

And this was the sweet peace of Daphne!

This the life's end of her ministers!

For this kings and princes gave of their revenues!

For this a crafty priesthood subordinated nature—her birds and brooks and lilies, the river, the labour of many hands, the sanctity of altars, the fertile power of the sun!

Better a law without love than a love without law.

Besides that, sympathy is in great degree a result of the mood we are in at the moment: anger forbids the emotion. On the other hand, it is easiest taken on when we are in a state of most absolute self-satisfaction. Ben-Hur walked with a quicker step, holding his head higher; and, while not less sensitive to the delightfulness of all about him, he made his survey with calmer spirit, though sometimes with curling lip; that is to say, he could not so soon forget how nearly he himself had been imposed upon.

CHAPTER 5

A NEW COMPANION

In front of Ben-Hur there was a forest of cypress-trees, each a column tall and straight as a mast. Venturing into the shady precinct, he heard a trumpet gaily blown, and an instant after saw lying upon the grass close by a countryman. The man arose and came to him.

"I give you peace," he said pleasantly.

"Thank you," Ben-Hur replied, then asked, "Go you my way?"

"I am for the stadium, if that is your way."

"The stadium!"

"Yes. The trumpet you heard but now was a call for the competitors."

"Good friend," said Ben-Hur frankly, "I admit my ignorance of the Grove; and if you will let me be your follower, I will be glad."

"That will delight me. Hark! I hear the wheels of the chariots. They are taking the track."

Ben-Hur listened a moment, then completed the introduction by laying his hand upon the man's arm, and saying, "I am the son of Arrius, the duumvir, and thou?"

"I am Malluch, a merchant of Antioch."

"Well, good Malluch, the trumpet and the gride of wheels, and the prospect of diversion excite me. I have some skill in the exercises. In the palæstræ of Rome I am not unknown. Let us to the course."

Malluch lingered to say quickly, "The duumvir was a Roman, yet I see his son in the garments of a Jew."

"The noble Arrius was my father by adoption," Ben-Hur answered.

"Ah! I see, and beg pardon."

Passing through the belt of forest, they came to a field with a track laid out upon it, in the shape and extent exactly like those of the stadia. The course, or track proper, was of soft earth, rolled and sprinkled, and on both sides defined by ropes, stretched loosely upon upright javelins. For the accommodation of spectators, and such as had interests reaching forward of the mere practice, there were several stands shaded by substantial awnings, and provided with seats in rising rows. In one of the stands the two new-comers found places.

Ben-Hur counted the chariots as they went by—nine in all.

"I commend the fellows," he said, with good-will. "Here in the East, I thought they aspired to nothing better than the two; but they are ambitious, and play with royal fours. Let us study their performance."

Eight of the fours passed the stand, some walking, others on the trot, and all unexceptionally handled; then the ninth one came on the gallop. Ben-Hur burst into exclamation.

"I have been in the stables of the Emperor, Malluch, but, by our father Abraham of blessed memory! I never saw the like of these."

The last four was then sweeping past. All at once they fell into confusion. Some one on the stand uttered a sharp cry. Ben-Hur turned, and saw an old man half-risen from an upper seat, his hands clenched and raised, his eyes fiercely bright, his long white beard fairly quivering. Some of the spectators nearest him began to laugh.

"They should respect his beard at least. Who is he?" asked Ben-Hur.

"A mighty man from the Desert, somewhere beyond Moab, and owner of camels in herds, and horses descended, they say, from the racers of the first Pharaoh—Sheik Ilderim by name and title."

Thus Malluch replied.

The driver meanwhile exerted himself to quiet the four, but without avail. Each ineffectual effort excited the sheik the more.

"Abaddon seize him!" yelled the patriarch shrilly. "Run! fly! do you hear, my children?" The question was to his attendants, apparently of the tribe. "Do you hear! They are Desert-born, like yourselves. Catch them—quick!"

The plunging of the animals increased.

"Accursed Roman!" and the sheik shook his fist at the driver. "Did he not swear he could drive them—swear it by all his brood of bastard Latin gods? Nay, hands off me—off, I say! They should run swift as eagles, and with the temper of hand-bred lambs, he swore. Cursed be he—cursed the mother of liars who calls him son! See them, the priceless! Let him touch one of them with a lash, and"—the rest of the sentence was lost in a furious grinding of his teeth. "To their heads, some of you, and speak them—a word, one is enough, from the tent-song your mothers sang you. Oh, fool, fool that I was to put trust in a Roman!"

Some of the shrewder of the old man's friends planted themselves between him and the horses. An opportune failure of breath on his part helped the stratagem.

Ben-Hur, thinking he comprehended the sheik, sympathized with him. Far more than mere pride of property—more than anxiety for the result of the race—in his view it was within the possible for the patriarch, according to his habits of thought and his ideas of the inestimable, to love such animals with a tenderness akin to the most sensitive passion.

Before the patriarch was done with his expletives, a dozen hands were at the bits of the horses, and their quiet assured. About that time, another chariot appeared upon the track; and, unlike the others, driver, vehicle, and racers were precisely as they would be presented in the Circus the day of final trial. For a reason which will presently be more apparent, it is desirable now to give this turn-out plainly to the reader.

There should be no difficulty in understanding the carriage known to us all as the chariot of classical renown. One has but to picture to himself a dray with low wheels and broad axle, surmounted by a box open at the tail end. Such was the primitive pattern. Artistic genius came along in time, and, touching the rude machine, raised it into a thing of beauty—that, for instance, in which Aurora, riding in advance of the dawn, is given to our fancy.

The jockeys of the ancients, quite as shrewd and ambitious as their successors of the present, called their humblest turn-out a *two*, and their best in grade a *four*; in the latter, they contested the Olympics and the other festal shows founded in imitation of them.

The same sharp gamesters preferred to put their horses to the chariot all abreast; and for distinction they termed the two next the pole *yoke-steeds*, and those on the right and left outside *trace-mates*. It was their judgment, also, that, by allowing the fullest freedom of action, the greatest speed was attainable; accordingly, the harness resorted to was peculiarly simple; in fact, there was nothing of it save a collar round the animal's neck, and a trace fixed to the collar, unless the lines and a halter fall within the term. Wanting to hitch up, the masters pinned a narrow wooden yoke, or cross-tree, near the end of the pole, and, by straps passed through rings at the end of the yoke, buckled the latter to the collar. The traces of the yoke-steeds they hitched to the axles: those of the trace-mates to the top rim of the chariot bed. There remained then but the adjustment of the lines, which, judged by the modern devices, was not the least curious part of the method. For this there was a large ring at the forward extremity of the pole; securing the ends to that ring first, they parted the lines so as to give one to each horse, and proceeded to pass them to the driver, slipping them separately through rings on the inner side of the halters at the mouth.

With this plain generalization in mind, all further desirable knowledge upon the subject can be had by following the incidents of the scene occurring.

The other contestants had been received in silence; the last comer was more fortunate. While moving towards the stand from which we are viewing the scene, his progress was signalized by loud demonstrations, by clapping of hands and cheers, the effect of which was to centre attention upon him exclusively. His yoke-steeds, it was observed, were black, while the trace-mates were snow-white. In conformity to the exacting canons of Roman taste, they had all four been mutilated; that is to say, their tails had been clipped, and, to complete the barbarity, their shorn manes were divided into knots tied with flaring red-and-yellow ribbons.

In advancing, the stranger at length reached a point where the chariot came into view from the stand, and its appearance would of itself have justified the shouting. The wheels were very marvels of construction. Stout bands of burnished bronze reinforced the hubs, otherwise very light; the spokes were sections of ivory tusks, set in with the natural curve outward to perfect the dishing, considered important then as now; bronze tyres held the fellies, which were of shining ebony. The axle, in keeping with the wheels, was tipped with heads of snarling tigers done in brass, and the bed was woven of willow wands gilded with gold.

The coming of the beautiful horses and resplendent chariot drew Ben-Hur to look at the driver with increased interest.

Who was he?

And directly the whole person of the driver was in view. A companion rode with him, in classic description a Myrtilus, permitted men of high estate indulging their passion for the race-course. Ben-Hur could see only the driver, standing erect in the chariot, with the reins passed several times round his body—a handsome figure, scantily covered by a tunic of light-red cloth; in the right hand a whip; in the other, the arm raised and lightly extended, the four lines. The pose was exceedingly graceful and animated. The cheers and clapping of hands were received with statuesque indifference. Ben-Hur stood transfixed—his instinct and memory had served him faithfully—*the driver was Messala!*

By the selection of horses, the magnificence of the chariot, the attitude and display of person—above all, by the expression of the cold, sharp, eagle features, imperialized in his countrymen by sway of the world through so many generations, Ben-Hur knew Messala unchanged, as haughty, confident, and audacious as ever, the same in ambition, cynicism, and mocking *insouciance*.

CHAPTER 6

BY THE FOUNTAIN

As Ben-Hur descended the steps of the stand, an Arab arose upon the last one at the foot, and cried out,—

"Men of the East and West—hearken! The good Sheik Ilderim giveth greeting. With four horses, sons of the favourites of Solomon the Wise, he hath come up against the best. Needs he most a mighty man to drive them. Whoso will take them to his satisfaction, to him he promiseth enrichment for ever. Here—there—in the city and in the

Circuses, and wherever the strong most do congregate, tell ye this his offer. So saith my master, Sheik Ilderim the Generous."

The proclamation awakened a great buzz among the people under the awning. By night it would be repeated and discussed in all the sporting circles of Antioch. Ben-Hur, hearing it, stopped and looked hesitatingly from the herald to the sheik. Malluch thought he was about to accept the offer, but was relieved when he presently turned to him, and asked, "Good Malluch, where to now?"

The worthy replied, with a laugh, "Would you liken yourself to others visiting the Grove for the first time, you will straightway to hear your fortune told."

"My fortune, said you? Though the suggestion has in it a flavour of unbelief, let us to the goddess at once."

They turned after a while into an avenue of oaks, where the people were going and coming in groups; footmen here, and horsemen; there women in litters borne by slaves; and now and then chariots rolled by thunderously.

At the end of the avenue the road, by an easy grade, descended into a lowland, where, on the right hand, there was a precipitous facing of grey rock, and on the left an open meadow of vernal freshness. Then they came in view of the famous Fountain of Castalia.

Edging through a company assembled at the point, Ben-Hur beheld a jet of sweet water pouring from the crest of a stone into a basin of black marble, where, after much boiling and foaming, it disappeared as through a funnel.

By the basin, under a small portico cut into the solid wall, sat a priest, old, bearded, wrinkled, cowled—never being more perfectly eremitish. From the manner of the people present, hardly might one say which was the attraction, the fountain, for ever sparkling, or the priest, for ever there. He heard, saw, was seen, but never spoke. Occasionally a visitor extended a hand to him with a coin in it. With a cunning twinkle of the eyes, he took the money, and gave the party in exchange a leaf of papyrus.

The receiver made haste to plunge the papyrus into the basin; then, holding the dripping leaf in the sunlight, he would be rewarded with a versified inscription upon its face; and the fame of the fountain seldom suffered loss by poverty of merit in the poetry. Before Ben-Hur could test the oracle, some other visitors were seen approaching across the meadow, and their appearance piqued the curiosity of the company, his not less than theirs.

He saw first a camel, very tall and very white, in leading of a driver on horseback. A houdah on the animal, besides being unusually large,

was of crimson and gold. Two other horsemen followed the camel with
tall spears in hand.

The camel seen at hand did not belie his appearance afar. A taller,
statelier brute of his kind no traveller at the fountain, though from the
remotest parts, had ever beheld. Such great black eyes! such exceedingly fine white hair! feet so contractile when raised, so soundless
in planting, so broad when set!—nobody had ever seen the peer of
this camel. And how well he became his housing of silk, and all its
frippery of gold in fringe and gold in tassel! The tinkling of silver
bells went before him, and he moved lightly, as if unknowing of his
burden.

But who were the man and woman under the houdah?

Every eye saluted them with the inquiry.

If the former were a prince or a king, the philosophers of the crowd
might not deny the impartiality of time. When they saw the thin,
shrunken face buried under an immense turban, the skin of the hue
of a mummy, making it impossible to form an idea of his nationality,
they were pleased to think the limit of life was for the great as well as
the small. They saw about his person nothing so enviable as the shawl
which draped him.

The woman was seated in the manner of the East, amidst veils and
laces of surpassing fineness. Above her elbows she wore armlets fashioned
like coiled asps, and linked to bracelets at the wrists by strands of gold;
otherwise the arms were bare and of singular natural grace, complemented with hands modelled daintily as a child's. One of the hands
rested upon the side of the carriage, showing tapered fingers glittering
with rings, and stained at the tips till they blushed like the pink of
mother-of-pearl. She wore an open caul upon her head, sprinkled with
beads of coral, and strung with coin-pieces called sunlets, some of which
were carried across her forehead, while others fell down her back, half-
smothered in the mass of her straight blue-black hair, of itself an in-
comparable ornament, not needing the veil which covered it, except
as a protection against sun and dust. From her elevated seat she looked
upon the people calmly, pleasantly, and apparently so intent upon
studying them as to be unconscious of the interest she herself was excit-
ing; and, what was unusual—nay, in violent contravention of the
custom among women of rank in public—she looked at them with an
open face.

It was a fair face to see; quite youthful; in form, oval: complexion
not white, like the Greek; nor brunette, like the Roman; nor blonde,
like the Gaul; but rather the tinting of the sun of the Upper Nile upon
a skin of such transparency that the blood shone through it on cheek

and brow with nigh the ruddiness of lamplight. The eyes, naturally large, were touched along the lids with the black paint immemorial throughout the East. The lips were slightly parted, disclosing, through their scarlet lake, teeth of glistening whiteness. To all these excellences of countenance the reader is finally besought to superadd the air derived from the pose of a small head, classic in shape, set upon a neck long, drooping, and graceful—the air, we may fancy, happily described by the word queenly.

As if satisfied with the survey of people and locality, the fair creature spoke to the driver—an Ethiopian of vast brawn, naked to the waist —who led the camel nearer the fountain, and caused it to kneel; after which he received from her hand a cup, and proceeded to fill it at the basin. That instant the sound of wheels and the trampling of horses in rapid motion broke the silence her beauty had imposed, and, with a great outcry, the bystanders parted in every direction, hurrying to get away.

"The Roman has a mind to ride us down. Look out!" Malluch shouted to Ben-Hur, setting him at the same time an example of hasty flight.

The latter faced to the direction the sounds came from, and beheld Messala in his chariot pushing the four straight at the crowd. This time the view was near and distinct.

The parting of the company uncovered the camel, which might have been more agile than his kind generally; yet the hoofs were almost upon him, and he resting with closed eyes, chewing the endless cud with such sense of security as long favouritism may be supposed to have bred in him. The Ethiopian wrung his hands afraid. In the houdah, the old man moved to escape; but he was hampered with age, and could not, even in the face of danger, forget the dignity which was plainly his habit. It was too late for the woman to save herself. Ben-Hur stood nearest them, and he called to Messala,

"Hold! Look where thou goest! Back, back!"

The patrician was laughing in hearty good-humour; and, seeing there was but one chance of rescue, Ben-Hur stepped in, and caught the bits of the left yoke-steed and his mate. "Dog of a Roman! Carest thou so little for life?" he cried, putting forth all his strength. The two horses reared, and drew the others round; the tilting of the pole tilted the chariot; Messala barely escaped a fall, while his complacent Myrtilus rolled back like a clod to the ground. Seeing the peril past, all the bystanders burst into derisive laughter.

The matchless audacity of the Roman then manifested itself. Loosing the lines from his body, he tossed them to one side, dismounted, walked

round the camel, looked at Ben-Hur, and spoke partly to the old man
and partly to the woman.

"Pardon, I pray you—I pray you both. I am Messala," he said; "and
by the old Mother of the earth, I swear I did not see you or your camel!
As to these good people—perhaps I trusted too much to my skill. I
sought a laugh at them—the laugh is theirs. Good may it do them!"

The good-natured, careless look and gesture he threw the bystanders
accorded well with the speech. To hear what more he had to say, they
became quiet. Assured of victory over the body of the offended, he
signed his companion to take the chariot to a safer distance, and
addressed himself boldly to the woman.

"Thou hast interest in the good man here, whose pardon, if not
granted now, I shall seek with the greater diligence hereafter; his
daughter, I should say."

At this point she broke in upon him.

"Wilt thou come here?" she asked, smiling, and with gracious bend
of the head to Ben-Hur.

"Take the cup and fill it, I pray thee," she said to the latter. "My
father is thirsty."

"I am thy most willing servant!"

Ben-Hur turned about to do the favour, and was face to face with
Messala. Their glances met: the Jew's defiant; the Roman's sparkling
with humour.

"O stranger, beautiful as cruel!" Messala said, waving his hand to
her. "If Apollo get thee not, thou shalt see me again. Not knowing
thy country, I cannot name a god to commend thee to; so, by all the
gods, I will commend thee to—myself!"

Seeing the Myrtilus had the four composed and ready, he returned to
the chariot. The woman looked after him as he moved away, and whatever else there was in her look, there was no displeasure. Presently she
received the water; her father drank; then she raised the cup to her
lips, and, leaning down, gave it to Ben-Hur; never action more graceful
and gracious.

"Keep it, we pray of thee! It is full of blessings—all thine!"

Immediately the camel was aroused, and on his feet, and about to
go, when the old man called,—

"Stand thou here."

Ben-Hur went to him respectfully.

"Thou hast served the stranger well to-day. There is but one God.
In His holy name I thank thee. I am Balthasar, the Egyptian. In the
Great Orchard of Palms, beyond the village of Daphne, in the shade of
the palms, Sheik Ilderim the Generous abideth in his tents, and we

are his guests. Seek us there. Thou shalt have welcome sweet with the savour of the grateful."

Ben-Hur was left in wonder at the old man's clear voice and reverend manner. As he gazed after the two departing, he caught sight of Messala going as he had come, joyous, indifferent, and with a mocking laugh.

CHAPTER 7

VENGEANCE PLANNED

As a rule, there is no surer way to the dislike of men than to behave well where they have behaved badly. In this instance, happily, Malluch was an exception to the rule. The affair he had just witnessed raised Ben-Hur in his estimation, since he could not deny him courage and address; could he now get some insight into the young man's history, the results of the day would not be at all unprofitable to good master Simonides.

On the latter point, referring to what he had as yet learned, two facts comprehended it all—the subject of his investigation was a Jew, and the adopted son of a famous Roman. Another conclusion which might be of importance was beginning to formulate itself in the shrewd mind of the emissary; between Messala and the son of the duumvir there was a connection of some kind. But what was it?—and how could it be reduced to assurance? With all his sounding, the ways and means of solution were not at all. In the heat of the perplexity, Ben-Hur himself came to his help. He laid his hand on Malluch's arm and drew him out of the crowd, which was already going back to its interest in the grey old priest and the mystic fountain.

"Good Malluch," he said, stopping, "may a man forget his mother?"

The question was abrupt and without direction, and therefore of the kind which leaves the person addressed in a state of confusion. Malluch looked into Ben-Hur's face for a hint of meaning, but saw, instead, two bright-red spots, one on each cheek, and in his eyes traces of what might have been repressed tears; then he answered mechanically, "No!" adding, with fervour, "never"; and a moment after, when he began to recover himself, "If he is an Israelite, never!" And when at length he was completely recovered—"My first lesson in the synagogue was the Shema; my next was the saying of the son of Sirach, 'Honour thy father with thy whole soul, and forget not the sorrows of thy mother.' "

The red spots on Ben-Hur's face deepened.

"My father," he said, "bore a good name, and was not without honour in Jerusalem, where he dwelt. My mother, at his death, was in the prime of womanhood; and it is not enough to say of her she was good and beautiful: in her tongue was the law of kindness, and her works were the praise of all in the gates, and she smiled at days to come. I had a little sister, and she and I were the family, and we were so happy that I, at least, have never seen harm in the saying of the old rabbi, 'God could not be everywhere, and, therefore, he made mothers.' One day an accident happened to a Roman in authority as he was riding past our house at the head of a cohort; the legionaries burst the gate and rushed in and seized us. I have not seen my mother or sister since. I cannot say they are dead or living. I do not know what became of them. But, Malluch, the man in the chariot yonder was present at the separation; he gave us over to the captors; he heard my mother's prayer for her children, and he laughed when they dragged her away. Hardly may one say which graves deepest in memory, love or hate. To-day I knew him afar—and, Malluch——"

He caught the listener's arm again.

"And, Malluch, he knows and takes with him now the secret I would give my life for: he could tell if she lives, and where she is, and her condition; if she—no, *they*—much sorrow has made the two as one—if they are dead, he could tell me where they died, and of what, and where their bones await my finding."

They took the road which led to the right across the meadow spoken of in the description of the coming to the fountain. Ben-Hur was first to break the silence.

"Do you know Sheik Ilderim the Generous?"

"Yes."

"Where is his Orchard of Palms? or, rather, Malluch, how far is it beyond the village of Daphne?"

"The Orchard of Palms lies beyond the village two hours by horse, and one by a swift camel."

"Thank you; and to your knowledge once more. Have the games of which you told me been widely published?"

"Oh yes, they will be of ample splendour. The prefect is rich, and could afford to lose his place; yet, as is the way with successful men, his love of riches is nowise diminished; and to gain a friend at court, if nothing more, he must make ado for the Consul Maxentius, who is coming hither to make final preparations for a campaign against the Parthians. A month ago heralds went to the four quarters to proclaim the opening of the Circus for the celebration. The name of the prefect would be of itself good guarantee of variety and magnificence, particularly throughout the East; but when to his promises Antioch joins hers, all the islands and the cities by the sea stand assured of the extraordinary, and will be here in person or by their most famous professionals. The fees offered are royal."

"One thing more now, O Malluch. When will the celebration be?"

"Ah! your pardon," the other answered. "To-morrow—and the next day," he said, counting aloud, "then, to speak in the Roman style, if the sea-gods be propitious, the consul arrives. Yes, the sixth day from this we have the games."

"The time is short, Malluch, but it is enough." The last words were spoken decisively. "By the prophets of our old Israel! I will take to the reins again. Stay! a condition; is there assurance that Messala will be a competitor?"

Malluch saw now the plan, and all its opportunities for the humiliation of the Roman; and he had not been true descendant of Jacob if, with all his interest wakened, he had not rushed to a consideration of the chances. His voice actually trembled as he said, "Have you the practice?"

"Fear not, my friend. The winners in the Circus Maximus have held their crowns these three years at my will. Ask them—ask the best of them, and they will tell you so. In the last great games the emperor himself offered me his patronage if I would take his horses in hand and run them against the entries of the world."

Malluch smiled and nodded as if saying, "Right, right—trust me a Jew to understand a Jew."

"The Messala will drive," he said directly. "He is committed to the race in many ways—by publication in the streets, and in the baths and theatres, the palace and barracks; and, to fix him past retreat, his name is on the tablets of every young spendthrift in Antioch."

"In wager, Malluch?"

"Yes, in wager; and every day he comes ostentatiously to practise, as you saw him."

"Ah! and that is the chariot, and those the horses, with which he will make the race? Thank you, thank you, Malluch! You have served me well already. I am satisfied. Now be my guide to the Orchard of Palms, and give me introduction to Sheik Ilderim the Generous."

"When?"

"To-day. His horses may be engaged to-morrow."

Malluch took a moment for reflection.

"It is best we go straight to the village, which is fortunately near by; if two swift camels are to be had for hire there, we will be on the road but an hour."

"Let us about it, then."

The village was an assemblance of palaces in beautiful gardens, interspersed with khans of princely sort. Dromedaries were happily secured, and upon them the journey to the famous Orchard of Palms was begun.

CHAPTER 8

THE ORCHARD OF PALMS

BEYOND the village the country was undulating and cultivated; in fact, it was the garden-land of Antioch, with not a foot lost to labour.

In course of their journey the friends came to the river, which they followed with the windings of the road, now over bold bluffs, and then into vales, all alike allotted for country-seats; and if the land was in full foliage of oak and sycamore and myrtle, and bay and arbutus, and perfuming jasmine, the river was bright with slanted sunlight, which would have slept where it fell but for ships in endless procession, gliding with the current, tacking for the wind, or bounding under the impulse of oars—some coming, some going, and all suggestive of the sea, and distant peoples, and famous places, and things coveted on account of their rarity. To the fancy there is nothing so winsome as a white sail seaward blown, unless it be a white sail homeward bound, its voyage happily done. And down the shore the friends went continuously till they came to a lake fed by back-water from the river, clear, deep, and without current. An old palm-tree dominated the angle of the inlet; turning to the left at the foot of the tree, Malluch clapped his hands and shouted,—

"Look, look! The Orchard of Palms!"

The scene was nowhere else to be found unless in the favoured oases of Arabia or the Ptolemæan farms along the Nile; and to sustain a sensation new as it was delightful, Ben-Hur was admitted into a tract of land apparently without limit and level as a floor.

The road wound in close parallelism with the shore of the lake; and when it carried the travellers down to the water's edge, there was always on that side a shining expanse limited not far off by the opposite shore, on which, as on this one, no tree but the palm was permitted.

"See that," said Malluch, pointing to a giant of the place. "Each ring upon its trunk marks a year of its life. Count them from root to branch, and if the sheik tells you the grove was planted before the Seleucidæ were heard of in Antioch, do not doubt him.

"You must know," Malluch continued, pausing now and then to dispose of a date, "that the merchant Simonides gives me his confidence, and sometimes flatters me by taking me into council; and as I attend him at his house, I have made acquaintance with many of his friends, who, knowing my footing with the host, talk to him freely in my presence. In that way I became somewhat intimate with Sheik Ilderim.

"A few weeks ago, the old Arab called on Simonides, and found me present. I observed he seemed much moved about something, and, in deference, offered to withdraw, but he himself forbade me. 'As you are an Israelite,' he said, 'stay, for I have a strange story to tell.' The emphasis on the word Israelite excited my curiosity. I remained, and this is in substance his story—I cut it short because we are drawing nigh the tent, and I leave the details to the good man himself. A good many years ago, three men called at Ilderim's tent out in the wilderness. They were all foreigners, a Hindoo, a Greek, and an Egyptian; and they had come on camels, the largest he had ever seen, and all white. He welcomed them, and gave them rest. Next morning they arose and prayed a prayer new to the sheik—a prayer addressed to God and His Son—this with much mystery besides. After breaking fast with him, the Egyptian told who they were, and whence they had come. Each had seen a star, out of which a voice had bidden them go to Jerusalem and ask, 'Where is He that is born King of the Jews?' They obeyed. From Jerusalem they were led by a star to Bethlehem, where, in a cave, they found a child newly born, which they fell down and worshipped; and after worshipping it, and giving it costly presents, and bearing witness of what it was, they took to their camels, and fled without pause to the sheik, because if Herod—meaning him surnamed the Great—could lay hands upon them, he would certainly kill them. And, faithful to his habit, the sheik took care of them, and kept them concealed for a year, when they departed, leaving with him gifts of great value, and each going a separate way."

"Has Ilderim nothing more of the three men?" asked Ben-Hur. "What became of them?"

"Ah, yes, that was the cause of his coming to Simonides the day of which I was speaking. Only the night before that day the Egyptian reappeared to him."

"Where?"

"Here at the door of the tent to which we are coming."

"How knew he the man?"

"As you knew the horses to-day—by face and manner."

"By nothing else?"

"He rode the same great white camel, and gave him the same name—Balthasar, the Egyptian."

"It is a wonder of the Lord's!"

Ben-Hur spoke with excitement.

And Malluch, wondering, asked, "Why so?"

"Balthasar, you said?"

"Yes. Balthasar, the Egyptian."

"That was the name the old man gave us at the fountain to-day."

Then, at the reminder, Malluch became excited.

"It is true," he said; "and the camel was the same—and you saved the man's life."

"And the woman," said Ben-Hur, like one speaking to himself—"the woman was his daughter."

He fell to thinking; and even the reader will say he was having a vision of the woman, and that it was more welcome than that of Esther, if only because it stayed longer with him; but no—

"Tell me again," he said presently. "Were the three to ask, 'Where is He that is to be King of the Jews?'

"Not exactly. The words were, *born to be King of the Jews.* Those were the words as the old sheik caught them first in the desert, and he has ever since been waiting the coming of the King; nor can any one shake his faith that He will come."

"How—as king?"

"Yes, and bringing the doom of Rome—so says the sheik."

Ben-Hur kept silent awhile, thinking and trying to control his feelings.

"The old man is one of many millions," he said slowly—"one of many millions each with a wrong to avenge; and this strange faith, Malluch, is bread and wine to his hope; for who but a Herod may be King of the Jews while Rome endures? But, following the story, did you hear what Simonides said to him?"

"If Ilderim is a grave man, Simonides is a wise one," Malluch replied. "I listened, and he said—— But hark! Some one comes overtaking us."

The noise grew louder, until presently they heard the rumble of wheels mixed with the beating of horse-hoofs—a moment later Sheik Ilderim himself appeared on horseback, followed by a train, among which were the four wine-red Arabs drawing the chariot. The sheik's chin, in its muffling of long white beard, was drooped upon his breast. Our friends had out-travelled him; but at sight of them, he raised his head, and spoke kindly.

"Peace to you!—Ah, my friend Malluch! Welcome! And tell me you are not going, but just come; that you have something for me from the good Simonides—may the Lord of his fathers keep him in life for many years to come! Ay, take up the straps, both of you, and follow me. I have bread and leben, or, if you prefer it, arrack, and the flesh of young kid. Come!"

They followed after him to the door of the tent, in which, when they were dismounted, he stood to receive them, holding a platter with three cups filled with creamy liquor just drawn from a great smoke-stained skin bottle, pendent from the central post.

"Drink," he said heartily, "drink, for this is the fear-naught of the tentmen."

They each took a cup, and drank till but the foam remained.

"Enter now, in God's name."

And when they were gone in, Malluch took the sheik aside, and spoke to him privately; after which he went to Ben-Hur and excused himself.

"I have told the sheik about you, and he will give you the trial of his horses in the morning. He is your friend. Having done for you all I can, you must do the rest, and let me return to Antioch. There is one there who has my promise to meet him to-night. I have no choice but to go. I will come back to-morrow prepared, if all goes well in the meantime, to stay with you until the games are over."

With blessings given and received, Malluch set out in return.

CHAPTER 9

MALLUCH'S REPORT

WHAT time the lower horn of a new moon touched the castellated piles on Mount Sulpius, and two-thirds of the people of Antioch were out on their house-tops comforting themselves with the night breeze when it blew, and with fans when it failed, Simonides sat in the chair which had come to be a part of him, and from the terrace looked down over the river, and his ships a-swing at their moorings. The wall at his back cast its shadow broadly over the water to the opposite shore. Above him the endless tramp upon the bridge went on. Esther was holding a plate for him containing his frugal supper—some wheaten cakes light as wafers, some honey, and a bowl of milk, into which he now and then dipped the wafers after dipping them into the honey.

"Malluch is a laggard to-night," he said, showing where his thoughts were.

"Do you believe he will come?" Esther asked.

"Unless he has taken to the sea or the desert, and is yet following on, he will come." Just then a footstep was heard upon the terrace—"Ha, Esther! said I not so? He is here—and we will have tidings. For thy sake, sweet child—my lily just budded—I pray the Lord God, who has not forgotten his wandering sheep of Israel, that they be good and comforting."

Malluch came to the chair.

"Peace to you, good master," he said, with a low obeisance—"and to you, Esther, most excellent of daughters."

He stood before them deferentially, and the attitude and the address left it difficult to define his relation to them; the one was that of a servant, the other indicated the familiar and friend. On the other side, Simonides, as was his habit in business, after answering the salutation went straight to the subject.

"What of the young man, Malluch?"

The events of the day were told quietly and in the simplest words, and until he was through there was no interruption; nor did the listener in the chair so much as move a hand during the narration; but for his eyes, wide open and bright, and an occasional long-drawn breath, he might have been accounted an effigy.

"Thank you, thank you, Malluch," he said heartily, at the conclusion; "you have done well—no one could have done better. Now what say you of the young man's nationality?"

"He is an Israelite, good master, and of the tribe of Judah."

"You are positive?"

"Very positive."

"He appears to have told you but little of his life."

"He has somewhere learned to be prudent. I might call him distrustful. He baffled all my attempts upon his confidence until we started from the Castalian fount going to the village of Daphne."

"In what he said or did, Malluch, could you in anywise detect his master-idea? You know they peep through cracks close enough to stop the wind."

"Give me to understand you," said Malluch, in doubt.

"Well, you know we nor speak nor act, much less decide grave questions concerning ourselves, except we be driven by a motive. In that respect, what made you of him?"

"As to that, Master Simonides, I can answer with much assurance. He is devoted to finding his mother and sister—that first. Then he has a grievance against Rome; and as the Messala of whom I told you had something to do with the wrong, the great present object is to humiliate him. The meeting at the fountain furnished an opportunity, but it was put aside as not sufficiently public."

"The Messala is influential," said Simonides thoughtfully.

"Yes; but the next meeting will be in the Circus."

"Well—and then?"

"The son of Arrius will win."

"How know you?"

Malluch smiled.

"I am judging by what he says."

"Is that all?"

"No; there is a much better sign—his spirit."

Simonides gazed for a time at the ships and their shadows slowly swinging together in the river; when he looked up, it was to end the interview.

"Enough, Malluch," he said. "Get you to eat, and make ready to return to the Orchard of Palms; you must help the young man in his coming trial. Come to me in the morning. I will send a letter to Ilderim." Then in an undertone, as if to himself, he added, "I may attend the Circus myself."

When Malluch, after the customary benediction given and received, was gone, Simonides took a deep draught of milk, and seemed refreshed and easy of mind.

"Put the meal down, Esther," he said; "it is over."

She obeyed.

"Here now."

She resumed her place upon the arm of the chair close to him.

She said with a simplicity, almost childish,—

"Send for him, father. Send for him to-night, and do not let him go into the Circus."

"Ah!" he said, prolonging the exclamation; and again his eyes fell upon the river, where the shadows were more shadowy than ever, since the moon had sunk far down behind Sulpius, leaving the city to the ineffectual stars. "Not go into the Circus, Esther! Why, child?"

"It is not a place for a son of Israel, father."

"Rabbinical, rabbinical, Esther! Is that all?"

The tone of the inquiry was searching, and went to her heart, which began to beat loudly,—so loudly she could not answer. A confusion new and strangely pleasant fell upon her.

"The young man is to have the fortune," he said, taking her hand and speaking more tenderly; "he is to have the ships and the shekels,— all, Esther, all. Yet I did not feel poor, for thou wert left me, and thy love so like the dead Rachel's. Tell me, is he to have that too?"

She bent over him, and laid her cheek against his head.

"Speak, Esther. I will be the stronger of the knowledge. In warning there is strength."

She sat up then, and spoke as if she were Truth's holy self.

"Comfort thee, father. I will never leave thee; though he take my love, I will be thy handmaid ever as now."

And, stooping, she kissed him.

"And more," she said, continuing; "he is comely in my sight, and the pleading of his voice drew me to him, and I shudder to think of him in danger. Yes, father, I would be more than glad to see him again. Still, the love that is unrequited cannot be perfect love, wherefore I will wait a time, remembering I am thy daughter and my mother's."

"A very blessing of the Lord art thou, Esther! A blessing to keep me rich, though all else be lost. And by His holy name and everlasting life, I swear thou shalt not suffer."

CHAPTER 10

A ROMAN REVEL

The palace across the river nearly opposite Simonides' place is said to have been completed by the famous Epiphanes, and was all such a habitation can be imagined; though he was a builder whose taste ran to the immense rather than the classical, now so called,—an architectural imitator, in other words, of the Persians instead of the Greeks.

As we have to do with but one apartment in the old pile, the residue of it is left to the reader's fancy; and, as pleases him, he may go through its garden, baths, halls, and labyrinths of rooms to the pavilions on the roof, all furnished as became a house of fame in a city which was more nearly Milton's "gorgeous East" than any other in the world.

There are five chandeliers hanging by sliding bronze chains from the ceiling,—one in each corner, and in the centre one,—enormous pyramids of lighted lamps, illuminating even the demoniac faces of the Atlantes and the complex tracery of the cornice. About tables, seated or standing, or moving restlessly from one to another, there are probably a hundred persons, whom we must study at least for a moment.

They are all young, some of them little more than boys. That they are Italians, and mostly Romans, is past doubt. They all speak Latin in purity, while each one appears in the indoor dress of the great capital on the Tiber,—that is, in tunics short of sleeve and skirt, a style of vesture well adapted to the climate of Antioch, and especially comfortable in the too close atmosphere of the saloon. On the divan here and there togas and lacernæ lie where they have been carelessly tossed, some of them significantly bordered with purple. On the divan also lie sleepers stretched at ease; whether they were overcome by the heat and fatigue of the sultry day or by Bacchus we will not pause to inquire.

A party entered the room, and, unnoticed at first, proceeded to the central table. The signs were that they had come from a revel just dismissed. Some of them kept their feet with difficulty. Around the leader's brow was a chaplet which marked him master of the feast, if not the giver. The wine had made no impression upon him unless to heighten his beauty, which was of the most manly Roman style. In going to the table, he made room for himself and his followers with little ceremony and no apologies; and when at length he stopped, and looked over it and at the players, they all turned to him, with a shout like a cheer.

"Messala! Messala!" they cried.

Messala took the demonstration indifferently, and proceeded presently to show the ground of his popularity.

"A health to thee, Drusus, my friend," he said to the player next at his right; "a health—and thy tablets a moment."

He raised the waxen boards, glanced at the memoranda of wagers, and tossed them down.

"Denarii, only denarii—coin of cartmen and butchers!" he said, with a scornful laugh. "By the drunken Semele, to what is Rome coming, when a Cæsar sits o' nights waiting a turn of fortune to bring him but a beggarly denarius!"

He turned the box upon the table and held it firmly over the dice.

And Drusus asked, "Did you ever see one Quintus Arrius?"

"The duumvir?"

"No—his son?"

"I knew not he had a son."

"Well, it is nothing," Drusus added indifferently; "only, my Messala, Pollux was not more like Castor than Arrius is like thee."

The remark had the effect of a signal: twenty voices took it up.

"True, true! His eyes—his face," they cried.

"What!" answered one, disgusted. "Messala is a Roman; Arrius is a Jew."

"Thou sayest right," a third exclaimed. "He is a Jew, or Momus lent his mother the wrong mask."

There was promise of a dispute; seeing which, Messala interposed. "The wine is not come, my Drusus; and, as thou seest, I have the freckled Pythias as they were dogs in leash. As to Arrius, I will accept thy opinion of him, so thou tell me more about him."

"Well, be he Jew or Roman—and, by the great god Pan, I say it not in disrespect of thy feelings, my Messala!—this Arrius is handsome and brave and shrewd. The emperor offered him favour and patronage, which he refused. He came up through mystery, and keepeth distance as if he felt himself better or knew himself worse than the rest of us. In the palæstræ he was unmatched; he played with the blue-eyed giants from the Rhine and the hornless bulls of Sarmatia as they were willow wisps. The duumvir left him vastly rich. He has a passion for arms, and thinks of nothing but war. Maxentius admitted him into his family, and he was to have taken ship with us, but we lost him at Ravenna. Nevertheless he arrived safely. We heard of him this morning. *Perpol!* Instead of coming to the palace or going to the citadel, he dropped his baggage at the khan, and hath disappeared again."

At the beginning of the speech Messala listened with polite indifference; as it proceeded, he became more attentive; at the conclusion, he took his hand from the dice-box, and called out, "Ho, my Caius! Dost thou hear?"

A youth at his elbow—his Myrtilus, or comrade, in the day's chariot practice—answered, much pleased with the attention, "Did I not, my Messala, I were not thy friend."

"Dost thou remember the man who gave thee the fall to-day?"

"By the love-locks of Bacchus, have I not a bruised shoulder to help me keep it in mind?" and he seconded the words with a shrug that submerged his ears.

"Well, be thou grateful to the fates—I have found thy enemy. Listen."

Thereupon Messala turned to Drusus.

"Tell us more of him—*perpol!*—of him who is both Jew and Roman by Phœbus, a combination to make a Centaur lovely! What garments doth he affect, my Drusus?"

"Those of the Jews."

"Hearest thou, Caius?" said Messala. "The fellow is young—one; he hath the visage of a Roman—two; he loveth best the garb of a Jew —three; and in the palæstræ fame and fortune come of arms to throw a horse or tilt a chariot, as the necessity may order—four. And Drusus, help thou my friend again. Doubtless this Arrius hath tricks of language; otherwise he could not so confound himself, to-day a Jew, to-morrow a Roman; but of the rich tongue of Athene—discourseth he in that as well?"

"With such purity, Messala, he might have been a contestant in the Isthmia."

"Art thou listening, Caius?" said Messala. "The fellow is qualified to salute a woman—for that matter, Aristomache herself—in the Greek; and as I keep the count, that is five. What sayest thou?"

"Thou hast found him, my Messala," Caius answered; "or I am not myself."

"Thy pardon, Drusus—and pardon of all—for speaking in riddles thus," Messala said, in his winsome way. "By all the decent gods, I would not strain thy courtesy to the point of breaking, but now help thou me. See!"—he put his hand on the dice-box again, laughing—"See how close I hold the Pythias and their secret! Thou didst speak, I think, of mystery in connection with the coming of the son of Arrius. Tell me of that."

" 'Tis nothing, Messala, nothing," Drusus replied; "a child's story. When Arrius, the father, sailed in pursuit of the pirates, he was without wife or family; he returned with a boy—him of whom we speak—and next day adopted him."

"Adopted him?" Messala repeated. "By the gods, Drusus, thou dost indeed interest me! Where did the duumvir find the boy? And who was he?"

"Who shall answer thee that, Messala? who but the young Arrius himself? *Perpol!* in the fight the duumvir—then but a tribune—lost his galley. A returning vessel found him and one other—all of the crew who survived—afloat upon the same plank. I give you now the story of the rescuers, which hath this excellence at least—it hath never been contradicted. They say, the duumvir's companion on the plank was a Jew——"

"A Jew!" echoed Messala.

"And a slave."

"How, Drusus? A slave?"

"When the two were lifted to the deck, the duumvir was in his tribune's armour, and the other in the vesture of a rower."

Messala arose from leaning against the table.

"A galley"—he checked the debasing word, and looked around, for once in his life at loss. Just then a procession of slaves filed into the room, some with great jars of wine, others with baskets of fruits and confections, others again with cups and flagons, mostly silver. There was inspiration in the sight. Instantly Messala climbed upon a stool.

"Men of the Tiber," he said, in a clear voice, "let us turn this waiting for our chief into a feast of Bacchus. Whom choose ye for master?"

Drusus arose.

"Who shall be master but the giver of the feast?" he said. "Answer, Romans."

They gave their reply in a shout.

Messala took the chaplet from his head, gave it to Drusus, who climbed upon the table, and, in the view of all, solemnly replaced it, making Messala master of the night.

"There came with me into the room," he said, "some friends just risen from table. That our feast may have the approval of sacred custom, bring hither that one of them most overcome by wine."

A din of voices answered, "Here he is, here he is!"

And from the floor where he had fallen, a youth was brought forward, so effeminately beautiful he might have passed for the drinking-god himself—only the crown would have dropped from his head, and the thyrsus from his hand.

"Lift him upon the table," the master said.

It was found he could not sit.

"Help him, Drusus, as the fair Nyone may yet help thee."

Drusus took the inebriate in his arms.

Then addressing the limp figure, Messala said, amidst profound silence, "O Bacchus! greatest of the gods, be thou propitious to-night. And for myself, and these thy votaries, I vow this chaplet"—and from his head he raised it reverently—"I vow this chaplet to thy altar in the Grove of Daphne."

He bowed, replaced the crown upon his locks, then stooped and uncovered the dice, saying, with a laugh, "See, my Drusus, by the ass of Silenus, the denarius is mine!"

There was a shout that set the floor to quaking, and the grim Atlantes to dancing, and the orgies began.

CHAPTER II

IN AN ARAB HOME

SHEIK ILDERIM was a man of too much importance to go about with a small establishment. He had a reputation to keep with his tribe, such as became a prince and patriarch of the greatest following in all the Desert east of Syria; with the people of the cities he had another reputation, which was that of one of the richest personages not a king in all the East; and, being rich in fact—in money as well as in servants, camels, horses, and flocks of all kinds—he took pleasure in a certain state, which, besides magnifying his dignity with strangers, contributed to his personal pride and comfort.

At the door of his tent we left Ben-Hur.

Servants were already waiting the master's direction. One of them took off his sandals; another unlatched Ben-Hur's Roman shoes; then the two exchanged their dusty outer garments for fresh ones of white linen.

"Enter—in God's name, enter, and take thy rest," said the host heartily, in the dialect of the Market-place of Jerusalem; forthwith he led the way to a divan.

"I will sit here," he said next, pointing; "and there the stranger."

A woman—in the old time she would have been called a handmaid —answered, and dexterously piled the pillows and bolsters as rests for the back; after which they sat upon the side of the divan, while water was brought fresh from the lake, and their feet bathed and dried with napkins.

The servant went away. Thereupon Ilderim settled himself upon the divan, as at this day merchants sit on their rugs in the bazaars of Damascus; and when fairly at rest, he stopped combing his beard, and said, gravely, "That thou art my guest, and hast drunk my leben, and art about to taste my salt, ought not to forbid a question: Who art thou?"

"Sheik, I am a Jew with a grievance against Rome, compared with which thine is not more than a child's trouble."

The old man combed his beard with nervous haste, and let fall his brows until even the twinkle of the eyes went out.

"Still further: I swear to thee, Sheik Ilderim—I swear by the covenant the Lord made with my fathers,—so thou but give me the revenge I seek, the money and the glory of the race shall be thine."

Ilderim's brows relaxed; his head arose; his face began to beam; and it was almost possible to see the satisfaction taking possession of him. He called to a servant: "Let my Arabs come!"

The man drew aside part of the division curtain of the tent, exposing to view a group of horses, who lingered a moment where they were as if to make certain of the invitation.

"Come!" Ilderim said to them. "Why stand ye there? What have I that is not yours? Come, I say!"

They stalked slowly in.

Ilderim's face beamed again, and he would have spoken.

"A moment, good sheik, a moment!" said Ben-Hur. "Let me say further. From the masters in Rome I learned many lessons, little thinking they would serve me in a time like this. I tell thee these thy sons of the Desert, though they have separately the speed of eagles and the endurance of lions, will fail if they are not trained to run together under the yoke. For bethink thee, sheik, in every four there is one the slowest and one the swiftest; and while the race is always to the slowest, the trouble is always with the swiftest. It was so to-day; the driver could not reduce the best to harmonious action with the poorest. My trial may have no better result; but if so, I will tell thee of it: that I swear. Wherefore, in the same spirit I say, can I get them to run together, moved by my will, the four as one, thou shalt have the sestertii and the crown, and I my revenge. What sayest thou?"

Ilderim listened, combing his beard the while. At the end he said, with a laugh, "I think better of thee, son of Israel. We have a saying in the Desert, 'If you will cook the meal with words, I will promise an ocean of butter.' Thou shalt have the horses in the morning."

At that moment there was a stir at the rear entrance to the tent.

"The supper—it is here! and yonder my friend Balthasar, whom thou shalt know. He hath a story to tell which an Israelite should never tire of hearing."

And to the servants he added,—

"Take the records away, and return my jewels to their apartment."

And they did as he ordered.

CHAPTER 12

ILDERIM'S SUPPER

THREE rugs were spread on the carpet within the space so nearly enclosed by the divan; a table not more than a foot in height was brought and set within the same place, and covered with a cloth. Off to one side a portable earthenware oven was established under the presidency of a woman whose duty it was to keep the company in bread, or, more precisely, in hot cakes of flour from the handmills grinding with constant sound in a neighbouring tent.

Meanwhile Balthasar was conducted to the divan, where Ilderim and Ben-Hur received him standing. A loose black gown covered his person; his step was feeble, and his whole movement slow and cautious, apparently dependent upon a long staff and the arm of a servant.

"Peace to you, my friend," said Ilderim respectfully. "Peace and welcome."

The Egyptian raised his head and replied, "And to thee, good sheik —to thee and thine, peace and the blessing of the One God—God, the true and loving."

The manner was gentle and devout, and impressed Ben-Hur with a feeling of awe; besides which the blessing included in the answering salutation had been partly addressed to him, and while that part was being spoken, the eyes of the aged guest, hollow yet luminous, rested upon his face long enough to stir an emotion new and mysterious, and so strong that he again and again during the repast scanned the much-wrinkled and bloodless face for its meaning; but always there was the expression bland, placid, and trustful as a child's. A little later he found that expression habitual.

"This is he, O Balthasar," said the sheik, laying his hand on Ben-Hur's arm, "who will break bread with us this evening."

Balthasar could no longer withhold explanation.

"To-day, O most generous sheik, my life was in peril, and would have been lost had not a youth, the counterpart of this one—if, indeed, he be not the very same—intervened when all others fled, and saved me." Then he addressed Ben-Hur directly, "Art thou not he?"

"I cannot answer so far," Ben-Hur replied, with modest deference. "I am he who stopped the horses of the insolent Roman when they were rushing upon thy camel at the Fountain of Castalia. Thy daughter left a cup with me."

From the bosom of his tunic he produced the cup, and gave it to Balthasar.

A glow lighted the faded countenance of the Egyptian.

"The Lord sent thee to me at the Fountain to-day," he said, in a tremulous voice, stretching his hand towards Ben-Hur; "and He sends thee to me now. I give Him thanks; and praise Him thou, for of His favour I have wherewith to give thee great reward, and I will. The cup is thine; keep it."

Ben-Hur took back the gift, and Balthasar, seeing the inquiry upon Ilderim's face, related the occurrence at the Fountain.

"What!" said the sheik to Ben-Hur. "Thou saidst nothing of this to me, when better recommendation thou couldst not have brought. Am I not an Arab, and sheik of my tribe of tens of thousands? And is not he my guest? And is it not in my guest-bond that the good or evil thou dost him is good or evil done to me? Whither shouldst thou go for reward but here? And whose the hand to give it but mine?"

His voice at the end of the speech rose to cutting shrillness.

"Good sheik, spare me, I pray. I came not for reward, great or small; and that I may be acquitted of the thought, I say the help I gave this excellent man would have been given as well to thy humblest servant."

"But he is my friend, my guest—not my servant; and seest thou not in the difference the favour of fortune?" Then to Balthasar the sheik subjoined, "Ah, by the splendour of God! I tell thee again he is not a Roman."

With that he turned away, and gave attention to the servants, whose preparations for the supper were about complete.

The table to which they immediately addressed themselves was, as may be thought, rich in the substantials and delicacies favourite in the East—in cakes hot from the oven, vegetables from the gardens, meats singly, compounds of meats and vegetables, milk of kine, and honey and butter—all eaten or drunk, it should be remarked, without any of the modern accessories—knives, forks, spoons, cups, or plates; and in this part of the repast but little was said, for they were hungry. But when the dessert was in course it was otherwise. They laved their hands again, had the lap-cloths shaken out, and with a renewed table and the sharp edge of their appetites gone, they were disposed to talk and listen.

With such a company—an Arab, a Jew, and an Egyptian, all believers alike in one God—there could be at that age but one subject of conversation; and of the three, which should be speaker but he to whom the Deity had been so nearly a personal appearance, who had seen Him in a star, had heard His voice in direction, had been led so far and so miraculously by His Spirit? And of what should he talk but that of which he had been called to testify?

When he had finished there was a long silence. Then he spake again.

"Good sheik," he said in his placid way, "to-morrow or the next day I will go up to the city for a time. My daughter wishes to see the preparations for the games. I will speak further about the time of our going. And, my son, I will see you again. To you both, peace and good-night."

They all arose from the table. The sheik and Ben-Hur remained looking after the Egyptian until he was conducted out of the tent.

"Sheik Ilderim," said Ben-Hur then, "I have heard strange things to-night. Give me leave, I pray, to walk by the lake that I may think of them."

"Go; and I will come after you."

They washed their hands again; after which, at a sign from the master, a servant brought Ben-Hur his shoes, and directly he went out.

CHAPTER 13

A REVERIE

UP a little way from the dowar there was a cluster of palms, which threw its shade half in the water, half on the land. A bulbul sang from the branches a song of invitation. Ben-Hur stopped beneath to listen. At any other time the notes of the bird would have driven thought away; but the story of the Egyptian was a burden of wonder, and he was a labourer carrying it, and, like other labourers, there was to him no music in the sweetest music until mind and body were happily attuned by rest.

The night was quiet. Not a ripple broke upon the shore. The old stars of the old East were all out, each in its accustomed place; and there was summer everywhere—on land, on lake, in the sky.

Ben-Hur's imagination was heated, his feelings aroused, his will all unsettled.

Now, as we have seen, from Balthasar himself Ben-Hur had the marvellous story. Was he satisfied?

There was a shadow upon him deeper than that of the cluster of palms—the shadow of a great uncertainty, which—take note, O reader! which pertained more to the kingdom than the King.

"What of this kingdom? And what is it to be?" Ben-Hur asked himself in thought.

In the midst of his reverie a hand was laid upon his shoulder.

"I have a word to say, O son of Arrius," said Ilderim, stopping by his side—"A word, and then I must return, for the night is going."

"I give you welcome, sheik."

"As to the things you have heard but now," said Ilderim, almost without pause, "take in belief all save that relating to the kind of kingdom the Child will set up when He comes; as to so much keep virgin mind until you hear Simonides the merchant—a good man here in Antioch, to whom I will make you known. The Egyptian gives you coinage of his dreams which are too good for the earth; Simonides is wiser; he will ring you the sayings of your prophet, giving book and page, so you cannot deny that the Child will be King of the Jews in fact—ay, by the splendour of God! a King as Herod was, only better and far more magnificent. And then, you see, we will taste the sweetness of vengeance. I have said. Peace to you!"

"Stay—sheik!"

If Ilderim heard his call, he did not stay.

"Simonides again!" said Ben-Hur bitterly. "Simonides here, Simonides there; from this one now, then from that! I am like to be well ridden by my father's servant, who knows at least to hold fast that which is mine; wherefore he is richer, if indeed he be not wiser, than the Egyptian. By the covenant! it is not to the faithless a man should go to find a faith to keep—and I will not. But, hark! singing—and the voice a woman's—or an angel's! It comes this way."

Down the lake towards the dowar came a woman singing. Her voice floated along the hushed water melodious as a flute, and louder growing each instant. Directly the dipping of oars was heard in slow measure; a little later the words were distinguishable—words in purest Greek, best fitted of all the tongues of the day for the expression of passionate grief.

At the conclusion of the song the singer was past the cluster of palms. The last word—farewell—floated past Ben-Hur weighted with all the sweet sorrow of parting. The passing of the boat was as the passing of a deeper shadow into the deeper night.

Ben-Hur drew a long breath hardly distinguishable from a sigh.

"I know her by the song—the daughter of Balthasar. How beautiful it was! And how beautiful is she!"

He recalled her large eyes curtained slightly by the drooping lids, the cheeks oval and rosy rich, the lips full and deep with dimpling in the corners, and all the grace of the tall lithe figure.

"How beautiful she is!" he repeated.

And his heart made answer by a quickening of its movement.

Then, almost the same instant, another face, younger and quite as beautiful—more childlike and tender, if not so passionate—appeared as if held up to him out of the lake.

"Esther!" he said, smiling. "As I wished, a star has been sent to me."

He turned, and passed slowly back to the tent.

His life had been crowded with griefs and with vengeful preparations—too much crowded for love. Was this the beginning of a happy change?

And if the influence went with him into the tent, whose was it?

Esther had given him a cup.

So had the Egyptian.

And both had come to him at the same time under the palms.

Which?

BOOK FIFTH

"Only the actions of the just
  Smell sweet and blossom in the dust."
                                        SHIRLEY
"And, through the heat of conflict, keeps the law,
  In calmness made, and sees what he foresaw."
                                        WORDSWORTH

CHAPTER I

GRATUS WARNED

THE morning after the bacchanalia in the saloon of the palace, the divan was covered with young patricians. When dawn began to peer through the skylights of the saloon, Messala arose, and took the chaplet from his head, in sign that the revel was at end; then he gathered his robe about him, gave a last look at the scene, and, without a word, departed for his quarters. Cicero could not have retired with more gravity from a night-long senatorial debate.

Three hours afterwards two couriers entered his room, and from his own hand received each a despatch, sealed and in duplicate, and consisting chiefly of a letter to Valerius Gratus, the procurator, still resident in Cæsarea. The importance attached to the speedy and certain delivery of the paper may be inferred. One courier was to proceed overland, the other by sea; both were to make the utmost haste.

It is of great concern now that the reader should be fully informed of the contents of the letter thus forwarded, and it is accordingly given:

"ANTIOCH, *XII. Kal. Jul.*
    "*Messala to Gratus.*

"O my Midas!

"I pray thou take no offence at the address, seeing it is one of love and gratitude, and an admission that thou art most fortunate among men; seeing, also, that thy ears are as they were derived from thy mother, only proportionate to thy matured condition.

"O my Midas!

"I have to relate to thee an astonishing event, which, though as

123

yet somewhat in the field of conjecture, will, I doubt not, justify thy instant consideration.

"Allow me first to revive thy recollection. Remember, a good many years ago, a family of a prince of Jerusalem, incredibly ancient and vastly rich—by name Ben-Hur. If thy memory have a limp or ailment of any kind, there is, if I mistake not, a wound on thy head which may help thee to a revival of the circumstance.

"Next, to arouse thy interest. In punishment of the attempt upon thy life—for dear repose of conscience, may all the gods forbid it should ever prove to have been an accident!—the family were seized and summarily disposed of, and their property confiscated. And inasmuch, O my Midas! as the action had the approval of our Cæsar, who was as just as he was wise—be there flowers upon his altars for ever!—there should be no shame in referring to the sums which were realized to us respectively from that source, for which it is not possible I can ever cease to be grateful to thee, certainly not while I continue, as at present, in the uninterrupted enjoyment of the part which fell to me.

"In vindication of thy wisdom—a quality for which, as I am now advised, the son of Gordius, to whom I have boldly likened thee, was never distinguished among men or gods—I recall further that thou didst make disposition of the family of Hur, both of us at the time supposing the plan hit upon to be the most effective possible for the purposes in view, which were silence and delivery over to inevitable but natural death. Thou wilt remember what thou didst with the mother and sister of the malefactor; yet, if now I yield to a desire to learn whether they be living or dead, I know, from knowing the amiability of thy nature, O my Gratus, that thou wilt pardon me as one scarcely less amiable than thyself.

"As more immediately essential to the present business, however, I take the liberty of inviting to thy remembrance that the actual criminal was sent to the galleys a slave for life—so the precept ran; and it may serve to make the event which I am about to relate the more astonishing by saying here that I saw and read the receipt for his body delivered in course to the tribune commanding a galley.

"Thou mayst begin now to give me more especial heed, O my most excellent Phrygian!

"Referring to the limit of life at the oar, the outlaw thus justly disposed of should be dead, or, better speaking, some one of the three thousand Oceanides should have taken him to husband at least five years ago. And if thou wilt excuse a momentary weakness, O most virtuous and tender of men! inasmuch as I loved him in childhood, and also because he was very handsome—I used in much admiration to call him my Ganymede—he ought in right to have fallen into the arms of the most beautiful daughter of the family. Of opinion, however, that he was certainly dead, I have lived quite five years in calm and innocent enjoyment of the fortune for which I am in a degree indebted to him. I make the admission of indebtedness without intending it to diminish my obligation to thee.

"Now I am at the very point of interest.

"Last night, while acting as master of the feast for a party just from Rome—their extreme youth and inexperience appealed to my compassion—I heard a singular story. Maxentius, the consul, as you know, comes to-day to conduct a campaign against the Parthians. Of the ambitious who are to accompany him there is one, a son of the late duumvir Quintus Arrius. I had occasion to inquire about him particularly. When Arrius set out in pursuit of the pirates, whose defeat gained him his final honours, he had no family; when he returned from the expedition, he brought back with him an heir. Now be thou composed as becomes the owner of so many talents in ready sestertia! The son and heir of whom I speak is he whom thou didst send to the galleys—the very Ben-Hur who should have died at his oar five years ago—returned now with fortune and rank, and possibly as a Roman citizen, to—— Well, thou art too firmly seated to be alarmed, but I, O my Midas! I am in danger—no need to tell thee of what. Who should know, if thou dost not?

"Sayst thou to all this, tut-tut?

"When Arrius, the father by adoption of this apparition from the arms of the most beautiful of the Oceanides (see above my opinion of what she should be), joined battle with the pirates, his vessel was sunk, and but two of all her crew escaped drowning—Arrius himself and this one, his heir.

"The officers who took them from the plank on which they were floating say the associate of the fortunate tribune was a young man who, when lifted to the deck, was in the dress of a galley slave.

"This should be convincing, to say least; but lest thou say tut-tut again, I tell thee, O my Midas! that yesterday, by good chance—I have a vow to Fortune in consequence—I met the mysterious son of Arrius face to face; and I declare now that, though I did not then recognise him, he is the very Ben-Hur who was for years my playmate; the very Ben-Hur who, if he be a man, though of the commonest grade, must this very moment of my writing be thinking of vengeance—for so would I were I he—vengeance not to be satisfied short of life; vengeance for country, mother, sister, self, and—

E

I say it last—though thou mayst think it should be first—for fortune lost.

"By this time, O good my benefactor and friend! my Gratus! in consideration of thy sestertia in peril, their loss being the worst which could befall one of thy high estate—I quit calling thee after the foolish old King of Phrygia—by this time, I say (meaning after having read me so far), I have faith to believe thou hast ceased saying tut-tut, and art ready to think what ought to be done in such emergency.

"It were vulgar to ask thee now what shall be done. Rather let me say I am thy client; or, better yet, thou art my Ulysses whose part it is to give me sound direction.

"And I please myself thinking I see thee when this letter is put into thy hands. I see thee read it once, thy countenance all gravity, and then again with a smile; then, hesitation ended, and thy judgment formed, it is this, or it is that; wisdom like Mercury's, promptitude like Cæsar's.

"The sun is now fairly risen. An hour hence two messengers will depart from my door, each with a sealed copy hereof, one of them will go by land, the other by sea, so important do I regard it that thou shouldst be early and particularly informed of the appearance of our enemy in this part of our Roman world.

"I will await thy answer here.

"Ben-Hur's going and coming will of course be regulated by his master, the consul, who, though he exert himself without rest day and night, cannot get away under a month. Thou knowest what work it is to assemble and provide for an army destined to operate in a desolate, townless country.

"I saw the Jew yesterday in the Grove of Daphne; and if he be not there now, he is certainly in the neighbourhood, making it easy for me to keep him in eye. Indeed, wert thou to ask me where he is now, I should say, with the most positive assurance, he is to be found at the old Orchard of Palms, under the tent of the traitor Sheik Ilderim, who cannot long escape our strong hand. Be not surprised if Maxentius, as his first measure, places the Arab on ship for forwarding to Rome.

"I am so particular about the whereabouts of the Jew because it will be important to thee, O illustrious! when thou comest to consider what is to be done; for already I know, and by the knowledge I flatter myself I am growing in wisdom, that in every scheme involving human action there are three elements always to be taken into account—time, place, and agency.

"If thou sayest this is the place, have thou then no hesitancy in trusting the business to thy most loving friend, who would be thy aptest scholar as well.

"MESSALA."

CHAPTER 2

PREPARATION

ABOUT the time the couriers departed from Messala's door with the despatches (it being yet the early morning hour), Ben-Hur entered Ilderim's tent.

The sheik saluted him from the divan.

"I give thee peace, son of Arrius," he said, with admiration, for, in truth, he had never seen a more perfect illustration of glowing, powerful, confident manhood. "I give thee peace and good-will. The horses are ready, I am ready. And thou?"

"The peace thou givest me, good sheik, I give thee in return. I thank thee for so much good-will. I am ready."

Ilderim clapped his hands.

"I will have the horses brought. Be seated."

"Are they yoked?"

"No."

"Then suffer me to serve myself," said Ben-Hur. "It is needful that I make the acquaintance of thy Arabs. I must know them by name, O sheik, that I may speak to them singly; nor less must I know their temper, for they are like men: if bold, the better of scolding; if timid, the better of praise and flattery. Let the servants bring me the harness."

"And the chariot?" asked the sheik.

"I will let the chariot alone to-day. In its place, let them bring me a fifth horse, if thou hast it; he should be barebacked, and fleet as the others."

Ilderim's wonder was aroused, and he summoned a servant immediately.

"Bid them bring the harness for the four," he said; "the harness for the four, and the bridle for Sirius."

Ilderim then arose.

"Sirius is my love, and I am his, O son of Arrius. We have been comrades for twenty years—in tent, in battle, in all stages of the desert we have been comrades. I will show him to you."

Going to the division curtain, he held it, while Ben-Hur passed under. The horses came to him in a body.

The harness was brought. With his own hands Ben-Hur equipped the horses; with his own hands he led them out of the tent, and there attached the reins.

"Bring me Sirius," he said.

An Arab could not have better sprung to seat on the courser's back. "And now the reins."

They were given him, and carefully separated.

"Good sheik," he said, "I am ready. Let a guide go before me to the field, and send some of thy men with water."

The field, when reached, proved ample and well fitted for the training, which Ben-Hur began immediately by driving the four at first slowly, and in perpendicular lines, and then in wide circles. Advancing a step in the course, he put them next into a trot; again progressing, he pushed into a gallop; at length he contracted the circles, and yet later drove eccentrically here and there, right, left, forward, and without a break. An hour was thus occupied. Slowing the gait to a walk, he drove up to Ilderim.

"The work is done, nothing now but practice," he said. "I give you joy, Sheik Ilderim, that you have such servants as these. See," he continued, dismounting and going to the horses, "see, the gloss of their red coats is without spot; they breathe lightly as when I began. I give thee great joy, and it will go hard if"—he turned his flashing eyes upon the old man's face—"if we have not the victory and our——"

He stopped, coloured, bowed. At the sheik's side he observed, for the first time, Balthasar, leaning upon his staff, and two women closely veiled. At one of the latter he looked a second time, saying to himself, with a flutter about his heart, " 'Tis she—'tis the Egyptian!" Ilderim picked up his broken sentence,—

"The victory, and our revenge!" Then he said aloud, "I am not afraid; I am glad. Son of Arrius, thou art the man. Be the end like the beginning, and thou shalt see of what stuff is the lining of the hand of an Arab who is able to give."

"I thank thee, good sheik," Ben-Hur returned modestly. "Let the servants bring drink for the horses."

With his own hands he gave the water.

In the midst of the exercises, and the attention they received from all the bystanders, Malluch came upon the ground, seeking the sheik.

"I have a message for you, O sheik," he said, availing himself of a moment he supposed favourable for the speech—"a message from Simonides, the merchant."

"Simonides!" ejaculated the Arab. "Ah! 'tis well. May Abaddon take all his enemies!"

"He bade me give thee first the holy peace of God," Malluch continued; "and then this despatch, with prayer that thou read it the instant of receipt."

Ilderim, standing in his place, broke the sealing of the package delivered to him, and from a wrapping of fine linen took two letters, which he proceeded to read.

[No. 1.]
"Simonides to Sheik Ilderim.

"O friend!

"Assure thyself first of a place in my inner heart.

"Then——

"There is in thy dowar a youth of fair presence, calling himself the son of Arrius; and such he is by adoption.

"He is very dear to me.

"He hath a wonderful history, which I will tell thee; come thou to-day or to-morrow, that I may tell thee the history, and have thy counsel.

"Meantime, favour all his requests, so they be not against honour. Should there be need of reparation, I am bound to thee for it.

"That I have interest in this youth, keep thou private.

"Remember me to thy other guests. He, his daughter, thyself, and all whom thou mayst choose to be of thy company, must depend upon me at the Circus the day of the games. I have seats already engaged.

"To thee and all thine, peace.

"What should I be, O my friend, but thy friend?

"SIMONIDES."

[No. 2.]
"Simonides to Sheik Ilderim.

"O friend!

"Out of the abundance of my experience, I send you a word.

"There is a sign which all persons not Romans, and who have moneys or goods subject to despoilment, accept as warning—that is, the arrival at a seat of power of some high Roman official charged with authority.

"To-day comes the Consul Maxentius.

"Be thou warned!

"Another word of advice.

"A conspiracy, to be of effect against thee, O friend, must include the Herods as parties; thou hast great properties in their dominions.

"Wherefore keep thou watch.

"Send this morning to thy trusty keepers of the roads leading south from Antioch, and bid them search every courier going and coming; if they find private despatches relating to thee or thy affairs, *thou shouldst see them.*

"You should have received this yesterday, though it is not too late, if you act promptly.

"If couriers left Antioch this morning, your messengers know the byways, and can get before them with your orders.

"Do not hesitate.

"Burn this after reading.

"O my friend! thy friend,

"SIMONIDES."

Ilderim read the letters a second time, and refolded them in the linen wrap, and put the package under his girdle.

The exercises in the field continued but a little longer—in all, about two hours. At their conclusion, Ben-Hur brought the four to a walk, and drove to Ilderim.

"With leave, O sheik," he said, "I will return thy Arabs to the tent, and bring them out again this afternoon."

Ilderim walked to him as he sat on Sirius, and said, "I give them to you, son of Arrius, to do with as you will until after the games. You have done with them in two hours what the Romans—may jackals gnaw his bones fleshless!—could not in as many weeks. We will win—by the splendour of God, we will win!"

At the tent Ben-Hur remained with the horses while they were being cared for; then, after a plunge in the lake and a cup of arrack with the sheik, whose flow of spirits was royally exuberant, he dressed himself in his Jewish garb again, and walked with Malluch on into the Orchard.

There was much conversation between the two, not all of it important. One part, however, must not be overlooked. Ben-Hur was speaking.

"I will give you," he said, "an order for my property stored in the khan this side the river by the Seleucian Bridge. Bring it to me to-day, if you can. And, good Malluch—if I do not overtask you——"

Malluch protested heartily his willingness to be of service.

"Thank you, Malluch, thank you," said Ben-Hur. "I will take you at your word, remembering that we are brethren of the old tribe, and that the enemy is a Roman. First, then—as you are a man of business, which I much fear Sheik Ilderim is not——"

"Arabs seldom are," said Malluch gravely.

"Nay, I do not impeach their shrewdness, Malluch. It is well, however, to look after them. To save all forfeit or hindrance in connection with the race, you would put me perfectly at rest by going to the office of the Circus, and seeing that he has complied with every preliminary rule; and if you can get a copy of the rules, the service may be of great avail to me. I would like to know the colours I am to wear, and particularly the number of the crypt I am to occupy at the starting; if it be next Messala's on the right or left, it is well; if not, and you can have it changed so as to bring me next the Roman, do so. Have you good memory, Malluch?"

"It has failed me, but never, son of Arrius, where the heart helped it as now."

"I will venture, then, to charge you with one further service. I saw yesterday that Messala was proud of his chariot, as he might be, for the best of Cæsar's scarcely surpass it. Can you not make its display an excuse which will enable you to find if it be light or heavy? I would like to have its exact weight and measurements—and, Malluch, though you fail in all else, bring me exactly the height his axle stands above the ground. You understand, Malluch? I do not wish him to have any actual advantage of me. I do not care for his splendour; if I beat him, it will make his fall the harder, and my triumph the more complete. If there are advantages really important, I want them."

"I see, I see!" said Malluch. "A line dropped from the centre of the axle is what you want."

"Thou hast it; and be glad, Malluch—it is the last of my commissions. Let us return to the dowar."

At the door of the tent they found a servant replenishing the smoke-stained bottles of leben freshly made, and stopped to refresh themselves. Shortly afterwards Malluch returned to the city.

During their absence, a messenger well mounted had been despatched with orders as suggested by Simonides. He was an Arab, and carried nothing written.

The landing was a simple affair, consisting of a short stairway, and a platform garnished by some lamp-posts; yet at the top of the steps he paused, arrested by what he beheld.

There was a shallop resting upon the clear water lightly as an egg-shell. An Ethiop—the camel-driver at the Castalian fount—occupied the rower's place, his blackness intensified by a livery of shining white. All the boat aft was cushioned and carpeted with stuffs brilliant with Tyrian red. On the rudder seat sat the Egyptian herself, sunk in Indian shawls and a very vapour of most delicate veils and scarfs. Her arms were bare to the shoulders; and, not merely faultless in shape, they had the effect of compelling attention to them—their pose, their action, their expression; the hands, the fingers even, seemed endowed with graces and meaning; each was an object of beauty. The shoulders and neck were protected from the evening air by an ample scarf, which yet did not hide them.

In the glance he gave her, Ben-Hur paid no attention to these details.

"Come," she said, observing him stop, "come, or I shall think you a poor sailor."

The red of his cheek deepened. Did she know anything of his life upon the sea? He descended to the platform at once.

"I was afraid," he said, as he took the vacant seat before her.

"Of what?"

"Of sinking the boat," he replied, smiling.

"Wait until we are in deeper water," she said, giving a signal to the black, who dipped the oars, and they were off.

If love and Ben-Hur were enemies, the latter was never more at mercy. The Egyptian sat where he could not but see her; she, whom he had already engrossed in memory as his ideal of the Shulamite. With her eyes giving light to his, the stars might come out, and he not see them; and so they did. The night might fall with unrelieved darkness everywhere else; her look would make illumination for him. And then, as everybody knows, given youth and such companionship, there is no situation in which the fancy takes such complete control as upon tranquil waters under a calm night sky, warm with summer. It is so easy at such time to glide imperceptibly out of the commonplace into the ideal.

CHAPTER 3

THE LETTER INTERCEPTED

ILDERIM returned to the dowar next day about the third hour. As he dismounted, a man whom he recognised as of his own tribe came to him and said, "O sheik, I was bidden give thee this package, with request that thou read it at once. If there be answer, I was to wait thy pleasure."

Ilderim gave the package immediate attention. The seal was already broken. The address ran, *To Valerius Gratus at Cæsarea.*

"Abaddon take him!" growled the sheik, at discovering a letter in Latin.

Had the missive been in Greek or Arabic, he could have read it; as it was, the utmost he could make out was the signature in bold Roman letters—Messala—whereat his eyes twinkled.

"Where is the young Jew?" he asked.

"In the field with the horses," a servant replied.

The sheik replaced the papyrus in its envelopes, and, tucking the package under his girdle, remounted the horse.

CHAPTER 4

BEN-HUR READS THE LETTER

The sheik waited, well satisfied, until Ben-Hur drew his horses off the field for the forenoon—well satisfied, for he had seen them, after being put through all the other paces, run full speed in such manner that it did not seem there were one the slowest and another the fastest—run, in other words, as the four were one.

At the door of the tent they dismounted.

"Son of Arrius"—Ilderim drew forth the package, and opened it slowly, while they walked to the divan and seated themselves—"son of Arrius, see thou here, and help me with thy Latin."

He passed the despatch to Ben-Hur.

"There; read—and read aloud, rendering what thou findest into the tongue of thy fathers. Latin is an abomination."

Ben-Hur was in good spirits, and began the reading carelessly. " '*Messala to Gratus!*' " He paused. A premonition drove the blood to his heart. Ilderim observed his agitation.

"Well; I am waiting."

Ben-Hur prayed pardon, and recommenced the paper, which, it is sufficient to say, was one of the duplicates of the letter despatched so carefully to Gratus by Messala the morning after the revel in the palace.

The sheik held his peace, listening closely, until Ben-Hur came to the paragraph in which he was particularly mentioned: " 'I saw the Jew yesterday in the Grove of Daphne;' " so ran the part, " 'and if he be not there now, he is certainly in the neighbourhood, making it easy for me to keep him in eye. Indeed, wert thou to ask me where he is now, I should say, with the most positive assurance, he is to be found at the old Orchard of Palms.' "

"A—h!" exclaimed Ilderim, in such a tone one might hardly say he was more surprised than angry; at the same time, he clutched his beard.

"'At the old Orchard of Palms,'" Ben-Hur repeated, "'under the tent of the traitor Sheik Ilderim.'"

"Traitor!—I?" the old man cried, in his shrillest tone, while lip and beard curled with ire, and on his forehead and neck the veins swelled and beat as they would burst.

"Yet a moment, sheik," said Ben-Hur, with a deprecatory gesture. "Such is Messala's opinion of you. Hear his threat." And he read on —"'under the tent of the traitor Sheik Ilderim, who cannot long escape our strong hand. Be not surprised if Maxentius, as his first measure, places the Arab on ship for forwarding to Rome.'"

"To Rome! Me—Ilderim—sheik of ten thousand horsemen with spears—me to Rome!"

He leaped rather than rose to his feet, his arms outstretched, his fingers spread and curved like claws, his eyes glittering like a serpent's.

"O God!—nay, by all the gods except of Rome!—when shall this insolence end? A freeman am I; free are my people. Must we die slaves? Or, worse, must I live a dog, crawling to a master's feet? Must I lick his hand lest he lash me? What is mine is not mine; I am not my own; for breath of body I must be beholden to a Roman. Oh, if I were young again! Oh, could I shake off twenty years—or ten— or five!"

He ground his teeth and shook his hands overhead; then, under the impulse of another idea, he walked away and back again to Ben-Hur swiftly, and caught his shoulder with a strong grasp.

"If I were as thou, son of Arrius—as young, as strong, as practised in arms; if I had a motive hissing me to revenge—a motive, like thine, great enough to make hate holy—Away with disguise on thy part and on mine! Son of Hur, son of Hur, I say——"

The sheik stopped for want of breath, panting, wringing his hands. And, sooth to say, of all the passionate burst Ben-Hur retained but a vague impression wrought by fiery eyes, a piercing voice, and a rage too intense for coherent expression.

For the first time in years, the desolate youth heard himself addressed by his proper name. One man at least knew him, and acknowledged it without demand of identity; and he an Arab fresh from the desert!

How came the man by his knowledge? The letter? No. It told the cruelties from which his family had suffered; it told the story of his own misfortunes, but it did not say he was the very victim whose escape from doom was the theme of the heartless narrative. That was the point of explanation he had notified the sheik would follow the reading of the letter. He was pleased, and thrilled with hope restored, yet kept an air of calmness.

"Good sheik, tell me how you came by this letter."

"My people keep the roads between cities," Ilderim answered bluntly. "They took it from a courier."

"Are they known to be thy people?"

"No. To the world they are robbers, whom it is mine to catch and slay."

"Again, sheik. You call me son of Hur—my father's name. I did not think myself known to a person on earth. How came you by the knowledge?"

Ilderim hesitated; but rallying, he answered, "I know you, yet I am not free to tell you more."

"Someone holds you in restraint?"

The sheik closed his mouth, and walked away; but, observing Ben-Hur's disappointment, he came back, and said, "Let us say no more about the matter now. I will go to town; when I return, I may talk to you fully. Give me the letter."

Ilderim rolled the papyrus carefully, restored it to its envelopes, and became once more all energy.

"What sayst thou?" he asked, while waiting for his horse and retinue.

"I intended to answer, sheik, and I will." Ben-Hur's countenance and voice changed with the feeling invoked. "I devoted myself to vengeance long ago. Every hour of the five years passed, I have lived with no other thought. I have taken no respite. I have had no pleasures of youth. The blandishments of Rome were not for me. I wanted her to educate me for revenge. I resorted to her most famous masters and professors—not those of rhetoric or philosophy: alas! I had no time for them. The arts essential to a fighting-man were my desire. I associated with gladiators, and with winners of prizes in the circus; and they were my teachers. The drill-masters in the great camp accepted me as a scholar, and were proud of my attainments in their line. O sheik, I am a soldier; but the things of which I dream require me to be a captain. With that thought, I have taken part in the campaign against the Parthians; when it is over, then, if the Lord spare my life and strength—then"—he raised his clenched hands, and spoke vehemently—"then I will be an enemy Roman-taught in all things; then Rome shall account to me in Roman lives for her ills. You have my answer, sheik."

Ilderim put an arm over his shoulder, and kissed him, saying passionately, "If thy God favour thee not, son of Hur, it is because He is dead. Take thou this from me—sworn to, if so thy preference run: thou shalt have my hands, and their fulness—men, horses, camels, and the desert for preparation. I swear it! For the present, enough. Thou shalt see or hear from me before night."

Turning abruptly off, the sheik was speedily on the road to the city.

CHAPTER 5

A SUMMONS

THE mid-day meal disposed of, still further to occupy himself, Ben-Hur had the chariot rolled out into the sunlight for inspection. The word but poorly conveys the careful study the vehicle underwent. No point or part of it escaped him. With a pleasure which will be better understood hereafter, he saw the pattern was Greek, in his judgment preferable to the Roman in many respects; it was wider between the wheels, and lower and stronger, and the disadvantage of greater weight would be more than compensated by the greater endurance of his Arabs. Speaking generally, the carriage-makers of Rome built for the games almost solely, sacrificing safety to beauty, and durability to grace; while the chariots of Achilles and "the king of men," designed for war and all its extreme tests, still ruled the tastes of those who met and struggled for the crowns Isthmian and Olympic.

Next he brought the horses, and, hitching them to the chariot, drove to the field of exercise, where, hour after hour, he practised them in movement under the yoke. When he came away in the evening, it was with restored spirit, and a fixed purpose to defer action in the matter of Messala until the race was won or lost. He could not forego the pleasure of meeting his adversary under the eyes of the East; that there might be other competitors seemed not to enter his thought. His confidence in the result was absolute; no doubt of his own skill; and as to the four, they were his full partners in the glorious game.

After nightfall, Ben-Hur sat by the door of the tent waiting for Ilderim, not yet returned from the city. He was not impatient, or vexed, or doubtful. The sheik would be heard from, at least. Indeed, whether it was from satisfaction with the performance of the four, or the refreshment there is in cold water succeeding bodily exercise, or supper partaken with royal appetite, or the reaction which, as a kindly provision of nature, always follows depression, the young man was in good humour verging upon elation. He felt himself in the hands of Providence no longer his enemy. At last there was a sound of horse's feet coming rapidly, and Malluch rode up.

"Son of Arrius," he said cheerily, after salutation, "I salute you for Sheik Ilderim, who requests you to mount and go to the city. He is waiting for you."

Ben-Hur asked no questions, but went in where the horses were feeding. Aldebaran came to him, as if offering his service. He played with him lovingly, but passed on, and chose another, not of the four—they were sacred to the race. Very shortly the two were on the road, going swiftly and in silence.

Some distance below the Seleucian Bridge they crossed the river by a ferry, and, riding far round on the right bank, and recrossing by another ferry, entered the city from the west. The detour was long, but Ben-Hur accepted it as a precaution for which there was good reason.

Down to Simonides' landing they rode, and in front of the great warehouse, under the bridge, Malluch drew rein.

"We are come," he said. "Dismount."

Ben-Hur recognised the place.

"Where is the sheik?" he asked.

"Come with me. I will show you."

A watchman took the horses, and almost before he realized it Ben-Hur stood once more at the door of the house up on the greater one, listening to the response from within—"In God's name, enter."

CHAPTER 6

ACKNOWLEDGED

MALLUCH stopped at the door; Ben-Hur entered alone.

Three persons were present, looking at him—Simonides, Ilderim, and Esther.

"Son of Hur——"

The guest turned to the speaker.

"Son of Hur," said Simonides, repeating the address slowly, and with distinct emphasis, as if to impress all its meaning upon him most interested in understanding it, "take thou the peace of the Lord God of our fathers—take it from me." He paused, and then added, "From me and mine."

"Simonides," Ben-Hur answered, much moved, "the holy peace you tender is accepted. As son to father, I return it to you. Only let there be perfect understanding between us."

Simonides bowed his acknowledgment.

"Esther, child, bring me the paper," he said, with a breath of relief. She went to a panel in the wall, opened it, took out a roll of papyri, and brought and gave it to him.

"Thou saidst well, son of Hur," Simonides began, while unrolling the sheets. "Let us understand each other. In anticipation of the demand—which I would have made hadst thou waived it—I have here a statement covering everything necessary to the understanding required. I could see but two points involved—the property first, and then our relation. The statement is explicit as to both. Will it please thee to read it now?"

Ben-Hur received the papers, but glanced at Ilderim.

"Nay," said Simonides, "the sheik shall not deter thee from reading. The account—such thou wilt find it—is of a nature requiring a witness. In the attesting place at the end thou wilt find, when thou comest to it, the name—Ilderim, Sheik. He knows all. He is thy friend. All he has been to me, that will he be to thee also."

Simonides looked at the Arab, nodding pleasantly, and the latter gravely returned the nod, saying, "Thou hast said."

Ben-Hur replied, "I know already the excellence of his friendship, and have yet to prove myself worthy of it." Immediately he continued, "Later, O Simonides, I will read the papers carefully; for the present, do thou take them, and if thou be not too weary, give me their substance."

Simonides took back the roll.

"This," said Simonides, drawing out the first leaf, "shows the money I had of thy father's, being the amount saved from the Romans; there was no property saved, only money, and that the robbers would have secured but for our Jewish custom of bills of exchange. The amount saved, being sums I drew from Rome, Alexandria, Damascus, Carthage, Valentia, and elsewhere within the circle of trade, was one hundred and twenty talents Jewish money."

He gave the sheet to Esther, and took the next one.

"With that amount—one hundred and twenty talents—I charged myself. Hear now my credits. I use the word, as thou wilt see, with reference rather to the proceeds gained from the use of the money."

From separate sheets he then read footings, which, fractions omitted, were as follows:

CR.

"By ships, ...	60 talents.
„ goods in store, ...	110 „
„ cargoes in transit, ...	75 „
„ camels, horses, etc., ...	20 „

„	warehouses,	.	.	.	.	.	10 „
„	bills due	.	.	.	.	.	54 „
„	money on hand and subject to draft,				.	224 „
	Total,	.	.	.	.	.	553 talents."

"To these now, to the five hundred and fifty-three talents gained, add the original capital I had from thy father, and thou hast SIX HUNDRED AND SEVENTY-THREE TALENTS!—and all thine—making thee, O son of Hur, the richest subject in the world."

He took the papyri from Esther, and, reserving one, rolled them and offered them to Ben-Hur. The pride perceptible in his manner was not offensive; it might have been from a sense of duty well done; it might have been for Ben-Hur without reference to himself.

"And there is nothing," he added, dropping his voice, but not his eyes—"there is nothing now thou mayest not do."

Taking the roll, Ben-Hur arose, struggling with emotion.

"All this is to me as a light from heaven, sent to drive away a night which has been so long I feared it would never end, and so dark I had lost the hope of seeing," he said, with a husky voice. He stretched his hand with the roll to Simonides.

"The things these papers take into account—all of them: ships, houses, goods, camels, horses, money; the least as well as the greatest—give I back to thee, O Simonides, making them all thine, and sealing them to thee and thine for ever."

Esther smiled through her tears; Ilderim pulled his beard with rapid motion, his eyes glistening like beads of jet. Simonides alone was calm.

"Sealing them to thee and thine for ever," Ben-Hur continued, with better control of himself, "with one exception, and upon one condition."

The breath of the listeners waited upon his words.

"The hundred and twenty talents which were my father's thou shalt return to me."

Ilderim's countenance brightened.

"And thou shalt join me in search of my mother and sister, holding all thine subject to the expense of discovery, even as I will hold mine."

Simonides was much affected. Stretching out his hand, he said, "I see thy spirit, son of Hur, and I am grateful to the Lord that He hath sent thee to me such as thou art. If I served well thy father in life, and his memory afterwards, be not afraid of default to thee; yet must I say the exception cannot stand."

Exhibiting, then, the reserved sheet, he continued,—

"Thou hast not all the account. Take this and read—read aloud."

Ben-Hur took the supplement, and read it.

"Statement of the servants of Hur, rendered by Simonides, steward of the estate.
1. Amrah, Egyptian, keeping the palace in Jerusalem.
2. Simonides, the steward, in Antioch.
3. Esther, daughter of Simonides."

Now, in all his thoughts of Simonides, not once had it entered Ben-Hur's mind that, by the law, a daughter followed the parent's condition. In all his visions of her, the sweet-faced Esther had figured as the rival of the Egyptian, and an object of possible love. He shrank from the revelation so suddenly brought him, and looked at her blushing; and, blushing, she dropped her eyes before him. Then he said, while the papyrus rolled itself together,—

"A man with six hundred talents is indeed rich, and may do what he pleases; but, rarer than the money, more priceless than the property, is the mind which amassed the wealth, and the heart it could not corrupt when amassed. O Simonides—and thou, fair Esther—fear not. Sheik Ilderim here shall be witness that in the same moment ye were declared my servants, that moment I declared ye free; and what I declare, that will I put in writing. Is it not enough? Can I do more?"

"Son of Hur," said Simonides, "verily thou dost make servitude lightsome. I was wrong; there are some things thou canst not do; thou canst not make us free in law. I am thy servant for ever, because I went to the door with thy father one day, and in my ear the awl-marks yet abide."

Ben-Hur walked the floor in pain of impotent wish.

"I was rich before," he said, stopping suddenly. "I was rich with the gifts of the generous Arrius; now comes this greater fortune, and the mind which achieved it. Is there not a purpose of God in it all? Counsel me, O Simonides! Help me to see the right and do it. Help me to be worthy my name, and what thou art in law to me, that will I be to thee in fact and deed. I will be thy servant for ever."

Simonides' face actually glowed.

"O son of my dead master! I will do better than help; I will serve thee with all my might of mind and heart. Body, I have not; it perished in thy cause; but with mind and heart I will serve thee. I swear it, by the altar of our God, and the gifts upon the altar! Only make me formally what I have assumed to be."

"Name it," said Ben-Hur eagerly.

"As steward, the care of the property will be mine."

"Count thyself steward now; or wilt thou have it in writing?"

"Thy word simply is enough; it was so with the father, and I will not more from the son. And now, if the understanding be perfect——" Simonides paused.

"It is with me," said Ben-Hur.

"And thou, daughter of Rachel, speak!" said Simonides, lifting her arm from his shoulder.

Esther, left thus alone, stood a moment abashed, her colour coming and going; then she went to Ben-Hur, and said, with a womanliness singularly sweet, "I am not better than my mother was; and, as she is gone, I pray you, O my master, let me care for my father."

Ben-Hur took her hand, and led her back to the chair, saying, "Thou art a good child. Have thy will."

Simonides replaced her arm upon his neck, and there was silence for a time in the room.

CHAPTER 7

THE PROGRAMME

THE day before the games, in the afternoon, all Ilderim's racing property was taken to the city, and put in quarters adjoining the Circus.

On the way, they came upon Malluch in waiting for them. He exchanged salutations as usual, and produced a paper, saying to the sheik, "I have here the notice of the editor of the games, just issued, in which you will find your horses published for the race. You will find in it also the order of exercises. Without waiting, good sheik, I congratulate you upon your victory."

He gave the paper over, and, leaving the worthy to master it, turned to Ben-Hur.

"To you also, son of Arrius, my congratulations. There is nothing now to prevent your meeting Messala. Every condition preliminary to the race is complied with. I have the assurance from the editor himself."

"I thank you, Malluch," said Ben-Hur.

Malluch proceeded:

"Your colour is white, and Messala's mixed scarlet and gold. The good effects of the choice are visible already. Boys are now hawking white ribbons along the streets; to-morrow every Arab and Jew in the city will wear them. In the Circus you will see the white fairly divide the galleries with the red."

And Malluch, greatly delighted, gave him parting salutation, and started to ride away, but returned presently.

"Your pardon," he said to Ben-Hur. "There was another matter. I could not get near Messala's chariot myself, but I had another measure it; and, from his report, its hub stands quite a palm higher from the ground than yours."

"A palm! So much?" cried Ben-Hur joyfully.

Then he leaned over to Malluch.

"As thou art a son of Judah, Malluch, and faithful to thy kin, get thee a seat in the gallery over the Gate of Triumph, down close to the balcony in front of the pillars, and watch well when we make the turns there; watch well, for if I have favour at all, I will—— Nay, Malluch, let it go unsaid! Only get thee there, and watch well."

At that moment a cry burst from Ilderim.

"Ha! By the spendour of God! what is this?"

He drew near Ben-Hur with a finger pointing on the face of the notice.

"Read," said Ben-Hur.

"No; better thou."

Ben-Hur took the paper, which, signed by the prefect of the province as editor, performed the office of a modern programme, giving particularly the several divertissements provided for the occasion. It informed the public that there would be first a procession of extraordinary splendour; that the procession would be succeeded by the customary honours to the god Consus, whereupon the games would begin; running, leaping, wrestling, boxing, each in the order stated. The names of the competitors were given, with their several nationalities and schools of training, the trials in which they had been engaged, the prizes won, and the prizes now offered; under the latter head the sums of money were stated in illuminated letters, telling of the departure of the day when the simple chaplet of pine or laurel was fully enough for the victor, hungering for glory as something better than riches, and content with it.

Over these parts of the programme Ben-Hur sped with rapid eyes. At last he came to the announcement of the race. He read it slowly. Attending lovers of the heroic sports were assured they would certainly be gratified by an Orestean struggle unparalleled in Antioch. The city offered the spectacle in honour of the consul. One hundred thousand sestertii and a crown of laurel were the prizes. Then followed the particulars. The entries were six in all—fours only permitted; and, to further interest in the performance, the competitors would be turned into the course together. Each four then received description.

"I. A four of Lysippus the Corinthian—two greys, a bay, and a black; entered at Alexandria last year, and again at Corinth, where they were winners. Lysippus, driver. Colour, yellow.

"II. A four of Messala of Rome—two white, two black; victors of the Circensian as exhibited in the Circus Maximus last year. Messala, driver. Colours, scarlet and gold.

"III. A four of Cleanthes the Athenian—three grey, one bay; winners at the Isthmian last year. Cleanthes, driver. Colour, green.

"IV. A four of Dicæus the Byzantine—two black, one grey, one bay; winners this year at Byzantium. Dicæus, driver. Colour, black.

"V. A four of Admetus the Sidonian—all greys. Thrice entered at Cæsarea, and thrice victors. Admetus, driver. Colour, blue.

"VI. A four of Ilderim, sheik of the Desert. All bays; first race. Ben-Hur, a Jew, driver. Colour, white."

Ben-Hur, a Jew, driver!

Why that name instead of Arrius?

Ben-Hur raised his eyes to Ilderim. He had found the cause of the Arab's outcry. Both rushed to the same conclusion.

The hand was the hand of Messala!

CHAPTER 8

THE CIRCUS

THE Circus at Antioch stood on the south bank of the river, nearly opposite the island, differing in no respect from the plan of such buildings in general.

In the purest sense, the games were a gift to the public; consequently, everybody was free to attend; and, vast as the holding capacity of the structure was, so fearful were the people, on this occasion, lest there should not be room for them, that, early the day before the opening of the exhibition, they took up all the vacant spaces in the vicinity, where their temporary shelter suggested an army in waiting.

At midnight the entrances were thrown wide, and the rabble, surging in, occupied the quarters assigned to them, from which nothing less than an earthquake or an army with spears could have dislodged them. They dozed the night away on the benches, and breakfasted there;

and there the close of the exercises found them, patient and sight-hungry as in the beginning.

The better people, their seats secured, began moving towards the Circus about the first hour of the morning, the noble and very rich among them distinguished by litters and retinues of liveried servants.

By the second hour, the efflux from the city was a stream unbroken and innumerable.

Exactly as the gnomon of the official dial up in the citadel pointed the second hour half gone, the legion, in full panoply, and with all its standards on exhibit, descended from Mount Sulpius; and when the rear of the last cohort disappeared in the bridge, Antioch was literally abandoned—not that the Circus could hold the multitude, but that the multitude was gone out to it, nevertheless.

A great concourse on the river shore witnessed the consul come over from the island in a barge of state. As the great man landed, and was received by the legion, the martial show for one brief moment transcended the attraction of the Circus.

At the third hour, the audience, if such it may be termed, was assembled; at last, a flourish of trumpets called for silence, and instantly the gaze of over a hundred thousand persons was directed towards a pile forming the eastern section of the building.

Slowly crossing the arena, the procession proceeds to make circuit of the course. The display is beautiful and imposing. Approval runs before it in a shout, as the water rises and swells in front of a boat in motion. If the dumb, figured gods make no sign of appreciation of the welcome, the editor and his associates are not so backward.

The reception of the athletes is even more demonstrative, for there is not a man in the assemblage who has not something in wager upon them, though but a mite or farthing. And it is noticeable, as the classes move by, that the favourites among them are speedily singled out: either their names are loudest in the uproar, or they are more profusely showered with wreaths and garlands tossed to them from the balcony.

CHAPTER 9

THE START

ABOUT three o'clock, speaking in modern style, the programme was concluded except the chariot-race. The editor, wisely considerate of the comfort of the people, chose that time for a recess. At once the *vomitoria* were thrown open, and all who could hastened to the portico outside where the restaurateurs had their quarters. Those who remained yawned, talked, gossiped, consulted their tablets, and, all distinctions else forgotten, merged into but two classes—the winners, who were happy, and the losers, who were glum and captious.

Now, however, a third class of spectators, composed of citizens who desired only to witness the chariot-race, availed themselves of the recess to come in and take their reserved seats; by so doing they thought to attract the least attention and give the least offence. Among these were Simonides and his party, whose places were in the vicinity of the main entrance on the north side, opposite the consul.

As the four stout servants carried the merchant in his chair up the aisle, curiosity was much excited. Presently some one called his name. Those about caught it and passed it on along the benches to the west; and there was hurried climbing on seats to get sight of the man about whom common report had coined and put in circulation a romance so mixed of good fortune and bad that the like had never been known or heard of before.

Ilderim was also recognised and warmly greeted; but nobody knew Balthasar or the two women who followed him closely veiled.

The people made way for the party respectfully, and the ushers seated them in easy speaking distance of each other down by the balustrade overlooking the arena. In providence of comfort, they sat upon cushions and had stools for foot-rests.

The women were Iras and Esther.

Upon being seated, the latter cast a frightened look over the Circus, and drew the veil closer about her face; while the Egyptian, letting her veil fall upon her shoulders, gave herself to view, and gazed at the scene with the seeming unconsciousness of being stared at, which, in a woman, is usually the result of long social habitude.

The new-comers generally were yet making their first examination of the great spectacle, beginning with the consul and his attendants, when some workmen ran in and commenced to stretch a chalked rope across the arena from balcony to balcony in front of the pillars of the first goal.

About the same time, also, six men came in through the Porta Pompæ and took post, one in front of each occupied stall; whereat there was a prolonged hum of voices in every quarter.

"See, see! The green goes to number four on the right; the Athenian is there."

"And Messala—yes, he is in number two."

"The Corinthian——"

"Watch the white! See, he crosses over, he stops; number one it is—number one on the left."

"No, the black stops there, and the white at number two."

"So it is."

These gatekeepers, it should be understood, were dressed in tunics coloured like those of the competing charioteers; so, when they took their stations, everybody knew the particular stall in which his favourite was that moment waiting.

At length the recess came to an end.

The trumpeters blew a call at which the absentees rushed back to their places. At the same time, some attendants appeared in the arena, and, climbing upon the division wall, went to an entablature near the second goal at the west end, and placed upon it seven wooden balls; then returning to the first goal, upon an entablature there they set up seven other pieces of wood hewn to represent dolphins.

"What shall they do with the balls and fishes, O sheik?" asked Balthasar.

"Hast thou never attended a race?"

"Never before; and hardly know I why I am here."

"Well, they are to keep the count. At the end of each round run thou shalt see one ball and one fish taken down."

The preparations were now complete, and presently a trumpeter in gaudy uniform arose by the editor, ready to blow the signal of commencement promptly at his order. Straightway the stir of the people and the hum of their conversation died away. Every face near-by, and every face in the lessening perspective, turned to the east, as all eyes settled upon the gates of the six stalls which shut in the competitors.

The unusual flush upon his face gave proof that even Simonides had caught the universal excitement. Ilderim pulled his beard fast and furious.

"Look now for the Roman," said the fair Egyptian to Esther, who did not hear her, for, with close-drawn veil and beating heart, she sat watching for Ben-Hur.

The structure containing the stalls, it should be observed, was in form of the segment of a circle, retired on the right so that its central point was projected forward, and midway the course, on the starting side of the first goal. Every stall, consequently, was equally distant from the starting-line or chalked rope above mentioned.

The trumpet sounded short and sharp; whereupon the starters, one for each chariot, leaped down from behind the pillars of the goal, ready to give assistance if any of the fours proved unmanageable.

Again the trumpet blew, and simultaneously the gatekeepers threw the stalls open.

First appeared the mounted attendants of the charioteers, five in all, Ben-Hur having rejected the service. The chalked line was lowered to let them pass, then raised again. They were beautifully mounted, yet scarcely observed as they rode forward; for all the time the trampling of eager horses, and the voices of drivers scarcely less eager, were heard behind in the stalls, so that one might not look away an instant from the gaping doors.

The chalked line up again, the gatekeepers called their men, instantly the ushers on the balcony waved their hands, and shouted with all their strength, "Down! down!"

As well have whistled to stay a storm.

Forth from each stall, like missiles in a volley from so many great guns, rushed the six fours; and up the vast assemblage arose, electrified and irrepressible, and, leaping upon the benches, filled the Circus and the air above it with yells and screams. This was the time for which they had so patiently waited!—this the moment of supreme interest treasured up in talk and dreams since the proclamation of the games!

"He is come—there—look!" cried Iras, pointing to Messala.

"I see him," answered Esther, looking at Ben-Hur.

The veil was withdrawn. For an instant the little Jewess was brave. An idea of the joy there is in doing an heroic deed under the eyes of a multitude came to her, and she understood ever after how, at such times, the souls of men, in the frenzy of performance, laugh at death or forget it utterly.

The competitors were now under view from nearly every part of the Circus, yet the race was not begun; they had first to make the chalked line successfully.

The line was stretched for the purpose of equalizing the start. If it were dashed upon, discomfiture of man and horses might be apprehended; on the other hand, to approach it timidly was to incur the hazard of being thrown behind in the beginning of the race; and that was certain forfeit of the great advantage always striven for—the position next the division wall on the inner line of the course.

The competitors having started, each on the shortest line for the position next the wall, yielding would be like giving up the race; and who dared yield? It is not in common nature to change a purpose in mid-career; and the cries of encouragement from the balcony were indistinguishable and indescribable; a roar which had the same effect upon all the drivers.

The fours neared the rope together. Then the trumpeter by the editor's side blew a signal vigorously. Twenty feet away it was not heard. Seeing the action, however, the judges dropped the rope, and not an instant too soon, for the hoof of one of Messala's horses struck it as it fell. Nothing daunted, the Roman shook out his long lash, loosed the reins, leaned forward, and, with a triumphant shout, took the wall.

"Jove with us! Jove with us!" yelled all the Roman faction, in a frenzy of delight.

As Messala turned in, the bronze lion's head at the end of his axle caught the fore-leg of the Athenian's right-hand trace-mate, flinging the brute over against its yoke-fellow. Both staggered, struggled, and lost their headway. The ushers had their will at least in part. The thousands held their breath with horror; only up where the consul sat was there shouting.

"Jove with us!" screamed Drusus frantically.

"He wins! Jove with us!" answered his associates, seeing Messala speed on.

Tablet in hand, Sanballat turned to them, to accept wagers from them at the suggestion of Simonides.

Messala having passed, the Corinthian was the only contestant on the Athenian's right, and to that side the latter tried to turn his broken four; and then, as ill-fortune would have it, the wheel of the Byzantine, who was next on the left, struck the tail-piece of his chariot, knocking his feet from under him. There was a crash, a scream of rage and fear, and the unfortunate Cleanthes fell under the hoofs of his own steeds; a terrible sight, against which Esther covered her eyes.

On swept the Corinthian, on the Byzantine, on the Sidonian.

Sanballat looked for Ben-Hur, and turned again to Drusus and his coterie.

"A hundred sestertii on the Jew!" he cried.

"Taken!" answered Drusus.

"Another hundred on the Jew!" shouted Sanballat.

Nobody appeared to hear him. He called again; the situation below was too absorbing, and they were too busy shouting, "Messala! Messala! Jove with us!"

When the Jewess ventured to look again, a party of workmen were removing the horses and broken car; another party were taking off the man himself; and every bench upon which there was a Greek was vocal with execrations and prayers for vengeance. Suddenly she dropped her hands; Ben-Hur, unhurt, was to the front, coursing freely forward along with the Roman! Behind them, in a group, followed the Sidonian, the Corinthian, and the Byzantine. The race was on; the souls of the racers were in it; over them bent the myriads.

CHAPTER 10

THE RACE

WHEN the dash for position began, Ben-Hur, as we have seen, was on the extreme left of the six. For a moment, like the others, he was half blinded by the light in the arena; yet he managed to catch sight of his antagonists and divine their purpose. At Messala, who was more than an antagonist to him, he gave one searching look. The air of passionless hauteur characteristic of the fine patrician face was there as of old, and so was the Italian beauty, which the helmet rather increased; but more—it may have been a jealous fancy, or the effect of the brassy shadow in which the features were at the moment cast, still the Israelite thought he saw the soul of the man as through a glass, darkly: cruel, cunning, desperate; not so excited as determined—a soul in a tension of watchfulness and fierce resolve.

In a time not longer than was required to turn his four again, Ben-Hur felt his own resolution harden to a like temper. At whatever cost, at all hazards, he would humble this enemy! Prize, friends, wagers, honour—everything that can be thought of as a possible interest in the race was lost in the one deliberate purpose. Regard for life even should not hold him back. Yet there was no passion on his part; no blinding rush of heated blood from heart to brain, and back again; no impulse to fling himself upon Fortune—he did not believe in Fortune; far otherwise. He had his plan, and, confiding in himself, he settled to the task never more observant, never more capable. The air about him seemed aglow with a renewed and perfect transparency.

When not half-way across the arena, he saw that Messala's rush would, if there was no collision, and the rope fell, give him the wall; that the rope would fall, he ceased as soon to doubt; and, further, it came to him, a sudden flash-like insight, that Messala knew it was to be let drop at the last moment (prearrangement with the editor could safely reach that point in the contest); and it suggested, what more Roman-like than for the official to lend himself to a countryman who, besides being so popular, had also so much at stake? There could be no other accounting for the confidence with which Messala pushed his four forward the instant his competitors were prudently checking their fours in front of the obstruction—no other except madness.

It is one thing to see a necessity and another to act upon it. Ben-Hur yielded the wall for the time.

The rope fell, and all the four but his sprang into the course under the urgency of voice and lash. He drew head to the right, and, with all the speed of his Arabs, darted across the trails of his opponents, the angle of movement being such as to lose the least time and gain the greatest possible advance. So, while the spectators were shivering at the Athenian's mishap, and the Sidonian, Byzantine, and Corinthian were striving, with such skill as they possessed, to avoid involvement in the ruin, Ben-Hur swept around and took the course neck and neck with Messala, though on the outside. The marvellous skill shown in making the change thus from the extreme left across to the right without appreciable loss did not fail the sharp eyes upon the benches; the Circus seemed to rock and rock again with prolonged applause. Then Esther clasped her hands in glad surprise; then Sanballat, smiling, offered his hundred sestertii a second time without a taker; and then the Romans began to doubt, thinking Messala might have found an equal, if not a master, and that in an Israelite!

And now, racing together side by side, a narrow interval between them, the two neared the second goal.

The pedestal of the three pillars there, viewed from the west, was a stone wall in the form of a half-circle, around which the course and opposite balcony were bent in exact parallelism. Making this turn was considered in all respects the most telling test of a charioteer; it was, in fact, the very feat in which Orestes failed. As an involuntary admission of interest on the part of the spectators, a hush fell over all the Circus, so that for the first time in the race the rattle and clang of the cars plunging after the tugging steeds were distinctly heard. Then, it would seem, Messala observed Ben-Hur, and recognised him; and at once the audacity of the man flamed out in an astonishing manner.

"Down Eros, up Mars!" he shouted, whirling his lash with practised hand—"Down Eros, up Mars!" he repeated, and caught the well-doing Arabs of Ben-Hur a cut the like of which they had never known.

The blow was seen in every quarter, and the amazement was universal. The silence deepened; up on the benches behind the consul the boldest held his breath, waiting for the outcome. Only a moment thus: then, involuntarily, down from the balcony, as thunder falls, burst the indignant cry of the people.

The four sprang forward affrighted. No hand had ever been laid upon them except in love; they had been nurtured ever so tenderly; and as they grew, their confidence in man became a lesson to men beautiful to see. What should such dainty natures do under such indignity but leap as from death?

Forward they sprang as with one impulse, and forward leaped the car. Past question, every experience is serviceable to us. Where got Ben-Hur the large hand and mighty grip which helped him now so well? Where but from the oar with which so long he fought the sea? And what was this spring of the floor under his feet to the dizzy eccentric lurch with which in the old time the trembling ship yielded to the beat of staggering billows, drunk with their power? So he kept his place, and gave the four free rein, and called to them in soothing voice, trying merely to guide them round the dangerous turn; and before the fever of the people began to abate, he had back the mastery. Nor that only; on approaching the first goal, he was again side by side with Messala, bearing with him the sympathy and admiration of every one not a Roman. So clearly was the feeling shown, so vigorous its manifestation, that Messala, with all his boldness, felt it unsafe to trifle further.

As the cars whirled round the goal, Esther caught sight of Ben-Hur's face—a little pale, a little higher raised, otherwise calm, even placid.

Immediately a man climbed on the entablature at the west end of the division wall, and took down one of the conical wooden balls. A dolphin on the east entablature was taken down at the same time.

In like manner, the second ball and second dolphin disappeared.

And then the third ball and third dolphin.

Three rounds concluded: still Messala held the inside position; still Ben-Hur moved with him side by side; still the other competitors followed as before. The contest began to have the appearance of one of the double races which became so popular in Rome during the later Cæsarean period—Messala and Ben-Hur in the first, the Corinthian, Sidonian, and Byzantine in the second. Meantime the ushers succeeded in returning the multitude to their seats, though the clamour continued to run the rounds, keeping, as it were, even pace with the rivals in the course below.

In the fifth round the Sidonian succeeded in getting a place outside Ben-Hur, but lost it directly.

The sixth round was entered upon without change of relative position.

Gradually the speed had been quickened—gradually the blood of the competitors warmed with the work. Men and beasts seemed to know alike that the final crisis was near, bringing the time for the winner to assert himself.

The interest which from the beginning had centred chiefly in the struggle between the Roman and the Jew, with an intense and general sympathy for the latter, was fast changing to anxiety on his account. On all the benches the spectators bent forward motionless, except as their faces turned following the contestants. Ilderim quitted combing his beard, and Esther forgot her fears.

"A hundred sestertii on the Jew!" cried Sanballat to the Romans under the consul's awning.

There was no reply.

"A talent—or five talents, or ten; choose ye!"

He shook his tablets at them defiantly.

"I will take thy sestertii," answered a Roman youth, preparing to write.

"Do not do so," interposed a friend.

"Why?"

"Messala hath reached his utmost speed. See him lean over his chariot-rim, the reins loose as flying ribbons. Look then at the Jew."

The first one looked.

"By Hercules!" he replied, his countenance falling. "The dog throws all his weight on the bits. I see, I see! If the gods help not our friend, he will be run away with by the Israelite. No, not yet. Look! Jove with us, Jove with us!"

The cry, swelled by every Latin tongue, shook the *velaria* over the consul's head.

If it were true that Messala had attained his utmost speed, the effort was with effect; slowly but certainly he was beginning to forge ahead. His horses were running with their heads low down; from the balcony their bodies appeared actually to skim the earth; their nostrils showed blood-red in expansion; their eyes seemed straining in their sockets. Certainly the good steeds were doing their best! How long could they keep the pace? It was but the commencement of the sixth round. On they dashed. As they neared the second goal, Ben-Hur turned in behind the Roman's car.

The joy of the Messala faction reached its bound: they screamed and howled, and tossed their colours; and Sanballat filled his tablets with wagers of their tendering.

Malluch, in the lower gallery over the Gate of Triumph, found it hard to keep his cheer. He had cherished the vague hint dropped to him by Ben-Hur of something to happen in the turning of the western pillars. It was the fifth round, yet the something had not come; and he had said to himself, the sixth will bring it; but, lo! Ben-Hur was hardly holding a place at the tail of his enemy's car.

Over in the east end, Simonides' party held their peace. The merchant's head was bent low. Ilderim tugged at his beard, and dropped his brows till there was nothing of his eyes but an occasional sparkle of light. Esther scarcely breathed. Iras alone appeared glad.

Along the home-stretch—sixth round—Messala leading, next him Ben-Hur.

Thus to the first goal, and round it. Messala, fearful of losing his place, hugged the stony wall with perilous clasp; a foot to the left, and he had been dashed to pieces; yet, when the turn was finished, no man, looking at the wheel-tracks of the two cars, could have said, here went Messala, there the Jew. They left but one trace behind them.

As they whirled by, Esther saw Ben-Hur's face again, and it was whiter than before.

Simonides, shrewder than Esther, said to Ilderim, the moment the rivals turned into the course, "I am no judge, good sheik, if Ben-Hur be not about to execute some design. His face hath that look."

To which Ilderim answered, "Saw you how clean they were and fresh? By the splendour of God, friend, they have not been running! But now watch!"

One ball and one dolphin remained on the entablatures; and all the people drew a long breath, for the beginning of the end was at hand.

First, the Sidonian gave the scourge to his four, and, smarting with fear and pain, they dashed desperately forward, promising for a brief time to go to the front. The effort ended in promise. Next, the Byzantine and Corinthian each made the trial with like result, after which they were practically out of the race. Thereupon, with a readiness perfectly explicable, all the factions except the Romans joined hope in Ben-Hur, and openly indulged their feeling.

"Ben-Hur! Ben-Hur!" they shouted, and the blent voices of the many rolled overwhelmingly against the consular stand.

From the benches above him as he passed, the favour descended in fierce injunctions.

"Speed thee, Jew!"

"Take the wall now!"

"Oh! loose the Arabs! Give them rein and scourge!"

"Let him not have the turn on thee again. Now or never!"

Over the balustrade they stooped low, stretching their hands imploringly to him.

Either he did not hear, or could not do better, for half-way round the course, and he was still following; at the second goal even still no change!

And now, to make the turn, Messala began to draw in his left-hand steeds, an act which necessarily slackened their speed. His spirit was high; more than one altar was richer of his vows; the Roman genius was still president. On the three pillars only six hundred feet away were fame, increase of fortune, promotions, and a triumph ineffably sweetened by hate, all in store for him! That moment Malluch, in the gallery, saw Ben-Hur lean forward over his Arabs, and give them the

reins. Out flew the many-folded lash in his hand; over the backs of the
startled steeds it writhed and hissed, and hissed and writhed again and
again; and though it fell not, there were both sting and menace in its
quick report; and as the man passed thus from quiet to resistless action,
his face suffused, his eyes gleaming, along the reins he seemed to flash
his will; and instantly not one, but the four as one, answered with a
leap that landed them alongside the Roman's car. Messala, on the
perilous edge of the goal, heard, but dared not look to see what the
awakening portended. From the people he received no sign. Above the
noises of the race there was but one voice, and that was Ben-Hur's. In
the old Aramaic, as the sheik himself, he called to the Arabs,—

"On, Atair! On, Rigel! What, Antares! dost thou linger now? Good
horse—oho, Aldebaran! I hear them singing in the tents. I hear the
children singing and the women—singing of the stars, of Atair, Antares,
Rigel, Aldebaran, victory!—and the song will never end. Well done!
Home to-morrow, under the black tent—home! On, Antares! The tribe
is waiting for us, and the master is waiting! 'Tis done! 'tis done! Ha,
ha! We have overthrown the proud. The hand that smote us is in the
dust. Ours the glory! Ha, ha!—steady! The work is done—soho!
Rest!"

There had never been anything of the kind more simple; seldom anything so instantaneous.

At the moment chosen for the dash, Messala was moving in a circle
round the goal. To pass him, Ben-Hur had to cross the track, and good
strategy required the movement to be in a forward direction; that is,
on a like circle limited to the least possible increase. The thousands on
the benches understood it all: they saw the signal given—the magnificent
response; the four close outside Messala's outer wheel; Ben-Hur's inner
wheel behind the other's car—all this they saw. Then they heard a
crash loud enough to send a thrill through the Circus, and, quicker
than thought, out over the course a spray of shining white-and-yellow
flinders flew. Down on its right side toppled the bed of the Roman's
chariot. There was a rebound as of the axle hitting the hard earth;
another and another; then the car went to pieces; and Messala, entangled
in the reins, pitched forward headlong.

To increase the horror of the sight by making death certain, the
Sidonian, who had the wall next behind, could not stop or turn out.
Into the wreck full speed he drove; then over the Roman, and into the
latter's four, all mad with fear. Presently, out of the turmoil, the fighting of horses, the resound of blows, the murky cloud of dust and sand,
he crawled, in time to see the Corinthian and Byzantine go on down
the course after Ben-Hur, who had not been an instant delayed.

The people arose, and leaped upon the benches, and shouted and screamed. Those who looked that way caught glimpses of Messala, now under the trampling of the fours, now under the abandoned cars. He was still; they thought him dead; but far the greater number followed Ben-Hur in his career. They had not seen the cunning touch of the reins by which, turning a little to the left, he caught Messala's wheel with the iron-shod point of his axle, and crushed it; but they had seen the transformation of the man, and themselves felt the heat and glow of his spirit, the heroic resolution, the maddening energy of action with which, by look, word, and gesture, he so suddenly inspired his Arabs. And such running! It was rather the long leaping of lions in harness; but for the lumbering chariot, it seemed the four were flying. When the Byzantine and Corinthian were half-way down the course, Ben-Hur turned the first goal.

And the race was WON!

The consul arose; the people shouted themselves hoarse; the editor came down from his seat, and crowned the victors.

The fortunate man among the boxers was a low-browed, yellow-haired Saxon, of such brutalized face as to attract a second look from Ben-Hur, who recognized a teacher with whom he himself had been a favourite at Rome. From him the young Jew looked up and beheld Simonides and his party on the balcony. They waved their hands to him. Esther kept her seat; but Iras arose, and gave him a smile and a wave of her fan—favours not the less intoxicating to him because we know, O reader, they would have fallen to Messala had he been the victor.

The procession was then formed, and, midst the shouting of the multitude which had had its will, passed out of the Gate of Triumph.

And the day was over.

CHAPTER II

AN INVITATION

BEN-HUR tarried across the river with Ilderim; for at midnight, as previously determined, they would take the road which the caravan, then thirty hours out, had pursued.

The sheik was happy; his offers of gifts had been royal; but Ben-Hur had refused everything, insisting that he was satisfied with the humiliation of his enemy. The generous dispute was long continued.

"Think," the sheik would say, "what thou hast done for me. In every black tent down to the Akaba and to the ocean, and across to the Euphrates, and beyond to the sea of the Scythians, the renown of my Mira and her children will go; and they who sing of them will magnify me, and forget that I am in the wane of life; and all the spears now masterless will come to me, and my sword-hands multiply past counting. Thou dost not know what it is to have sway of the desert such as will now be mine. I tell thee it will bring tribute incalculable from commerce, and immunity from kings. Ay, by the sword of Solomon! doth my messenger seek favour for me of Cæsar, that will he get. Yet nothing—nothing?"

And Ben-Hur would answer,—

"Nay, sheik, have I not thy hand and heart? Let thy increase of power and influence inure to the King who comes. Who shall say it was not allowed thee for Him? In the work I am going to, I may have great need. Saying no now will leave me to ask of thee with better grace hereafter."

In the midst of a controversy of the kind, two messengers arrived— Malluch and one unknown. The former was admitted first.

The good fellow did not attempt to hide his joy over the event of the day.

"But, coming to that with which I am charged," he said, "the master Simonides sends me to say that, upon the adjournment of the games, some of the Roman faction made haste to protest against payment of the money prize."

Ilderim started up, crying, in his shrillest tones,—

"By the splendour of God! the East shall decide whether the race was fairly won."

"Nay, good sheik," said Malluch, "the editor has paid the money."

" 'Tis well."

"When they said Ben-Hur struck Messala's wheel, the editor laughed, and reminded them of the blow the Arabs had at the turn of the goal."

"And what of the Athenian?"

"He is dead."

"Dead!" cried Ben-Hur.

"Dead!" echoed Ilderim. "What fortune these Roman monsters have! Messala escaped!"

"Escaped—yes, O sheik, with life; but it shall be a burden to him. The physicians say he will live, but never walk again."

Ben-Hur looked silently up to heaven. He had a vision of Messala, chair-bound like Simonides, and, like him, going abroad on the shoulders of servants. The good man had abode well; but what would this one with his pride and ambition?

"Simonides bade me say, further," Malluch continued, "Sanballat is having trouble. Drusus, and those who signed with him, referred the question of paying the five talents they lost to the Consul Maxentius, and he has referred it to Cæsar. Messala also refused his losses, and Sanballat, in imitation of Drusus, went to the consul, where the matter is still in advisement. The better Romans say the protestants shall not be excused; and all the adverse factions join with them. The city rings with the scandal."

"What says Simonides?" asked Ben-Hur.

"The master laughs, and is well pleased. If the Roman pays, he is ruined; if he refuses to pay, he is dishonoured. The imperial policy will decide the matter. To offend the East would be a bad beginning with the Parthians; to offend Sheik Ilderim would be to antagonize the Desert, over which lie all Maxentius's lines of operation. Wherefore Simonides bade me tell you to have no disquiet; Messala will pay."

Ilderim was at once restored to his good humour.

"Let us be off now," he said, rubbing his hands. "The business will do well with Simonides. The glory is ours. I will order the horses."

"Stay," said Malluch. "I left a messenger outside. Will you see him?"

"By the splendour of God! I forgot him."

Malluch retired, and was succeeded by a lad of gentle manners and delicate appearance, who knelt upon one knee, and said, winningly, "Iras, the daughter of Balthasar, well known to good Sheik Ilderim, hath intrusted me with a message to the sheik, who, she saith, will do her great favour so he receive her congratulations on account of the victory of his four."

"The daughter of my friend is kind," said Ilderim, with sparkling eyes. "Do thou give her this jewel, in sign of the pleasure I have from her message."

He took a ring from his finger as he spoke.

"I will as thou sayest, O sheik," the lad replied, and continued, "The daughter of the Egyptian charged me further. She prays the good Sheik Ilderim to send word to the youth Ben-Hur that her father hath taken residence for a time in the palace of Idernee, where she will receive the youth after the fourth hour to-morrow. And if, with her congratulations, Sheik Ilderim will accept her gratitude for this other favour done, she will be ever so pleased."

The sheik looked at Ben-Hur, whose face was suffused with pleasure.

"What will you?" he asked.

F

"By your leave, O sheik, I will see the fair Egyptian."

Ilderim laughed, and said, "Shall not a man enjoy his youth?"

Then Ben-Hur answered the messenger.

"Say to her who sent you that I, Ben-Hur, will see her at the palace of Idernee, wherever that may be, to-morrow at noon."

The lad arose, and, with silent salute, departed.

At midnight Ilderim took the road, having arranged to leave a horse and a guide for Ben-Hur, who was to follow him.

CHAPTER 12

ENTRAPPED

GOING next day to fill his appointment with Iras, Ben-Hur turned from the Omphalus, which was in the heart of the city, into the Colonnade of Herod, and came shortly to the palace of Idernee.

From the street he passed first into a vestibule, on the sides of which were stairways under cover, leading up to a portico. Winged lions sat by the stairs; in the middle there was a gigantic ibis spouting water over the floor; the lions, ibis, walls, and floor were reminders of the Egyptians: everything, even the balustrading of the stairs, was of massive grey stone.

Above the vestibule, and covering the landing of the steps, arose the portico, a pillared grace, so light, so exquisitely proportioned, it was at that period hardly possible of conception except by a Greek. Of marble snowy white, its effect was that of a lily dropped carelessly upon a great bare rock.

Ben-Hur paused in the shade of the portico to admire its tracery and finish, and the purity of its marble; then he passed on into the palace. Ample folding doors stood open to receive him. The passage into which he first entered was high, but somewhat narrow; red tiling formed the floor, and the walls were tinted to correspond. Yet this plainness was a warning of something beautiful to come.

The passage brought him to a closed door, in front of which he paused; and, as he did so, the broad leaves began to open of themselves, without creak or sound of lock or latch, or touch of foot or finger. The singularity was lost in the view that broke upon him.

Standing in the shade of the dull passage, and looking through the doorway, he beheld the atrium of a Roman house, roomy and rich to a fabulous degree of magnificence.

Still in his dreamful mood, Ben-Hur sauntered about, charmed by all he beheld, and waiting. He did not mind a little delay; when Iras was ready she would come or send a servant. In every well-regulated Roman house the atrium was the reception chamber for visitors.

Twice, thrice, he made the round. As often he stood under the opening in the roof, and pondered the sky and its azure depth; then, leaning against a pillar, he studied the distribution of light and shade, and its effects; here a veil diminishing objects, there a brilliance exaggerating others; yet nobody came. He listened, but there was not a sound; the palace was still as a tomb.

There might be a mistake. No, the messenger had come from the Egyptian, and this was the palace of Idernee.

He went to a door. Though he walked ever so lightly, the sound of his stepping was loud and harsh, and he shrank from it. He was getting nervous. The cumbrous Roman lock resisted his first effort to raise it; and the second—the blood chilled in his cheeks—he wrenched with all his might; in vain—the door was not even shaken. A sense of danger seized him, and for a moment he stood irresolute.

Who in Antioch had the motive to do him harm?

Messala!

And this palace of Idernee? He had seen Egypt in the vestibule, Athens in the snowy portico; but here, in the atrium, was Rome; everything about him betrayed Roman ownership. True, the site was on the great thoroughfare of the city, a very public place in which to do him violence; but for that reason it was more accordant with the audacious genius of his enemy. The atrium underwent a change; with all its elegance and beauty, it was no more than a trap. Apprehension always paints in black.

The idea irritated Ben-Hur.

Half an hour passed—a much longer period to Ben-Hur—when the door which had admitted him opened and closed noiselessly as before, and without attracting his attention.

The moment of the occurrence he was sitting at the farther end of the room. A footstep startled him.

"At last she has come!" he thought, with a throb of relief and pleasure, and arose.

The step was heavy, and accompanied with the gride and clang of coarse sandals. The gilded pillars were between him and the door; he advanced quietly, and leaned against one of them. Presently he heard voices—the voices of men—one of them rough and guttural. What was said he could not understand, as the language was not of the East or South of Europe.

After a general survey of the room, the strangers crossed to their left, and were brought into Ben-Hur's view—two men, one very stout, both tall, and both in short tunics. They had not the air of masters of the house or domestics. Everything they saw appeared wonderful to them; everything they stopped to examine they touched. They were vulgarians. The atrium seemed profaned by their presence. At the same time, their leisurely manner and the assurance with which they proceeded pointed to some right or business; if business, with whom?

With much jargon they sauntered this way and that, all the time gradually approaching the pillar by which Ben-Hur was standing. Off a little way, where a slanted gleam of the sun fell with a glare upon the mosaic of the floor, there was a statue which attracted their notice. In examining it, they stopped in the light.

The mystery surrounding his own presence in the palace tended, as we have seen, to make Ben-Hur nervous; so now, when in the tall stout stranger he recognized the Northman whom he had known in Rome, and seen crowned only the day before in the Circus as the winning pugilist; when he saw the man's face, scarred with the wounds of many battles, and imbruted by ferocious passions; when he surveyed the fellow's naked limbs, very marvels of exercise and training, and his shoulders of Herculean breadth, a thought of personal danger started a chill along every vein. A sure instinct warned him that the opportunity for murder was too perfect to have come by chance; and here now were the myrmidons, and their business was with him. He turned an anxious eye upon the Northman's comrade—young, black-eyed, black-haired, and altogether Jewish in appearance; he observed also that both the men were in costume exactly such as professionals of their class were in the habit of wearing in the arena. Putting the several circumstances together, Ben-Hur could not be longer in doubt: he had been lured into the palace with design. Out of reach of aid, in this splendid privacy, he was to die!

He undid the sash around his waist, and, baring his head and casting off his white Jewish gown, stood forth in an under-tunic not unlike those of the enemy, and was ready, body and mind. Folding his arms, he placed his back against the pillar, and calmly waited.

The examination of the statue was brief. Directly the Northman turned, and said something in the unknown tongue; then both looked at Ben-Hur. A few more words, and they advanced towards him.

"Who are you?" he asked in Latin.

The Northman fetched a smile which did not relieve his face of its brutalism, and answered,—

"Barbarians."

"This is the palace of Idernee. Whom seek you? Stand and answer."

The words were spoken with earnestness. The strangers stopped; and in his turn the Northman asked, "Who are you?"

"A Roman."

The giant laid his head back upon his shoulders.

"Ha, ha, ha! I have heard how a god once came from a cow licking a salted stone; but not even a god can make a Roman of a Jew."

The laugh over, he spoke to his companion again, and they moved nearer.

"Hold!" said Ben-Hur, quitting the pillar. "One word."

They stopped again.

"A word!" replied the Saxon, folding his immense arms across his breast, and relaxing the menace beginning to blacken his face. "A word! Speak."

"You are Thord the Northman."

The giant opened his blue eyes.

"You were *lanista* in Rome."

Thord nodded.

"I was your scholar."

"No," said Thord, shaking his head. "By the beard of Irmin, I had never a Jew to make a fighting-man of."

"But I will prove my saying."

"How?"

"You came here to kill me."

"That is true."

"Then let this man fight me singly, and I will make the proof on his body."

A gleam of humour shone in the Northman's face. He spoke to his companion, who made answer; then he replied with the *naïveté* of a diverted child,—

"Wait till I say begin."

By repeated touches of his foot, he pushed a couch out on the floor, and proceeded leisurely to stretch his burly form upon it; when perfectly at ease, he said, simply, "Now begin."

Without ado, Ben-Hur walked to his antagonist.

"Defend thyself," he said.

The man, nothing loath, put up his hands.

As the two thus confronted each other in approved position, there was no discernible inequality between them; on the contrary, they were as like as brothers. To the stranger's confident smile Ben-Hur opposed an earnestness which, had his skill been known, would have accepted fair warning of danger. Both knew the combat was to be mortal.

Ben-Hur feinted with his right hand. The stranger warded, slightly advancing his left arm. Ere he could return to guard, Ben-Hur caught him by the wrist in a grip which years at the oar had made terrible as a vice. The surprise was complete, and no time given. To throw himself forward; to push the arm across the man's throat and over his right shoulder, and turn him left side front; to strike surely with the ready left hand; to strike the bare neck under the ear—were but petty divisions of the same act. No need of a second blow. The myrmidon fell heavily, and without a cry, and lay still.

Ben-Hur turned to Thord.

"Ha! What! By the beard of Irmin!" the latter cried in astonishment, rising to a sitting posture. Then he laughed.

"Ha, ha, ha. I could not have done it better myself."

He viewed Ben-Hur coolly from head to foot, and, rising, faced him with undisguised admiration.

"It was my trick—the trick I have practised for ten years in the schools of Rome. You are not a Jew. Who are you?"

"You knew Arrius the duumvir."

"Quintus Arrius? Yes, he was my patron."

"He had a son."

"Yes," said Thord, his battered features lighting dully, "I knew the boy. He would have made a king gladiator. Cæsar offered him his patronage. I taught him the very trick you played on this one here— a trick impossible except to a hand and arm like mine. It has won me many a crown."

"I am that son of Arrius."

Thord drew nearer, and viewed him carefully; then his eyes brightened with genuine pleasure, and, laughing, he held out his hand.

"Ha, ha, ha! He told me I would find a Jew here—a Jew—a dog of a Jew—killing whom was serving the gods."

"Who told you so?" asked Ben-Hur, taking the hand.

"He—Messala—ha, ha, ha!"

"When, Thord?"

"Last night."

"I thought he was hurt."

"He will never walk again. On his bed he told me between groans."

A very vivid portrayal of hate in a few words; and Ben-Hur saw that the Roman, if he lived, would still be capable and dangerous, and follow him unrelentingly. Revenge remained to sweeten the ruined life; therefore the clinging to fortune lost in the wager with Sanballat. Ben-Hur ran the ground over, with a distinct foresight of the many ways in which it would be possible for his enemy to interfere with him in the work he had undertaken for the King who was coming. Why not he resort to the Roman's methods? The man hired to kill him could be hired to strike back. It was in his power to offer higher wages. The temptation was strong; and, half yielding, he chanced to look down at his late antagonist lying still, with white upturned face, so like himself. A light came to him, and he asked, "Thord, what was Messala to give you for killing me?"

"A thousand sestertii."

"You shall have them yet; and so you do now what I tell you, I will add three thousand more to the sum."

The giant reflected aloud,—

"I won five thousand yesterday; from the Roman one—six. Give me four, good Arrius—four more—and I will stand firm for you, though old Thor, my namesake, strike me with his hammer. Make it four, and I will kill the lying patrician, if you say so. I have only to cover his mouth with my hand—thus."

He illustrated the process by clapping his hand over his own mouth.

"I see," said Ben-Hur; "ten thousand sestertii is a fortune. It will enable you to return to Rome, and open a wine-shop near the Great Circus, and live as becomes the first of the *lanistæ*."

The very scars on the giant's face glowed afresh with the pleasure the picture gave him.

"I will make it four thousand," Ben-Hur continued; "and in what you shall do for the money there will be no blood on your hands, Thord. Hear me now. Did not your friend here look like me?"

"I would have said he was an apple from the same tree."

"Well, if I put on his tunic, and dress him in these clothes of mine, and you and I go away together, leaving him here, can you not get your sestertii from Messala all the same? You have only to make him believe it me that is dead."

Thord laughed till the tears ran into his mouth.

"Ha, ha, ha! Ten thousand sestertii were never won so easily. And a wine-shop by the Great Circus!—all for a lie without blood in it! Ha, ha, ha! Give me thy hand, O son of Arrius. Get on now, and—ha, ha, ha!—if ever you come to Rome, fail not to ask for the wine-shop of Thord the Northman. By the beard of Irmin, I will give you the best, though I borrow it from Cæsar!"

They shook hands again; after which the exchange of clothes was effected. It was arranged then that a messenger should go at night to Thord's lodging-place with the four thousand sestertii. When they were done, the giant knocked at the front door; it opened to him; and, passing out of the atrium, he led Ben-Hur into a room adjoining, where the latter completed his attire from the coarse garments of the dead pugilist. They separated directly in the Omphalus.

"Fail not, O son of Arrius, fail not the wine-shop near the Great Circus! Ha, ha, ha! By the beard of Irmin, there was never fortune gained so cheap. The gods keep you!"

Upon leaving the atrium, Ben-Hur gave a last look at the myrmidon as he lay in the Jewish vestments, and was satisfied. The likeness was striking. If Thord kept faith, the cheat was a secret to endure for ever.

.   .   .   .   .

At night, in the house of Simonides, Ben-Hur told the good man all that had taken place in the palace of Idernee; and it was agreed that, after a few days, public inquiry should be set afloat for the discovery of the whereabouts of the son of Arrius. Eventually the matter was to be carried boldly to Maxentius; then, if the mystery came not out, it was concluded that Messala and Gratus would be at rest and happy, and Ben-Hur free to betake himself to Jerusalem, to make search for his lost people.

At the leave-taking, Simonides sat in his chair out on the terrace overlooking the river, and gave his farewell and the peace of the Lord with the impressment of a father. Esther went with the young man to the head of the steps.

"If I find my mother, Esther, thou shalt go to her at Jerusalem, and be a sister to Tirzah."

And with the words he kissed her.

Was it only a kiss of peace?

He crossed the river next to the late quarters of Ilderim, where he found the Arab who was to serve him as guide. The horses were brought out.

"This one is thine," said the Arab.

Ben-Hur looked, and, lo! it was Aldebran, the swiftest and brightest of the sons of Mira, and, next to Sirius, the beloved of the sheik; and he knew the old man's heart came to him along with the gift.

The corpse in the atrium was taken up and buried by night; and, as part of Messala's plan, a courier was sent off to Gratus to make him at rest by the announcement of Ben-Hur's death—this time past question.

Ere long a wine-shop was opened near the Circus Maximus, with the inscription over the door:

THORD THE NORTHMAN.

BOOK SIXTH

"Is that a Death? and are there two?
Is Death that woman's mate?
. . . .
Her skin was as white as leprosy,
The Nightmare Life-in-Death was she,
Who thicks man's blood with cold."
COLERIDGE

CHAPTER I

THE PRISONERS

OUR story moves forward now thirty days from the night Ben-Hur left
Antioch to go out with Sheik Ilderim into the desert.

A great change has befallen—great at least as respects the fortunes
of our hero. *Valerius Gratus has been succeeded by Pontius Pilate!*

The removal, it may be remarked, cost Simonides exactly five talents
Roman money in hand paid to Sejanus, who was then in height of
power as imperial favourite; the object being to help Ben-Hur, by lessening his exposure while in and about Jerusalem attempting discovery of
his people. To such pious use the faithful servant put the winnings
from Drusus and his associates; all of whom, having paid their wagers,
became at once and naturally the enemies of Messala, whose repudiation
was yet an unsettled question in Rome.

Brief as the time was, already the Jews knew the change of rulers was
not for the better.

The worst of men do once in a while vary their wickednesses by
good acts; so with Pilate. He ordered an inspection of all the prisons
in Judea, and a return of the names of the persons in custody, with a
statement of the crimes for which they had been committed. The
revelations were astonishing. Hundreds of persons were released against
whom there were no accusations; many others came to light who had
long been accounted dead; yet more amazing, there was opening of
dungeons not merely unknown at the time by the people, but actually
forgotten by the prison authorities. With one instance of the
latter kind we have now to deal; and, strange to say, it occurred in
Jerusalem.

The Tower of Antonia, which will be remembered as occupying two-thirds of the sacred area on Mount Moriah, was originally a castle built by the Macedonians. All through the administration of Gratus it had been a garrisoned citadel and underground prison terrible to revolutionists. Woe when the cohorts poured from its gates to suppress disorder! Woe not less when a Jew passed the same gates going in under arrest!

With this explanation, we hasten to our story.

·　　·　　·　　·　　·

The order of the new procurator requiring a report of the persons in custody was received at the Tower of Antonia, and promptly executed; and two days have gone since the last unfortunate was brought up for examination. The tabulated statement, ready for forwarding, lies on the table of the tribune in command; in five minutes more it will be on the way to Pilate, sojourning in the palace up on Mount Zion.

The tribune's office is spacious and cool, and furnished in a style suitable to the dignity of the commandant of a post in every respect so important. Looking in upon him about the seventh hour of the day, the officer appears weary and impatient; when the report is despatched, he will to the roof of the colonnade for air and exercise, and the amusement to be had watching the Jews over in the courts of the Temple. His subordinates and clerks share his impatience.

In the spell of waiting a man appeared in a doorway leading to an adjoining apartment. He rattled a bunch of keys, each heavy as a hammer, and at once attracted the chief's attention.

"Ah, Gesius! come in," the tribune said.

As the new-comer approached the table behind which the chief sat in an easy-chair, everybody present looked at him, and, observing a certain expression of alarm and mortification on his face, became silent that they might hear what he had to say.

"O tribune!" he began, bending low, "I fear to tell what now I bring you."

"Another mistake—ha, Gesius?"

"If I could persuade myself it is but a mistake, I would not be afraid."

"A crime then—or, worse, a breach of duty. Thou mayst laugh at Cæsar, or curse the gods, and live; but if the offence be to the eagles—ah, thou knowest, Gesius—go on!"

"It is now about eight years since Valerius Gratus selected me to be keeper of prisoners here in the Tower," said the man deliberately. "I remember the morning I entered upon the duties of my office. There had been a riot the day before, and fighting in the streets. We slew many Jews, and suffered on our side. The affair came, it was said, of an attempt to assassinate Gratus, who had been knocked from his horse by a tile thrown from a roof. I found him sitting where you now sit, O tribune, his head swathed in bandages. He told me of my selection, and gave me these keys, numbered to correspond with the numbers of the cells; they were the badges of my office, he said, and not to be parted with. There was a roll of parchment on the table. Calling me to him, he opened the roll, 'Here are maps of the cells,' said he. There were three of them. 'This one,' he went on, 'shows the arrangement of the upper floor; this second one gives you the second floor; and this last is of the lower floor. I give them to you in trust.' I took them from his hand, and he said further, 'Now you have the keys and the maps; go immediately, and acquaint yourself with the whole arrangement; visit each cell, and see to its condition. When anything is needed for the security of a prisoner, order it according to your judgment, for you are the master under me, and no other.'

"I saluted him, and turned to go away; he called me back. 'Ah, I forgot,' he said. 'Give me the map of the third floor.' I gave it to him, and he spread it upon the table. 'Here, Gesius,' he said, 'see this cell.' He laid his finger on the one numbered V. 'There are three men confined in that cell, desperate characters, who by some means got hold of a State secret, and suffer for their curiosity, which'—he looked at me severely—'in such matters is worse than a crime. Accordingly, they are blind and tongueless, and are placed there for life. They shall have nothing but food and drink, to be given them through a hole, which you will find in the wall covered by a slide. Do you hear, Gesius?' I made him answer. 'It is well,' he continued. 'One thing more which you shall not forget, or'—he looked at me threateningly —'The door of their cell—cell No. V on the same floor—this one, Gesius'—he put his finger on the particular cell to impress my memory —'shall never be opened for any purpose, neither to let one in nor out, not even yourself.' 'But if they die?' I asked. 'If they die,' he said, 'the cell shall be their tomb. They were put there to die, and be lost. The cell is leprous. Do you understand?' With that he let me go."

Gesius stopped, and from the breast of his tunic drew three parchments, all much yellowed by time and use; selecting one of them, he spread it upon the table before the tribune, saying simply, "This is the lower floor."

The whole company looked at—

THE MAP.

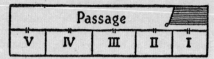

"This is exactly, O tribune, as I had it from Gratus. See, there is cell number V," said Gesius.

"I see," the tribune replied. "Go on now. The cell was leprous, he said."

"I would like to ask you a question," remarked the keeper modestly. The tribune assented.

"Had I not a right, under the circumstances, to believe the map a true one?"

"What else couldst thou?"

"Well, it is not a true one."

The chief looked up surprised.

"It is not a true one," the keeper repeated. "It shows, but five cells upon that floor, while there are six."

"Six, sayest thou?"

"I will show you the floor as it is—or as I believe it to be."

Upon a page of his tablets, Gesius drew the following diagram, and gave it to the tribune:

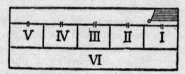

"Thou has done well," said the tribune, examining the drawing, and thinking the narrative at an end. "I will have the map corrected, or, better, I will have a new one made, and given thee. Come for it in the morning."

So saying, he arose.

"But hear me further, O tribune."

"To-morrow, Gesius, to-morrow."

"That which I have yet to tell will not wait."

The tribune good-naturedly resumed his chair.

"I will hurry," said the keeper humbly, "only let me ask another question. Had I not a right to believe Gratus in what he further told me as to the prisoners in cell number V?"

"Yes, it was thy duty to believe there were three prisoners in the cell—prisoners of state—blind and without tongues."

"Well," said the keeper, "that was not true either."

"No!" said the tribune, with returning interest.

"Hear, and judge for yourself, O tribune. As required, I visited all the cells, beginning with those on the first floor, and ending with those on the lower. The order that the door of number V should not be opened had been respected; through all the eight years food and drink for three men had been passed through a hole in the wall. I went to the door yesterday, curious to see the wretches who, against all expectation, had lived so long. The locks refused the key. We pulled a little, and the door fell down, rusted from its hinges. Going in, I found but one man, old, blind, tongueless, and naked. His hair dropped in stiffened mats below his waist. His skin was like the parchment there. He held his hands out, and the finger-nails curled and twisted like the claws of a bird. I asked him where his companions were. He shook his head in denial. Thinking to find the others, we searched the cell. The floor was dry; so were the walls. If three men had been shut in there, and two of them had died, at least their bones would have endured."

"Wherefore thou thinkest——"

"I think, O tribune, there has been but one prisoner there in the eight years."

The chief regarded the keeper sharply, and said, "Have a care; thou art more than saying Valerius lied."

Gesius bowed, but said, "He might have been mistaken."

"No, he was right," said the tribune warmly. "By thine own statement he was right. Didst thou not say but now that for eight years food and drink had been furnished three men?"

The bystanders approved the shrewdness of their chief; yet Gesius did not seem discomfited.

"You have but half the story, O tribune. When you have it all, you will agree with me. You know what I did with the man: that I sent him to the bath, and had him shorn and clothed, and then took him to the gate of the Tower, and bade him go free. I washed my hands of him. To-day he came back, and was brought to me. By signs and tears, he at last made me understand he wished to return to his cell, and I so ordered. As they were leading him off, he broke away and kissed my feet, and, by piteous dumb imploration, insisted I should go with him; and I went. The mystery of the three men stayed in my mind. I was not satisfied about it. Now I am glad I yielded to his entreaty."

The whole company at this point became very still.

"When we were in the cell again, and the prisoner knew it, he caught my hand eagerly, and led me to a hole like that through which we were accustomed to pass him his food. Though large enough to push your helmet through, it escaped me yesterday. Still holding my hand, he put his face to the hole and gave a beast-like cry. A sound came faintly back. I was astonished, and drew him away, and called out, 'Ho, here!' At first there was no answer. I called again, and received back these words, 'Be thou praised, O Lord!' Yet more astonishing, O tribune, the voice was a woman's. And I asked, 'Who are you?' and had reply, 'A woman of Israel, entombed here with her daughter. Help us quickly, or we die.' I told them to be of cheer, and hurried here to know your will."

The tribune arose hastily.

"Thou wert right, Gesius," he said, "and I see now. The map was a lie, and so was the tale of the three men. There have been better Romans than Valerius Gratus."

"Yes," said the keeper. "I gleaned from the prisoner that he had regularly given the women of the food and drink he had received."

"It is accounted for," replied the tribune, and observing the countenances of his friends, and reflecting how well it would be to have witnesses, he added, "Let us rescue the women. Come all."

Gesius was pleased.

"We will have to pierce the wall," he said. "I found where a door had been, but it was filled solidly with stones and mortar."

The tribune stayed to say to a clerk, "Send workmen after me with tools. Make haste; but hold the report, for I see it will have to be corrected."

In a short time they were gone.

CHAPTER 2

THE LEPERS

"A woman of Israel entombed here with her daughter. Help us quickly, or we die."

Such was the reply Gesius, the keeper, had from the cell which appears on his amended map as VI. The reader, when he observed the answer, knew who the unfortunates were, and, doubtless, said to himself, "At last the mother of Ben-Hur, and Tirzah, his sister!"

And so it was.

The morning of their seizure, eight years before, they had been carried to the Tower, where Gratus proposed to put them out of the way. He had chosen the Tower for the purpose as more immediately in his own keeping, and cell VI because, first, it could be better lost than any other; and, secondly, it was infected with leprosy; for these prisoners were not merely to be put in a safe place, but in a place to die. They were, accordingly, taken down by slaves in the night-time, when there were no witnesses of the deed; then, in completion of the savage task, the same slaves walled up the door, after which they were themselves separated, and sent away never to be heard of more. To save accusation, and, in the event of discovery, to leave himself such justification as might be allowed in a distinction between the infliction of a punishment and the commission of a double murder, Gratus preferred sinking his victims where natural death was certain, though slow. That they might linger along, he selected a convict who had been made blind and tongueless, and sank him in the only connecting cell, there to serve them with food and drink. Under no circumstances could the poor wretch tell the tale or identify either the prisoners or their doomsman. So, with a cunning partly due to Messala, the Roman, under colour of punishing a brood of assassins, smoothed a path to confiscation of the estate of the Hurs, of which no portion ever reached the imperial coffers.

As the last step in the scheme, Gratus summarily removed the old keeper of the prisons; not because he knew what had been done—for he did not—but because, knowing the underground floors as he did, it would be next to impossible to keep the transaction from him. Then, with masterly ingenuity, the procurator had new maps drawn for delivery to a new keeper, with the omission, as we have seen, of cell VI. The instructions given the latter, taken with the omission on the map, accomplished the design—the cell and its unhappy tenants were all alike lost.

The cell VI was in form as Gesius drew it on his map. Of its dimensions but little idea can be had; enough that it was a roomy, roughened interior, with ledged and broken walls and floor.

In the beginning, the site of the Macedonian Castle was separated from the site of the Temple by a narrow but deep cliff, somewhat in shape of a wedge. The workmen, wishing to hew out a series of chambers, made their entry in the north face of the cleft, and worked in, leaving a ceiling of the natural stone; delving farther, they executed the cells V, IV, III, II, I, with no connection with number VI except through number V. In like manner, they constructed the passage and stairs to the floor above. The process of the work was precisely that resorted to in carving out the Tombs of the Kings, yet to be seen a short distance north of Jerusalem; only when the cutting was done, cell VI was enclosed on its outer side by a wall of prodigious stones, in which, for ventilation, narrow apertures were left bevelled like modern port-holes. Herod, when he took hold of the Temple and Tower, put a facing yet more massive upon this outer wall, and shut up all the apertures but one, which yet admitted a little vitalizing air, and a ray of light not nearly strong enough to redeem the room from darkness.

Such was cell VI.

Startle not now!

The description of the blind and tongueless wretch just liberated from cell V may be accepted to break the horror of what is coming.

The two women are grouped close by the aperture; one is seated, the other is half reclining against her; there is nothing between them and the bare rock. The light, slanting upwards, strikes them with ghastly effect, and we cannot avoid seeing they are without vesture or covering. At the same time we are helped to the knowledge that love is there yet, for the two are in each other's arms. Riches take wings, comforts vanish, hope withers away, but love stays with us. Love is God.

Where the two are thus grouped the stony floor is polished shining smooth. Who shall say how much of the eight years they have spent in that space there in front of the aperture, nursing their hope of rescue by that timid yet friendly ray of light? When the brightness came creeping in, they knew it was dawn, when it began to fade, they knew the world was hushing for the night, which could not be anywhere so long and utterly dark as with them.

Our recollections of them in former days enjoin us to be respectful; their sorrows clothe them with sanctity. Without going too near, across the dungeon, we see they have undergone a change of appearance not to be accounted for by time or long confinement. The mother was beautiful as a woman, the daughter beautiful as a child; not even love could say so much now. Their hair is long, unkempt, and strangely white; they make us shrink and shudder with an indefinable repulsion, though the effect may be from an illusory glozing of the light glimmering dismally through the unhealthy murk; or they may be enduring the tortures of hunger and thirst, not having had to eat or drink since their servant, the convict, was taken away—that is, since yesterday.

Tirzah, reclining against her mother in half-embrace, moans piteously.

"Water, mother, water, though but a drop."

The mother stares around in blank helplessness. She has named God so often, and so often promised in His name, the repetition is beginning to have a mocking effect upon herself. A shadow passes before her dimming the dim light, and she is brought down to think of death as very near, waiting to come in as her faith goes out. Hardly knowing what she does, speaking aimlessly, because speak she must, she says again,—

"Patience, Tirzah; they are coming—they are almost here."

She thought she heard a sound over by the little trap in the partition-wall through which they held all their actual communication with the world. And she was not mistaken. A moment, and the cry of the convict rang through the cell. Tirzah heard it also; and they both arose, still keeping hold of each other.

"Praised be the Lord for ever!" exclaimed the mother, with the fervour of restored faith and hope.

"Ho, there!" they heard next; and then, "Who are you?"

The voice was strange. What matter? Except from Tirzah, they were the first and only words the mother had heard in eight years. The revulsion was mighty—from death to life—and so instantly!

"A woman of Israel, entombed here with her daughter. Help us quickly, or we die."

"Be of cheer. I will return."

The women sobbed aloud. They were found; help was coming. From wish to wish hope flew as the twittering swallows fly. They were found; they would be released. And restoration would follow—restoration to all they had lost—home, society, property, son and brother! The scanty light glozed them with the glory of day, and forgetful of pain and thirst and hunger, and of the menace of death, they sank upon the floor and cried, keeping fast hold of each other the while.

And this time they had not long to wait. Gesius, the keeper, told his tale methodically, but finished it at last. The tribune was prompt.

"Within there!" he shouted through the trap.

"Here!" said the mother, rising.

Directly she heard another sound in another place, as of blows on the wall—blows quick, ringing, and delivered with iron tools. She did not speak, nor did Tirzah, but they listened, well knowing the meaning of it all—that a way to liberty was being made for them. So men a long time buried in deep mines hear the coming of rescuers, heralded by thrust of bar and beat of pick, and answer gratefully with heart-throbs, their eyes fixed upon the spot whence the sounds proceed; and they cannot look away, lest the work should cease, and they be returned to despair.

The arms outside were strong, the hands skilful, the will good.

Each instant the blows sounded more plainly; now and then a piece fell with a crash; and liberty came nearer and nearer. Presently the workmen could be heard speaking. Then—O happiness!—through a crevice flashed a red ray of torches. Into the darkness it cut incisive as diamond brilliance, beautiful as if from a spear of the morning.

"It is he, mother, it is he! He has found us at last!" cried Tirzah, with the quickened fancy of youth.

But the mother answered meekly, "God is good!"

A block fell inside, and another—then a great mass, and the door was open. A man grimed with mortar and stone dust stepped in, and stopped, holding a torch over his head. Two or three others followed with torches, and stood aside for the tribune to enter.

Respect for women is not all a conventionality, for it is the best proof of their proper nature. The tribune stopped, because they fled from him—not with fear, be it said, but shame; nor yet, O reader, from shame alone! From the obscurity of their partial hiding he heard these words, the saddest, most dreadful, most utterly despairing of the human tongue,—

"Come not near us—unclean, unclean."

The men flared their torches while they stared at each other.

"Unclean, unclean!" came from the corner again, a slow tremulous wail exceedingly sorrowful. With such a cry we can imagine a spirit vanishing from the gates of Paradise, looking back the while.

So the widow and mother performed her duty, and in the moment realized that the freedom she had prayed for and dreamed of, fruit of scarlet and gold seen afar, was but an apple of Sodom in the hand.

She and Tirzah were—LEPERS!

Possibly the reader does not know all the word means. Let him be told it with reference to the law of that time, only a little modified in this.

"These four are accounted as dead—the blind, the leper, the poor, and the childless." Thus the Talmud.

That is, to be a leper was to be treated as dead—to be excluded from the city as a corpse; to be spoken to by the best beloved and most loving only at a distance; to dwell with none but lepers; to be utterly unprivileged; to be denied the rites of the Temple and the synagogue; to go about in rent garments and with covered mouth, except when crying, "Unclean, unclean!" to find home in the wilderness or in abandoned tombs; to become a materialized spectre of Hinnom and

Gehenna; to be at all times less a living offence to others than a breathing torment to self; afraid to die, yet without hope except in death.

Once—she might not tell the day or the year, for down in the haunted hell even time was lost—once the mother felt a dry scurf in the palm of her right hand, a trifle which she tried to wash away. It clung to the member pertinaciously; yet she thought but little of the sign till Tirzah complained that she, too, was attacked in the same way. The supply of water was scant, and they denied themselves drink, that they might use it as a curative. At length the whole hand was attacked; the skin cracked open, the finger-nails loosened from the flesh. There was not much pain withal, chiefly a steadily increasing discomfort. Later their lips began to parch and seam. One day the mother, who was cleanly to godliness, and struggled against the impurities of the dungeon with all ingenuity, thinking the enemy was taking hold on Tirzah's face, led her to the light, and, looking with the inspiration of a terrible dread, lo! the young girl's eyebrows were white as snow.

Oh, the anguish of that assurance!

The mother sat a while speechless, motionless, paralysed of soul, and capable of but one thought—leprosy, leprosy!

When she began to think, mother-like, it was not of herself, but her child, and, mother-like, her natural tenderness turned to courage, and she made ready for the last sacrifice of perfect heroism. She buried her knowledge in her heart; hopeless herself, she redoubled her devotion to Tirzah, and with wonderful ingenuity—wonderful chiefly in its very inexhaustibility—continued to keep the daughter ignorant of what they were beset with, and even hopeful that it was nothing. She repeated her little games, and retold her stories, and invented new ones, and listened with ever so much pleasure to the songs she would have from Tirzah, while on her own wasting lips the psalms of the singing king of their race served to bring soothing of forgetfulness, and keep alive in them both the recollection of the God who would seem to have abandoned them—the world not more lightly or utterly.

Slowly, steadily, with horrible certainty, the disease spread, after a while bleaching their heads white, eating holes in their lips and eyelids, and covering their bodies with scales; then it fell to their throats, shrilling their voices, and to their joints, hardening the tissues and cartilages —slowly, and, as the mother well knew, past remedy, it was affecting their lungs and arteries and bones, at each advance making the sufferers more and more loathsome; and so it would continue till death, which might be years before them.

Another day of dread at length came—the day the mother, under impulsion of duty, at last told Tirzah the name of their ailment; and the two, in agony of despair, prayed that the end might come quickly.

Still, as is the force of habit, these so afflicted grew in time not merely to speak composedly of their disease; they beheld the hideous transformation of their persons as of course, and in despite clung to existence. One tie to earth remained to them; unmindful of their own loneliness, they kept up a certain spirit by talking and dreaming of Ben-Hur. The mother promised reunion with him to the sister, and she to the mother, not doubting, either of them, that he was equally faithful to them, and would be equally happy of the meeting. And with the spinning and re-spinning of this slender thread they found pleasure, and excused their not dying. In such manner as we have seen, they were solacing themselves the moment Gesius called them, at the end of twelve hours' fasting and thirst.

The torches flashed redly through the dungeon, and liberty was come. "God is good," the widow cried—not for what had been, O reader, but for what was. In thankfulness for present mercy, nothing so becomes us as losing sight of past ills.

The tribune came directly; then in the corner to which she had fled, suddenly a sense of duty smote the elder of the women, and straightway the awful warning,—

"Unclean, unclean!"

The tribune heard it with a tremor, but kept his place.

"Who are you?" he asked.

"Two women dying of hunger and thirst. Yet"—the mother did not falter—"come not near us, nor touch the floor or the wall. Unclean, unclean!"

"Give me thy story, woman—thy name, and when thou wert put here, and by whom, and for what."

"There was one in this city of Jerusalem a Prince Ben-Hur, the friend of all generous Romans, and who had Cæsar for his friend. I am his widow, and this one with me is his child. How may I tell you for what we were sunk here, when I do not know, unless it was because we were rich? Valerius Gratus can tell you who our enemy was, and when our imprisonment began. I cannot. See to what we have been reduced —oh, see, and have pity!"

The air was heavy with the pest and the smoke of the torches, yet the Roman called one of the torch-bearers to his side, and wrote the answer nearly word for word. It was terse and comprehensive, containing at once a history, an accusation, and a prayer. No common person could have made it, and he could not but pity and believe.

"Thou shalt have relief, woman," he said, closing the tablets. "I will send thee food and drink."

"And raiment, and purifying water, we pray you, O generous Roman!"

"As thou wilt," he replied.

"God is good," said the widow, sobbing. "May His peace abide with you!"

"And, further," he added, "I cannot see thee again. Make preparation, and to-night I will have thee taken to the gate of the Tower, and set free. Thou knowest the law. Farewell."

He spoke to the men, and went out the door.

Very shortly some slaves came to the cell with a large gurglet of water, a basin and napkins, a platter with bread and meat, and some garments of women's wear; and, setting them down within reach of the prisoners, they ran away.

About the middle of the first watch, the two were conducted to the gate, and turned into the street.

CHAPTER 3

THE OLD HOME

ABOUT the hour Gesius, the keeper, made his appearance before the tribune in the Tower of Antonia, a footman was climbing the eastern face of Mount Olivet. On the summit—to reach which he bent his steps somewhat right of the beaten path—he came to a dead stop, arrested as if by a strong hand. Then one might have seen his eyes dilate, his cheeks flush, his breath quicken, effects all of one bright sweeping glance at what lay before him.

The traveller, good reader, was no other than Ben-Hur; the spectacle, Jerusalem.

The sun stooped low in its course. Awhile the flaring disc seemed to perch itself on the far summit of the mountains in the west, brazening all the sky above the city, and rimming the walls and towers with the brightness of gold. Then it disappeared as with a plunge. The quiet turned Ben-Hur's thought homeward. There was a point in the sky a little north of the peerless front of the Holy of Holies upon which he fixed his gaze; under it, straight as a lead-line would have dropped, lay his father's house, if yet the house endured.

Out in the desert while with Ilderim, looking for strong places and acquainting himself with it generally, as a soldier studies a country in which he has projected a campaign, a messenger came one evening with the news that Gratus was removed, and Pontius Pilate sent to take his place.

Messala was disabled and believed him dead; Gratus was powerless and gone; why should Ben-Hur longer defer the search for his mother and sister? There was nothing to fear now. If he could not himself see into the prisons of Judea, he could examine them with the eyes of others. If the lost were found, Pilate could have no motive in holding them in custody—none, at least, which could not be overcome by purchase. If found, he would carry them to a place of safety, and then, in calmer mind, his conscience at rest, this one first duty done, he could give himself more entirely to the King Who Was Coming. He resolved at once. That night he counselled with Ilderim, and obtained his assent. Three Arabs came with him to Jericho, where he left them and the horses, and proceeded alone and on foot. Malluch was to meet him in Jerusalem.

Ben-Hur's scheme, be it observed, was as yet a generality.

Where to begin was the first point. He had no clear idea about it. His wish was to commence with the Tower of Antonia. Tradition not of long standing planted the gloomy pile over a labyrinth of prison-cells, which, more even than the strong garrison, kept it a terror to the Jewish fancy. A burial, such as his people had been subjected to, might be possible there.

Under this inclination, moreover, there was a hope which he could not forego. From Simonides he knew Amrah, the Egyptian nurse, was living. It will be remembered, doubtless, that the faithful creature, the morning the calamity overtook the Hurs, broke from the guard and ran back into the palace, where, along with other chattels, she had been sealed up. During the years following, Simonides kept her supplied; so she was there now, sole occupant of the great house, which, with all his offers, Gratus had not been able to sell. The story of its rightful owners sufficed to secure the property from strangers, whether purchasers or mere occupants. People going to and fro passed it with whispers. Its reputation was that of a haunted house; derived probably from the infrequent glimpses of poor old Amrah, sometimes on the roof, sometimes in a latticed window.

So, first of all things, he would go to the old house, and look for Amrah.

He came, at length, to his father's house.

At the gate on the north side of the old house Ben-Hur stopped. In the corners the wax used in the sealing up was still plainly seen, and across the valves was the board with the inscription—

"This is the Property of
THE EMPEROR."

Nobody had gone in or out the gate since the dreadful day of the separation. Should he knock as of old? It was useless, he knew; yet he could not resist the temptation. Amrah might hear, and look out of one of the windows on that side. Taking a stone, he mounted the broad stone step, and tapped three times. A dull echo replied. He tried again, louder than before; and again, pausing each time to listen. The silence was mocking. Retiring into the street, he watched the windows; but they too, were lifeless. The parapet on the roof was defined sharply against the brightening sky; nothing could have stirred upon it unseen by him, and nothing did stir.

From the north side he passed to the west, where there were four windows which he watched long and anxiously, but with as little effect.

Silently, then, he stole round to the south. There, too, the gate was sealed and inscribed. The mellow splendour of the August moon, pouring over the crest of Olivet, since termed the Mount of Offence, brought the lettering boldly out; and he read, and was filled with rage. All he could do was to wrench the board from its nailing, and hurl it into the ditch. Then he sat upon the step, and prayed for the New King, and that His coming might be hastened. As his blood cooled, insensibly he yielded to the fatigue of long travel in the summer heat, and sank down lower, and at last slept.

About that time two women came down the street from the direction of the Tower of Antonia, approaching the palace of the Hurs. They advanced stealthily, with timid steps, pausing often to listen. At the corner of the rugged pile, one said to the other, in a low voice,—

"This is it, Tirzah!"

And Tirzah, after a look, caught her mother's hand, and leaned upon her heavily, sobbing but silent.

"Let us go on, my child, because"—the mother hesitated and trembled; then, with an effort to be calm, continued—"because when morning comes they will put us out of the gate of the city to—return no more."

Casting one look back and up to the windows on the west side, she stepped out into the light, drawing Tirzah after her; and the extent of their affliction was then to be seen—on their lips and cheeks, in their bleared eyes, in their cracked hands; especially in the long, snaky locks, stiff with loathsome ichor, and, like their eyebrows, ghastly white. Nor was it possible to have told which was mother, which daughter; both alike seemed witch-like old.

"Hist!" said the mother. "There is some one lying upon the step— a man. Let us go round him."

They crossed to the opposite side of the street quickly, and, in the shade there, moved on till before the gate, where they stopped.

"He is asleep, Tirzah!"

The man was very still.

"Stay here, and I will try the gate."

So saying, the mother stole noiselessly across and ventured to touch the wicket; she never knew if it yielded, for that moment the man sighed, and, turning restlessly, shifted the handkerchief on his head in such manner that the face was left upturned and fair in the broad moonlight. She looked down at it and started; then looked again, stooping a little, and arose and clasped her hands and raised her eyes to heaven in mute appeal. An instant so, and she ran back to Tirzah.

"As the Lord liveth, the man is my son—thy brother!" she said, in an awe-inspiring whisper.

"My brother?—Judah?"

The mother caught her hand eagerly.

"Come!" she said, in the same enforced whisper, "Let us look at him together—once more—only once—then help Thou Thy servants, Lord!"

They crossed the street hand in hand ghostly-quick, ghostly-still. When their shadows fell upon him, they stopped. One of his hands was lying out upon the step palm up. Tirzah fell upon her knees, and would have kissed it; but the mother drew her back.

"Not for thy life; not for thy life! Unclean, unclean!" she whispered.

Tirzah shrank from him, as if he were the leprous one.

He stirred, and tossed his hand. They moved back, but heard him mutter in his dream,—

"Mother! Amrah! Where is——"

He fell off into the deep sleep.

Tirzah stared wistfully. The mother put her face in the dust, struggling to suppress a sob so deep and strong it seemed her heart was bursting. Almost she wished he might waken.

He had asked for her; she was not forgotten; in his sleep he was thinking of her. Was it not enough?

Presently the mother beckoned to Tirzah, and they arose, and taking one more look, as if to print his image past fading, hand in hand they recrossed the street. Back in the shade of the wall there, they retired and knelt, looking at him, waiting for him to wake—waiting some revelation, they knew not what. Nobody has yet given us a measure for the patience of a love like theirs.

By and by, the sleep being yet upon him, another woman appeared at the corner of the palace. The two in the shade saw her plainly in the light; a small figure, much bent, dark-skinned, grey-haired, dressed neatly in servant's garb, and carrying a basket full of vegetables.

At sight of the man upon the step the new-comer stopped; then, as if decided, she walked on—very lightly as she drew near the sleeper. Passing round him, she went to the gate, slid the wicket latch easily to one side, and put her hand in the opening. One of the broad boards in the left valve swung ajar without noise. She put the basket through, and was about to follow, when, yielding to curiosity, she lingered to have one look at the stranger whose face was below her in open view.

The spectators across the street heard a low exclamation, and saw the woman rub her eyes as if to renew their power, bend closer down, clasp her hands, gaze wildly around, look at the sleeper, stoop and raise the outlying hand, and kiss it fondly—that which they wished so mightily to do, but dared not.

Awakened by the action, Ben-Hur instinctively withdrew the hand; as he did so, his eyes met the woman's.

"Amrah! O Amrah, is it thou?" he said.

The good heart made no answer in words, but fell upon his neck crying for joy.

Gently he put her arms away, and lifting the dark face wet with tears, kissed it, his joy only a little less than hers. Then those across the way heard him say,—

"Mother—Tirzah—O Amrah, tell me of them! Speak, speak, I pray thee!"

Amrah only cried afresh.

"Thou hast seen them, Amrah. Thou knowest where they are; tell me they are at home."

Tirzah moved, but the mother, divining her purpose, caught her and whispered, "Do not go—not for life. Unclean, unclean!"

Her love was in tyrannical mood. Though both their hearts broke, he should not become what they were; and she conquered.

Meantime Amrah, so entreated, only wept the more.

"Wert thou going in?" he asked, presently seeing the board swung back. "Come, then. I will go with thee." He arose as he spoke.

A moment and they were gone, leaving the two in the shade to behold the gate staring blankly at them—the gate which they might not ever enter more. They nestled together in the dust.

Next morning they were found and driven out of the city with stones.

"Begone! Ye are of the dead; go to the dead!"

With the doom ringing in their ears, they went forth.

CHAPTER 4

AMRAH'S FIDELITY

NOWADAYS travellers in the Holy Land looking for the famous place with the beautiful name, the King's Garden, descend the bed of the Cedron or the curve of Gihon and Hinnom as far as the old well Enrogel, take a drink of the sweet living water, and stop, having reached the limit of the interesting in that direction. They look at the great stones with which the well is curbed, ask its depth, smile at the primitive mood of drawing the purpling treasure, and waste some pity on the ragged wretch who presides over it. When that view has been enjoyed, and is sufficiently impressed upon the memory, the travellers glance at the Mount of Offence standing in rugged stateliness at their right hand, and then at the Hill of Evil Counsel over on the left, in which, if they be well up in Scriptural history and in the traditions rabbinical and monkish, they will find a certain interest not to be overcome by superstitious horror.

It were long to tell all the points of interest grouped around that hill; for the present purpose, enough that its feet are planted in the veritable orthodox Hell of the moderns—the Hell of brimstone and fire—in the old nomenclature Gehenna; and that now, as in the days of Christ, its bluff face opposite the city on the south and south-east is seamed and pitted with tombs which have been immemorially the dwelling-places of lepers, not singly, but collectively. There they set up their government and established their society; there they founded a city and dwelt by themselves, avoided as the accursed of God.

The second morning after the incidents of the preceding chapter, Amrah drew near the well En-rogel, and seated herself upon a stone. She brought with her a water-jar and a basket, the contents of the latter covered with a snow-white napkin.

The sun made its appearance, yet she sat watching and waiting; and while she thus waits, let us see what her purpose is.

The pleasure she derived from the presence of Ben-Hur in the old house once more may be imagined. She had nothing to tell him of her mistress or Tirzah—nothing. He would have had her move to a place not so lonesome; she refused. She would have had him take his own room again, which was just as he had left it; but the danger of discovery was too great, and he wished above all things to avoid inquiry. He would come and see her as often as possible. Coming in the night, he would also go away in the night. She was compelled to be satisfied, and at once occupied herself contriving ways to make him happy. So next night, earlier than usual, she stole out with her basket, and went over to the Fish Gate Market. Wandering about, seeking the best honey, she chanced to hear a man telling a story.

What the story was the reader can arrive at with sufficient certainty when told that the narrator was one of the men who had held torches for the commandant of the Tower of Antonia when, down in cell VI, the Hurs were found. The particulars of the finding were all told, and she heard them, with the names of the prisoners, and the widow's account of herself.

The feelings with which Amrah listened to the recital were such as became the devoted creature she was. She made her purchases, and returned home in a dream. What a happiness she had in store for her boy! She had found his mother!

She put the basket away, now laughing, now crying. Suddenly she stopped and thought. It would kill him to be told that his mother and Tirzah were lepers. He would go through the awful city over on the Hill of Evil Counsel—into each infected tomb he would go without rest, asking for them, and the disease would catch him, and their fate would be his. She wrung her hands. What should she do?

The lepers, she knew, were accustomed of mornings to come down from their sepulchral abodes in the hill, and take a supply of water for the day from the well En-rogel. Bringing their jars, they would set them on the ground and wait, standing afar until they were filled. To that the mistress and Tirzah must come; for the law was inexorable, and admitted no distinction. A rich leper was no better than a poor one.

So Amrah decided not to speak to Ben-Hur of the story she had heard, but go alone to the well and wait. Hunger and thirst would drive the unfortunates thither, and she believed she could recognise them at sight; if not, they might recognise her.

Shortly after sunrise, when business at the well was most pressing, and the drawer of water most hurried; when, in fact, half a dozen buckets were in use at the same time, everybody making haste to get away before the cool of the morning melted into the heat of the day, the tenantry of the hill began to appear and move about the doors of their tombs. Somewhat later they were discernible in groups, of which not a few were children so young that they suggested the holiest relation. Numbers came momentarily around the turn of the bluff—women with jars upon their shoulders, old and very feeble men hobbling along on staffs and crutches. Some leaned upon the shoulders of others; a few —the utterly helpless—lay, like heaps of rags, upon litters. Even that community of superlative sorrow had its love-light to make life endurable and attractive. Distance softened without entirely veiling the misery of the outcasts.

Now, quite at the base of the bluff there was a tomb which had more than once attracted Amrah by its wide gaping. A stone of large dimensions stood near its mouth. The sun looked into it through the hottest hours of the day, and altogether it seemed uninhabitable by anything living, unless, perchance, by some wild dogs returning from scavenger duty down in Gehenna. Thence, however, and greatly to her surprise, the patient Egyptian beheld two women come, one half supporting, half leading, the other. They were both white-haired; both looked old; but their garments were not rent, and they gazed about them as if the locality were new. The witness below thought she even saw them shrink terrified at the spectacle offered by the hideous assemblage of which they found themselves part.

The two remained by the stone awhile; then they moved slowly, painfully, and with much fear towards the well, whereat several voices were raised to stop them; yet they kept on. The drawer of water picked up some pebbles, and made ready to drive them back. The company cursed them. The greater company on the hill shouted shrilly, "Unclean, unclean!"

"Surely," thought Amrah of the two, as they kept coming—"surely, they are strangers to the usage of lepers."

She arose, and went to meet them, taking the basket and jar. The alarm at the well immediately subsided.

"What a fool," said one, laughing, "what a fool to give good bread to the dead in that way!"

Amrah, with better impulse, proceeded. If she should be mistaken! Her heart arose into her throat. And the farther she went, the more doubtful and confused she became. Four or five yards from where they stood waiting for her she stopped.

"These are old women," she said to herself. "I never saw them before. I will go back."

She turned away.

"Amrah," said one of the lepers.

The Egyptian dropped the jar and looked back, trembling.

"Who called me?" she asked.

"Amrah."

The servant's wondering eyes settled upon the speaker's face.

"Who are you?" she cried.

"We are they you are seeking."

Amrah fell upon her knees.

"O my mistress, my mistress! As I have made your God my God, be He praised that He has led me to you!"

And upon her knees the poor overwhelmed creature began moving forward.

"Stay, Amrah! Come not nearer. Unclean, unclean!"

The words sufficed. Amrah fell upon her face, sobbing so loud the people at the well heard her. Suddenly she arose upon her knees again.

"O my mistress, where is Tirzah?"

"Here I am, Amrah, here! Will you not bring me a little water?"

The habit of the servant renewed itself. Putting back the coarse hair fallen over her face, Amrah arose and went to the basket and uncovered it.

"See," she said, "here are bread and meat."

She would have spread the napkin upon the ground, but the mistress spoke again,—

"Do not so, Amrah. Those yonder may stone you, and refuse us drink. Leave the basket with me. Take up the jar and fill it, and bring it here. We will carry them to the tomb with us. For this day you will then have rendered all the service that is lawful. Haste, Amrah."

The people under whose eyes all this had passed made way for the servant, and even helped her fill the jar, so piteous was the grief her countenance showed.

"Who are they?" a woman asked.

Amrah meekly answered, "They used to be good to me."

Raising the jar upon her shoulder, she hurried back. In forgetfulness, she would have gone to them, but the cry "Unclean, unclean! Beware!" arrested her. Placing the water by the basket, she stepped back, and stood off a little way.

"Thank you, Amrah," said the mistress, taking the articles into possession. "This is very good of you."

"Is there nothing more I can do?" asked Amrah.

The mother's hand was upon the jar, and she was fevered with thirst; yet she paused, and rising, said firmly, "Yes, I know that Judah has come home. I saw him at the gate the night before last asleep on the step. I saw you wake him."

Amrah clasped her hands.

"O my mistress! You saw it, and did not come!"

"That would have been to kill him. I can never take him in my arms again. I can never kiss him more. O Amrah, Amrah, you love him, I know!"

"Yes," said the true heart, bursting into tears again, and kneeling. "I would die for him."

"Prove to me what you say, Amrah."

"I am ready."

"Then you shall not tell him where we are, or that you have seen us—only that, Amrah."

"But he is looking for you. He has come from afar to find you."

"He must not find us. He shall not become what we are. Hear, Amrah. You shall serve us as you have this day. You shall bring us the little we need—not long now—not long. You shall come every morning and evening thus, and—and"—the voice trembled, the strong will almost broke down—"and you shall tell us of him, Amrah; but to him you shall say nothing of us. Hear you?"

"The burden will be heavy, O my mistress, and hard to bear," said Amrah, falling upon her face.

"How much harder would it be to see him as we are!" the mother answered as she gave the basket to Tirzah. "Come again this evening," she said, taking up the water, and starting for the tomb.

Amrah waited kneeling until they had disappeared; then she took the road sorrowfully home.

In the evening she returned; and thereafter it became her custom to serve them in the morning and evening, so that they wanted for nothing needful. The tomb, though ever so stony and desolate, was less cheerless than the cell in the Tower had been. Daylight gilded its door, and it was in the beautiful world. Then, one can wait death with so much more faith out under the open sky.

The morning of the first day of the seventh month Ben-Hur arose from his couch in the khan ill satisfied with the whole world.

Little time had been lost in consultation upon the arrival of Malluch. The latter began the search at the Tower of Antonia, and began it boldly, by a direct inquiry of the tribune commanding.

In reply the tribune stated circumstantially the discovery of the women in the Tower, and permitted a reading of the memorandum he had taken of their account of themselves; when leave to copy it was prayed, he even permitted that.

Malluch thereupon hurried to Ben-Hur.

It were useless to attempt description of the effect the terrible story had upon the young man. The pain was not relieved by tears or passionate outcries; it was too deep for any expression. He sat still a long time, with pallid face and labouring heart. Now and then, as if to show the thoughts which were most poignant, he muttered,—

"Lepers, lepers! They—my mother and Tirzah—they lepers! How long, how long, O Lord!"

One moment he was torn by a virtuous rage of sorrow, next by a longing for vengeance which, it must be admitted, was scarcely less virtuous.

At length he arose.

"I must look for them. They may be dying."

"Where will you look?" asked Malluch.

"There is but one place for them to go."

Malluch interposed, and finally prevailed so far as to have the management of the further attempt intrusted to him. Together they went to the gate over on the side opposite the Hill of Evil Counsel, immemorially the lepers' begging-ground. There they stayed all day, giving alms, asking for the two women, and offering rich rewards for their discovery. So they did in repetition day after day through the remainder of the fifth month, and all the sixth. There was diligent scouring of the dread city on the hill by lepers to whom the rewards offered were mighty incentives, for they were only dead in law. Over and over again the gaping tomb down by the well was invaded, and its tenants subjected to inquiry; but they kept their secret fast. The result was failure. And now, the morning of the first day of the seventh month, the extent of the additional information gained was that not long before two leprous women had been stoned from the Fish Gate by the authorities. A little pressing of the clue, together with some shrewd comparison of dates, led to the sad assurance that the sufferers were the Hurs, and left the old questions darker than ever. Where were they? And what had become of them?

BOOK SEVENTH

"And, waking, I beheld her there
Sea-dreaming in the moted air,
A siren lithe and debonair,
With wristlets woven of scarlet weeds,
And oblong lucent amber beads
Of sea-kelp shining in her hair."

THOMAS BAILEY ALDRICH

CHAPTER I

THE HERALD

BEN-HUR went with the Galileans into their country, where his exploits gave him fame and influence. Before the winter was gone he raised three legions, and organized them after the Roman pattern. He could have had as many more, for the martial spirit of that gallant people never slept. The proceeding, however, required careful guarding as against both Rome and Herod Antipas. Contenting himself for the present with the three, he strove to train and educate them for systematic action. For that purpose he carried the officers over into the lava-beds of Trachonitis, and taught them the use of arms, particularly the javelin and sword, and the manœuvring peculiar to the legionary formation; after which he sent them home as teachers. And soon the training became a pastime of the people.

As may be thought, the task called for patience, skill, zeal, faith, and devotion on his part—qualities into which the power of inspiring others in matters of difficulty is always resolvable; and never man possessed them in greater degree, or used them to better effect. How he laboured! And with utter denial of self! Yet withal he would have failed but for the support he had from Simonides, who furnished him arms and money, and from Ilderim, who kept watch and brought him supplies. And still he would have failed but for the genius of the Galileans.

Under that name were comprehended the four tribes—Asher, Zebulon, Issachar, and Naphtali—and the districts originally set apart to them. The Jew born in sight of the Temple despised these brethren of the north; but the Talmud itself has said, "The Galilean loves honour, and the Jew money."

So with Ben-Hur the winter months rolled by, and spring came, with gladdening showers blown over from the summering sea in the west; and by that time so earnestly and successfully had he toiled that he could say to himself and his followers, "Let the good King come. He has only to tell us where He will have His throne set up. We have the sword-hands to keep it for Him."

And in all his dealings with the many men, they knew him only as a son of Judah, and by that name.

. . . . .

One evening, over in Trachonitis, Ben-Hur was sitting with some of his Galileans at the mouth of the cave in which he quartered, when an Arab courier rode to him, and delivered a letter. Breaking the package, he read:

"JERUSALEM, *Nisan IV.*

"A prophet has appeared who men say is Elias. He has been in the wilderness for years, and to our eyes he is a prophet; and such also is his speech, the burden of which is of One much greater than himself, who, he says, is to come presently, and for whom he is now waiting on the eastern shore of the River Jordan. I have been to see and hear him, and the One he is waiting for is certainly the King you are awaiting. Come and judge for yourself.

"All Jerusalem is going out to the prophet, and with many people else the shore on which he abides is like Mount Olivet in the last days of the Passover.

"MALLUCH."

Ben-Hur's face flushed with joy.

"By this word, O my friends," he said, "by this word, our waiting is at an end. The herald of the King has appeared and announced Him."

Upon hearing the letter read, they also rejoiced at the promise it held out.

"Get ready now," he added, "and in the morning set your faces homeward; when arrived there, send word to those under you, and bid them be ready to assemble as I may direct. For myself and you, I will go see if the King be indeed at hand, and send you report. Let us, in the meantime, live in the pleasure of the promise."

Going into the cave, he addressed a letter to Ilderim, and another to Simonides, giving notice of the news received, and of his purpose to go up immediately to Jerusalem. The letters he despatched by swift messengers. When night fell, and the stars of direction came out, he mounted, and with an Arab guide set out for the Jordan, intending to strike the track of the caravans between Rabbath-Ammon and Damascus.

The guide was sure, and Aldebaran swift; so by midnight the two were out of the lava fastness speeding southward.

CHAPTER 2

A SURPRISE

It was Ben-Hur's purpose to turn aside at the break of day, and find a safe place in which to rest; but the dawn overtook him while out in the Desert, and he kept on, the guide promising to bring him after-while to a vale shut in by great rocks, where there were a spring, some mulberry-trees, and herbage in plenty for the horses.

As he rode thinking of the wondrous events so soon to happen, and of the changes they were to bring about in the affairs of men and nations, the guide, ever on the alert, called attention to an appearance of strangers behind them.

"It is a camel with riders," the guide said directly.

"Are there others behind?" said Ben-Hur.

"It is alone. No, there is a man on horseback—the driver, probably."

A little later Ben-Hur himself could see the camel was white and unusually large, reminding him of the wonderful animal he had seen bring Balthasar and Iras to the fountain in the Grove of Daphne. There could be no other like it. Thinking then of the fair Egyptian, insensibly his gait became slower, and at length fell into the merest loiter, until finally he could discern a curtained houdah, and two persons seated within it. If they were Balthasar and Iras! Should he make himself known to them? But it could not be: this was the Desert—and they were alone. But while he debated the question, the long swinging stride of the camel brought its riders up to him. He heard the ringing of the tiny bells, and beheld the rich housings which had been so attractive to the crowd at the Castalian fount. He beheld also the Ethiopian, always attendant upon the Egyptians. The tall brute stopped close by his horse, and Ben-Hur, looking up, lo! Iras herself under the raised curtain looking down at him, her great swimming eyes bright with astonishment and inquiry!

"The blessing of the true God upon you!" said Balthasar in his tremulous voice.

"And to thee and thine be the peace of the Lord," Ben-Hur replied.

"My eyes are weak with years," said Balthasar; "but they approve you that son of Hur whom lately I knew an honoured guest in the tent of Ilderim the Generous."

"And thou art that Balthasar, the wise Egyptian, whose speech concerning certain holy things in expectation is having so much to do with the finding me in this waste place."

Afterwhile the party came to a shallow wady, down which, turning to the right hand, the guide led them. The bed of the cut was somewhat soft from recent rains, and quite bold in its descent. Momentarily, however, it widened; and ere long the sides became bluffs ribbed with rocks much scarred by floods rushing to lower depths ahead. Finally, from a narrow passage, the travellers entered a spreading vale which was very delightful; but come upon suddenly from the yellow, unrelieved, verdureless plain, it had the effect of a freshly discovered Paradise. The water-channels winding here and there, definable by crisp, white shingling, appeared like threads tangled among islands green with grasses and fringed with reeds. Up from the final depths of the valley of the Jordan some venturous oleanders had crept, and with their large bloom now starred the sunken place. One palm-tree arose in royal assertion.

"Bring me a cup," Iras said, with some impatience.

From the houdah the slave brought her a crystal goblet; then she said to Ben-Hur,—

"I will be your servant at the fountain."

They walked to the pool together. He would have dipped the water for her, but she refused his offer, and kneeling, held the cup to be filled by the stream itself; nor yet content, when it was cooled and over-running, she tendered him the first draught.

"No," he said, putting the graceful hand aside, and seeing only the large eyes half hidden beneath the arches of the upraised brows, "be the service mine, I pray."

She persisted in having her way.

"In my country, O son of Hur, we have a saying, 'Better a cup-bearer to the fortunate than minister to a king.' "

"Fortunate!" he said.

There were both surprise and inquiry in the tone of his voice and in his look, and she said quickly,—

"The gods give us success as a sign by which we may know them on our side. Were you not winner in the Circus?"

Before he could answer the allusion to the little Jewess, Balthasar came to the pool.

"We are greatly indebted to you, son of Hur," he said, in his grave manner. "This vale is very beautiful; the grass, the trees, the shade, invite us to stay and rest, and the spring here has the sparkle of diamonds in motion, and sings to me of a loving God. It is not enough to thank you for the enjoyment we find; come sit with us, and taste our bread."

"Suffer me first to serve you."

With that Ben-Hur filled the goblet, and gave it to Balthasar, who lifted his eyes in thanksgiving.

Immediately the slave brought napkins; and after laving their hands and drying them, the three seated themselves in Eastern style under the tent which years before had served the Wise Men at the meeting in the Desert. And they ate heartily of the good things taken from the camel's pack.

CHAPTER 3

THE HERALD AND HIS KING

THE caravan, stretched out upon the Desert, was very picturesque; in motion, however, it was like a lazy serpent. By and by its stubborn dragging became intolerably irksome to Balthasar, patient as he was; so, at his suggestion, the party determined to go on by themselves.

If the reader be young, or if he has yet a sympathetic recollection of the romanticisms of his youth, he will relish the pleasure with which Ben-Hur, riding near the camel of the Egyptians, gave a last look at the head of the straggling column almost out of sight on the shimmering plain.

To be definite as may be, and perfectly confidential, Ben-Hur found a certain charm in Iras's presence. If she looked down upon him from her high place, he made haste to get near her; if she spoke to him, his heart beat out of its usual time.

For that there is no logic in love, nor the least mathematical element, it is simply natural that she shall fashion the result who has the wielding of the influence.

To quicken the conclusion, there were signs, too, that she well knew the influence she was exercising over him. From some place under hand she had since morning drawn a caul of golden coins, and adjusted it so the gleaming strings fell over her forehead and upon her cheeks, blending lustrously with the flowing of her blue-black hair. From the same safe deposit she had also produced articles of jewellery—rings for her finger and ear, bracelets, a necklace of pearls—also, a shawl embroidered with threads of fine gold—the effect of all which she softened with a scarf of Indian lace skilfully folded about her throat and shoulders. And so arrayed, she plied Ben-Hur with countless coquetries of speech and manner; showering him with smiles; laughing in flute-like tremolo —and all the while following him with glances, now melting-tender, now sparkling-bright. By such play Antony was weaned from his glory; yet she who wrought his ruin was really not half so beautiful as this her country-woman.

And so to them the morning came, and the evening.

The sun at its going down behind a spur of the old Bashan, left the party halted by a pool of clear water of the rains out in the Abilene Desert. There the tent was pitched, the supper eaten, and preparations made for the night.

The second watch was Ben-Hur's; and he was standing, spear in hand, within arm-reach of the dozing camel, looking awhile at the stars, then over the veiled land. The stillness was intense; only after long spells a warm breath of wind would sough past, but without disturbing him, for yet in thought he entertained the Egyptian, recounting her charms, and sometimes debating how she came by his secrets, the uses she might make of them, and the course he should pursue with her. And through all the debate Love stood off but a little way—a strong temptation, the stronger of a gleam of policy behind. At the very moment he was most inclined to yield to the allurement, a hand very fair even in the moonless gloaming was laid softly upon his shoulder.

The third day of the journey the party nooned by the river Jabbok, where there were a hundred or more men, mostly of Peræa, resting themselves and their beasts. Hardly had they dismounted, before a man came to them with a pitcher of water and a bowl, and offered them drink; as they received the attention with much courtesy, he said, looking at the camel, "I am returning from the Jordan, where just now there are many people from distant parts, travelling as you are, illustrious friend; but they had none of them the equal of your servant here. A very noble animal. May I ask of what breed he is sprung?"

Balthasar answered, and sought his rest; but Ben-Hur, more curious, took up the remark.

"At what place on the river are the people?" he asked.

"At Bethabara."

"It used to be a lonesome ford," said Ben-Hur. "I cannot understand how it can have become of such interest."

"I see," the stranger replied; "you, too, are from abroad, and have not heard the good tidings."

"What tidings?"

"Well, a man has appeared out of the wilderness—a very holy man—with his mouth full of strange words, which take hold of all who hear them. He calls himself John the Nazarite, son of Zacharias, and says he is the messenger sent before the Messiah."

Even Iras listened closely while the man continued,—

"They say of this John that he has spent his life from childhood in a cave down by En-gedi, praying and living more strictly than the Essenes. Crowds go to hear him preach. I went to hear him with the rest."

"Have all these, your friends, been there?"

"Most of them are going; a few are coming away."

"What does he preach?"

"A new doctrine—one never before taught in Israel, as all say. He calls it repentance and baptism. The rabbis do not know what to make of him; nor do we. Some have asked him if he is the Christ, others if he is Elias; but to them all he has the answer, 'I am the voice of one crying in the wilderness, Make straight the way of the Lord!'"

At this point the man was called away by his friends; as he was going, Balthasar spoke.

"Good stranger!" he said tremulously, "tell us if we shall find the preacher at the place you left him."

"Yes, at Bethabara."

"Who should this Nazarite be!" said Ben-Hur to Iras, "if not the herald of our King?"

In so short a time he had come to regard the daughter as more interested in the mysterious personage he was looking for than the aged father! Nevertheless, the latter with a positive glow in his sunken eyes half arose, and said,—

"Let us make haste. I am not tired."

They turned away to help the slave.

There was little conversation between the three at the stopping-place for the night west of Ramoth-Gilead.

"Let us arise early, son of Hur," said the old man. "The Saviour may come, and we not there."

"The King cannot be far behind His herald," Iras whispered, as she prepared to take her place on the camel.

"To-morrow we will see!" Ben-Hur replied, kissing her hand.

Next day about the third hour, they caught sight of booths and tents and tethered animals; and then of the river, and a multitude collected down close by the bank, and yet another multitude on the western shore. Knowing that the preacher was preaching, they made greater haste; yet, as they were drawing near, suddenly there was a commotion in the mass, and it began to break up and disperse.

They were too late!

"Let us stay here," said Ben-Hur to Balthasar, who was wringing his hands. "The Nazarite may come this way."

When some hundreds were gone by, and it seemed the opportunity to so much as see the Nazarite was lost to the latter, up the river not far away they beheld a person coming towards them of such singular appearance they forgot all else.

Outwardly the man was rude and uncouth, even savage. Over a thin, gaunt visage of the hue of brown parchment, over his shoulders and down his back below the middle, in witch-like locks, fell a covering of sun-scorched hair. His eyes were burning-bright. All his right side was naked, and of the colour of his face, and quite as meagre; a shirt of the coarsest camel's-hair—coarse as Bedouin tent-cloth—clothed the rest of his person to the knees, being gathered at the waist by a broad girdle of untanned leather. His feet were bare. A scrip, also of untanned leather, was fastened to the girdle. He used a knotted staff to help him forward. His movement was quick, decided, and strangely watchful. Every little while he tossed the unruly hair from his eyes, and peered round as if searching for somebody.

In this time of such interest to the new-comers, and in which they were so differently moved, another man had been sitting by himself on a stone at the edge of the river, thinking yet, probably, of the sermon he had been hearing. Now, however, he arose, and walked slowly up from the shore, in a course to take him across the line the Nazarite was pursuing and bring him near the camel.

And the two—the preacher and the stranger—kept on until they came, the former within twenty yards of the animal, the latter within ten feet. Then the preacher stopped, and flung the hair from his eyes, looked at the stranger, threw his hands up as a signal to all the people in sight; and they also stopped, each in the pose of a listener; and when the hush was perfect, slowly the staff in the Nazarite's right hand came down pointed at the stranger.

All those who before were but listeners became watchers also.

At the same instant, under the same impulse, Balthasar and Ben-Hur fixed their gaze upon the man pointed out, and both took the same impression, only in different degree. He was moving slowly towards them in a clear space a little to their front, a form slightly above the average in stature, and slender, even delicate. His action was calm and deliberate, like that habitual to men much given to serious thought upon grave subjects; and it well became his costume, which was an under-garment full-sleeved and reaching to the ankles, and an outer robe called the talith; on his left arm he carried the usual handkerchief for the head, the red fillet swinging loose down his side. Except the fillet and a narrow border of blue at the lower edge of the talith, his attire was of linen yellowed with dust and road-stains. Possibly the exception should be extended to the tassels, which were blue and white, as prescribed by law for rabbis. His sandals were of the simplest kind. He was without scrip or girdle or staff.

These points of appearance, however, the three beholders observed briefly, and rather as accessories to the head and face of the man, which —especially the latter—were the real sources of the spell they caught in common with all who stood looking at him.

The head was open to the cloudless light, except as it was draped with hair long and slightly waved, and parted in the middle, and auburn in tint, with a tendency to reddish golden where most strongly touched by the sun. Under a broad, low forehead, under black well-arched brows, beamed eyes dark-blue and large, and softened to exceeding tenderness by lashes of the great length sometimes seen on children, but seldom, if ever, on men. As to the other features, it would have been difficult to decide whether they were Greek or Jewish. The delicacy of the nostrils and mouth was unusual to the latter type; and when it was taken into account with the gentleness of the eyes, the pallor of the complexion, the fine texture of the hair, and the softness of the beard, which fell in waves over his throat to his breast, never a soldier but would have laughed at him in encounter, never a woman who would not have confided in him at sight, never a child that would not, with quick instinct, have given him its hand and whole artless trust; nor might any one have said he was not beautiful.

The features, it should be further said, were ruled by a certain expression which, as the viewer chose, might with equal correctness have been called the effect of intelligence, love, pity, or sorrow; though, in better speech, it was a blending of them all—a look easy to fancy as the mark of a sinless soul doomed to the sight and understanding of the utter sinfulness of those among whom it was passing; yet withal no one could have observed the face with a thought of weakness in the man; so, at least, would not they who know that the qualities mentioned— love, sorrow, pity—are the results of a consciousness of strength to bear suffering oftener than strength to do: such has been the might of martyrs and devotees and the myriads written down in saintly calendars. And such, indeed, was the air of this One.'

Slowly He drew near—nearer the three.

Now Ben-Hur, mounted and spear in hand, was an object to claim the glance of a king; yet the eyes of the man approaching were all the time raised above him—and not to Iras, whose loveliness has been so often remarked, but to Balthasar, the old and unserviceable.

The hush was profound.

Presently the Nazarite, still pointing with his staff, cried in a loud voice,—

"Behold the Lamb of God, which taketh away the sin of the world!"

Balthasar fell upon his knees. For him there was no need of explanation; and as if the Nazarite knew it, he turned to those more immediately about him staring in wonder, and continued,—

"This is He of whom I said, After me cometh a man which is preferred before me; for He was before me. And I knew Him not: but that He should be manifest to Israel, therefore am I come baptizing with water. I saw the Spirit descending from heaven like a dove, and it abode upon Him. And I knew Him not: but He that sent me to baptize with water, the same said unto me, Upon whom thou shalt see the Spirit descending and remaining on Him, the same is He which baptizeth with the Holy Ghost. And I saw and bare record, that this"—he paused, his staff still pointing at the stranger in the white garments, as if to give a more absolute certainty to both his words and the conclusions intended—"I bare record, *that this is the* SON OF GOD!"

"It is He, it is He!" Balthasar cried, with upraised tearful eyes. Next moment he sank down insensible.

Ben-Hur leaped from his horse to render homage to his benefactor; but Iras cried to him, "Help, son of Hur, help, or my father will die!"

He stopped, looked back, then hurried to her assistance. She gave him a cup; and leaving the slave to bring the camel to its knees, he ran to the river for water. The stranger was gone when he came back.

At last Balthasar was restored to consciousness. Stretching forth his hands, he asked feebly, "Where is He?"

"Who?" asked Iras.

An intense instant interest shone upon the good man's face, as if a last wish had been gratified, and he answered,—

"He—the Redeemer—the son of God, whom I have seen again."

"Believest thou so?" Iras asked in a low voice of Ben-Hur.

"The time is full of wonders; let us wait," was all he said.

And next day, while the three were listening to him, the Nazarite broke off in mid-speech, saying reverently, "Behold the Lamb of God!"

Looking to where he pointed, they beheld the stranger again. As Ben-Hur surveyed the slender figure, and holy beautiful countenance compassionate to sadness, a new idea broke upon him.

"Balthasar is right—so is Simonides. May not the Redeemer be a King also?"

And he asked one at his side, "Who is the man walking yonder?"

The other laughed mockingly, and replied,—

"He is the son of a carpenter over in Nazareth."

BOOK EIGHTH

"Who could resist? Who in this universe?
  She did so breathe ambrosia, so immerse
  My fine existence in a golden clime.
  She took me like a child of suckling time,
  And cradled me in roses. Thus condemn'd,
  The current of my former life was stemm'd,
  And to this arbitrary queen of sense
  I bow'd a tranced vassal."—KEATS, *Endymion*
    "I am the resurrection and the life."

CHAPTER I

ANTICIPATION

"ESTHER—Esther! Speak to the servant below that he may bring me a cup of water."

"Would you not rather have wine, father?"

"Let him bring both."

This was in the summer-house upon the roof of the old palace of the Hurs in Jerusalem. From the parapet overlooking the court-yard Esther called to a man in waiting there; at the same moment another man-servant came up the steps and saluted respectfully.

"A package for the master," he said, giving her a letter enclosed in linen cloth, tied and sealed.

For the satisfaction of the reader, we stop to say that it is the twenty-first day of March, nearly three years after the annunciation of the Christ at Bethabara.

In the meanwhile, Malluch, acting for Ben-Hur, who could not longer endure the emptiness and decay of his father's house, had bought it from Pontius Pilate.

Now it should not be inferred from this explanation that Ben-Hur had publicly assumed ownership of the property. In his opinion, the hour for that was not yet come. Neither had he yet taken his proper name. Passing the time in the labours of preparation in Galilee, he waited patiently the action of the Nazarene, who became daily more and more a mystery to him, and by prodigies done, often before his eyes, kept him in a state of anxious doubt both as to His character and mission. Occasionally he came up to the Holy City, stopping at the paternal house; always, however, as a stranger and a guest.

These visits of Ben-Hur, it should also be observed, were for more than mere rest from labour. Balthasar and Iras made their home in the palace; and the charm of the daughter was still upon him with all its original freshness, while the father, though feebler in body, held him an unflagging listener to speeches of astonishing power, urging the divinity of the wandering miracle-worker of whom they were all so expectant.

As to Simonides and Esther, they had arrived from Antioch only a few days before this their reappearance—a wearisome journey to the merchant, borne, as he had been, in a palanquin swung between two camels, which, in their careening, did not always keep the same step. But now that he was come, the good man, it seemed, could not see enough of his native land. He delighted in the perch upon the roof, and spent most of his day hours there seated in an arm-chair, the duplicate of that one kept for him in the cabinet over the store-house by the Orontes.

Esther read aloud the letter that the messenger had brought.

"*Nisan*, 8th *day*.

"On the road from Galilee to Jerusalem.

"The Nazarene is on the way also. With Him, though without His knowledge, I am bringing a full legion of mine. A second legion follows. The Passover will excuse the multitude. He said upon setting out, 'We will go up to Jerusalem, and all things that are written by the prophets concerning Me shall be accomplished.'

"Our waiting draws to an end.

"In haste.

"Peace to thee, Simonides.

BEN-HUR."

Esther returned the letter to her father, while a choking sensation gathered in her throat. There was not a word in the missive for her—not even in the salutation had she a share—and it would have been so easy to have written "and to thine, peace." For the first time in her life she felt the smart of a jealous sting.

"The eighth day," said Simonides, "the eighth day; and this, Esther, this is the——"

"The ninth," she replied.

"Ah, then, they may be in Bethany now."

"And possibly we may see him to-night," she added, pleased into momentary forgetfulness.

"It may be, it may be! To-morrow is the Feast of Unleavened Bread, and he may wish to celebrate it; so may the Nazarene; and we may see him—we may see both of them, Esther."

At this point the servant appeared with the wine and water. Esther helped her father, and in the midst of the service Iras came upon the roof.

To the Jewess the Egyptian never appeared so very, very beautiful as at that moment. Her gauzy garments fluttered about her like a little cloud of mist; her forehead, neck, and arms glittered with the massive jewellery so affected by her people. Her countenance was suffused with pleasure. She moved with buoyant steps, and self-conscious, though without affectation. Esther at the sight shrank within herself, and nestled closer to her father.

"Peace to you, Simonides, and to the pretty Esther peace," said Iras, inclining her head to the latter. "You remind me, good master—if I may say it without offence—you remind me of the priests in Persia who climb their temples at the decline of day to send prayers after the departing sun——"

A sound of some one walking swiftly along the street below interrupted the speech, and she leaned over the parapet to see. Then she drew back, and cried, with hands clasped above her head, "Now blessed be Isis! 'Tis he—Ben-Hur himself! That he should appear while I had such thought of him! There are no gods if it be not a good omen."

Esther saw her disappear down the steps, when, putting her hands over her face, she burst into tears so they ran scalding through her fingers.

And all the stars were out, burning low above the city and the dark wall of mountains about it, before she recovered enough to go back to the summer-house, and in silence take her accustomed place at her father's side, humbly waiting his pleasure. To such duty it seemed her youth, if not her life, must be given. And, let the truth be said, now that the pang was spent, she went not unwillingly back to the duty.

CHAPTER 2

BEN-HUR'S RELATION

An hour or thereabouts after the scene upon the roof, Balthasar and Simonides, the latter attended by Esther, met in the great chamber of the palace; and while they were talking, Ben-Hur and Iras came in together.

The young Jew, advancing in front of his companion, walked first to Balthasar, and saluted him, and received his reply; then he turned to Simonides, but paused at sight of Esther.

He paused in surprise at seeing Esther a woman now, and so beautiful; and as he stood looking at her, a still voice reminded him of broken vows and duties undone; almost his old self returned.

For an instant he was startled; but recovering, he went to Esther, and said, "Peace to thee, sweet Esther—peace; and thou, Simonides"—he looked to the merchant as he spoke—"the blessing of the Lord be thine, if only because thou hast been a good father to the fatherless."

Esther heard him with downcast face; Simonides answered,—

"I repeat the welcome of the good Balthasar, son of Hur—welcome to thy father's house; and sit and tell us of thy travels, and of thy work, and of the wonderful Nazarene—who is He, and what. If thou art not at ease here, who shall be? Sit, I pray—there, between us, that we may all hear."

Esther stepped out quickly and brought a covered stool, and set it for him.

"Thanks," he said to her gratefully.

When seated, after some other conversation, he addressed himself to the men.

"I have come to tell you of the Nazarene."

The two became instantly attentive.

"For many days now I have followed Him with such watchfulness as one may give another upon whom he is waiting so anxiously. I have seen Him under all circumstances said to be trials and tests of men; and while I am certain He is a man as I am, not less certain am I that He is something more."

"What more?" asked Simonides.

"I will tell you——"

Some one coming into the room interrupted him; he turned, and arose with extended hands.

"Amrah! Dear old Amrah!" he cried.

She came forward; and they, seeing the joy in her face, thought not once how wrinkled and tawny it was. She knelt at his feet, clasped his knees, and kissed his hands over and over; and when he could he put the lank grey hair from her cheeks, and kissed them, saying, "Good Amrah, have you nothing, nothing of them—not a word—not one little sign?"

Then she broke into sobbing which made him answer plainer even than the spoken word.

"God's will has been done," he next said solemnly, in a tone to make each listener know he had no hope more of finding his people. In his eyes there were tears which he would not have them see, because he was a man.

When he could again, he took seat, and said, "Come, sit by me, Amrah—here. No? then at my feet; for I have much to say to these good friends of a wonderful man come into the world."

But she went off, and stooping with her back to the wall, joined her hands before her knees, content, they all thought, with seeing him. Then Ben-Hur, bowing to the old men, began again,—

"I fear to answer the question asked me about the Nazarene without first telling you some of the things I have seen Him do; and to that I am the more inclined, my friends, because to-morrow He will come to the city, and go up into the Temple, which He calls His Father's house, where, it is further said, He will proclaim Himself. So, whether you are right, O Balthasar, or you, Simonides, we and Israel shall know to-morrow."

Balthasar rubbed his hands tremulously together, and asked, "Where shall I go to see Him?"

"The pressure of the crowd will be very great. Better, I think, that you all go upon the roof above the cloisters—say upon the Porch of Solomon."

"Can you be with us?"

"No," said Ben-Hur, "my friends will require me, perhaps, in the procession."

"Procession!" exclaimed Simonides. "Does He travel in state?"

Ben-Hur saw the argument in mind.

"He brings twelve men with Him, fishermen, tillers of the soil, one a publican, all of the humbler class; and He and they make their journeys on foot, careless of wind, cold, rain, or sun. Seeing them stop by the wayside at nightfall to break bread or lie down to sleep, I have been reminded of a party of shepherds going back to their flocks from market, not of nobles and kings. Only when He lifts the corners of His handkerchief to look at some one or shake the dust from His head, I am made known He is their teacher as well as their companion —their superior not less than their friend."

"The Greeks would call him a philosopher," said Iras.

"Nay, daughter," said Balthasar, "the philosophers had never the power to do such things as this man has."

"How know you this man has?"

Ben-Hur answered quickly, "I saw Him turn water into wine."

"Very strange, very strange," said Simonides; "but it is not so strange to me as that He should prefer to live poor when He could be so rich. Is He so poor?"

"He owns nothing, and envies nobody his owning. He pities the rich. But passing that, what would you say to see a man multiply seven loaves and two fishes, all his store, into enough to feed five thousand people, and have full baskets over? That I saw the Nazarene do."

"You saw it!" exclaimed Simonides.

"Ay, and ate of the bread and fish."

"More marvellous still," Ben-Hur continued, "what would you say of a man in whom there is such healing virtue that the sick have but to touch the hem of His garment to be cured, or cry to Him afar? That, too, I witnessed, not once, but many times. As we came out of Jericho two blind men by the wayside called to the Nazarene, and He touched their eyes, and they saw. So they brought a palsied man to Him, and He said merely, 'Go unto thy house,' and the man went away well. What say you to these things?"

The merchant had no answer.

"Think you now, as I have heard others argue, that what I have told you are tricks of jugglery? Let me answer by recalling greater things which I have seen Him do. Look first to that curse of God— comfortless, as you all know, except by death—leprosy."

At these words Amrah dropped her hands to the floor, and in her eagerness to hear him half arose.

"What would you say," said Ben-Hur, with increased earnestness— "what would you say to have seen that I now tell you? A leper came to the Nazarene while I was with Him down in Galilee, and said, 'Lord, if Thou wilt, Thou canst make me clean.' He heard the cry, and touched the outcast with His hand, saying, 'Be thou clean'; and forthwith the man was himself again, healthful as any one of us who beheld the cure, and we were a multitude."

Here Amrah arose, and with her gaunt fingers held the wiry locks from her eyes. The brain of the poor creature had long since gone to heart, and she was troubled to follow the speech.

"Then, again," said Ben-Hur, without stop, "ten lepers came to Him one day in a body, and falling at His feet, called out—I saw and heard it all—called out, 'Master, Master, have mercy upon us!' He told them, 'Go, show yourselves to the priest, as the law requires; and before you are come there ye shall be healed.'"

"And were they?"

"Yes. On the road going their infirmity left them, so that there was nothing to remind us of it except their polluted clothes."

"Such thing was never heard before—never in all Israel!" said Simonides in undertone.

And then, while he was speaking, Amrah turned away, and walked noiselessly to the door, and went out; and none of the company saw her go.

"The thoughts stirred by such things done under my eyes I leave you to imagine," said Ben-Hur continuing; "but my doubts, my misgivings, my amazement, were not yet at the full. The people of Galilee are, as you know, impetuous and rash; after years of waiting their swords burned their hands; nothing would do them but action. 'He is slow to declare Himself; let us force Him,' they cried to me. And I too became impatient. If He is to be King, why not now? The legions are ready. So as He was once teaching by the seaside we would have crowned Him whether or not; but He disappeared, and was next seen on a ship departing from the shore. Good Simonides, the desires that make other men mad—riches, power, even kingships offered out of great love by a great people—move this One not at all. What say you?"

The merchant's chin was low upon his breast; raising his head, he replied resolutely, "The Lord liveth, and so do the words of the prophets. Time is in the green yet; let to-morrow answer."

"Be it so," said Balthasar, smiling.

And Ben-Hur said, "Be it so." Then he went on: "But I have not yet done. From these things, not too great to be above suspicion by such as did not see them in performance, as I did, let me carry you now to others infinitely greater, acknowledged since the world began to be past the power of man. Tell me, has any one to your knowledge ever reached out and taken from Death what Death has made his own? Who ever gave again the breath of a life lost? Who but——"

"God!" said Balthasar reverently.

Ben-Hur bowed.

"O wise Egyptian! I may not refuse the name you lend me. What would you—or you, Simonides—what would you either or both have said had you seen, as I did, a man, with few words and no ceremony, without effort more than a mother's when she speaks to wake her child asleep, undo the work of Death? It was down at Nain. We were about going into the gate, when a company came out bearing a dead man. The Nazarene stopped to let the train pass. There was a woman among them crying. I saw His face soften with pity. He spoke to her, then went and touched the bier, and said to him who lay upon it dressed for burial, 'Young man, I say unto thee, Arise!' And instantly the dead sat up and talked."

"God only is so great," said Balthasar to Simonides.

"Mark you," Ben-Hur proceeded, "I do but tell you things of which I was a witness, together with a cloud of other men. On the way hither I saw another act still more mighty. In Bethany there was a man named Lazarus, who died and was buried; and after he had lain four days in a tomb, shut in by a great stone, the Nazarene was shown to the place. Upon rolling the stone away, we beheld the man lying inside bound and rotting. There were many people standing by, and we all heard what the Nazarene said, for He spoke in a loud voice: 'Lazarus, come forth!' I cannot tell you my feelings when in answer, as it were, the man arose and came out to us with all his cerements about him. 'Loose him,' said the Nazarene next, 'loose him, and let him go.' And when the napkin was taken from the face of the resurrected, lo, my friends! the blood ran anew through the wasted body, and he was exactly as he had been in life before the sickness that took him off. He lives yet, and is hourly seen and spoken to. You may go see him to-morrow. And now, as nothing more is needed for the purpose, I ask you that which I came to ask, it being but a repetition of what you asked me, O Simonides, What more than a man is this Nazarene?"

The question was put solemnly, and long after midnight the company sat and debated it; Simonides being yet unwilling to give up his understanding of the sayings of the prophets, and Ben-Hur contending that the elder disputants were both right—that the Nazarene was the Redeemer, as claimed by Balthasar, and also the destined King the merchant would have.

"To-morrow we will see. Peace to you all."

So saying, Ben-Hur took his leave, intending to return to Bethany.

CHAPTER 3

GLAD TIDINGS

THE first person to go out of the city upon the opening of the Sheep's Gate next morning was Amrah, basket on arm. No questions were asked her by the keepers, since the morning itself had not been more regular in coming than she; they knew her somebody's faithful servant, and that was enough for them.

As the reader must by this time have surmised, she was going to her mistress, whose tomb, it will be remembered, overlooked the well En-rogel.

Early as it was, the unhappy woman was up and sitting outside, leaving Tirzah asleep within. The course of the malady had been terribly swift in the three years. Conscious of her appearance, with the refined instincts of her nature, she kept her whole person habitually covered. Seldom as possible she permitted even Tirzah to see her.

This morning she was taking the air with bared head, knowing there was no one to be shocked by the exposure. The light was not full, but enough to show the ravages to which she had been subject. In the sky—clear, fair, inviting—one would think she might have found some relief to her ache of mind; but, alas! in making the beautiful elsewhere the sun served her never so unfriendly—it did but disclose her growing hideousness. But for the sun, she would not have been the horror she was to herself, nor been waked so cruelly from dreams of Tirzah as she used to be. The gift of seeing can be sometimes a dreadful curse.

Does one ask why she did not make an end to her sufferings?

The Law forbade her!

A Gentile may smile at the answer; but so will not a son of Israel.

While she sat there peopling the dusky solitude with thoughts even more cheerless, suddenly a woman came up the hill staggering and spent with exertion.

The widow arose hastily, and covering her head, cried, in a voice unnaturally harsh, "Unclean, unclean!"

In a moment, heedless of the notice, Amrah was at her feet. All the long-pent love of the simple creature burst forth: with tears and passionate exclamations she kissed her mistress's garments, and for a while the latter strove to escape from her; then, seeing she could not, she waited till the violence of the paroxysm was over.

"What have you done, Amrah?" she said. "Is it by such disobedience you prove your love for us? Wicked woman! You are lost; and he—your master—you can never, never go back to him."

Amrah grovelled sobbing in the dust.

Here Tirzah, awakened by the noise, appeared at the door of the tomb. The pen shrinks from the picture she presented. In the half-clad apparition, patched with scales, lividly seamed, nearly blind, its limbs and extremities swollen to grotesque largeness, familiar eyes however sharpened by love could not have recognized the creature of childish grace and purity we first beheld her.

"Is it Amrah, mother?"

The servant tried to crawl to her also.

"Stay, Amrah!" the widow cried imperiously. "I forbid you touching her. Rise, and get you gone before any at the well see you here. Nay, I forgot—it is too late! You must remain now and share our doom. Rise, I say!"

Amrah rose to her knees, and said, brokenly and with clasped hands, "O good mistress! I am not false—I am not wicked. I bring you good tidings."

"Of Judah?" and as she spoke, the widow half withdrew the cloth from her head.

"There is a wonderful man," Amrah continued, "who has power to cure you. He speaks a word, and the sick are made well, and even the dead come to life. I have come to take you to Him."

"Poor Amrah!" said Tirzah compassionately.

"No," cried Amrah, detecting the doubt underlying the expression—"no, as the Lord lives, even the Lord of Israel, my God as well as yours, I speak the truth. Go with me, I pray, and lose no time. This morning He will pass by on His way to the city. See! the day is at hand. Take the food here—eat, and let us go."

The mother listened eagerly. Not unlikely she had heard of the wonderful man, for by this time His fame had penetrated every nook in the land.

"Who is He?" she asked.

"A Nazarene."

"Who told you about Him?"

"Judah."

"Judah told you. Is he at home?"

"He came last night."

The widow, trying to still the beating of her heart, was silent awhile.

"Did Judah send you to tell us this?" she next asked.

"No. He believes you dead."

"There was a prophet once who cured a leper," the mother said thoughtfully to Tirzah; "but he had his power from God." Then addressing Amrah, she asked, "How does my son know this man so possessed?"

"He was travelling with Him, and heard the lepers call, and saw them go away well. First there was one man; then there were ten; and they were all made whole."

The elder listener was silent again. The skeleton hand shook. We may believe she was struggling to give the story the sanction of faith, which is always an absolutist in demand, and that it was with her as with the men of the day, eye-witnesses of what was done by the Christ, as well as the myriads who have succeeded them. She did not question the performance, for her own son was the witness testifying through the servant; but she strove to comprehend the power by which work so astonishing could be done by a man. Well enough to make inquiry as to the fact; to comprehend the power, on the other hand, it is first necessary to comprehend God; and he who waits for that will die waiting. With her, however, the hesitation was brief. To Tirzah she said,—

"This must be the Messiah!"

She spoke not coldly, like one reasoning a doubt away, but as a woman of Israel familiar with the promises of God to her race—a woman of understanding, ready to be glad over the least sign of the realization of the promises.

"There was a time when Jerusalem and all Judea were filled with a story that He was born. I remember it. By this time He should be a man. It must be—it is He. Yes," she said to Amrah, "we will go with you. Bring the water which you will find in the tomb in a jar, and set the food for us. We will eat and be gone."

The breakfast, partaken under excitement, was soon despatched, and the three women set out on their extraordinary journey. As Tirzah had caught the confident spirit of the others, there was but one fear that troubled the party. Bethany, Amrah said, was the town the man was coming from; now from that to Jerusalem there were three roads, or rather paths—one over the first summit of Olivet, a second at its base, a third between the second summit and the Mount of Offence. The three were not far apart; far enough, however, to make it possible for the unfortunates to miss the Nazarene if they failed the one He chose to come by.

A little questioning satisfied the mother that Amrah knew nothing of the country beyond the Cedron, and even less of the intentions of the man they were going to see, if they could. She discerned, also, that both Amrah and Tirzah—the one from confirmed habits of servitude,

the other from natural dependency—looked to her for guidance; and
she accepted the charge.

"We will go first to Bethphage," she said to them. "There, if the
Lord favour us, we may learn what else to do."

They descended the hill to Tophet and the King's Garden, and
paused in the deep trail furrowed through them by centuries of way-
faring.

"I am afraid of the road," the matron said. "Better that we keep
to the country among the rocks and trees. This is feast-day, and on the
hill-sides yonder I see signs of a great multitude in attendance. By
going across the Mount of Offence here we may avoid them."

Tirzah had been walking with great difficulty; upon hearing this her
heart began to fail her.

"The mount is steep, mother; I cannot climb it."

"Remember we are going to find health and life. See, my child, how
the day brightens around us! And yonder are women coming this way
to the well. They will stone us if we stay here. Come, be strong this
once."

Thus the mother, not less tortured herself, sought to inspire the
daughter; and Amrah came to her aid. To this time the latter had
not touched the persons of the afflicted, nor they her; now, in disregard
of consequences as well as of command, the faithful creature went to
Tirzah, and put her arm over her shoulder, and whispered, "Lean on
me. I am strong, though I am old; and it is but a little way off. There
—now we can go."

The face of the hill they essayed to cross was somewhat broken with
pits, and ruins of old structures; but when at last they stood upon the
top to rest, and looked at the spectacle presented them over in the
north-west—at the Temple and its courtly terraces, at Zion, at the enduring towers white beetling into the sky beyond—the mother was
strengthened with a love of life for life's sake.

From the side of the middle summit garnished green with myrtle and
olive trees, they saw, upon looking that way next, thin columns of
smoke rising lightly and straight up into the pulseless morning, each a
warning of restless pilgrims astir, and of the flight of the pitiless hours,
and the need of haste.

Though the good servant toiled faithfully to lighten the labour in
descending the hill-side, not sparing herself in the least, the girl moaned
at every step; sometimes in extremity of anguish she cried out. Upon
reaching the road—that is, the road between the Mount of Offence and
the middle or second summit of Olivet—she fell down exhausted.

"Go on with Amrah, mother, and leave me here," she said faintly.

"No, no, Tirzah. What would the gain be to me if I were healed and you not? When Judah asks for you, as he will, what would I have to say to him were I to leave you?"

"Tell him I loved him."

The elder leper arose from bending over the fainting sufferer, and gazed about her with that sensation of hope perishing which is more nearly like annihilation of the soul than anything else. The supremest joy of the thought of cure was inseparable from Tirzah, who was not too old to forget, in the happiness of healthful life to come, the years of misery by which she had been so reduced in body and broken in spirit. Even as the brave woman was about leaving the venture they were engaged in to the determination of God, she saw a man on foot coming rapidly up the road from the east.

"Courage, Tirzah! Be of cheer," she said. "Yonder I know is one to tell us of the Nazarene."

Amrah helped the girl to a sitting posture, and supported her while the man advanced.

"In your goodness, mother, you forget what we are. The stranger will go around us; his best gift to us will be a curse, if not a stone."

"We will see."

There was no other answer to be given, since the mother was too well and sadly acquainted with the treatment outcasts of the class to which she belonged were accustomed to at the hands of her country-men.

As has been said, the road at the edge of which the group was posted was little more than a worn path or trail, winding crookedly through tumuli of limestone. If the stranger kept it, he must meet them face to face; and he did so, until near enough to hear the cry she was bound to give. Then, uncovering her head, a further demand of the law, she shouted shrilly,—

"Unclean, unclean!"

To her surprise, the man came steadily on.

"What would you have?" he asked, stopping opposite them not four yards off.

"Thou seest us. Have a care," the mother said, with dignity.

"Woman, I am the courier of Him who speaketh but once to such as thou and they are healed. I am not afraid."

"The Nazarene?"

"The Messiah," he said.

"Is it true that He cometh to the city to-day?"

"He is now at Bethphage."

"On what road, master?"

"This one."

She clasped her hands, and looked up thankfully.

"For whom takest thou Him?" the man asked, with pity.

"The Son of God," she replied.

"Stay thou here then; or, as there is a multitude with Him, take thy stand by the rock yonder, the white one under the tree; and as He goeth by fail not to call to Him; call, and fear not. If thy faith but equal thy knowledge, He will hear thee though all the heavens thunder. I go to tell Israel, assembled in and about the city, that He is at hand, and to make ready to receive Him. Peace to thee and thine, woman."

The stranger moved on.

"Did you hear, Tirzah? Did you hear? The Nazarene is on the road, on this one, and He will hear us. Once more, my child—oh, only once! and let us to the rock. It is but a step."

Thus encouraged, Tirzah took Amrah's hand and arose; but as they were going, Amrah said, "Stay; the man is returning." And they waited for him.

"I pray your grace, woman," he said, upon overtaking them. "Remembering that the sun will be hot before the Nazarene arrives, and that the city is near by to give me refreshment should I need it, I thought this water would do thee better than it will me. Take it and be of good cheer. Call to Him as He passes."

He followed the words by offering her a gourd full of water, such as foot-travellers sometimes carry with them in their journeys across the hills; and instead of placing the gift on the ground for her to take up when he was at a safe distance, he gave it into her hand.

"Art thou a Jew?" she asked, surprised.

"I am that, and better; I am a disciple of the Christ who teacheth daily by word and example this thing which I have done unto you. The world hath long known the word charity without understanding it. Again I say, peace and good cheer to thee and thine."

He went on, and they went slowly to the rock he had pointed out to them, high as their heads, and scarcely thirty yards from the road on the right. Standing in front of it, the mother satisfied herself they could be seen and heard plainly by passers-by whose notice they desired to attract. There they cast themselves under the tree in its shade, and drank of the gourd, and rested refreshed. Ere long Tirzah slept, and fearing to disturb her, the others held their peace.

CHAPTER 4

HEALED

DURING the third hour the road in front of the resting-place of the lepers became gradually more and more frequented by people going in the direction of Bethphage and Bethany; now, however, about the commencement of the fourth hour, a great crowd appeared over the crest of Olivet, and as it defiled down the road, thousands in number, the two watchers noticed with wonder that every one in it carried a palm-branch freshly cut. As they sat absorbed by the novelty, the noise of another multitude approaching from the east drew their eyes that way. Then the mother awoke Tirzah.

"What is the meaning of it all?" the latter asked.

"He is coming," answered the mother. "These we see are from the city going to meet Him; those we hear in the east are his friends bearing Him company; and it will not be strange if the processions meet here before us."

"I fear, if they do, we cannot be heard."

The same thought was in the elder's mind.

"Amrah," she asked, "when Judah spoke of the healing of the ten, in what words did he say they called to the Nazarene?"

"Either they said, 'Lord, have mercy upon us,' or 'Master, have mercy.'"

"Only that?"

"No more that I heard."

"Yet it was enough," the mother added to herself.

"Yes," said Amrah, "Judah said he saw them go away well."

Meantime the people in the east came up slowly. When at length the foremost of them were in sight, the gaze of the lepers fixed upon a man riding in the midst of what seemed a chosen company which sang and danced about Him in extravagance of joy. The Rider was bare-headed and clad all in white. Behind Him the irregular procession, pouring forward with continuous singing and shouting, extended out of view. There was no need of any one to tell the lepers that this was He—the wonderful Nazarene!

"He is here, Tirzah," the mother said; "He is here. Come, my child."

As she spoke she glided in front of the white rock and fell upon her knees.

Directly the daughter and servant were by her side. Then at sight of the procession in the east, the thousands from the city halted, and began to wave their green branches, shouting, or rather chanting (for it was all in one voice),—

"Blessed is the King of Israel that cometh in the name of the Lord!"

And all the thousands who were of the Rider's company, both those near and those afar, replied so the air shook with the sound, which was as a great wind threshing the side of the hill. Amidst the din, the cries of the poor lepers were not more than the twittering of dazed sparrows.

The moment of the meeting of the hosts was come, and with it the opportunity the sufferers were seeking; if not taken, it would be lost for ever, and they would be lost as well.

"Nearer, my child—let us get nearer. He cannot hear us," said the mother.

She arose, and staggered forward. Her ghastly hands were up, and she screamed with horrible shrillness. The people saw her—saw her hideous face, and stopped awe-struck—an effect for which extreme human misery, visible as in this instance, is as potent as majesty in purple and gold. Tirzah, behind her a little way, fell down too faint and frightened to follow farther.

"The lepers! the lepers!"

"Stone them!"

"The accursed of God! Kill them!"

These, with other yells of like import, broke in upon the hosannas of the part of the multitude too far removed to see and understand the cause of the interruption. Some there were, however, near by familiar with the nature of the man to whom the unfortunates were appealing— some who, by long intercourse with Him, had caught somewhat of His divine compassion: they gazed at Him, and were silent while, in fair view, He rode up and stopped in front of the woman. She also beheld His face—calm, pitiful, and of exceeding beauty, the large eyes tender with benignant purpose.

And this was the colloquy that ensued:

"O Master, Master! Thou seest our need; Thou canst make us clean. Have mercy upon us—mercy!"

"Believest thou I am able to do this?" He asked.

"Thou art He of whom the prophets spake—Thou art the Messiah!" she replied.

His eyes grew radiant, His manner confident.

"Woman," he said, "great is thy faith; be it unto thee even as thou wilt."

He lingered an instant after, apparently unconscious of the presence of the throng—an instant—then He rode away.

To the heart divinely original, yet so human in all the better elements of humanity, going with sure prevision to a death of all the inventions of men the foulest and most cruel, breathing even then in the forecast shadow of the awful event, and still as hungry and thirsty for love and faith as in the beginning, how precious and ineffably soothing the farewell exclamation of the grateful woman:

"To God in the highest, glory! Blessed, thrice blessed, the Son whom He hath given us!"

Immediately both the hosts, that from the city and that from Bethphage, closed around Him with their joyous demonstrations, with hosannas and waving of palms, and so He passed from the lepers for ever. Covering her head the elder hastened to Tirzah, and folded her in her arms, crying, "Daughter, look up! I have His promise; He is indeed the Messiah. We are saved—saved!" And the two remained kneeling while the procession, slowly going, disappeared over the mount. When the noise of its singing afar was a sound scarcely heard, the miracle began.

There was first in the hearts of the lepers a freshening of the blood; then it flowed faster and stronger, thrilling their wasted bodies with an infinitely sweet sense of painless healing. Each felt the scourge going from her; their strength revived; they were returning to be themselves. Directly, as if to make the purification complete, from body to spirit the quickening ran, exalting them to a very fervour of ecstasy. The power possessing them to this good end was most nearly that of a draught of swift and happy effect; yet it was unlike and superior in that its healing and cleansing were absolute, and not merely a delicious consciousness while in progress, but the planting, growing, and maturing all at once of a recollection so singular and so holy, that the simple thought of it should be of itself ever after a formless yet perfect thanksgiving.

To this transformation—for such it may be called quite as properly as a cure—there was a witness other than Amrah. The reader will remember the constancy with which Ben-Hur had followed the Nazarene throughout His wanderings; and now, recalling the conversation of the night before, there will be little surprise at learning that the young Jew was present when the leprous woman appeared in the path of the pilgrims. He heard her prayer, and saw her disfigured face; he heard the answer also, and was not so accustomed to incidents of the kind, frequent as they had been, as to have lost interest in them. Had such thing been possible with him, still the bitter disputation always excited by the simplest display of the Master's curative gift would have sufficed to keep his curiosity alive. Besides that, if not above it as an incentive, his hope to satisfy himself upon the vexed question of the mission of the mysterious man was still upon him strong as in the beginning; we might indeed say even stronger, because of a belief that now quickly, before the sun went down, the man Himself would make all known by public proclamation. At the close of the scene, consequently, Ben-Hur had withdrawn from the procession, and seated himself upon a stone to wait its passage.

From his place he nodded recognition to many of the people—Galileans in his league, carrying short swords under their long abbas. After a little a swarthy Arab came up leading two horses; at a sign from Ben-Hur he also drew out.

"Stay here," the young master said, when all were gone by, even the laggards. "I wish to be at the city early, and Aldebaran must do me service."

He stroked the broad forehead of the horse, now in its prime of strength and beauty, then crossed the road towards the two women.

They were to him, it should be borne in mind, strangers in whom he felt interest only as they were subjects of a superhuman experiment, the result of which might possibly help him to solution of the mystery that had so long engaged him. As he proceeded, he glanced casually at the figure of the little woman over by the white rock, standing there her face hidden in her hands.

"As the Lord liveth, it is Amrah!" he said to himself.

He hurried on, and passing by the mother and daughter, still without recognising them, he stopped before the servant.

"Amrah," he said to her, "Amrah, what do you here?"

She rushed forward, and fell upon her knees before him, blinded by her tears, nigh speechless with contending joy and fear.

"O master, master! Thy God and mine, how good He is!"

The knowledge we gain from much sympathy with others passing through trials is but vaguely understood; strangely enough, it enables us, among other things, to merge our identity into theirs often so completely that their sorrows and their delights become our own. So poor Amrah, aloof and abiding her face, knew the transformation the lepers were undergoing without a word spoken to her—knew it, and shared all their feeling to the full. Her countenance, her words, her whole manner, betrayed her condition; and with swift presentiment he connected it with the women he had just passed: he felt her presence there at that time was in some way associated with them, and turned hastily as they rose to their feet. His heart stood still; he became rooted in his tracks—dumb past outcry—awe-struck.

The woman he had seen before the Nazarene was standing with her hands clasped and eyes streaming, looking towards heaven. The mere transformation would have been a sufficient surprise; but it was the least of the causes of his emotion. Could he be mistaken? Never was there in life a stranger so like his mother; and like her as she was the day the Roman snatched her from him. There was but one difference to mar the identity—the hair of this person was a little streaked with grey; yet that was not impossible of reconcilement, since the intelligence which had directed the miracle might have taken into consideration the natural effects of the passage of years. And who was it by her side, if not Tirzah?—fair, beautiful, perfect, more mature, but in all other respects exactly the same in appearance as when she looked with him over the parapet the morning of the accident to Gratus. He had given them over as dead, and time had accustomed him to the bereavement; he had not ceased mourning for them, yet, as something distinguishable, they had simply dropped out of his plans and dreams. Scarcely believing his senses, he laid his hand upon the servant's head, and asked, tremulously,—

"Amrah, Amrah—my mother! Tirzah! tell me if I see aright."

"Speak to them, O master, speak to them!" she said.

He waited no longer, but ran, with outstretched arms, crying, "Mother! mother! Tirzah! Here I am!"

They heard his call, and with a cry as loving started to meet him. Suddenly the mother stopped, drew back, and uttered the old alarm,—

"Stay, Judah, my son; come not nearer. Unclean, unclean!"

The utterance was not from habit, grown since the dread disease struck her, as much as fear; and the fear was but another form of the ever-thoughtful maternal love. Though they were healed in person, the taint of the scourge might be in their garments ready for communication. He had no such thought. They were before him; he had called them, they had answered. Who or what should keep them from him now? Next moment the three, so long separated, were mingling their tears in each other's arms.

The first ecstasy over, the mother said, "In this happiness, O my children, let us not be ungrateful. Let us begin life anew by acknowledgement of Him to whom we are all so indebted."

They fell upon their knees, Amrah with the rest; and the prayer of the elder outspoken was as a psalm.

Tirzah repeated it word for word; so did Ben-Hur, but not with the same clear mind and questionless faith, for when they were risen, he asked,—

"In Nazareth, where the man was born, mother, they call Him the son of a carpenter. What is He?"

Her eyes rested upon him with all their old tenderness, and she answered as she had answered the Nazarene Himself,—

"He is the Messiah."

"And whence has He His power?"

"We may know by the use He makes of it. Can you tell me any ill He has done?"

"No."

"By that sign then I answer, He has His power from God."

It is not an easy thing to shake off in a moment the expectations nurtured through years until they have become essentially a part of us; and though Ben-Hur asked himself what the vanities of the world were to such a One, his ambition was obdurate and would not down. He persisted as men do yet every day in measuring the Christ by himself. How much better if we measured ourselves by the Christ!

Naturally, the mother was the first to think of the cares of life.

"What shall we do now, my son? Where shall we go?"

Then Ben-Hur, recalled to duty, observed how completely every trace of the scourge had disappeared from his restored people; that each had back her perfection of person; that, as with Naaman when he came up out of the water, their flesh had come again like unto the flesh of a little child; and he took off his cloak, and threw it over Tirzah.

"Take it," he smiled; "the eye of the stranger would have shunned you before, now it shall not offend you."

The act exposed a sword belted to his side.

"Is it a time of war?" asked the mother anxiously.

"No."

"Why, then, are you armed?"

"It may be necessary to defend the Nazarene."

Thus Ben-Hur evaded the whole truth.

"Has He enemies? Who are they?"

"Alas, mother, they are not all Romans!"

"Is He not of Israel, and a man of peace?"

"There was never one more so; but in the opinion of the rabbis and teachers, He is guilty of a great crime."

"What crime?"

"In His eyes the uncircumcised Gentile is as worthy favour as a Jew of the strictest habit. He preaches a new dispensation."

The mother was silent, and they moved to the shade of the tree by the rock. Calming his impatience to have them home again and hear their story, he showed them the necessity of obedience to the law governing in cases like theirs, and in conclusion called the Arab, bidding him take the horses to the gate by Bethesda and await him there; whereupon they set out by the way of the Mount of Offence. The return was very different from the coming; they walked rapidly and with ease, and in good time reached a tomb newly made near that of Absalom, overlooking the depths of Cedron. Finding it unoccupied, the women took possession, while he went on hastily to make the preparations required for their new condition.

Ben-Hur pitched two tents out on the Upper Cedron east a short space of the Tombs of the Kings, and furnished them with every comfort at his command; and thither without loss of time, he conducted his mother and sister, to remain until the examining priest could certify their perfect cleansing.

Nor should it be forgotten that these incidents occurred between the twenty-first day of March—counting by the modern calendar—and the twenty-fifth. The evening of the latter day Ben-Hur yielded and rode to the city, leaving behind him a promise to return in the night.

CHAPTER 5

UNMASKED

BEN-HUR alighted at the gate of the khan from which the three Wise Men more than thirty years before departed, going down to Bethlehem. There, in keeping of his Arab followers, he left the horse, and shortly after was at the wicket of his father's house, and in a yet briefer space in the great chamber. He called for Malluch first; that worthy being out, he sent a salutation to his friends the merchant and the Egyptian. They were being carried abroad to see the celebration. The latter, he was informed, was very feeble, and in a state of deep dejection.

While the servant was answering for the elder, the curtain of the doorway was drawn aside, and the younger Egyptian came in, and walked—or floated, upborne in a white cloud of the gauzy raiment she so loved and lived in—to the centre of the chamber, where the light cast by lamps from the seven-armed brazen stick planted upon the floor was the strongest. With her there was no fear of light.

The servant left the two alone.

In the excitement occasioned by the events of the few days past, Ben Hur had scarcely given a thought to the fair Egyptian. If she came to his mind at all, it was merely as a briefest pleasure, a suggestion of a delight which could wait for him, and was waiting.

But now the influence of the woman revived with all its force the instant Ben-Hur beheld her. He advanced to her eagerly, but stopped and gazed. Such a change he had never seen!

She was the first to speak.

"Your coming is timely, O son of Hur," she said, in a voice sharply distinct. "I wish to thank you for hospitality; after to-morrow I may not have the opportunity to do so."

Ben-Hur bowed slightly, without taking his eyes from her.

"I have heard of a custom which the dice-players observe with good result among themselves," she continued. "When the game is over, they refer to their tablets and cast up their accounts; then they libate the gods and put a crown upon the happy winner. We have had a game—it has lasted through many days and nights. Why, now that it is at an end, shall not we see to which the chaplet belongs?"

Yet very watchful, Ben-Hur answered lightly, "A man may not balk a woman bent on having her way."

"Tell me," she continued, inclining her head, and permitting the sneer to become positive—"tell me, O prince of Jerusalem, where is He, that Son of the carpenter of Nazareth, and Son not less of God, from whom so lately such mighty things were expected?"

He waved his hand impatiently, and replied, "I am not His keeper."

The beautiful head sank forward yet lower.

"Has He broken Rome to pieces?"

Again, but with anger, Ben-Hur raised his hand in deprecation.

"Where has He seated His capital?" she continued. "Cannot I go see His throne and its lions of bronze? And His palace—He raised the dead; and to such a One, what is it to raise a golden house? He has but to stamp His foot and say the word, and the house is, pillared like Karnak, and wanting nothing."

There was by this time slight ground left to believe her playing; the questions were offensive, and her manner pointed with unfriendliness; seeing which, he on his side became more wary, and said, with good humour, "O Egypt, let us wait another day, even another week, for Him, the lions, and the palace."

She went on without noticing the suggestion.

"And how is it I see you in that garb? Such is not the habit of governors in India or vice-kings elsewhere. I saw the satrap of Teheran once, and he wore a turban of silk and a cloak of cloth of gold, and the hilt and scabbard of his sword made me dizzy with their splendour of precious stones. I thought Osiris had lent him a glory from the sun. I fear you have not entered upon your kingdom—the kingdom I was to share with you."

"The daughter of my wise guest is kinder than she imagines herself; she is teaching me that Isis may kiss a heart without making it better."

Ben-Hur spoke with cold courtesy, and Iras, after playing with the pendent solitaire of her necklace of coins, rejoined, "For a Jew, the son of Hur is clever. I saw your dreaming Cæsar make His entry into Jerusalem. You told us He would that day proclaim Himself King of the Jews from the steps of the Temple. I beheld the procession descend the mountain bringing Him. I heard their singing. They were beautiful with palms in motion. I looked everywhere among them for a figure with a promise of royalty—a horseman in purple, a chariot with a driver in shining brass, a stately warrior behind an orbed shield, rivalling his spear in stature. I looked for His guard. It would have been pleasant to have seen a prince of Jerusalem and a cohort of the legions of Galilee."

She flung her listener a glance of provoking disdain, then laughed heartily, as if the ludicrousness of the picture in her mind were too strong for contempt.

"Instead of a Sesostris returning in triumph or a Cæsar helmed and sworded—ha, ha, ha!—I saw a man with a woman's face and hair, riding an ass's colt, and in tears. The King! the Son of God! the Redeemer of the world! Ha, ha, ha!"

In spite of himself, Ben-Hur winced.

"Daughter of Balthasar," he said, with dignity, "if this be the game of which you spoke to me, take the chaplet—I accord it yours. Only let us make an end of words. That you have a purpose I am sure. To it, I pray, and I will answer you; then let us go our several ways, and forget we ever met. Say on; I will listen, but not to more of that which you have given me."

She regarded him intently a moment, as if determining what to do—possibly she might have been measuring his will—then she said coldly, "You have my leave—go."

"Peace to you," he responded, and walked away.

As he was about passing out of the door, she called to him.

"A word."

He stopped where he was, and looked back.

"Consider all I know about you."

"O most fair Egyptian," he said, returning, "what all do you know about me?"

She looked at him absently.

H

"You are more of a Roman, son of Hur, than any of your Hebrew brethren."

"Am I so unlike my countrymen?" he asked indifferently.

"The demi-gods are all Roman now," she rejoined.

"And therefore you will tell me what more you know about me?"

"The likeness is not lost upon me. It might induce me to save you."

"Save me!"

The pink-stained fingers toyed daintily with the lustrous pendant at the throat, and her voice was exceeding low and soft; only a tapping on the floor with her silken sandal admonished him to have a care.

"There was a Jew, an escaped galley-slave, who killed a man in the palace of Idernee," she began slowly.

Ben-Hur was startled.

"The same Jew has three trained legions from Galilee to seize the Roman governor to-night; the same Jew has alliances perfected for war upon Rome, and Ilderim the Sheik is one of his partners."

Drawing nearer him, she almost whispered,—

"You have lived in Rome. Suppose these things repeated in ears we know of. Ah! you change colour."

He drew back from her with somewhat of the look which may be imagined upon the face of a man who, thinking to play with a kitten, has run upon a tiger; and she proceeded,—

"You are acquainted in the antechamber, and know the Lord Sejanus. Suppose it were told him with the proofs in hand—or without the proofs—that the same Jew is the richest man in the East—nay, in all the empire. The fishes of the Tiber would have fattening other than that they dig out of its ooze, would they not? And while they were feeding—ha! son of Hur!—what splendour there would be on exhibition in the Circus! Amusing the Roman people is a fine art; getting the money to keep them amused is another art even finer; and was there ever an artist the equal of the Lord Sejanus?"

Hur drew a breath and said lightly, "Thanks. It were not well to keep the Lord Sejanus waiting for you. The Desert is not so sensitive. Again, O Egypt, peace!"

To this time he had been standing uncovered; now he took the hand-kerchief from his arm where it had been hanging, and adjusting it upon his head, turned to depart. But she arrested him; in her eagerness, she even reached a hand to him.

"Stay," she said.

He looked back at her, but without taking the hand, though it was very noticeable for its sparkling of jewels; and he knew by her manner that the reserved point of the scene which was so surprising to him was now to come.

"Stay, and do not distrust me, O son of Hur, if I declare I know why the noble Arrius took you for his heir. And, by Isis! by all the gods of Egypt! I swear I tremble to think of you, so brave and generous, under the hand of the remorseless minister. You have left a portion of your youth in the atria of the great capital; consider, as I do, what the Desert will be to you in contrast of life. Oh, I give you pity—pity! And if you but do what I say, I will save you. That also, I swear, by our holy Isis!"

Words of entreaty and prayer these, poured forth volubly and with earnestness and the mighty sanction of beauty.

"Almost—almost I believe you," Ben-Hur said, yet hesitatingly, and in a voice low and indistinct; for a doubt remained with him grumbling against the yielding tendency of the man—a good sturdy doubt, such a one as has saved many a life and fortune.

"The perfect life for a woman is to live in love; the greatest happiness for a man is the conquest of himself; and that, O prince, is what I have to ask of you."

She spoke rapidly, and with animation; indeed, she had never appeared to him so fascinating.

"You had once a friend," she continued. "It was in your boyhood. There was a quarrel, and you and he became enemies. He did you wrong. After many years you met him again in the Circus at Antioch."

"Messala!"

"Yes, Messala. You are his creditor. Forgive the past; admit him to friendship again; restore the fortune he lost in the great wager; rescue him. The six talents are as nothing to you; not so much as a bud lost upon a tree already in full leaf; but to him—Ah, he must go about with a broken body; wherever you meet him, he must look up to you from the ground. O Ben-Hur, noble prince! to a Roman descended as he is, beggary is the other most odious name for death. Save him from beggary!"

If the rapidity with which she spoke was a cunning invention to keep him from thinking, either she never knew or else had forgotten that there are convictions which derive nothing from thought, but drop into place without leave or notice. It seemed to him, when at last she paused to have an answer, that he could see Messala himself peering at him over her shoulder; and in its expression the countenance of the Roman was not that of a mendicant or a friend; the sneer was as patrician as ever, and the fine edge of the hauteur as flawless and irritating.

"The appeal has been decided then, and for once a Messala takes nothing. I must go and write it in my book of great occurrences—a judgment by a Roman against a Roman! But did he—did Messala send you to me with this request, O Egypt?"

"He has a noble nature, and judged you by it."

Ben-Hur took the hand upon his arm.

"As you know him in such friendly way, fair Egyptian, tell me, would he do for me, there being a reversal of the conditions, that he asks of me? Answer, by Isis! Answer, for the truth's sake!"

There was insistence in the touch of his hand, and in his look also.

"Oh!" she began, "he is——"

"A Roman, you were about to say; meaning that I, a Jew, must not determine dues from me to him by any measure of dues from him to me; being a Jew, I must forgive him my winnings because he is a Roman. If you have more to tell me, daughter of Balthasar, speak quickly, quickly; for by the Lord God of Israel, when this heat of blood, hotter waxing, attains its highest, I may not be able longer to see that you are a woman, and beautiful! I may see but the spy of a master the more hateful because the master is a Roman. Say on, and quickly."

She threw his hand off and stepped back into the full light, with all the evil of her nature collected in her eyes and voice.

"Thou drinker of lees, feeder upon husks! To think I could love thee, having seen Messala! Such as thou were born to serve him. He would have been satisfied with release of the six talents; but I say to the six thou shalt add twenty—twenty, dost thou hear? The kissings of my little finger which thou hast taken from him, though with my consent, shall be paid for; and that I have followed thee with affectation of sympathy, and endured thee so long, enter into the account not less because I was serving him. The merchant here is thy keeper of moneys. If by to-morrow at noon he has not thy order acted upon in favour of my Messala for six-and-twenty talents—mark the sum!—thou shalt settle with the Lord Sejanus. Be wise and—farewell."

As she was going to the door, he put himself in her way.

"The old Egypt lives in you," he said. "Whether you see Messala to-morrow or the next day, here or in Rome, give him this message. Tell him I have back the money, even the six talents, he robbed me of by robbing my father's estate; tell him I survived the galleys to which he had me sent, and in my strength rejoice in his beggary and dishonour; tell him I think the affliction of body which he has from my hand is the curse of our Lord God of Israel upon him more fit than death for his crimes against the helpless; tell him my mother and sister whom he had sent to a cell in Antonia that they might die of leprosy, are alive and well, thanks to the power of the Nazarene whom you so despise; tell him that, to fill my measure of happiness, they are restored to me, and that I will go hence to their love, and find in it more than compensation for the impure passions which you leave me to take to him; tell him—this for your comfort, O cunning incarnate, as much as his—tell him that when the Lord Sejanus comes to despoil me he will find nothing; for the inheritance I had from the duumvir, including the villa by Misenum, has been sold, and the money from the sale is out of reach, afloat in the marts of the world as bills of exchange; and that this house and the goods and merchandise and the ships and caravans with which Simonides plies his commerce with such princely profits are covered by imperial safeguards—a wise head having found the price of the favour, and the Lord Sejanus preferring a reasonable gain in the way of gift to much gain fished from pools of blood and wrong; tell him if all this were not so, if the money and property were all mine, yet should he not have the least part of it, for when he finds our Jewish bills, and forces them to give up their values, there is yet another resort left me—a deed of gift to Cæsar—so much, O Egypt, I found out in the atria of the great capital; tell him that along with my defiance I do not send him a curse in words, but, as a better expression of my undying hate, I send him one who will prove to him the sum of all curses; and when he looks at you repeating this my message, daughter of Balthasar, his Roman shrewdness will tell him all I mean. Go now —and I will go."

He conducted her to the door, and, with ceremonious politeness, held back the curtain while she passed out.

"Peace to you," he said, as she disappeared.

CHAPTER 6

BETRAYAL

THE streets were full of people going and coming, or grouped about the fires roasting meat, and feasting and singing, and happy. The odour of scorching flesh mixed with the odour of cedar-wood aflame and smoking loaded the air; and as this was the occasion when every son of Israel was full brother to every other son of Israel, and hospitality was without bounds, Ben-Hur was saluted at every step, while the groups by the fires insisted, "Stay and partake with us. We are brethren in the love of the Lord." But with thanks to them he hurried on, intending to take horse at the khan and return to the tents on the Cedron.

To make the place, it was necessary for him to cross the thoroughfare so soon to receive sorrowful Christian perpetuation. There also the pious celebration was at its height. Looking up the street, he noticed the flames of torches in motion streaming out like pennons; then he observed that the singing ceased where the torches came. His wonder rose to its highest, however, when he became certain that amidst the smoke and dancing sparks he saw the keener sparkling of burnished spear-tips, arguing the presence of Roman soldiers. What were they, the scoffing legionaries, doing in a Jewish religious procession? The circumstance was unheard of, and he stayed to see the meaning of it.

The moon was shining its best; yet, as if the moon and the torches, and the fires in the street, and the rays streaming from windows and open doors were not enough to make the way clear, some of the processionists carried lighted lanterns; and fancying he discovered a special purpose in the use of such equipments, Ben-Hur stepped into the street so close to the line of march as to bring every one of the company under view while passing. The torches and the lanterns were being borne by servants, each of whom was armed with a bludgeon or a sharpened stave. Their present duty seemed to be to pick out the smoothest paths among the rocks in the street for certain dignitaries among them— elders and priests; rabbis with long beards, heavy brows, and beaked noses; men of the class potential in the councils of Caiaphas and Hannas. Where could they be going? Not to the Temple, certainly, for the route to the sacred house from Zion, whence these appeared to be coming, was by the Xystus. And their business—if peaceful, why the soldiers?

As the procession began to go by Ben-Hur, his attention was particularly called to three persons walking together. They were well towards the front, and the servants who went before them with lanterns appeared unusually careful in the service. In the person moving on the left of this group he recognized a chief policeman of the Temple; the one on the right was a priest; the middle man was not at first so easily placed, as he walked leaning heavily upon the arms of the others, and carried his head so low upon his breast as to hide his face. His appearance was that of a prisoner not yet recovered from the fright of arrest, or being taken to something dreadful—to torture or death. The dignitaries helping him on the right and left, and the attention they gave him, made it clear that if he were not himself the object moving the party, he was at least in some way connected with the object—a witness or a guide, possibly an informer. So, if it could be found who he was, the business in hand might be shrewdly guessed. With great assurance, Ben-Hur fell in on the right of the priest, and walked along with him. Now if the man would lift his head! And presently he did so, letting the light of the lanterns strike full in his face, pale, dazed, pinched with dread; the beard roughed; the eyes filmy, sunken, and despairing. In much going about following the Nazarene, Ben-Hur had come to know His disciples as well as the Master; and now, at sight of the dismal countenance, he cried out,—

"The 'Scariot!"

Slowly the head of the man turned until his eyes settled upon Ben-Hur, and his lips moved as if he were about to speak; but the priest interfered.

"Who art thou? Begone!" he said to Ben-Hur, pushing him away.

The young man took the push good-naturedly, and, waiting an opportunity, fell into the procession again. Thus he was carried passively along down the street, through the crowded lowlands between the hill Bezetha and the Castle of Antonia, and on by Bethesda reservoir to the Sheep Gate. There were people everywhere, and everywhere the people were engaged in sacred observances.

It being Passover night, the valves of the Gate stood open. The keepers were off somewhere feasting. In front of the procession as it passed out unchallenged was the deep gorge of the Cedron, with Olivet beyond, its dressing of cedar and olive trees darker of the moonlight silvering all the heavens. Two roads met and merged into the street at the gate— one from the north-east, the other from Bethany. Ere Ben-Hur could finish wondering whether he were to go further, and if so, which road was to be taken, he was led off down into the gorge. And still no hint of the purpose of the midnight march.

Down the gorge and over the bridge at the bottom of it. There was a great clatter on the floor as the crowd, now a straggling rabble, passed over beating and pounding with their clubs and staves. A little farther, and they turned off to the left in the direction of an olive orchard enclosed by a stone wall in view from the road. Ben-Hur knew there was nothing in the place but old gnarled trees, the grass, and a trough hewn out of a rock for the treading of oil after the fashion of the country. While, yet more wonder-struck, he was thinking what could bring such a company at such an hour to a quarter so lonesome, they were all brought to a standstill. Voices called out excitedly in front; a chill sensation ran from man to man; there was a rapid falling back, and a blind stumbling over each other. The soldiers alone kept their order.

It took Ben-Hur but a moment to disengage himself from the mob and run forward. There he found a gateway without a gate admitting to the orchard, and he halted to take in the scene.

A man in white clothes, and bareheaded, was standing outside the entrance, His hands crossed before Him—a slender, stooping figure, with long hair and thin face—in an attitude of resignation and waiting.

It was the Nazarene!

Behind Him, next the gateway, were the disciples in a group; they were excited, but no man was ever calmer than He. The torchlight beat redly upon Him, giving His hair a tint ruddier than was natural to it; yet the expression of the countenance was as usual all gentleness and pity.

Opposite this most unmartial figure stood the rabble, gaping, silent, awed, cowering—ready at a sign of anger from Him to break and run. And from Him to them—then at Judas, conspicuous in their midst—Ben-Hur looked—one quick glance, and the object of the visit lay open to his understanding. Here was the betrayer, there the betrayed; and these with clubs and staves, and the legionaries, were brought to take Him.

A man may not always tell what he will do until the trial is upon him. This was the emergency for which Ben-Hur had been for years preparing. The man to whose security he had devoted himself, and upon whose life he had been building so largely, was in personal peril; yet he stood still. Such contradictions are there in human nature! To say truth, O reader, the very calmness with which the mysterious Person confronted the mob held him in restraint by suggesting the possession of a power in reserve more than sufficient for the peril. Peace and good-will, and love and non-resistance, had been the burden of the Nazarene's teaching; would He put His preaching into practice? He was master of life; He could restore it when lost; He could take it at pleasure. What use would He make of the power now? Defend Himself? And how? A word—a breath—a thought were sufficient. That there would be some signal exhibition of astonishing force beyond the natural Ben-Hur believed, and in that faith waited. And in all this he was still measuring the Nazarene by himself—by the human standard.

Presently the clear voice of the Christ arose.

"Whom seek ye?"

"Jesus of Nazareth," the priest replied.

"I am He."

At these simplest of words, spoken without passion or alarm, the assailants fell back several steps, the timid among them cowering to the ground; and they might have let Him alone and gone away had not Judas walked over to Him.

"Hail, Master!"

With this friendly speech, he kissed Him.

"Judas," said the Nazarene mildly, "betrayest thou the Son of man with a kiss? Wherefore art thou come?"

Receiving no reply, the Master spoke to the crowd again.

"Whom seek ye?"

"Jesus of Nazareth."

"I have told you that I am He. If, therefore, you seek me, let these go their way."

At these words of entreaty the rabbis advanced upon Him; and, seeing their intent, some of the disciples for whom He interceded drew nearer; one of them cut off a man's ear, but without saving the Master from being taken. And yet Ben-Hur stood still! Nay, while the officers were making ready with their ropes, the Nazarene was doing His greatest charity—not the greatest in deed, but the very greatest in illustration of His forbearance, so far surpassing that of men.

"Suffer ye thus far," He said to the wounded man, and healed him with a touch.

Both friends and enemies were confounded—one side that He could do such a thing, the other that He would do it under the circumstances.

"Surely He will not allow them to bind Him!"

Thus thought Ben-Hur.

"Put up thy sword into the sheath; the cup which My Father hath given Me, shall I not drink it?" From the offending follower, the Nazarene turned to His captors. "Are you come out as against a thief, with swords and staves to take Me? I was daily with you in the Temple, and you took Me not; but this is your hour, and the power of darkness."

The posse plucked up courage and closed about Him; and when Ben-Hur looked for the faithful they were gone—not one of them remained.

The crowd about the deserted man seemed very busy with tongue, hand, and foot. Over their heads, between the torch-sticks, through the smoke, sometimes in openings between the restless men, Ben-Hur caught momentary glimpses of the prisoner. Never had anything struck him as so piteous, so unfriended, so forsaken! Yet, he thought, the man could have defended Himself—He could have slain His enemies with a breath, but He would not. What was the cup His Father had given Him to drink? And who was the Father to be so obeyed? Mystery upon mystery—not one, but many.

Directly the mob started in return to the city, the soldiers in the lead. Ben-Hur became anxious; he was not satisfied with himself. Where the torches were in the midst of the rabble, he knew the Nazarene was to be found. Suddenly he resolved to see Him again. He would ask Him one question.

Taking off his long outer garment and the handkerchief from his head, he threw them upon the orchard wall, and started after the posse, which he boldly joined. Through the stragglers he made way, and by little at length reached the man who carried the ends of the rope with which the prisoner was bound.

The Nazarene was walking slowly, His head down, His hands bound behind Him; the hair fell thickly over His face, and He stooped more than usual; apparently He was oblivious to all going on around Him. In advance a few steps were priests and elders talking and occasionally looking back. When at length they were all near the bridge in the gorge, Ben-Hur took the rope from the servant who had it, and stepped past him.

"Master, Master!" he said hurriedly, speaking close to the Nazarene's ear. "Dost thou hear, Master? A word—one word. Tell me——"

The fellow from whom he had taken the rope now claimed it.

"Tell me," Ben-Hur continued, "goest Thou with these of Thine own accord?"

The people were come up now, and in his own ears asking angrily, "Who art thou, man?"

"O Master," Ben-Hur made haste to say, his voice sharp with anxiety, "I am Thy friend and lover. Tell me, I pray thee, if I bring rescue, wilt Thou accept it."

The Nazarene never so much as looked up or allowed the slightest sign of recognition; yet the something which when we are suffering is always telling it to such as look at us, though they be strangers, failed not now. "Let Him alone," it seemed to say; "He has been abandoned by His friends; the world has denied Him; in bitterness of spirit, He has taken farewell of men; He is going He knows not where, and He cares not. Let Him alone."

And to that Ben-Hur was now driven. A dozen hands were upon him, and from all sides there was shouting, "He is one of them. Bring him along; club him—kill him!"

With a gust of passion which gave him many times his ordinary force, Ben-Hur raised himself, turned once about with his arms outstretched, shook the hands off, and rushed through the circle which was fast hemming him in. The hands snatching at him as he passed tore his garments from his back, so he ran off the road naked; and the gorge, in keeping of the friendly darkness, darker there than else-where, received him safe.

Reclaiming his handkerchief and outer garments from the orchard wall, he followed back to the city gate; thence he went to the khan, and on the good horse rode to the tents of his people out by the Tombs of the Kings.

As he rode, he promised himself to see the Nazarene on the morrow —promised it, not knowing that the unfriended man was taken straight-way to the house of Hannas to be tried that night.

CHAPTER 7

NEAR THE END

Next morning, about the second hour, two men rode full speed to the doors of Ben-Hur's tents, and dismounting, asked to see him. He was not yet risen, but gave directions for their admission.

"Peace to you, brethren," he said, for they were of his Galileans, and trusted officers. "Will you be seated?"

"Nay," the senior replied bluntly, "to sit and be at ease is to let the Nazarene die. Rise, son of Judah, and go with us. The judgment has been given. The tree of the cross is already at Golgotha."

Ben-Hur stared at them.

"The cross!" was all he could for the moment say.

"They took Him last night, and tried Him," the man continued. "At dawn they led Him before Pilate. Twice the Roman denied His guilt; twice he refused to give Him over. At last he washed his hands, and said, 'Be it upon you, then;' and they answered——"

"Who answered?"

"They the priests and people—'His blood be upon us and our children.'"

"Holy father Abraham!" cried Ben-Hur; "a Roman kinder to an Israelite than his own kin! And if—ah, if He should indeed be the Son of God, what shall ever wash His blood from their children? It must not be—'tis time to fight!"

His face brightened with resolution, and he clapped his hands.

"The horses—and quickly!" he said to the Arab who answered the signal. "And bid Amrah send me fresh garments, and bring my sword! It is time to die for Israel, my friends. Tarry without till I come."

He ate a crust, drank a cup of wine, and was soon upon the road.

"Whither would you go first?" asked the Galilean.

"To collect the legions."

"Alas!" the man replied, throwing up his hands.

"Why alas?"

"Master"—the man spoke with shame—"master, I and my friend here are all that are faithful. The rest do follow the priests."

"Seeking what?" and Ben-Hur drew rein.

"To kill Him."

"Not the Nazarene?"

"You have said it."

"Let us go, brethren; let us to Golgotha."

They passed through excited crowds of people going south, like themselves. All the country north of the city seemed aroused and in motion.

Hearing that the procession with the condemned might be met with somewhere near the great white towers left by Herod, the three friends rode thither, passing round south-east of Akra. In the valley below the Pool of Hezekiah, passage way against the multitude became impossible, and they were compelled to dismount, and take shelter behind the corner of a house and wait.

The waiting was as if they were on a river bank, watching a flood go by, for such the people seemed.

Half an hour—an hour—the flood surged by Ben-Hur and his companions within arm's reach, incessant, undiminished.

The going was singularly quiet. A hoof-stroke upon a rock, the glide and rattle of revolving wheels, voices in conversation, and now and then a calling voice, were all the sounds heard above the rustle of the mighty movement. Yet was there upon every countenance the look with which men make haste to see some dreadful sight, some sudden wreck, or ruin, or calamity of war. And by such signs Ben-Hur judged that these were the strangers in the city come up to the Passover, who had no part in the trial of the Nazarene, and might be His friends.

At length, from the direction of the great towers, Ben-Hur heard, at first faint in the distance, a shouting of many men.

"Hark! they are coming now," said one of his friends.

The people in the street halted to hear; but as the cry rang over their heads, they looked at each other, and in shuddering silence moved along.

The shouting drew nearer each moment; and the air was already full of it and trembling, when Ben-Hur saw the servants of Simonides coming with their master in his chair, and Esther walking by his side; a covered litter was next behind them.

"Peace to you, O Simonides—and to you, Esther," said Ben-Hur, meeting them. "If you are for Golgotha, stay until the procession passes; I will then go with you. There is room to turn in by the house here."

The merchant's large head rested heavily upon his breast; rousing himself, he answered, "Speak to Balthasar; his pleasure will be mine. He is in the litter."

Ben-Hur hastened to draw aside the curtain. The Egyptian was lying within, his wan face so pinched as to appear like a dead man's. The proposal was submitted to him.

"Can we see Him?" he inquired faintly.

"The Nazarene? yes; He must pass within a few feet of us."

"Dear Lord!" the old man cried fervently. "Once more, once more! Oh, it is a dreadful day for the world!"

Meantime the flood poured along, if anything, more densely than before; and the shouting came nearer, shrill up in the air, hoarse along the earth, and cruel. At last the procession was up.

"See!" said Ben-Hur bitterly; "that which cometh now is Jerusalem."

The advance was in possession of an army of boys, hooting and screaming, "The King of the Jews! Room, room for the King of the Jews!"

A band of legionaries fully armed followed next, marching in sturdy indifference, the glory of burnished brass about them the while.

Then came the NAZARENE!

He was nearly dead. Every few steps He staggered as if He would fall. A stained gown badly torn hung from His shoulders over a seamless under-tunic. His bare feet left red splotches upon the stones. An inscription on a board was tied to His neck. A crown of thorns had been crushed hard down upon His head, making cruel wounds, from which streams of blood, now dry and blackened, had run over His face and neck. The long hair, tangled in the thorns, was clotted thick. The skin, where it could be seen, was ghastly white. His hands were tied before Him. Back somewhere in the city He had fallen exhausted under the transverse beam of His cross, which, as a condemned person, custom required Him to bear to the place of execution; now a countryman carried the burden in His stead. Four soldiers went with Him as a guard against the mob, who sometimes, nevertheless, broke through, and struck Him with sticks, and spit upon Him. Yet no sound escaped Him, neither remonstrance nor groan; nor did He look up until He was nearly in front of the house sheltering Ben-Hur and his friends, all of whom were moved with quick compassion. Esther clung to her father; and he, strong of will as he was, trembled. Balthasar fell down speechless. Even Ben-Hur cried out, "O my God, my God!" Then, as if He divined their feelings or heard the exclamation, the Nazarene turned His wan face towards the party, and looked at them each one, so they carried the look in memory through life. They could see He was thinking of them, not Himself, and the dying eyes gave them the blessing He was not permitted to speak.

CHAPTER 8

THE END

WHEN the party—Balthasar, Simonides, Ben-Hur, Esther, and two faithful Galileans—reached the place of crucifixion, Ben-Hur was in advance leading them. How they had been able to make way through the great press of excited people, he never knew; no more did he know the road by which they came, or the time it took them to come. He had walked in total unconsciousness, neither hearing nor seeing anybody or anything, and without a thought of where he was going, or the ghostliest semblance of a purpose in his mind. In such condition a little child could have done as much as he to prevent the awful crime he was about to witness. The intentions of God are always strange to us; but not more so than the means by which they are wrought out, and at last made plain to our belief.

Ben-Hur came to a stop; those following him also stopped. As a curtain rises before an audience, the spell holding him in its sleep-awake rose, and he saw with a clear understanding.

There was a space upon the top of a low knoll rounded like a skull, and dry, dusty, and without vegetation, except some scrubby hyssop. The boundary of the space was a living wall of men, with men behind struggling, some to look over, others to look through it. An inner wall of Roman soldiery held the dense outer wall rigidly to its place. A centurion kept eye upon the soldiers. Up to the very line so vigilantly guarded, Ben-Hur had been led; at the line he now stood, his face to the north-west. The knoll was the old Aramaic Golgotha—in Latin, Calvaria; Anglicized, Calvary; translated, The Skull.

On its slopes, in the low places, on the swells and higher hills, the earth sparkled with a strange enamelling. Look where he would outside the walled space, he saw no patch of brown soil, no rock, no green thing; he saw only thousands of eyes in ruddy faces; off a little way in the perspective only ruddy faces without eyes; off a little farther only a broad, broad circle, which the nearer view instructed him was also of faces. And this was the ensemble of three millions of people; under it three millions of hearts throbbing with passionate interest in what was taking place upon the knoll; indifferent as to the thieves, caring only for the Nazarene, and for Him only as He was an object of hate or fear or curiosity—He who loved them all, and was about to die for them.

In the spectacle of a great assemblage of people there are always the bewilderment and fascination one feels while looking over a stretch of sea in agitation, and never had this one been exceeded; yet Ben-Hur gave it but a passing glance, for that which was going on in the space described would permit no division of his interest.

Up on the knoll so high as to be above the living wall, and visible over the heads of an attending company of notables, conspicuous because of his mitre and vestments and his haughty air, stood the high priest. Up the knoll still higher, up quite to the round summit, so as to be seen far and near, was the Nazarene, stooped and suffering, but silent. The wit among the guard had complemented the crown upon His head by putting a reed in His hand for a sceptre. Clamours blew upon him like blasts—laughter—execrations—sometimes both together indistinguishably.

From this dreamy state Ben-Hur was aroused by the sound of hammering. On the summit of the knoll he observed then what had escaped him before—some soldiers and workmen preparing the crosses. The holes for planting the trees were ready, and now the transverse beams were being fitted to their places.

"Bid the men make haste," said the high priest to the centurion. "These"—and he pointed to the Nazarene—"must be dead by the going down of the sun, and buried, that the land may not be defiled. Such is the law."

With a better mind, a soldier went to the Nazarene and offered Him something to drink, but He refused the cup. Then another went to Him and took from His neck the board with the inscription upon it, which he nailed to the tree of the cross—and the preparation was complete.

"The crosses are ready," said the centurion to the pontiff, who received the report with a wave of the hand and the reply,—

"Let the Blasphemer go first. The Son of God should be able to save Himself. We will see."

The people to whom the preparation in its several stages was visible, and who to this time had assailed the hill with incessant cries of impatience, permitted a lull which directly became a universal hush. The part of the infliction most shocking, at least to the thought, was reached—the men were to be nailed to their crosses. When for that purpose the soldiers laid their hands upon the Nazarene first, a shudder passed through the great concourse; the most brutalized shrank with dread. Afterwards there were those who said the air suddenly chilled and made them shiver.

"How very still it is!" Esther said, as she put her arm about her father's neck.

And remembering the torture he himself had suffered, he drew her face down upon his breast, and sat trembling.

"Avoid it, Esther, avoid it!" he said. "I know not but all who stand and see it—the innocent as well as the guilty—may be cursed from this hour."

Balthasar sank upon his knees.

"Son of Hur," said Simonides, with increasing excitement—"son of Hur, if Jehovah stretch not forth His hand, and quickly, Israel is lost —and we are lost."

Ben-Hur answered calmly, "I have been in a dream, Simonides, heard in it why all this should be, and why it should go on. It is the will of the Nazarene—it is God's will. Let us do as the Egyptian here—let us hold our peace and pray."

As he looked up on the knoll again, the words were wafted to him through the awful stillness,—

"I AM THE RESURRECTION AND THE LIFE."

He bowed reverently as to a person speaking.

Up on the summit meantime the work went on. The guard took the Nazarene's clothes from Him; so that He stood before the millions naked. The stripes of the scourging He had received in the early morning were still bloody upon His back; yet He was laid pitilessly down, and stretched upon the cross—first, the arms upon the transverse beam; the spikes were sharp—a few blows, and they were driven through the tender palms; next, they drew his knees up until the soles of the feet rested flat upon the tree; then they placed one foot upon the other, and one spike fixed both of them fast. The dulled sound of the hammering was heard outside the guarded space; and such as could not hear, yet saw the hammer as it fell, shivered with fear. And withal not a groan, or cry, or word of remonstrance from the sufferer; nothing at which an enemy could laugh; nothing a lover could regret.

"Which way wilt thou have Him faced?" asked a soldier bluntly.

"Towards the Temple," the pontiff replied. "In dying, I would have Him see the holy house hath not suffered by Him."

The workmen put their hands to the cross, and carried it, burden and all, to the place of planting. At a word, they dropped the tree into the hole; and the body of the Nazarene also dropped heavily, and hung by the bleeding hands. Still no cry of pain—only the exclamation, divinest of all recorded exclamations,—

"Father, forgive them, for they know not what they do."

The cross, reared now above all other objects, and standing singly out against the sky, was greeted with a burst of delight; and all who could see and read the writing upon the board over the Nazarene's head made haste to decipher it. Soon as read, the legend was adopted by them and communicated, and presently the whole mighty concourse was ringing with salutation from side to side, and repeating it with laughter and groans.

"King of the Jews! Hail, King of the Jews!"

The pontiff, with a clearer idea of the import of the inscription, protested against it, but in vain; so the titled King, looking from the knoll with dying eyes, must have had the city of His fathers at rest below Him—she who had so ignominiously cast Him out.

The sun was rising rapidly to noon; the hills bared their brown breasts lovingly to it; the more distant mountains rejoiced in the purple with which it so regally dressed them. In the city, the temples, palaces, towers, pinnacles, and all points of beauty and prominence seemed to lift themselves into the unrivalled brilliance, as if they knew the pride they were giving the many who from time to time turned to look at them. Suddenly a dimness began to fill the sky and cover the earth—at first no more than a scarce perceptible fading of the day; a twilight out of time; an evening gliding in upon the splendours of noon. But it deepened, and directly drew attention; whereat the noise of the shouting and laughter fell off, and men, doubting their senses, gazed at each other curiously: then they looked to the sun again; then at the mountains, getting farther away; at the sky and the near landscape, sinking in shadow; at the hill upon which the tragedy was enacting; and from all these they gazed at each other again, and turned pale, and held their peace.

"It is only a mist or passing cloud," Simonides said soothingly to Esther, who was alarmed. "It will brighten presently."

Ben-Hur did not think so.

"It is not a mist or a cloud," he said. "The spirits who live in the air—the prophets and saints—are at work in mercy to themselves and nature. I say to you, O Simonides, truly as God lives, He who hangs yonder is the Son of God."

And leaving Simonides lost in wonder at such a speech from him, he went where Balthasar was kneeling near by, and laid his hand upon the good man's shoulder.

"O wise Egyptian, hearken!—Thou alone wert right—the Nazarene is indeed the Son of God."

Balthasar drew him down to him, and replied feebly, "I saw Him a Child in the manger where He was first laid; it is not strange that I knew Him sooner than thou; but oh that I should live to see this day! Would I had died with my brethren! Happy Melchior! Happy, happy Gaspar!"

"Comfort thee!" said Ben-Hur. "Doubtless they too are here."

The dimness went on deepening into obscurity, and that into positive darkness, but without deterring the bolder spirits upon the knoll. One after the other the thieves were raised on their crosses, and the crosses planted. The guard was then withdrawn, and the people set free closed in upon the height, and surged up it, like a converging wave. A man might take a look, when a new-comer would push him on, and take his place, to be in turn pushed on—and there were laughter and ribaldry and revilements, all for the Nazarene.

"Ha, ha! If Thou be King of the Jews, save Thyself," a soldier shouted.

"Ay," said a priest, "if He will come down to us now, we will believe in Him."

Others wagged their heads wisely, saying, "He would destroy the Temple, and rebuild it in three days, but cannot save Himself."

Others still: "He called Himself the Son of God; let us see if God will save Him."

What all there is in prejudice no one has ever said. The Nazarene had never harmed the people; far the greater part of them had never seen Him except in this His hour of calamity; yet—singular contrariety! —they loaded Him with their curses, and gave their sympathy to the thieves.

The supernatural night, dropped thus from the heavens, affected Esther as it began to affect thousands of others braver and stronger.

"Let us go home," she prayed—twice, three times—saying, "It is the frown of God, father. What other dreadful things may happen, who can tell? I am afraid."

Simonides was obstinate. He said little, but was plainly under great excitement. Observing, about the end of the first hour, that the violence of the crowding up on the knoll was somewhat abated, at his suggestion the party advanced to take position near the crosses. Ben-Hur gave his arm to Balthasar; yet the Egyptian made the ascent with difficulty. From their new stand, the Nazarene was imperfectly visible, appearing to them not more than a dark suspended figure. They could hear Him, however—hear His sighing, which showed an endurance or exhaustion greater than that of His fellow-sufferers; for they filled every lull in the noises with their groans and entreaties.

The second hour after the suspension passed like the first one. To the Nazarene they were hours of insult, provocation, and slow dying. He spoke but once in the time. Some women came and knelt at the foot of His cross. Among them He recognised His mother with the beloved disciple.

"Woman," He said, raising His voice, "Behold thy son!" And to the disciple, "Behold thy mother!"

The third hour came, and still the people surged round the hill, held to it by some strange attraction, with which, in probability, the night in mid-day had much to do. They were quieter than in the preceding hour; yet at intervals they could be heard off in the darkness shouting to each other, multitude calling unto multitude. It was noticeable, also, that coming now to the Nazarene, they approached His cross in silence, took the look in silence, and so departed. This change extended even to the guard, who so shortly before had cast lots for the clothes of the crucified; they stood with their officers a little apart, more watchful of the one convict than of the throngs coming and going. If He but breathed heavily, or tossed His head in a paroxysm of pain, they were instantly on the alert. Most marvellous of all, however, was the altered behaviour of the high priest and his following, the wise men who had assisted him in the trial in the night, and, in the Victim's face, kept place by him with zealous approval. When the darkness began to fall, they began to lose their confidence. There were among them many learned in astronomy, and familiar with the apparitions so terrible in those days to the masses; much of the knowledge was descended to them from their fathers far back; some of it had been brought away at the end of the Captivity; and the necessities of the Temple service kept it all bright. These closed together when the sun commenced to fade before their eyes, and the mountains and hills to recede; they drew together in a group around their pontiff, and debated what they saw. "The moon is at its full," they said, with truth, "and this cannot be an eclipse." Then, as no one could answer the question common with them all—as no one could account for the darkness, or for its occurrence at that particular time, in their secret hearts they associated it with the Nazarene, and yielded to an alarm which the long continuance of the phenomenon steadily increased. In their place behind the soldiers, they noted every word and motion of the Nazarene, and hung with fear upon His sighs, and talked in whispers. The man might be the Messiah, and then—— But they would wait and see!

In the meantime Ben-Hur was not once visited by the old spirit. The perfect peace abode with him. He prayed simply that the end might be hastened. He knew the condition of Simonides' mind—that he was hesitating on the verge of belief. He could see the massive face weighed down by solemn reflection. He noticed him casting inquiring glances at the sun, as seeking the cause of the darkness. Nor did he fail to notice the solicitude with which Esther clung to him, smothering her fears to accommodate his wishes.

"Be not afraid," he heard him say to her; "but stay and watch with me. Thou mayst live twice the span of my life, and see nothing of human interest equal to this; and there may be revelations more. Let us stay to the close."

When the third hour was about half gone, some men of the rudest class—wretches from the tombs about the city—came and stopped in front of the centre cross.

"This is He, the new King of the Jews," said one of them.

The others cried, with laughter, "Hail, all hail, King of the Jews!" Receiving no reply, they went closer.

"If Thou be King of the Jews, or son of God, come down," they said loudly.

At this, one of the thieves quit groaning, and called to the Nazarene, "Yes, if Thou be Christ, save Thyself and us."

The people laughed and applauded; then, while they were listening for a reply, the other felon was heard to say to the first one, "Dost thou not fear God? We receive the due rewards of our deeds; but this man hath done nothing amiss."

The bystanders were astonished; in the midst of the hush which ensued, the second felon spoke again, but this time to the Nazarene,—

"Lord," he said, "remember me when Thou comest into Thy kingdom."

Simonides gave a great start. "When Thou comest into Thy kingdom!" It was the very point of doubt in his mind; the point he had so often debated with Balthasar.

"Didst thou hear?" said Ben-Hur to him. "The kingdom cannot be of this world. Yon witness saith the King is but going to His kingdom."

"Hush!" said Simonides, more imperiously than ever before in speech to Ben-Hur. "Hush, I pray thee! If the Nazarene should answer——"

And as he spoke the Nazarene did answer, in a clear voice, full of confidence,—

"Verily I say unto thee, To-day shalt thou be with Me in Paradise!"

Simonides waited to hear if that were all; then he folded his hands and said, "No more, no more, Lord! The darkness is gone; I see with other eyes—even as Balthasar, I see with eyes of perfect faith."

The faithful servant had at last his fitting reward. His broken body might never be restored; nor was there riddance of the recollection of his sufferings, or recall of the years embittered by them; but suddenly a new life was shown him, with assurance that it was for him—a new life lying just beyond this one—and its name was Paradise. There he would find the Kingdom of which he had been dreaming, and the King. A perfect peace fell upon him.

Over the way, in front of the cross, however, there were surprise and consternation. The cunning casuists there put the assumption underlying the question and the admission underlying the answer together. For saying through the land that He was the Messiah, they had brought the Nazarene to the cross; and, lo! on the cross, more confidently than ever, He had not only reasserted Himself, but promised enjoyment of His Paradise to a malefactor. They trembled at what they were doing. The pontiff, with all his pride, was afraid. Where got the man His confidence except from Truth? And what should the Truth be but God? A very little now would put them all to flight.

The breathing of the Nazarene grew harder; His sighs became great gasps. Only three hours upon the cross, and He was dying!

The intelligence was carried from man to man, until every one knew it; and then everything hushed; the breeze faltered and died; a stifling vapour loaded the air; heat was superadded to darkness: nor might any one unknowing the fact have thought that off the hill, out under the overhanging pall, there were three millions of people waiting awe-struck what should happen next—they were so still!

Then there went out through the gloom, over the heads of such as were on the hill within hearing of the dying man, a cry of despair, if not reproach,—

"My God! My God! why hast Thou forsaken Me?"

The voice startled all who heard it. One it touched uncontrollably.

The soldiers in coming had brought with them a vessel of wine and water, and set it down a little way from Ben-Hur. With a sponge dipped into the liquor, and put on the end of a stick, they could moisten the tongue of a sufferer at their pleasure. An impulse seized him; catching up the sponge, he dipped it into the vessel and started for the cross.

"Let Him be!" the people in the way shouted angrily. "Let Him be!"

Without minding them, he ran on, and put the sponge to the Nazarene's lips.

Too late, too late!

The face then plainly seen by Ben-Hur, bruised and black with blood and dust as it was, lighted nevertheless with a sudden glow; the eyes opened wide, and fixed upon some One visible to them alone in the far heavens; and there were content and relief, even triumph, in the shout the victim gave.

"It is finished! It is finished!"

So a hero, dying in the doing a great deed, celebrates his success with a last cheer.

The light in the eyes went out; slowly the crowned head sank upon the labouring breast. Ben-Hur thought the struggle over; but the fainting soul recollected itself, so that he and those around him caught the other and last words, spoken in a low voice, as if to one listening close by,—

"Father, into Thy hands I commend My spirit."

A tremor shook the tortured body; there was a scream of fiercest anguish, and the mission and the earthly life were over at once. The heart, with all its love, was broken; for of that, O reader, the man died!

Ben-Hur went back to his friends, saying simply, "It is over; He is dead."

In a space incredibly short the multitude was informed of the circumstance. No one repeated it aloud; there was a murmur which spread from the knoll in every direction; a murmur that was little more than a whispering, "He is dead! He is dead!" and that was all. The people had their wish; the Nazarene was dead; yet they stared at each other aghast. His blood was upon them! And while they stood staring at each other, the ground commenced to shake; each man took hold of his neighbour to support himself; in a twinkling the darkness disappeared, and the sun came out; and everybody, as with the same glance, beheld the crosses upon the hill all reeling drunk-like in the earthquake. They beheld all three of them; but the one in the centre was arbitrary; it alone would be seen; and for that it seemed to extend itself upwards, and lift its burden, and swing it to and fro higher and higher in the blue of the sky. And every man among them who had jeered at the Nazarene; every one who had struck Him; every one who had voted to crucify Him; every one who had marched in the procession from the city; every one who had in his heart wished Him dead, and they were as ten to one, felt that he was in some way individually singled out from the many, and that if he would live he must get away quickly as possible from that menace in the sky. They started to run; they ran with all their might; on horseback, and camels, and in chariots they ran, as well as on foot; but then, as if it were mad at them for what they had done, and had taken up the cause of the unoffending and friendless dead, the earthquake pursued them, and tossed them about, and flung them down, and terrified them yet more by the horrible noise of great rocks grinding and rending beneath them. They beat their breasts and shrieked with fear. His blood was upon them! The home-bred and the foreign, priest and layman, beggar, Sadducee, Pharisee, were overtaken in the race, and tumbled about indiscriminately. If they called on the Lord, the outraged earth answered for Him in fury, and dealt them all alike. It did not even know wherein the high priest was better than his guilty brethren; overtaking him, it tripped him up also, and smirched the fringing of his robe, and filled the golden bells with sand, and his mouth with dust. He and his people were alike in the one thing at least—the blood of the Nazarene was upon them all!

When the sunlight broke upon the crucifixion, the mother of the Nazarene, the disciple, and the faithful women of Galilee, the centurion and his soldiers, and Ben-Hur and his party, were all who remained upon the hill. These had not time to observe the flight of the multitude; they were too loudly called upon to take care of themselves.

"Seat thyself here," said Ben-Hur to Esther, making a place for her at her father's feet. "Now cover thine eyes, and look not up; but put thy trust in God, and the spirit of yon just Man so foully slain."

"Nay," said Simonides reverently, "let us henceforth speak of Him as the Christ."

"Be it so," said Ben-Hur.

Presently a wave of the earthquake struck the hill. The shrieks of the thieves upon the reeling crosses were terrible to hear. Though giddy with the movements of the ground, Ben-Hur had time to look at Balthasar, and beheld him prostrate and still. He ran to him and called—there was no reply. The good man was dead! Then Ben-Hur remembered to have heard a cry in answer, as it were, to the scream of the Nazarene in His last moment; but he had not looked to see from whom it had proceeded; and ever after he believed the spirit of the Egyptian accompanied that of his Master over the boundary into the kingdom of Paradise. The idea rested not only upon the cry heard, but upon the exceeding fitness of the distinction. If faith were worthy reward in the person of Gaspar, and love in that of Melchior, surely he should have some special meed who through a long life had so excellently illustrated the three virtues in combination—Faith, Love, and Good Works.

The servants of Balthasar had deserted their master; but when all was over, the two Galileans bore the old man in his litter back to the city.

It was a sorrowful procession that entered the south gate of the palace of the Hurs about the set of sun that memorable day. About the same hour the body of the Christ was taken down from the cross.

The remains of Balthasar were carried to the guest-chamber. All the servants hastened weeping to see him; for he had the love of every living thing with which he had in anywise to do; but when they beheld his face, and the smile upon it, they dried their tears, saying, "It is well. He is happier this evening than when he went out in the morning."

Ben-Hur would not trust a servant to inform Iras what had befallen her father. He went himself to see her and bring her to the body. He imagined her grief; she would now be alone in the world; it was a time to forgive and pity her. He remembered he had not asked why she was not of the party in the morning, or where she was; he remembered he had not thought of her; and, from shame, he was ready to make any amends, the more so as he was about to plunge her into such acute grief.

He shook the curtains of her door; and though he heard the ringing of the little bells echoing within, he had no response; he called her name, and again he called—still no answer. He drew the curtain aside and went into the room; she was not there. He ascended hastily to the roof in search of her; nor was she there. He questioned the servants; none of them had seen her during the day. After a long quest everywhere through the house, Ben-Hur returned to the guest-chamber, and took the place by the dead which should have been hers; and he bethought him there how merciful the Christ had been to His aged servant. At the gate of the kingdom of Paradise happily the afflictions of this life, even its desertions, are left behind and forgotten by those who go in and rest.

When the gloom of the burial was nigh gone, on the ninth day after the healing, the law being fulfilled, Ben-Hur brought his mother and Tirzah home; and from that day in that house the most sacred names possible of utterance by men were always coupled worshipfully together—

GOD THE FATHER AND CHRIST THE SON.

CHAPTER 9

THE CATACOMB

ABOUT five years after the crucifixion, Esther, the wife of Ben-Hur, sat in her room in the beautiful villa by Misenum. It was noon, with a warm Italian sun making summer for the roses and vines outside. Everything in the apartment was Roman, except that Esther wore the garments of a Jewish matron. Tirzah and two children at play upon a lion's skin on the floor were her companions; and one had only to observe how carefully she watched them to know that the little ones were hers.

Time had treated her generously. She was more than ever beautiful, and in becoming mistress of the villa, she had realized one of her cherished dreams.

In the midst of this simple, home-like scene, a servant appeared in the doorway, and spoke to her.

"A woman in the atrium to speak with the mistress."

"Let her come. I will receive her here."

Presently the stranger entered. At sight of her the Jewess arose, and was about to speak; then she hesitated, changed colour, and finally drew back, saying, "I have known you, good woman. You are——"

"I was Iras, the daughter of Balthasar."

Esther conquered her surprise, and bade the servant bring the Egyptian a seat.

"No," said Iras coldly. "I will retire directly."

The two gazed at each other. We know what Esther presented—a beautiful woman, a happy mother, a contented wife. On the other side, it was very plain that fortune had not dealt so gently with her former rival. The tall figure remained with some of its grace; but an evil life had tainted the whole person. The face was coarse; the large eyes were red and pursed beneath the lower lids; there was no colour in her cheeks. The lips were cynical and hard, and general neglect was leading rapidly to premature old age. Her attire was ill chosen and draggled. The mud of the road clung to her sandals. Iras broke the painful silence.

"These are thy children?"

Esther looked at them, and smiled.

"Yes. Will you not speak to them?"

"I would scare them," Iras replied. Then she drew closer to Esther, and seeing her shrink, said, "Be not afraid. Give thy husband a message for me. Tell him his enemy is dead, and that for the much misery he brought me I slew him."

"His enemy!"

"The Messala. Further, tell thy husband that for the harm I sought to do him I have been punished until even he would pity me."

Tears arose in Esther's eyes, and she was about to speak.

"Nay," said Iras, "I do not want pity or tears. Tell him, finally, I have found that to be a Roman is to be a brute. Farewell."

She moved to go. Esther followed her.

"Stay and see my husband. He has no feeling against you. He sought for you everywhere. He will be your friend. I will be your friend. We are Christians."

The other was firm.

"No; I am what I am of choice. It will be over shortly."

"But"—Esther hesitated—"have we nothing you would wish; nothing to—to——"

The countenance of the Egyptian softened; something like a smile played about her lips. She looked at the children upon the floor.

"There is something," she said.

Esther followed her eyes, and with quick perception answered, "It is yours."

Iras went to them, and knelt on the lion's skin, and kissed them both. Rising slowly, she looked at them; then passed to the door and out of it without a parting word. She walked rapidly, and was gone before Esther could decide what to do.

Ben-Hur, when he was told of the visit, knew certainly what he had long surmised—that on the day of the crucifixion Iras had deserted her father for Messala. Nevertheless, he set out immediately and hunted for her vainly; they never saw her more, or heard of her. The blue bay, with all its laughing under the sun, has yet its dark secrets. Had it a tongue, it might tell us of the Egyptian.

Simonides lived to be a very old man. In the tenth year of Nero's reign, he gave up the business so long centred in the warehouse at Antioch. To the last he kept a clear head and a good heart, and was successful.

One evening, in the year named, he sat in his arm-chair on the terrace of the warehouse. Ben-Hur and Esther, and their three children, were with him. The last of the ships swung at mooring in the current of the river; all the rest had been sold. In the long interval between this and the day of the crucifixion but one sorrow had befallen them:

'that was when the mother of Ben-Hur died; and then and now their grief would have been greater but for their Christian faith.

The ship spoken of had arrived only the day before, bringing intelligence of the persecution of Christians begun by Nero in Rome, and the party on the terrace were talking of the news when Malluch, who was still in their service, approached and delivered a package to Ben-Hur.

"Who brings this?" the latter asked, after reading.

"An Arab."

"Where is he?"

"He left immediately."

"Listen," said Ben-Hur to Simonides.

He then read the following letter:

"I, Ilderim, the son of Ilderim the Generous, and sheik of the tribe of Ilderim, to Judah, son of Hur.

"Know, O friend of my father's, how my father loved you. Read what is herewith sent, and you will know. His will is my will; therefore what he gave is thine.

"All the Parthians took from him in the great battle in which they slew him I have retaken—this writing, with other things, and vengeance, and all the brood of that Mira who in his time was mother of so many stars.

"Peace be to you and all yours.

"This voice out of the desert is the voice of

"ILDERIM, *Sheik*."

Ben-Hur next unrolled a scrap of papyrus yellow as a withered mulberry leaf. It required the daintiest handling. Proceeding, he read:

"Ilderim, surnamed the Generous, sheik of the tribe of Ilderim, to the son who succeeds me.

"All I have, O son, shall be thine in the day of thy succession, except that property by Antioch known as the Orchard of Palms; and it shall be to the son of Hur who brought us such glory in the Circus—to him and his for ever.

"Dishonour not thy father.

"ILDERIM THE GENEROUS, *Sheik*."

"What say you?" asked Ben-Hur of Simonides.

Esther took the papers pleased, and read them to herself. Simonides remained silent. His eyes were upon the ship; but he was thinking. At length he spoke.

"Son of Hur," he said gravely, "the Lord has been good to you in these later years. You have much to be thankful for. Is it not time to decide finally the meaning of the gift of the great fortune now all in your hand, and growing?"

"I decided that long ago. The fortune was meant for the service of the Giver; not a part, Simonides, but all of it. The question with me has been, How can I make it most useful, in His cause? And of that tell me, I pray you."

Simonides answered,—

"The great sums you have given to the Church here in Antioch, I am witness to. Now, instantly almost with this gift of the generous sheik's, comes the news of the persecution of the brethren in Rome. It is the opening of a new field. The light must not go out in the capital."

"Tell me how I can keep it alive."

"I will tell you. The Romans, even this Nero, hold two things sacred —I know of no others they so hold—they are the ashes of the dead and all places of burial. If you cannot build temples for the worship of the Lord above ground, then build them below the ground; and to keep them from profanation, carry to them the bodies of all who die in the faith."

Ben-Hur arose excitedly.

"It is a great idea," he said. "I will not wait to begin it. Time forbids waiting. The ship that brought the news of the suffering of our brethren shall take me to Rome. I will sail to-morrow."

He turned to Malluch.

"Get the ship ready, Malluch, and be thou ready to go with me."

"It is well," said Simonides.

"And thou, Esther, what sayest thou?" asked Ben-Hur.

Esther came to his side, and put her hand on his arm, and answered,—

"So wilt thou best serve the Christ. O my husband, let me not hinder, but go with thee and help."

· · · · ·

If any of my readers, visiting Rome, will make the short journey to the Catacomb of San Calixto, which is more ancient than that of San Sebastiano, he will see what became of the fortune of Ben-Hur, and give him thanks. Out of that vast tomb Christianity issued to supersede the Cæsars.